W9-DDA-598

Deadly Blessings

Other Five Star Titles
by Julie Hyzy:

Artistic License

Deadly Blessings

Julie Hyzy

Five Star • Waterville, Maine

First Edition
First Printing: June 2005

Published in 2005 in conjunction with
Tekno Books and Ed Gorman.

Set in 11 pt. Plantin by Al Chase.

Printed in the United States on permanent paper.

Library of Congress Cataloging-in-Publication Data

Hyzy, Julie A.
    Deadly blessings / by Julie Hyzy.—1st ed.
      p. cm.
    ISBN 1-59414-290-4 (hc : alk. paper)
    I. Title.
PS3608.Y98D43 2005
   813'.6—dc22
                                     2005004993

In memory of Mom and Dad,
Whose words of wisdom I miss every day.

"Don't let little things bother you."
—Ed Garbarczyk

*"Smile through your troubles;
you'll build character that way."*
—Margot Garbarczyk

Acknowledgments

Believe me when I tell you there are more people to thank than I have pages in this book.

My heartfelt thanks to my wonderful family: Curt, Robyn, Sara, Biz, and Paul. Your support, encouragement, and love have given me wings.

And my deepest thanks to my writing group for the past four years—The Southland Scribes: Linda Cochran, Sandi Tatara, Ralph Horner, Sherry Cole, Jane Andringa, George Kulles, and Ryan O'Reilly. Great people, great writers. A very special thanks to our leader, Helen Osterman, who went above and beyond the call of duty in helping me meet my deadline.

I'll always have a special spot in my heart for the Otsego, Michigan library ladies, especially Marg Murphy who supports new authors with unparalleled warmth and enthusiasm.

Memories of a cold Hell Night served to inspire a key scene in *Deadly Blessings*. Thanks to my fraternity brothers, the Gamma Pi chapter of Delta Sigma Pi—you know who you are.

The folks at Five Star Publishing are amazing. I've never met such a cheerful group of people, who are pleased and proud of what they do. As they should be. I can't say enough about what a great group the Five Star team is. Thank you to all the wonderful people who made me feel welcome out there at Authors' Day, especially my editor, Mary P. Smith; thanks also to John Helfers, and everyone at Tekno Books; and to

Debbie Brod, good friend, and editor extraordinaire.

I would be remiss without mentioning my entire Garbarczyk Family clan; my buddy and movie-reviewer colleague, Mary Fliris; my mini-grouper cohorts, Earl Merkel and John Welsh; The WAMers; J. Michael Major, who gave me lots of great suggestions; and my closest friends: Rene, Mike, Karen, Dennis, Maureen, and Redreid, all of whom keep my spirits soaring.

And of course, thank you to Michael A. Black, my writing partner, trusted first reader, and dear friend, for believing in me. His talent, encouragement, and guidance inspire me to write every day.

Chapter One

The problem was, I couldn't leave.

My cell phone chirped, shattering the awkward, magazine-reading silence of the crowded waiting room. In the quick moment it took me to haul my purse from the floor to my lap, the phone chirped again, and the two strangers flanking me shook their heads in annoyance.

As the phone continued its high-pitched signal, I scrambled out of my seat, dug for the handset, and headed toward the wall-mounted display of blank adoption file requests in the far corner. The space afforded me a modicum of privacy as I checked Caller ID, then answered.

"What's up, Jordan?"

Back in Chicago, my assistant talked fast. I could tell by the hollow sound of her voice that she kept a hand cupped over the mouthpiece. "Bass is furious. He wants to know where you are."

Bass was always furious about something, but the tension in Jordan's voice—practically pinging over the connection—had me worried.

"Why? What happened?"

"Don't know. He isn't saying much, except for bugging me to find out where you are."

"What did you tell him?"

I could almost see her dark face grimace. "I sure as hell didn't let on you were in Springfield, if that's what you're asking," she said. I could always count on Jordan for sass. A beat later, her conspiratorial tone returned. "What do you want me to say?"

My mind raced. "Tell him I have a doctor's appointment. I'll be in as soon as I can."

"A doctor's appointment? Girl, you're four hours away. He's not going to believe any doctor's appointment takes that long."

"Tell him it's female troubles. That'll make him squirm."

She let out a short laugh, then sobered. "You best get back here as soon as you can. I think it's something to do with that priest story of yours."

"Oh, shit," I said, hoping no one nearby heard me, cupping my own hand over the phone now, too. "Did Milla change her mind about talking to us on camera?"

"Bass hasn't told me squat about what's going on. All I know is, he's been on the phone all morning, screaming at people. He's flipping out, let me tell you. And he says you better get back here, pronto. Otherwise . . ."

"Otherwise what?"

A stern voice from behind the far desk called out my name. "Alexandrine St. James?"

"I gotta go, Jordan," I said. "They just called me." I waved to the woman, who acknowledged me with an absent-minded nod. Making my way toward her, I spoke into the phone again. "I'll call you when I'm done here. Hold him off as long as you can."

"You got it, Alex, but he said if you aren't back by lunch time, your ass is grass."

With a tight smile stretching my face, I waited in the warm cubicle, seconds ticking by like years. I sat up a little straighter, allowing trickles of perspiration an express path down my back. "Guess I'm getting a late start on this search, compared to most folks, huh?" I said, trying to both break the ice and quicken my caseworker's pace.

My fingers drummed a silent beat against my leg as the woman scanned my adoption request.

I wore a khaki skirt and white sleeveless blouse, hoping my look said "trustworthy." In any event, I was glad to have chosen something cool. It was unseasonably warm for October, and I'd debated wearing a business suit.

"No," she answered, not looking up. "We get all kinds."

All kinds. Like me.

I was living on borrowed time and I knew it. Bass expected me back in our Chicago office any minute, while I sat—trying to look patient—two hundred miles south, in Springfield, Illinois. The realization made my smile muscles ache. I was on borrowed time in another sense too. Every day I waited made it ever more unlikely that I'd find the man and woman who'd put me up for adoption more than thirty years ago.

The woman seated across from me had all that information at her fingertips. And maybe if I played this right, I'd be heading back to Chicago with my biological parents' names in my pocket in plenty of time to keep Bass happy.

Jordan had mentioned the Milla feature story. I hoped to God the girl hadn't gotten cold feet about appearing on camera. I knew I should try to put it out of my head, just for now, but found that impossible to do. I needed to get back to Chicago, posthaste.

I smiled harder. Never too proud to suck up.

My caseworker, Marlene, looked like someone who might be swayed by a little apple-polishing. Her sausage fingers, with their gleaming pearlescent nails, hit the keyboard with a vengeance, now that she'd perused my file.

I released a sigh of gratitude. We were starting to move.

Clicking at the keyboard so fast I thought the letters might start bouncing up, she glanced at me. "Give me your name again, honey."

"Alex," I said. "Alexandrine St. James. Also Szatjemski." I spelled it for her. Polish last name, dark-Irish looks. An adoption office was the one place where unusual combinations like that wouldn't raise eyebrows.

"Szatjemski your maiden name?"

"No, I'm not married. My dad had it changed."

She glanced over the rims of her half-moon glasses. "I'll deal with that later." I didn't think that bode well for me. She seemed the sort of person for whom rules were everything. Her smiles were doled out at prescribed intervals—when she introduced herself, and again when she sat down behind her desk. My fear was that she'd have another ready, a sad smile this time, when she told me that there was nothing she could do to help me.

She looked up again.

"Middle initial?"

"P."

"Thank you." Her tone was automatic, without inflection, and she moved into a rhythm. Typing while wrinkling her nose at the computer, she'd stop, hands poised over the keyboard, and tilt her head up to peer through her glasses at the screen, while making a little "o" with her mouth. Type, stop, type, stop. Tiny beads of sweat formed a perfect outline of her upper lip. The cubicle was warm, making me doubly glad I'd chosen something sleeveless. They say women don't sweat; they glisten. Blowing out a breath to calm myself, I knew I was glistening but good.

I scooted forward till I perched at the edge of my chair, hoping for a glimpse of the computer display, but it was blocked from my view by a gizmo I'd never seen before. Much like the blinders they put on horses before a race, the side of the monitor near to me had a plastic barricade. Set on a hinge, it was designed to flip across the front of the monitor with a quick push of the fingers, should the need arise.

I imagined they got a lot of adoptees craning their necks to catch a glimpse of otherwise classified information.

Marlene didn't seem to notice my eyes make their futile stray toward her monitor. "You know . . ." She typed a few more characters, her tiny clacking movements slower than before. "I should run two separate inquiries here. As if I'm following two cases. To be sure that we cover both last names."

I nodded encouragement and thanked her. It wouldn't hurt for her to know I appreciated her efforts. The nose wrinkled again. I was getting used to it.

If I could only get access to the computer system. For just one minute.

She turned to me. "I'm sorry," she said. My heart dropped before she added, "This computer is so slow today. And we have the problem about your last name. It makes things much more complicated." This last admonishment was accompanied by a little shake of her head, as though it had been my fault that my parents had changed it.

But at least she was still looking.

Margot and Ed Szatjemski, my adoptive parents, had recently retired to Arkansas with the hope of enjoying those much-advertised bubbling hot springs. They didn't know I was here today, didn't know I'd taken some extra time after my visit with them before heading back to Chicago. But my mother might have suspected something. She asked me at least four times why I hadn't brought Lucy along.

Lucy didn't know I'd made the trip, actually. My parents' biological child, and three years my senior, Lucy suffered from Williams Syndrome. As handicaps go, it's a cheerful one, but its ravages left her without the necessary skills to live on her own. Pulling her out of the group home to have her tag along would have jeopardized my quest, so I'd lied and told my mother that I was under deadline this week. No time.

"Hmmph," Marlene said again. But this time, she pushed her chair back and lifted a finger to her lips. "I can't get this to tell me if your birth mother is open to contact. Let me get the file and I'll check. Just a minute."

I sat back as she got up, listening to the quiet hum and murmurs of conversations in the cubicles around me. The place was hopping. Most of the others in the waiting room had been in their late teens, early twenties. I was a late bloomer where this investigation was concerned. My parents would be crushed if they knew I was here today. Until they'd retired and moved out of state, I hadn't even risked an attempt for fear they'd find out.

I peered around the corner of Marlene's cubicle to watch her depart. I lost sight of her just about the same time I could no longer hear the slapping of her sandals against the bottoms of her feet. No one was walking the short corridor she'd just left, everyone busy in small conversations and smaller cubicles of their own.

I eased into her seat and adjusted the monitor toward me. It squeaked on its plastic stand and I held my breath for a moment, worried that some matron-like administrator would pounce on me, slap my hands for sneaking around, and banish me from the records office forever.

The blinder that Marlene had flipped across the front of it opened with no problem, but she hadn't simply minimized the file, she'd exited.

I grabbed the mouse, moving to access most recently viewed files. It had to be there. And it was. Szatjemski, A. P. My breath fell out in a whoosh so loud that it echoed in my ears.

With what seemed like slow-motion movements, I double-clicked, my foot tapping out a staccato rhythm of nervousness under the pressure of Marlene's return. The little timer came up and I know I made a sound of frustration, keeping one ear open even as the cheerful cybersand thing turned one way, then another. "C'mon," I whispered.

Beep. Beep. Beep.

My pager blared, clanging like a gong on my belt.

I panicked. My fingers flew to my side and I hit the silent button. It took all of a second and a half but it felt like forever.

Breathe, I told myself.

In those scant seconds that I silenced the alarm, the timer stopped turning and the computer sounded an indignant beep. A tiny gray box appeared mid-screen, asking me for the code to access this record.

My file was password-protected.

Damn.

Frustrated, I closed the request and returned the squeaky monitor back to its original position, before moving back to my own chair. I wouldn't have guessed Marlene would have had the foresight to close it so quickly. But she probably dealt with dozens of us every day. And desperate people do desperate things.

After checking the number on my pager, I dug my cell phone out and put in a quick call to Bass. His assistant, Frances, was no help. After he beeped me, he'd apparently walked away. She transferred me to Jordan, and I got her voicemail. I left a message to call me only if it was life or death.

Something was up.

Tucking the phone into my purse, I sat back to wait.

Having my parents out of state gave me latitude in my adoption quest. Caring people, my parents, they were also just a bit protective. I'd gotten used to it, the way people get used to annoying habits of people they love. You either accept them the way they are, blowing off their idiosyncrasies, or you learn to live without them in your life. For me it was an easy choice.

Of course, when eccentricities become annoying to the point of distraction, it might be time to rethink a relationship.

Which reminded me that I hadn't spoken with Dan for two days.

My pager sounded again. This time, without fear of getting caught snooping, I didn't jump. But I'd inadvertently buried the thing in my purse and the beeping mocked my unsuccessful efforts to dig it out quickly.

Marlene's backless shoes made their slapping sound as she returned from the back room. She took her seat again, her eyebrows raised as I fumbled through my purse, finally hitting the silent button. A quick look at the display confirmed that it was work calling me again.

I knew I should have called back that moment, but Marlene had a manila folder in her hands. *My* manila folder—with at least a half-inch worth of papers and forms. I decided to wait.

She opened it on her lap, in front of me, careful to keep one side up so that I couldn't read any of the papers inside. "Let's see here," she said.

In my job, I'm calm. Cool. I have to be. Our weekly broadcast of *Midwest Focus Television NewsMagazine* brings us situations that run the gamut of feel-good to make-your-skin-crawl. My job is to investigate, to find the story that will touch the hearts of the viewing public. To interview, to evaluate, to winnow through the chaff to find wheat worth disseminating.

I talk to hundreds of folks every year. I hear their stories. Some will do anything for that fifteen minutes of fame.

Others will break your heart with their willingness to share their lives. But I maintain an even keel. Always. I have to. It's a defense mechanism, most likely. But it's also an effective tool to getting the job done well.

But right now my hands were sweating. My feet, crossed and shoved far beneath the chair, were wiggling to the beat of fear. I wasn't about to rush Marlene.

"We-ll," she finally said, stringing the word out into two syllables, "I don't see that either of your biological parents have filed the 'Open to Contact' form." She let the thought hang as she flipped through the file again.

This was the moment of decision for her. I knew it. I just knew she was considering throwing me a bone. Something small. The town where I was born? The name of the hospital? Maybe even a hint about my mother's last name? I said nothing, but tried my best to look hopeful and sincere.

"Legally," she said, her eyes meeting mine, "there's nothing in here I can tell you . . ."

I returned her nod. Her eyes were a watery shade of brown. Eyebrows carefully penciled into tadpole shapes over draped lids.

". . . but you've made this long trip down, and I understand how hard it has to be . . ."

I wanted to shout, "Yes? Yes?" but my cell phone shattered the moment. My face must have registered both my frustration, and my moment of indecision.

"Do you have to get that?" Marlene asked.

Digging through my purse again, I nodded. The timing couldn't be worse, I thought, mentally cursing whoever was calling. At the same time I knew that I needed to sound pleasant, or risk ruining the impression Marlene had of me, thus far. She still smiled. Maybe all wasn't lost, yet.

The caller ID number told me it was Bass. "Alex here."

17

His voice boomed over the tiny handset and I knew Marlene could hear every word. "Where the hell are you?"

"I'm at an appointment, Mr. Bassett."

That took him aback, I knew. I never called him Mr. Bassett.

"Well, how long till your return, Ms. St. James?" Oh, he was in a rare mood. "We got a situation here."

Marlene shook her head in a commiserating way. I was engendering sympathy. Good.

"It might be a couple of hours."

"Why? Where the hell are you?"

"I'm on personal time, Mr. Bassett."

"I don't give a rat's ass what kind of time you're on. Get moving. This one ain't gonna wait. It's that case you were following. The one we've been waiting on?" He ended his sentence as a question. I knew Bass didn't trust cell phones. He thought there was a network of satellites that singled him out and paid attention to every one of his personal conversations. So I wasn't going to get anything specific from him here. As though to make his meaning clear, he enunciated his next words with care: "The one with your unique perspective?"

Aha. So it was the priest story after all—the holy man had impregnated a twenty-two-year-old Polish immigrant and had then fled to Brazil when the truth came to light. Being the only member of the investigative team fluent in Polish, I'd landed this one. And it was a plum.

"Okay," I said. "I'll be there as soon as I can."

"You got till noon."

He hung up.

I'd never make it. I blew out a breath of frustration, thinking that I'd call him again on the drive back to massage his ruffled feathers.

"I'm sorry," I said. Flustered by Bass's call and whatever

18

information Marlene was about to impart, I didn't pay attention as I tucked the phone away. I snagged the tiny antenna in the front pocket of my purse. Open, it somersaulted off my lap to the floor, spilling its contents as it tumbled.

I could have lived through the embarrassment of having my mints, my change purse, even my feminine products strewn across the industrial carpeting. But what sealed my fate was my press pass. It landed, smiling skyward, at Marlene's feet.

She leaned over to pick it up. "Oh," she said, stringing the word out, "you're with the media?"

I opened my mouth to answer.

"Sorry." Her eyes had changed. No longer empathetic, she'd morphed into an efficient clerk, wary of evil investigators. Tapping the manila folder with a proprietary little pat-pat, she said, "These records are sealed."

Chapter Two

"What do you mean you gave it to Fenton? Who the *hell* is Fenton?"

As though they'd conspired to make me feel loud and obnoxious, with my voice raised at least two octaves and twenty decibels, the entire office staff took that very moment to fall completely silent.

Bass was loving this. I knew he was. Glee danced in his hazel eyes.

He and I were standing in the hub, the nerve center of our television station's administrative office. Support staff desks made up this center section, set at ten-foot intervals across the spacious floor. The hub was home to six assistants, all women, who fielded calls, made appointments, and moved at the speed of light, as they often did, to help us get a story together. And right now every single one of them had her eyes glued on me.

Bass smirked, letting the silence hang there a moment, long enough for the water cooler thirty feet away to gurgle before answering me. The bastard.

Philip J. Bassett hated being called Bass. Which was why I did it. It was a career decision. Succumbing to the temptation of calling the boss "prick" to his face could get a person fired. Calling him by a nickname got his ire up, but since the ire was usually way up there anyway where I was concerned, there was no real harm done. I figured he should be happy I didn't call him "Hound" instead.

How he came to be known as Bass, I didn't know. It started before my time, back in the good old days by the good old boys. Back then, it might have even been an affectionate nickname. Now, not even close. It was my rebellion, my chance to get back at the little jerk. And little he was.

I stood a full inch taller than he did, and in heels I towered over him. So much so, I had to resist the constant urge to reach down and flick ever-present dandruff flakes off the top of his head. Winter or summer, it always looked like he just stepped in from a light flurry. And when he shook his head—something he did often and with vehemence—rather than fly about, the little flakes hung on for dear life, stuck as they were to his greasy hair gel. He'd been raised in the Brylcreem era, and he must have stocked up.

Even with the thick-soled shoes he wore, he wasn't a breath over five-foot-five. Petite, diminutive, the guy, with his full head of brown hair and clean-shaven looks, had the advantage of looking closer to mid-forties than his actual age of sixty-something.

"Fenton," he said, in a patronizing voice, "is new."

"And you gave him *my* story?"

"Look, Alex, this one's turned into a heater." Another thing, Bass was a policeman wannabe. He loved to sprinkle his conversation with law enforcement vernacular. I suspected that he'd been turned down from applying due to his lack of stature. Either that, or he watched a lot of those shows on TV. The man was a veritable lexicon of cop-speak.

I struggled to lower my voice. "You told me to get back here fast. I got here as quick as I could."

"I told you to get back here by noon, or you were outta luck."

Like they were watching a tennis match, I was aware of the staff's eyeballs, six sets of them, flicking from me to Bass and

21

back again. Like a freeze-frame in a movie, the women were stock-still, fingers suspended over their keyboards, or handing off folders, or poised to get up from their seats. Not moving. Like being in a wax museum, with a little sign underneath: "Busy office, circa early 21st century." Except for their watchful eyes and the performance Bass and I were providing, the place was still.

I'd made record time flying up I-55. Fueled by anger and frustration, I'd taken my mood out on the gas pedal, breaking every speed limit I saw. I knew that if I'd gotten stopped, I would've had no defense. But I didn't care.

As I drove, I'd phoned Bass. Repeatedly. But he wouldn't take any of my calls. Frances, standing behind him now, had sworn he wasn't avoiding me. She wouldn't tell me what the scoop was, only that something big had happened. I hate it when people tell you that something's up, but won't tell you what it is. Makes my imagination work overtime. I had twenty possibilities to my immoral priest story running through my brain.

But I hadn't expected to hear that the young woman had been murdered.

Twenty-two years old, Milla Voight had maintained she didn't know that Father Carlos de los Santos was a priest until after she confronted him with the news of her pregnancy. A recent immigrant to the United States from Poland, she'd worked as a shampoo girl at a north side hair salon, making minimum wage and hoping for a better life. She'd been in the States no more than a month when she'd been introduced to the handsome de los Santos through a mutual acquaintance.

The story might have remained quiet if Milla hadn't attempted to terminate her pregnancy at the very abortion clinic where Father Carlos was staging a peaceful sit-in demonstration. Rumor was, she knew he'd be there, and had seen it as an opportunity to make him feel remorse for the situation he'd put her in, while bringing her plight to the attention of his colleagues.

Instead, feeling the tug of his priestly collar perhaps, he'd taken the occasion to lecture her on the sanctity of life. She'd reacted with hysterics borne of frustration. And the entire exchange had been recorded by an industrious second-string reporter who watched with delight as his interview made the headline story on the ten o'clock news.

Milla didn't get the abortion. What she got was instant fame and an eager attorney willing to take her case, pro bono.

And a month later when, about to be subpoenaed, Father Carlos of the Saints fled in haste to Brazil, her story made it to my desk as a possible feature for investigation. When Bass had learned that I spoke Polish, he was so tickled that I thought he might wet himself. Milla spoke almost no English and I'd planned to arrange a meeting after my jaunt to Springfield.

I'd never get that chance now. How lonely it had to be, how overwhelming the odds against a young girl new to the country, pregnant, and taking on an institution as powerful as the Catholic Church. And now both she and her unborn child were dead. Unceremoniously dumped in the Cal Sag channel, found floating by a homeless guy who'd gone down there to take a leak.

Something reeked to high heaven on this one.

Before speaking again, I chanced a look over Bass's head to Frances, who stood behind him. Tall, and svelte, the fifty-something woman sported maroon hair, spiked in a style more suited to a person three decades younger. She rolled her eyes, and gave an almost imperceptible shake of her head. I was gonna lose this one.

I took a deep breath and blew it out slowly.

"Okay," I said, "just tell me why. And don't give me because I took a half-day vacation. I know that's not it."

Bass was not a magnanimous kinda guy. Here I was, acquiescing, giving up quicker than I normally would, a combination of the day's aggravation and the look on Frances's face telling me it wasn't worth fighting the Hundred Years' War on this one—and Bass wasn't smirking. Wasn't even smiling. He looked . . . beaten.

"It came down from on high. Can't tell you the specifics, just that the new guy, Fenton . . ." he said this, elongating the man's name in such a way that I got the distinct impression that Fenton wasn't high on Bass's favorite person list, either. Hey, maybe I even moved up a notch. Hard to get lower than the bottom, I supposed. ". . . He's our best shot for breaking out of the number two position and knocking *Up Close Issues* off its mighty perch."

I raised an eyebrow. Just one.

The office staff was moving again. The fireworks were over.

Bass put up his hands in a gesture of trying to ward me off. Again, he seemed more resigned than triumphant. "Don't ask."

"Fine," I said. "It's been a lousy day, and now that I don't have this 'heater' case to work on, I'm heading home."

"Ah . . ."

"What?"

Bass scratched the top of his greasy head. Several flakes inched away in fear. "You've been assigned a different story. Remember the beauty salons?"

Dread kicked in. "No."

Bass grinned. His malicious humor was back. "Yes, Ma'am. Gabriela will be here in fifteen minutes with all the details."

★ ★ ★ ★ ★

I shut the door to my office, not caring that it made a tell-tale "whump" as I dropped backward to lean against it, massaging my eyes with my free hand. I still held my purse in the other. Remembering the fiasco down at the State Adoption Records office, I frowned at it and flung it into a nearby chair.

My office was precisely as I'd left it. Cluttered. Jordan knew better than to let anyone mess with my mess while I was out. I could tell you what color notepaper each tiny bit of information had been recorded on. I could tell you what color ink I used. I could tell you which pile every note was hidden in. What I couldn't do was reach into a cabinet and pull out the proper file. Because I never put anything away.

Once a case was closed, the story finished, written, and filmed, Jordan came in and cleared it away, working her magic to encourage order in my wayward office.

I walked beyond my desk and stood at the picture window overlooking the Chicago River and the Michigan Avenue Bridge. The day sparkled, almost to the point where it hurt to look at the bright, white Wrigley Building across the river, reflecting the sunshine.

The window and its vista over the city was my favorite part of the room. And my desk was arranged to accommodate the splendor of it all. It had taken me a couple of weeks working here before it dawned on me that the gorgeous view sprawled behind me—that guests sitting across from me could enjoy it, but that I was missing out on the world going by.

One night, after I'd worked late, I picked my head up from a couple hours of concentration to find the office completely quiet, completely dark. The only light in the whole place came from the Tiffany-style, Wal-Mart-priced lamp that I'd bought to cozy up my office a little.

But it wasn't only the dark and quiet office that had surprised me, it was the shimmer of the city lights that met me when I turned around. Just past Thanksgiving, the city had been strung with the glow of Christmas. Tiny white glints lit up the night. Across the river, the massive evergreen in front of the Tribune towers was so coated with light, the beauty of it caught in my throat.

Despite the fact that I was bone-tired and had a headache from twelve hours of work, I saw possibility. Drawing on energy reserves that unfailingly appear when an appealing idea dawns, I managed to move the heavy desk, so that it now sat perpendicular to the window, allowing me to view my slice of the city all the time.

The following morning, everyone who stopped in gave me a curious look, but no one said a word. Not only was I the only female in a managerial role, but I was also the eccentric one as well.

That was then. Right now, I needed to call Dan. Another fun thing on the agenda for the day. We still had issues to work out. *If* we were going to work them out. Dropping into my chair, I pulled the phone over and dialed.

His "hi" was tentative. "How was your trip to Springfield?"

After I told him, he said, "Tough break."

At that moment, I could hear his mind get up and leave the conversation, looking for something more interesting to engage itself in.

"Yeah," I said. I let the silence hang. "And I lost the priest story."

That got his attention.

Dan worked for the competition, *Up Close Issues*, the number one locally-filmed television newsmagazine. They were so far ahead of us in ratings that they'd recently moved from the weekly format we followed, to twice weekly. And they were trouncing us further.

Dan and I had met at a fancy-shmancy television awards dinner over a year ago, right after I started at *Midwest*. Dan was the anchor, which meant he got much better pay than I did. Although most of the time we weren't working on the same feature, or the same angle, we still enjoyed discussing our "cases." This time, as luck would have it, we'd both drawn the "fleeing priest" gig. Dan had been assigned first. When he'd heard that I'd gotten the nod, too, he'd brought home champagne to celebrate. Not only was this a big one, but he was expecting to benefit from whatever information I uncovered. After all, I'd be able to interview Milla without the impediment of an interpreter. Not to mention that my being a woman and Catholic would likely encourage her to open up more.

Sure, I would have shared some information. Not everything, of course. I had a responsibility to my station, after all. But over time, Dan and I had developed a symbiotic relationship with regard to breaking news, and there was room for cooperation.

"What? They can't do that."

"They did."

"Shit." I could tell by the way he spat the word that he wasn't upset solely on my behalf.

"Let's talk about it later," I said, changing the subject. "I was hoping to cut out early, but Bass has me following something else. I thought I might get back around seven."

"You mean my apartment?" he said, sounding slow and stupid.

So, it was "my apartment" now, even though I'd been staying there for most of the past six months. "Yeah . . ." I let the sentence hang.

"I thought you were staying at your folks' old house for another week or so. Till everything was settled with their move."

"Everything *is* settled with their move. Remember?"

"Oh, yeah," he said, but something was wrong. "Listen, why don't you take it easy and not worry about making it back to my place tonight? You've had a rough day."

I knew we weren't the stuff of which long relationships are made, but his easy dismissal bugged me. Stung, I forced myself to say, "Okay, sure. Not a problem."

"Maybe you and I can have dinner tomorrow night? What do you think? Give us a chance to talk?"

"Yeah, that's probably a good idea." I wondered if my voice sounded as fake as it felt.

"Catch you later," he said. He started talking to someone nearby and hung up before I had a chance to respond.

They say bad news always comes in threes. I couldn't wait to see what was next.

"Here she comes."

At Jordan's whispered warning, my eyes shot up. Emerging from the elevators, Gabriela, an "I just broke a nail" expression on her face, walked with that famous-person wiggle of hers toward the glass doors at the front of our office. Even from this distance, I could tell that her eyes were focused on the reflective surface, checking out her flawless looks, no doubt. One hand reached up to pat the side of her face, tucking aside errant hairs. Then, with a flash of a grimace, she stopped her approach, taking a moment to reach inside her open suit jacket and, giving a bit of a squirm, she straightened out her snug red dress. With a happy little tilt of her head, she plastered a mega-watt smile on her face and came through the doors.

While Gabriela rarely graced us with her presence here in

the newsroom, she had to know that we'd been able to see every move she made as she approached. Maybe she just didn't care.

I exchanged a look with Jordan before returning my attention to the files on the desk before us. As assistants go, I couldn't ask for a better friend. Jordan had come to the station fresh out of secretarial school, pride in her top grades evident on her café-au-lait face. A beautiful girl, she reminded me of Halle Berry. The resemblance was so strong that when I interviewed her, I'd expected a prima donna attitude, but she surprised me with a maturity and enthusiasm that the other candidates for the job couldn't match. My instincts hadn't let me down; I was lucky to have Jordan on my team.

Most of the secretaries in the hub nearly fell over themselves whenever Gabriela stopped by. Their brush with glamour, I supposed. I felt a tinge of regret for having taken that wide-eyed awe away from Jordan. Through lack of tact, lack of being able to hold my tongue, and the occasional, yet intentional, disparaging comment, I believed I had single-handedly influenced her cynical views of our star.

Gabriela made a beeline for my office, stopping up short at Jordan's desk as though surprised. Almost like she'd expected me to scurry back to my office when I saw her approach.

"Alex."

I knew my name. While I assumed she knew hers as well, just to be sure I said, "Gabriela."

Her face went through a curious blinking, pursed-lip movement. Then she scrunched her nose. At last year's Christmas party, drunk, she told me she'd hired an image consultant. Cost her a bundle, but through hiccups and grins, she admitted that it was money well spent. The guy, whose client base was so stellar that he refused to name names, had told her that the nose scrunching was her signature. That she should use it. I'd never reminded her of our conversation; I'm sure she wouldn't recall it anyway. But now, with her scrunching that perfect little nose at me, I had to fight the urge to make a biting, un-PC wisecrack.

She expected me to ask what she needed. I knew that, but the woman was such a priss that I decided to make her ask for it herself.

I gave her a little smile, resisting the temptation to scrunch my nose, and turned back to Jordan. "Will you be able to get this done by three?"

Jordan avoided looking Gabriela's way. "Not a problem." With a nearly imperceptible grin, she took the folder from my hand. That left me with Gabriela still hovering in the area of my right shoulder.

"Alex?"

Oh, this time we were going to phrase my name as a question.

"Yes, Gabriela."

"Did Mr. Bassett speak with you about my story?"

They were all her stories. Week after week, feature after feature, it was Gabriela's visage that took up the screen, commenting and narrating the adventures we investigators had researched for her, explained to her, and coached her through pronunciations for. From the viewers' perspective, she never took a vacation. We did double-duty several weeks a year so that Gabriela could continue reporting the stories, uninterrupted. Local magazine and newspaper interviewers often asked what drove her to push herself. After all, other stations had substitute anchors who were generally well-received by the public.

Gabriela's pat line was that she'd worked so hard to

achieve a bond with her loyal viewers that she would hate to ever let them down.

The truth, I believed, was that Gabriela was afraid of giving up her anchor spot, even for a week. Being in second place in the ratings meant that the powers-that-be were always looking for a way to nudge our numbers upward. Gabriela's face was synonymous with our station, and I knew she wanted to keep it that way.

She'd taken an unusual interest in the recent replacement of one of the national news anchors who'd done the unthinkable. Taken maternity leave. It was a tidbit that often made it into Gabriela's conversation. Gabriela wasn't married, but I knew the fact that another mouthpiece had been so easily replaced bugged her.

"Your story?" I was being difficult, I know, but I swear I wasn't in the mood to deal with her.

"Can we . . ." she made a wiggly-finger gesture toward my office, and scrunched her nose yet again.

I sighed. "Sure. C'mon in."

Actually, me positioned behind my organizationally challenged desk, and she across from me, wasn't a bad setup at all. Half-turned toward the window, I could appear to be paying attention and still watch the little boats go by on the river in my peripheral vision. Leaning back, I watched Gabriela talk without really hearing her. Until she added, ". . . which is another reason why we think you're the best one for this story."

"Say that again?"

She had the decency to shoot an embarrassed smile. "Well, it isn't as though you're, you know, big into image or anything. Not that that's bad." She tucked a perfect hair behind a perfect ear with a perfectly manicured acrylic nail. I'd had fake nails, once. Never again. Felt like I was typing with tiny shoes on my fingers.

Still, I wasn't clear on what she meant, so I leaned forward, elbows on the desk. I thought if I arranged myself into a listening position, maybe I could corral my wayward thoughts into behaving. "We're supposed to be doing an exposé on hair salons . . ." I affected a dramatic tone, ". . . and the devastating effect mistakes can have on their clients." She didn't seem to enjoy my humor. "Bass told me you had some acquaintances lined up for me to interview. Women who had some really bad hair days."

It was her turn to lean forward. Even though my door was closed, she lowered her voice, like we were girlfriends about to share some delicious secret. "Well, of course, that's the focus, but Mr. Bassett and I discussed this at length. We thought it would be so much more exciting if you went undercover and visited a few of these places, you know, to see how they operate?"

I shook my head, "Bass wants me to go 'undercover'?"

"Well, it was my idea, actually, but Bass loved it. Not just because you could get so much more information that way, you know, that 'in-depth' stuff you're always so excited about, but because the station would be paying for you to visit these salons, and . . ." she grinned one of those cat-that-ate-the-canary smiles, "you'll be getting all these free makeovers at places. Maybe you'll be able find a look that suits you."

Her triumphant smile attempted guilelessness. Failed.

I hate the feeling of knowing that if you just had a couple of extra seconds, you could come back with a perfect retort. I suspected that my mouth hung open. While I knew it was trying to form those witty words, it was more likely looking like I didn't comprehend.

"Here," she thrust a paper at me. A sheet of her personal

stationery: heavyweight, cream color, with her name in deep blue script centered at the top. I remembered when she ordered it. When the first batch came in, she'd stormed into Bass's office waving a stack of them, screaming something about having ordered "Dress Blue" not "Navy Blue."

Whatever shade this was, it was wonderful. I held it up to the light. Watermark and everything. Maybe I could talk Bass into ordering me some of this stuff.

"That's a list of all the salons I want you to visit."

I did a quick count. "There are *ten* places on this list."

"And these," she handed up yet another personalized page, "are the people you need to interview. It's such a shame." She shook her head, staring at the paper till I took it. "So much suffering."

I tried to detect humor in her delivery. None whatsoever. This was the woman who sat at the anchor desk and reported mass murderers, child molesters, and global terrorism. Weekly. And her eyes were getting glassy over bad haircuts?

There had to be twenty names staring up at me. She provided phone numbers, both home and cell for each, along with e-mail addresses. I fought and won a small victory over my emotions—restraining myself from rolling my eyes.

She was sitting on the edge of her chair. Just itching for a fight; I could tell.

But then again, so was I.

The manila files in the center of my desk were chock full of information on Milla Voight, Father de los Santos, the priesthood, and Brazil. I placed the two sheets of information from Gabriela with them, one atop the other, aligning the papers' corners with the tips of my fingers. Movements this precise usually heralded an explosion on my part.

"Tell you what," I said attempting a reasonable voice, but coming across more like I was teaching English as a second language. "I'll look over these lists and pick out the ones that look the most promising, okay?"

"I worked hard getting that information together."

"I'm sure you did. And I appreciate it." I detected a slight relaxation on her part as I lied, easily. "Let me spend some time doing research before I come up with our guests, okay? You know this will take time, and we're not going to be able to broadcast interviews with this many women, or salons. Not in one show."

I knew what she was going to say, so I interrupted, "And I don't think Bass is going to be up for a two-parter."

Nose-scrunch again, but she smiled this time, uncrossing her legs and standing up. "Okay, I know you usually do a pretty good job, but I thought you might like just a teensy bit of help. Especially since you lost that big story."

This time I did roll my eyes.

"Too bad, but isn't it kind of ironic?" Gabriela said.

I never would have imagined Gabriela using "ironic" in a sentence. "How so?"

"Well that girl who got murdered was a hair washer at a salon. Not one of these, of course," she said as she tapped the paper in front of me. "But this new story is about disasters at hair salons. I'd have to say that hers was probably one of the worst disasters of all."

"Worst" doesn't begin to describe it, I thought, as she left.

I looked at the list of salons she'd given me. Murdered Milla Voight's salon hadn't made this cut. But that didn't mean I couldn't start my hair investigation there.

Chapter Three

I stood outside the Hair to Dye For salon at ten-thirty Tuesday morning. Just a few blocks off the intersection of Chicago Avenue and Rush Street, it was considered near-north rather than downtown. The hand-lettered, *"Mowimy Po Polsku"* sign in the window was unusual. I found it odd that they would advertise speaking Polish in such an urban and trendy area. I was also surprised by the salon's nondescript presence on the bustling street.

I mean, I heard of hiding your light under a bushel basket, but this was ridiculous. I passed it twice before the process of elimination of addresses left me no other option. Not that it was shabby. On the contrary, it was a gem, a converted two-story brownstone, with potted geraniums atop the wide, concrete arms of the cement stairs. The two floors above sported window boxes efflorescent with colorful trailing petunias, despite it being October. As much as I enjoyed the color and brightness of the flowering display, part of me longed for the cool crispness of fall. The way things were going, however, we'd probably skip it altogether and head right into the bite of winter.

What had once been the garden apartment, set below sidewalk level and protected by black wrought-iron fencing, was now the salon. There was no sign on the street to direct pedestrian attention downward. Maybe they got enough business that they didn't need people to notice them. For my own sake, I hoped so. I was about to put my hair in their hands.

I noticed a gate in the wrought-iron. Its squeak made me wince. Narrow stone-encrusted steps led downward into the garden of the apartment. Really, it was no more than a small patch of lawn. Ten-by-ten at best.

As I approached the picture window front of the salon, I was struck by the image of mannequins coming suddenly to life. The staff, all young, all attractive in a Barbie doll way, their skin clear, their hair perfect, their bodies curvy but slim, had been virtually immobile until they spotted me. Like one of those old-fashioned boxes with figures inside. Put in a quarter and watch them move.

The image wasn't contradicted, even as I pulled open the glass door to ringing chimes—one of those bell-sets they hang on the opening mechanism. I would have expected something more state-of-the art. But it gave the place charm.

As peroxide and hairspray smells swirled up to meet me, I noticed that the girls' movements were off. Like I was hearing music in my head, and they were struggling to keep with the beat. One had been sweeping, two others leafing through magazines. Another behind a high counter, about to scratch her head. Or so it seemed. They all had stopped, and now that they moved, they looked at me. If I read their expressions right, they were surprised, and curious. Like clinker notes clumsily hit in the middle of a familiar song, something was not right; I couldn't put my finger on it.

A young woman, with chunked magenta streaks in her long blond hair, smiled at me as I rested my elbows atop the counter between us. "I have an appointment," I said, giving her my name.

"Yes, I have it here." While her English was clear, she spoke with an accent that could have either been Polish or Czech. Her bright blue eyes looked up at me with a quizzical look. "You are Alex?"

I nodded, wondering if this girl had known Milla Voight. Even though I was off the story, her murder was still fresh in the newspapers, and I wanted to see if there was anything I could learn. Milla had been employed here from the time she'd arrived from Poland till the time of her death. Surely she'd made a friend or two along the way. With any luck I'd get a little more information about the girl whom I hadn't had the chance to know.

The shop consisted of two aisles, a front reception area where I stood, and a back place which, when I craned my neck a bit, I could tell housed three washing sinks. The aisle to my right was lined with dryers, the one to my left—seven stations with those cool chairs that spin, raise, and lower with the touch of a foot.

There were a couple of other clients, one of them sat at a station deep to my left. Her white hair was being set in scratchy-looking rollers, kept in place with long pink plastic pins that had gone out of use in the seventies.

Even as the counter girl walked me over to the white vinyl and chrome chairs lining the window, I knew that this was a silly venture on my part. What was I going to do? Find some key piece of information and hand it over to this new guy Fenton? Not a chance on that.

But what other options did I have? In my personal fantasy, I would walk in with some great human interest angle on the story of Milla's murder and demand that Bass return the story to me. Once he saw the in-depth investigation I'd done, he'd have no choice but to give in, and I'd be looking at a shot at the coveted Davis award.

The girl handed me one of those oversized hardbound books. Not a lot of pages, but every single one had some gorgeous model looking impossibly fabulous in a wacky hair style—the kind that if I wore them, would make small children shriek with laughter and think I was about to make a little doggie for them out of balloons.

I sighed; the magenta-streaked blonde said, "You like it?"

I had turned to a page featuring a stunning redhead with hair piled up on her head, a lot like the style mom-types wore in the fifties for a night on the town. This redhead, whose photograph was so close up that her pores should have come up the size of dimes, had the most flawless complexion I'd ever seen. The hairstyle was awful, but on her it looked great.

"Yeah," I said, with a laugh, "if I looked like her, I suppose I would." The girl grinned, which I took for comprehension and a sharing of the joke, but when she returned to the phone, she spoke only Polish.

Little did she know, with my dark hair and freckles, that I could understand every word, as she discussed schedule conflicts and trading days off.

Most of the girls were pretty, all with that indefinable quality that let me know that they were foreign, even before they opened their mouths to speak in heavily-accented English. I found it interesting that there was this cache of Polish folk in this snazzy area, and they were making a go of it. According to the information I'd gleaned, the Hair to Dye For Salon had been in business under the same owner for the past seven years.

At a movement to my immediate left, I looked up. A slim, dark-haired girl stood, her head half-bowed. Wearing fashionable too-short black flare pants and a tight, black, silky shirt that exposed her navel, she was one of those "Goth" types that I thought had gone out of style in the last decade. No apparent piercings other than her ears, but the dark lipstick did nothing for her pale face.

She lifted her right hand in a way that let me know she wanted me to follow her. No smile, not a word. She was a few inches shorter than my five-foot-six, which made her pretty tiny. The hair, a page-boy in a deep maroon, was obviously dyed.

"Hi," I said, "are you my stylist?"

She turned and shrugged in a way that let me know she not only didn't understand English, but that she was not about to start a conversation. This was one shy chick.

I was about to try again when, with another little hand movement, she gestured me into a chair by the wash sinks. And then she was gone.

I'm hair-challenged. Always have been. My idea of accoutrement is a rubber band. I like my hair pulled off my face, out of my way. For a while, in my early twenties, I went through this period of hair-worry, investing in hot rollers, two different barrel-size curling irons, and a whole battery of goop to make my hair look natural. I gave up when it took me longer to "style" in the morning than it did for me to commute. Plus the fact that any wind, any rain . . . heck, even the thought of rain made my locks go straight and lifeless.

Right now, my hair, chestnut brown, was just past shoulder length. Perfect for rubber-banding in place. If I was going somewhere fancy, I simply side-parted it and let it hang. Someone once told me that I should go shorter, and that bangs would help camouflage my high forehead, but I liked it simple. And my hair was exactly that. Despite Gabriela's insistence that I could use a new look, I wasn't willing to suffer through more than a trim for the benefit of one of her stories.

Several girls were still sweeping the floor, although it seemed to me it was already clean enough to eat off of. The white of the tile sparkled, but broom after broom continued to sweep invisible dirt away. Two girls were cleaning the mirrors. Again, they were spotless, but still were being shined and polished as though to get them cleaner.

Other girls straightened magazine racks and hair care displays, taking each bottle and jar down one at a time to dust, then replacing it on the now-cleaned, clean shelf.

I wondered how they could afford to keep such a large staff on duty all day. And why they chose to. These women clearly had nothing to do, and yet they didn't sit down to gossip; they worked as they gossiped. Must be why the prices were so high.

They spoke in Polish, some of them racing through conversation in a dialect I couldn't quite follow. I'd been raised on my parents' English-bastardized version of the language.

"Hallo," a voice behind me said. I turned to greet a young woman, about twenty-four years old. She must have come from the back room, because I hadn't seen her before. She was a bigger girl than I was; she had me by about three inches in height and at least thirty pounds in weight. But she carried it well. Like Marilyn Monroe, she had a voluptuous, curvy look. And like Marilyn, she was an attractive girl. Until she smiled.

She tried to keep her mouth closed, but her pronounced overbite and large teeth marred what could have been a stunning face. When she grinned, which she did when I said "hi," her whole face lit up, and the pink of her rounded cheeks deepened. I liked her immediately.

"I am Sophia," she said with a little lilt, like a question, as she pointed to her chest.

"I'm Alex."

"Alex?" she tilted her head. "This is name for boy, no?"

"I guess," I said, sitting back down at the sink chair.

Sophia reached over and fingered my hair, making appraising noises as she did so. I couldn't guess at what she meant as she lifted strands and slid them through her fingers.

"Cut?" she finally said.

"Just a trim."

She led me to a different chair by the mirrors and I obediently sat. Standing behind me, she pulled the ends of my hair up in such a way that it looked as though she'd lopped off a good four inches. The new length hit just above my earlobe. Way too short.

"Umm," I said, "I like to keep it up in a ponytail."

"No ponytail. No." She lowered her head till it was next to mine and smiled into the mirror at me as she let my hair drop. "You see? You have long face. Long hair make it drag." She pulled it up again, this time holding it, bun-like at the back of my head, then pulled a few wisps in front of my eyes and did some sort of contortion with them that made me look as though I sported bangs. "Look now. You see? Different. Pretty blue eyes. You got boyfriend?"

"Uh, yeah."

"He will tell you how beautiful you are."

I laughed. She obviously didn't know Dan. "I'd rather keep it long," I said, though I had to admit she was probably right. The shorter look did seem to frame my face better than the straggly brown mess I was used to. "Just a trim," I repeated.

Her look told me she was disappointed in my decision. She stood back and gave me another appraising look. "You try maybe highlights?"

The broken English was starting to get to me. I thought life might be easier if I told her I spoke Polish, and then, once we got started on the hair, I could put my feelers out about Milla Voight, but I was interrupted before I could start. The front door made its tinkling announcement and a young man strode in, every tense inch of him telegraphing anger.

He made his way directly toward us, waving a newspaper

in my stylist's face, calling to her in Polish, making her name sound like Zophia. My knee-jerk reaction was that he was her boyfriend, but the twin expressions of warning on their faces as they stared each other down made me reassess.

This had to be her brother. From the looks of it, younger, by about three or four years.

They spoke so fast, and with so much emotion, that I had a hard time keeping up with the conversation. I arranged my expression into careful nonchalance, but paid close attention.

"Matthew," she said in English, her voice low. "I have client here."

He gave me a cursory look, and a polite nod, as if to acknowledge my presence. If it slowed him down, the effect was temporary. Fair-haired and handsome, Matthew was a bigger, more masculine version of his sister. Over six feet tall, he had the clear peaches-and-cream complexion and bright blue eyes his sister had, but as though a sculptor had sat down to work with two identical lumps of clay, each maintained a strength of gender—though the resemblance was uncanny.

His face set in a scowl, I couldn't help but think about how handsome he would be if he smiled. He was a bit too young for my tastes, but I could nonetheless appreciate his attractiveness. And while he had a small overbite, and the same large teeth that Sophia did, it wasn't quite so pronounced on his larger frame.

Their Polish became clearer as I began to catch the rhythm of their speech.

"So tell me Sophia, tell me again about your great future in this place," he said, hissing the sibilant consonants. "What kind of future does Milla have now?"

Milla? Had to be Milla Voight.

"Please," she said. It wasn't a request. "I have no time for this, Matthew."

She placed both of her hands on my head, one on each side of my part, as though ready to commence styling. My inner alarm went off. No!

I sensed it was an attempt to dismiss him, but he walked around in front of me. Even if I weren't a people-watcher by nature, my interest would have been piqued when he held up the article that had apparently precipitated this angry outburst. The Polish newspaper's headline story featured a large picture of Milla Voight and a very small one of Father de los Santos. But it seemed that it was the priest who had gotten the brother's ire up.

I felt like the salami in a sandwich, the two of them arguing over me, close, invading my space. Sophia's hands had moved to my shoulders, preventing me from getting up. She couldn't know that I was understanding this conversation and there was no chance I'd try to get away.

I caught a glimpse of her nails, ragged and bitten to the quick. She held a comb, tight in her right hand. "Please," she said again in her native language, "this woman is a paying customer."

"Yes," he said, derision obvious in his tone. He wagged his head. "What would Mama think?"

Sophie moved closer to him, placing one hand on his arm.

He shook it off, but his tone softened. "We can go somewhere else. Another city. Start again."

Her hands twitched with tension. "Matthew, let's talk about this later. At home. All right?"

Behind me, at the back of the shop, a door opened. I might have missed the noise and the movement, had it not been for the reaction of the staff. By the time the knob clicked closed, everyone's eyes had shot toward the sound. As of course, did mine.

A large man had emerged and was making his way toward

us. Scary large. His clothes were not cheap, that much I could tell, but he wore them too small. My guess was that this bruiser did that on purpose, to emphasize the muscles in his chest and the bulge in his pants.

His thick, dark hair was so short that it spiked out around his massive head, and he sported a neat Fu Manchu. Olive-complected, he was the sort of fellow who steps out of the shadows in movies just to make the protagonist nervous. Which was exactly the effect he was having on Sophie and her brother. I felt like a rapt audience member, itching to see what would happen next. Except I wasn't used to sitting this close to the action.

"Problem, Sophia?" he asked in clear, unaccented English. Despite the calm his dark eyes exuded, there was an alertness, a wariness, within them.

"Oh. . . . No. My brother has a disagreement," she said with what looked like a forced smile, "with . . . with our landlord." I watched Milla's face disappear into the newspaper's fold as Matthew tucked it under his arm.

Except for the old lady customer who sat reading *Cosmo* under the hum of a dryer, her foot tapping a rhythm that nobody else could hear, everyone's attention was on us. No secrets in this place, I thought.

The receptionist called out: "Hey, Ro? When you have a minute?"

Like a bear in the zoo on a hot summer day, the guy turned with movements both graceful and powerful. This was not a man in a hurry. Ro looked at the girl who'd called to him, nodded, then turned back to Matthew. "Let me know if there's anything I can do. Any brother of Sophie's is a friend of mine." He didn't wait for a response before heading over to the receptionist, who led him to the back of the shop.

As soon as he was out of earshot, Matthew lapsed back

into Polish again. "I'm going to prove it to you," he said, dropping the folded paper onto her shelf of supplies.

Prove what? I wondered.

"Matthew," she said, but he'd turned to leave. "Please, don't do anything foolish . . . Matthew!"

He yanked the front door open hard enough to send the bells into jangle spasms. They reverberated through the now-silent salon for what had to be seconds but felt like hours. Sophie bit the insides of her mouth, pulling her cheeks in, like a fish. Her fists gripped the gray comb so hard I could see the knuckles go white.

Chapter Four

My pager sounded just as I settled up with Sophie. Pressing my card into her hand, along with a sizeable tip, I whispered to her in Polish, "Call me, if there's anything I can do; I might be able to help, somehow." My sixth sense told me there was a story here.

The realization that I'd heard and understood the conversation between her and Matthew flashed into her eyes and she stopped for a moment, speechless. Pushing my luck, I continued, "If you ever want to talk about your friend Milla, or if you need help . . ." I left the statement intentionally vague, hoping she'd fill in the blanks herself and take a chance on me. She hadn't exactly opened up during the hair styling, but we'd established a rapport of sorts. I could only hope.

When I left the salon, she hadn't smiled, but I saw her pocket my business card.

I pulled out my cell phone when I got back into my car. The interior had been warmed by the October sun and now smelled a bit like French fries. I'd caught a glimpse of myself in the ubiquitous mirrors in the salon, but I just had to take another gander before calling in. I pulled down the visor mirror for a good hard look.

The first word that had gone through my mind at the salon was "beehive," and my style hadn't miraculously changed in the past five minutes. Unfortunately. The receptionist had pulled Sophie over to the side while the highlights I'd reluctantly agreed to, "processed." I can only assume she told Sophie how much I liked the 'do in that one book. My sarcasm had been lost on my audience. Well, it wouldn't be the first time.

Grimacing, I flipped the visor back up. It came out of its little hinge-y thing and I spent another minute or so fixing it. As cars go, mine is pretty utilitarian. People make jokes about Fords, and when I bought this one brand-spanking new four years ago, I'd half-expected problems to surface right away. So far, however, it had been a dream. My little white Escort was small, easy to maneuver, and cheap. Exactly what I wanted in a vehicle.

Settled, I punched in the phone number to the office.

Jordan answered on the second ring, "Alex St. James' office."

"Hey, Jordan, I got the page, but I'm running late. Think you can get Bass to stall the meeting for about—"

"The meeting's been rescheduled for two, but you better get down here. That's why I beeped you."

"What's up?"

She made a noise and I could almost see the look on her face. Combination annoyance and puzzlement. "Something big is brewing around here. Mr. Mulhall's coming."

"Hank? What for?"

"They're making this new guy thing into a big deal. And—now this is just a rumor—so don't quote me . . ."

Jordan's rumors were nothing to be ignored. "Yeah?"

"I heard that they're letting folks go. We're supposed to find out right before the meeting, but I been hearing that heads are gonna roll."

"But they just hired . . ."

"Yeah. Fenn-ton." She elongated the name in a sing-song way.

"Have you met him?"

"Unfortunately."

"And?"

Jordan snorted. A very unladylike sound. "I give him two months."

I smiled as I pulled into traffic, my cell tucked safely back in my purse. Not enough time to make it home and revamp my hair. I stole another glance, this time in the foreshortened rearview mirror. It wasn't so bad, after all. And what the heck, I was on a story. Just one of the hazards of the job.

Maybe I underestimated my new look, I thought later, as I walked into the office. I'd given Sophie the go-ahead on highlights and a free hand in styling, hoping to get her to talk more about Milla. I'd been half-successful. I had new hair.

Expressions on the assistants' faces as I passed ranged from stunned to confused. That's how I read them, at least. I couldn't find Jordan at the moment, which annoyed me to hell. She would have told me how it really looked.

Comments varied from benign, "Wow, Alex, new 'do?" to "What in the world happened?"

Feeling as though I was running a gauntlet in order to get to my office, I felt my mood growing ever more dark. I wished I'd taken the time, now, to pull it down. But the meeting awaited and I figured I'd just take my lumps. Jordan had said heads were going to roll. I hoped mine wasn't going to be one of them, but if it was, at least it would be stylin'.

Standing in the doorway to my office was a young man I'd never seen before. I took a chance. "Fenton?"

Okay, I'll admit, with a name like Fenton, I expected someone older, and this guy didn't even look legal drinking age. I wondered if he had to shave yet. He turned toward me with a head-to-toe raking glance. Too slowly, he forced his hand out toward me. "You must be Alexandra. Not too hard to figure out . . ." his eyes focused on my chest, then moved to my face with a self-satisfied smile. "My aunt told me there was a babe on board."

His aunt? Who could that be, I wondered, as I shook his hand and pasted a smile on my face. "Nice to meet you. But call me Alex." He wasn't much taller than I was, maybe five-foot-seven, and his face was slim, with pinched-in cheeks, like a guitarist in an acid rock band. He had brown hair, lots of it, and it fell long and straight past his forehead to hang into his eyes. If he hadn't been wearing Dockers and a button-down collared shirt, I would have taken him for a time-warped hippie.

He lifted half his mouth in a smirk. "I don't do nicknames, Alexandra. So, if you don't mind . . ."

I wanted to slap his silly little face. "As a matter of fact, Fenton, I do mind."

"Well," he said, affecting a huff. "If you like being called by a man's name . . ." His eyes raked over me again and I could only imagine what was going on in his tiny brain.

We were off to a bad start here. I took a deep breath and decided to try again. But I could feel the bright lights of anger flash inside my head and my words came out sharp.

"First of all, Fenton, my given name is not Alexandra. And I *do* like nicknames. Mine especially. And unless you'd like me to come up with one for you . . ." With effort, I tempered my words, smiling, as though we were old buddies and I was making a joke, "I suggest you call me Alex. Just . . . Alex. Got it?"

I walked away before he answered and worried for a half-second about the repercussions about that little interchange. Sometimes I had such a hard time holding my tongue.

Dropping my stuff on my desk, I picked up a notebook and a couple of folders for the meeting and headed out the door, nearly colliding with Bass I did so.

"Geez!" he said, in a perturbed voice, "where are you

heading?" His mouth dropped open and his eyes widened. "And what the hell happened to your hair?"

I gritted my teeth. "We've got a meeting scheduled, don't we?"

"Yeah, but it's not in my office, it's in the conference room. And you won't need that stuff." He waited while I put the folders back, then started down the corridor. I fell into step with him. Ahead of us, Fenton sauntered into the conference room and I slowed Bass down with a hand on his arm.

"What's up, Bass? And what's with the conference room?" I was wary. We never used that. Not unless it was a big deal.

The look on his face before he spoke was unreadable. "We need the space. We've got two new men we're introducing to the staff. I figured it's best to gather everyone at once rather than walk desk-to-desk with them." He gave an embarrassed shrug, "And the producer popped for some . . . appetizers and things. It's all set up in there."

Bass hadn't walked *me* desk-to-desk for introductions when *I* started. And they'd certainly not put out hors d'oeuvres either. When I arrived my first day, Bass had looked up, handed off some files and pointed to my office. It'd been up to me to get to know who was who and what was what on my own.

Even though he'd hired me, it had been under duress. The station wanted to be seen as "with it" and forward-thinking. Sure. I was, in fact, the only female on the investigative team. Their token. I knew it, but I was good at my job and tried not to let the old-boy network get to me.

I wondered again what was causing Bass to behave in a manner completely foreign to him. When he'd said turning the priest story over to Fenton came from on high, he must have meant it. "Two?" I knew about this Fenton fellow, but hadn't heard about anyone else.

"Yeah, Fenton Foss and another guy, William Armstrong."

"They're *both* new investigators?" If they were getting a reception like this, I could see my control of the good stories going down the tubes. Fast.

"No. Just Fenton. Armstrong's our new scriptwriter. I'm assigning him to you."

I stopped in my tracks. "What?"

Bass faced me. "They're waiting for us in there. Let's go."

"No, no, no. Wait a minute. What happened to Tony?"

His hands came up. "It will all be explained. There was a management shakeup over the weekend. The powers that be. . . ." He stopped himself and I didn't know why, but when he continued, his entire tone had changed, as though to convince me while he convinced himself. "We are really fortunate to get William Armstrong. He's young. He's energetic. And he comes to us with an impressive resume. I have no doubt he'll infuse new life into your stories, Alex."

Young? Like Fenton? Just what I needed.

My head gave one of those nasty wiggle-tilts that means I'm really mad. "I wasn't aware that my stories needed new life infused into them, Philip." I rarely used Bass's first name. He had to know I was angry. "Tony Wender may be an older guy, but he knows what he's doing."

In fact, Tony was my buddy. He'd taken me under his wing when all the other good old boys had shut their doors. He had some stodgy ways about him, and should probably have retired a decade ago, but I liked him. And I was worried for him. He hadn't struck me as the type who'd go down without a fight.

"Just wait. You'll like this Armstrong guy. I think you and him will make an excellent team."

"Oh you do, do you? Well, if he's anything like this Fenton

51

character, you can keep him. I'll write my own flipping scripts and you can tell golden boy number two to keep his greasy little paws off of my stories."

Bass shot me such a look of panic as I finished my spiel that there could be only one possibility. I clenched shut my eyes for a half-second. Then turned around.

"Hello," the man said.

I think I made a noise that came out something like "hurmulp."

He offered his hand. "Ms. St. James?" he said. "I'm William Armstrong. Pleased to meet you."

I managed to put my hand in his, as warmth from my chest raced up my neck to my face. Sweat beads popped out at my hairline—and I remembered with a suddenness that made me sweat all the more, the ridiculous hairstyle I sported from today's adventures.

William Armstrong was a doll. Of course he was. Just over six feet tall, with a crop of slightly wavy, light brown hair, he was solid and sturdy, looking at me through eyes that sparkled bright blue. His face impassive, I couldn't tell if he was amused or angry, or if he'd even heard my crazed diatribe. Fenton might have been a child, but this William was a man. With the kind of looks I'd cross the street to say hello to.

His hand was warm, and it gripped mine with friendly pressure, as I finally found my voice. "Nice to meet you." A bubble of embarrassment shot through me. In sticky situations I find myself prone to giggling; I was having a hell of a time keeping my composure.

"Yes, I gathered that," he said, utterly deadpan.

So he *had* heard.

I went into damage control. "What I meant was . . ."

He let go of my hand. "Don't worry about it."

As we were walking in, he turned to me, holding his palm

out as though to let me examine it. "It wasn't too greasy, was it?"

Humor glinted in his eyes, but I would have felt better if he'd smiled or something. I processed that even as other thoughts ran through my mind. I wished my hair didn't look so stupid, I wished I'd kept my mouth shut a moment ago with Bass, and I wondered how I'd ever make up for looking like such an idiot.

Bass stood next to me and actually tugged at my sleeve, like a little kid. "C'mon, we've got the meeting. They're waiting."

When I walked into the conference room, an enormous high-ceilinged corner space, I was taken aback. Not by the view; I'd been in here plenty of times before. Windows overlooked both the sparkling yet dirty Chicago River to the north and busy, dark Wabash Avenue to the east. What surprised me was the group.

Not only was the support staff present—I'd expected that as we'd made our way through the uninhabited hub—but everyone, from Gabriela, and our hotshot producer Hank, who almost never showed up here, to Dennis, the mailroom guy. There must have been thirty people milling about, all going through the polite nibble, sip, chat motions so common to business get-togethers.

The two men had allowed me first passage into the conference room. Since it was already crowded, I took the opportunity to escape from William—maybe he'd forget he met me and tomorrow we could try again—and moved toward Tony Wender, who I spotted standing in the far corner, holding a clear plastic cup of white wine. Wine? In the middle of the day? Something was up. And it appeared that I'd be finding out soon what it was.

I made my way around the huge oak table. A perfect circle,

it must have been at least eight feet in diameter and took up a good percentage of the room. I sidled up next to Tony and he grinned at me through glassy eyes. Must have been at the wine for a little while. One bony hand held the cup and the other reached up to run through his hair. Tony tended to hunch over. Although he wasn't too tall, he was very skinny, and he had a full crop of salt-and-pepper hair that he was extremely proud not to have lost yet.

"Didja hear?" he asked me, in an almost-shout.

I shook my head and moved closer, hoping he'd take the hint and lower his voice. Even though the room was doing a murmur-level hum, his pronouncement boomed loud enough to make the gaggle of secretaries hovering around one of the many cheese trays look up.

He boomed again. "They're putting me out to pasture." He gave me one of those drunken nods that people do when they've just imparted some pearl of information and want you to grasp the significance.

This was surreal. As though my life as I knew it had suddenly been repositioned, like one of those flat puzzle games where you have to get the numbers in sequential order between one and fifteen, by sliding them around. My fifteen constants, which had been nicely aligned, were now all jumbled up, and part of me wondered if through some great cosmic equalizing algorithm, my foray into the adoption question had started the game. Payback for digging where I should have left well-enough alone.

At least everyone else was as confused as I was. Or, at least, they looked it.

"What happened?" I asked Tony.

Instead of answering, he tipped his plastic tumbler toward the far end of the table, where Hank stood. Hank, his white hair gleaming in the brightness of the overhead lights, his tall, portly body the picture of a well-to-do successful businessman, focused his gaze on person after person, to quiet the chatter.

For all I knew, he was about to put me out to pasture, too.

Jordan made her way toward me. She maneuvered her way in so that she could stand next to me and still keep an eye on the proceedings. We both faced Hank, leaning back as we rested our butts on the low red-oak cabinets behind us. She raised her glass up to about mouth height, folding her other arm underneath as though to cover up the fact that she was talking. Like anyone who looked our way wouldn't know.

"What's with the hair?" she asked, not looking at me.

Hank was waiting. The room would be quiet in moments.

"Long story. I didn't have a chance to take it down." I glanced over to her. "How appalling is it?"

Her brown eyes moved my way for a moment and I watched her take a long, appraising look. "Actually, it's not bad. You don't like it?"

I shook my head.

"You're just not used to it. And it's a little fancy for the office, maybe." She waggled her head a bit. "But if you were going to a wedding or something, I think it's a good look. Frames your face better than your usual."

"Thanks," I whispered. The fact that Jordan didn't think I looked hideous gave me a measure of comfort.

"Dan called, by the way," she added as Hank cleared his throat to begin his speech. "He's dropping by here around four."

Dinner tonight. I'd almost forgotten.

Our dinner plates cleared away, Dan drained his third French Burgundy before the subject came up. Up to that point we'd stayed on safer ground.

"You look nice," he'd said when we first sat down. The lilt to his voice called his sincerity into question. "Any reason for the fancy ' 'do'?"

"I'm working on a story."

"Really?" he said in skeptical tone. "Did you wear an evening gown as you investigated?"

"Ha ha." I shot him a lips-only smile. A flash of his old humor shone in his eyes and for a split-second I thought I might regret tonight's impending breakup. But not really. Better now. The longer you wait in relationships sometimes, the harder it gets to break up. That was a lesson I'd learned a long time ago and I didn't want to make that mistake again. And deep in my heart I knew it would never work out between us. Maybe I'd known it all along.

Dan, handsome and suave, with the kind of allure you'd find in the glossy pages of Abercrombie and Fitch catalogs, was a shade too old to be one of their models, but his age suited him. He'd crossed thirty-five early this year, which made him a bit older than me, but he had an almost chameleon-like ability to look just the perfect age and maturity level to get what he wanted, when he wanted it. He should have been a salesman. A year selling brushes door-to-door, he could have retired.

"Seriously," he said, "what was up at your office today? You looked pretty frazzled when you came out of that meeting."

I was sure I had. Dan had been early, and the meeting had run late. In addition to announcing the hiring of Fenton and William, Hank had taken the opportunity to explain the "shake-up."

"We're reorganizing," I said, not feeling much like talking about it, but Dan persisted.

"Bankrupt?"

"No, not like that. Hank is always chasing you guys. He wants that number one position like crazy."

"Not if I can help it."

"Yeah, well, they want to shoot new blood into the works. It seemed to me that they picked off anyone over sixty. Except Bass."

"Tony?"

"Gone. With a nice package and a promise that they'll use him on a consulting basis. And we've pared down my team. Two investigators, me and Fenton."

"Who's this Fenton?"

I rolled my eyes. "Hank's nephew. Well, actually, his wife's nephew. Fresh out of school. Thinks he's God's gift to the station."

"Geez," Dan shook his head as he made commiserating noises.

I wasn't as surprised as Dan seemed to be that they'd decided to keep Bass on. Despite his idiosyncrasies and his age, he was a force to be reckoned with. Nothing went to production without his approval, and his standards were high. Except for the fact that his personal habits drove me insane, I respected the guy. It was nice to realize that Hank did, too.

I shrugged, as though the changes didn't bother me. "They're spinning this like it's the best thing to hit the station since we went on the air. And Bass is just hopping with nervous relief. I swear—if I thought he was unbearable before . . ." I let the sentence hang, more to gauge if Dan was listening than anything else.

Dan played with his crystal wineglass, making indentations on the linen tablecloth with its base. For several minutes we both watched as the circles disappeared almost as quickly as they were made. With each tilt and spin of the glass, the remaining puddle of ruby liquid left in the bottom of his glass drifted from side to side. A hypnotic rhythm.

I wanted to cut to the chase. I mean, really. Part of me wanted to lean forward, wink, and say, "Hey, it's been fun," and be done with it.

Instead, having pushed my own glass of wine to the side, a single and yet unfinished German Riesling, I sat back to stare out the floor-to-ceiling window to my right. We overlooked North Michigan Avenue from this fifth-floor perch, and now, at night, the sight was spectacular. It made me feel wealthy just to sit in a restaurant like this, looking down at the crowds who waited for walk signals before crossing streets en masse.

After tonight I'd be a free woman again. Although I might come to regret that when invited to couples-only doings, I knew I could live with it. Easily.

I gave a small chuckle. Some romance. Maybe that's why I was feeling less than morose this evening. Our being together made terrific sense—the way these things sometimes do—and people would shake their heads in wonder saying, "Wow, aren't they just the perfect couple?"

But I knew better. And I hoped he did too. We looked good on paper, two-dimensional and flat. But I wanted all three dimensions. I wanted togetherness in mind, body, and spirit.

The background music was perfect for tonight. A slow, melancholy tune, with a hint of Spanish guitar, it suited my mood to a T.

The minimal light in the restaurant and the smoked-glass walls that separated us from the other diners was what had drawn us here the first time, and had kept us coming back. A fat, white candle, flickering within its cylindrical glass enclosure atop a sterling base, sat between us. I ran an index finger over the tip of the flame and smiled at the line of soot I came up with. The fire danced as I did it again.

Wiping my finger on the linen napkin, I focused back on Dan, who continued to play with his wineglass. He looked up to signal our waiter. I guess he was going for that fourth Burgundy.

"Would you care for another?"

I tapped my half-filled glass. "I'm fine."

Now, he gave me a once-over and grinned.

"So, your priest story. What's the status on that?"

"Not mine anymore, remember? Fenton's."

He shot me a quizzical look, then shrugged and stared at his hands as he spoke. "Doesn't make sense to take you off it. I was hoping we could compare notes on this one. It's big."

I felt lousy enough about losing the story. His mood was starting to bring me down even further. I considered telling him about Sophie and the opening I'd almost crow-barred at the hairdresser's this morning, but all of a sudden I realized how desperate that sounded. Like I was grasping at straws. Too self-conscious to admit that I'd followed the story through that channel, I kept silent.

He tilted the glass against his open mouth, draining the last few drops.

"I still can't believe they gave the priest story to the new guy. Why would they do that?"

I brought myself mentally back to the table. It bugged me that he wasn't letting the subject go. My words came out peeved, snappish, "How should I know?"

"Well," he said, tugging at his sleeves, the way men used to do when they wore cufflinks, till the white oxford cloth showed the proper amount from the edge of his suit jacket. Tiny, perfectly embroidered initials in a deep maroon DBS, for Daniel B. Starck, faced back at him. I always wondered about the purpose for the embellishment. To remind him of his name, perhaps? "Maybe that's just a cover," he said.

"A cover? What in the world would they be covering for?"

"Not them. You."

I sat up straighter. Confused would be an understatement at this point.

"You aren't holding out on me, are you?" he asked, then responded to my look of puzzlement. "I mean, you said that Hank's breathing down your neck about trying to stretch to the number one spot. Maybe you're still on the story, but you just don't want to tell me about it?" He gave a half-shrug as though my answer to that wouldn't matter a whit to him.

I was pissed. No matter that I actually *had* followed the story down to Milla's place of business and had chosen to keep that quiet, I'd been taken off the hottest story in months and that ticked me off. But not as much as his suggestion that I was being duplicitous. "They gave Fenton my story," I said, punctuating each word with a pause for effect. "I'm stuck with this stupid hair-care feature that Gabriela came up with."

Dan's face was blank.

"Look at me." I pointed to the pile of hair atop my head. "Why in the world do you think I let someone do this to me if it wasn't for a story?"

"Well . . ." he said, and his brown eyes told me he was being totally honest here, "I thought you got all dolled up on purpose."

"On purpose?" I repeated, dully. "For the big meeting at the station today?"

"No. To impress me. To—you know—keep me."

The small area we sat in seemed to close around me. They say that happens when your mind can't quite grasp a situation. It was happening now. I wasn't understanding and yet I knew that when I finally did, I wasn't going to like it.

"Pretend like I'm dense, okay? Explain that."

Dan looked around the restaurant before leaning forward, as though searching for the right words. Like they were at the next table, ready to jump over at his beck and call. He took a deep breath and it occurred to me that he was uncomfortable. "We both know we're here tonight to talk about our . . . relationship, right?"

My turn to shrug.

"Well, I knew it was going to be tough on you and I wanted to let you down easy but now, you went and did your hair. And I like it, by the way."

Tough on me? Let *me* down easy? As if my words were knives, I could feel the sharpness of them as they left my mouth. "I didn't get my hair done for you."

"Whatever," he said, clearly not believing me. "Be that as it may, I hope we can stay friends," he winked at me as he reached for the check two heartbeats too long after the waiter dropped it off.

Still fuming I nodded. "Sure."

"Maybe you and I can have lunch next week and talk about . . . *Fenton's* . . . progress on the priest story."

And then, he winked again.

Chapter Five

For being mid-morning, my office was pretty dark. Roiling black clouds from a thunderstorm that had made its way across Lake Michigan onto Chicago's shores shadowed the skyline. The storm was intensifying by the moment, scary in that awesome way that made me fear the power of nature, even as I sat safe and dry in the dusky gloom. I'd been staring at my computer screen, my left hand gripping a large chunk of hair atop my head as I studied the display and tried to make sense of my notes. Every so often a burst of lightning caused my eyes to flick upward in surprise, as though someone had just taken my picture.

"So, your real name's . . . Alexis? Or is it Alexa?" a voice asked, pulling me from my concentration.

My gaze meandered up at the voice. It belonged to Fenton, leaning in my doorway, wearing a smug smile. With his skinny arms folded and feet spread in an arrogant stance, he lifted his chin in anticipation of my response.

Since the notes on my screen had nothing to do with the hair interviews I had scheduled for today and everything to do with Milla Voight's murder, I hit the "close" button before answering.

"Nope."

"I dated an Alexis once."

Like I cared. "That's nice."

His hands came up in a quick gesture of frustration and he took on a petulant tone that made me revise downward my original guess at his age, his emotional age anyway. This guy was a case of arrested development at the level of junior high. "Come on. What *is* your name? Might as well tell me. We're going to be working together, you know." Then he did this head movement thing that until this moment I hadn't realized was a habit. Kind of like a horse whose bridle was too tight, he would lift his head and shake it, to get the hair out of his eyes. Brown eyes. Or at least they looked it from here.

"Actually, we don't ever need to work together. You handle your stories; I handle mine."

He moved into the room and glanced at my computer screen. I caught the quick assessment he made. Piles of information were scattered all over my credenza and on a set of filing cabinets across the room from me. Because I had interviews scheduled, I'd taken a few minutes to tidy things up and my desk looked, if not clean, at least orderly. "So, what are you working on?" he asked.

I generally don't mind people asking me that. And sometimes I even have an answer. But this Fenton guy's very existence grated on my nerves.

"A hair story," I said. "Nothing exciting."

"I noticed you're a lot less dolled-up today." He pulled one of my chairs back and settled into it, his elbows on the wooden arms, his fingers interlaced.

Give him a point for observational skills. Today, almost back to normal, my hair hung loose, skimming my shoulders, straight. But the wispy bangs Sophie had cut in and the highlights were still there. I had to admit, when I'd checked them out in the bathroom mirror this morning, I kinda liked the change.

I fixed my gaze on him, hoping to make him wither and leave. Didn't work. He fidgeted in his seat. Belatedly, I realized he was here because he wanted something.

"Mr. Bassett told me you had a file on that Millie girl who was murdered."

"Milla. Her name was Milla."

"Yeah. Whatever. Can I have it?"

Sometimes I wonder if aliens haven't invaded our planet after all. This Fenton sure qualified. What else could explain the sort of mindset that allows a person to meet, insult and then ask a favor of another—someone they've known for all of twenty-four hours?

"Tell you what, Fent," I said, getting extreme and perverse satisfaction from the cringe on his face as I truncated his name, "I'll make a copy for you in a little bit. Let me just finish up here."

"I'll wait."

I shook my head.

His face started a shift from pale to red as he spoke, "Listen, there's no reason for you to be difficult about this. I know it was your story, but you have to give me whatever you've got. Otherwise Mr. Bassett is going to hear about it."

I felt like we were two little kids fighting over a toy, and Fenton was the whiny one ready to break into tears and run to tell his mommy.

Giving a sigh, I shook my head again. "I'm not being difficult." Not much, at least. "Look around. I've got lots of notes here. In lots of different places. It's going to take me a little bit to get it together. But I promise you'll have it. By this afternoon. Okay?"

Mollified, he nodded. "When you do, can we sit down and go over it then? So you can bring me up to speed? Give me an idea of how to go about putting the story together for the scripter?"

"Gabriela's got three women coming in to visit with me

64

today for this other story. Don't know that I'll have any free time."

"But I'm supposed to have it done by the end of business tomorrow."

Of course it had to be finished tomorrow. But I didn't see the reason for the whiny voice. This story was one that would just about write itself. "Shouldn't be a problem," I said.

"Maybe not for you, but I never . . ."

I waited, but he didn't finish his sentence.

"You've never researched a story before?"

Making an "ugh, that smells" face, he shrugged. "I don't think it'll be all that tough."

There was no more perfect response he could have given to provide me reason to blow him off. In the interest of fairness, and more importantly, to cover my ass so no one could accuse me of sabotage, he'd get his folder. Yup. He would get every single solitary fact about the case. All my suppositions, conjecture, notes, and leads, however—the ones I'd tracked down myself and had hoped to follow—those would stay with me.

"Well, it's good to see you have the right attitude," I said, with a beaming smile. "I'll get that information to you lickety-split."

Jordan knocked at the doorframe. My ten o'clock appointment, one of the hair fiasco women, stood next to her, looking wealthy, polished and terrified at the same time.

I was thrilled to see her.

"Duty calls," I said, gesturing toward them.

Looking painfully confused, Fenton stood up and walked out without saying another word.

After cursory introductions, Wilda Lassiter took a seat across from me.

"That's an interesting first name," I said, just to put her at ease, "Is it short for anything?"

I'm no detective, though I've secretly harbored the desire to be one for as long as I can remember. Probably how I came to work in this particular field of research. My job entails more than just fact-gathering and verification. I have to decide which of the many people I meet are good candidates for on-screen interviews, and who's going to take a seat beneath the glaring lights, get one look at the camera rolling, and freeze. Conversely, I need to determine which of my interviewees are going to see this as a shot at their fifteen minutes of fame and try to upstage Gabriela. She hates when that happens.

As do I, actually. Ham interviews are generally not audience-pleasers. But good-looking people who genuinely break down during the telling of their tale of woe, are. Wilda Lassiter, a dark blonde, dressed in at least five shades and textures of pale brown, looked like a tall, beige sparrow, moving her head with nervous jerks as her bright, dark eyes took in my office, one portion at a time. I could tell she wasn't actually seeing anything. She was trying to look at ease. Failing miserably. But she had the look of an onscreen winner.

Startled by the question, she shot her attention my way and gave a small smile. "My grandmother's name was Wilda. It's odd, I know, but no matter where I am, I'm always the only one."

Wilda looked to me like a woman who didn't like to waste time. The prim way she held her French-manicured hands atop her Chanel purse (I can recognize Chanel, even if I can't afford it), and her slightly forward lean, made me jump right in. "Gabriela told me that you had some problems with a salon?"

"I'll say."

She didn't expand immediately, but I took it more as a chance to gather her thoughts than an unwillingness to talk. Rather than press, I waited. She studied her hands as they crossed and recrossed themselves atop her purse, then gave a tiny shake of her blond head.

She didn't let me down.

"It was the worst experience of my life," she said with emotion. Her eyes widened and she pointed her index finger upward. I could see it tremble, even as her face maintained calm. "My regular designer, Bethany, was off on maternity leave. I swear, she picked the worst possible time to take off. I had three formal dinners coming up. Three! And every single one of them was key. I couldn't afford to miss them."

I glanced at my notes. "Did these have to do with your line of work?"

Her face conveyed the message that I'd asked a stupid question. I get used to that with interviewees sometimes. In this case, I hoped it meant she was becoming a bit more at ease. "No, of course not. I don't have a job." I'd never heard "job" come out in two syllables before. "I'm on the board of several philanthropic organizations. And it was Christmastime, just when we all have our end-of-the-year banquets."

I started to worry that her story wasn't going to play well with our viewers. "Okay, so tell me about your hair experience."

"Well." She tugged at her short brown skirt and shifted her weight from one cheek to the other as she settled herself to talk. "Do you have anything to drink? Bottled water, perhaps?"

She was definitely more at ease now.

"Of course. Sorry, I wasn't thinking," I said as I hit the intercom button on my phone and asked Jordan if she could oblige.

"As I was saying . . . Bethany was off, gone for at least three months, and I was more than a little skittish about trusting my hair to someone else. I'd been with Bethany for about five years, and she *knew* my hair. Knew it like she knew her own. And when you find a designer like that, it's like finding gold. You know what I mean, don't you?"

I felt her glance take in my straight, though recently high-lighted tresses.

I didn't want to go down *that* road, so I just nodded. "So, what happened?"

"They assigned me to Antonio." The way she said his name made me want to laugh. She rolled her eyes in sync with the syllables as she drew them out, long and melodiously. "Highly recommended. Their top designer. Some stylist. He was an ass. A pompous ass."

I had another appointment at ten-thirty. I knew I should push Wilda to get to the nitty-gritty, but she'd warmed to the subject and I get so much more information when a subject tells me their story in their own way.

"First off, he gives a look, like I'm the bride of Franken-stein, or something. And he tells me my color is all wrong for my face. That Bethany was a nice girl but she didn't have an eye for color. That if I followed his advice, I'd look ten years younger.

"I didn't like the way he talked about Bethany, but he told me that he'd just come from a seminar that introduced him to all new procedures, things that other salons wouldn't hear about for six months. Things that Bethany might have learned if she hadn't left to have a baby. He convinced me to trust him. He said I wouldn't recognize myself when he was finished." She made a noise then, that in a woman less cultured-looking, I'd have to call a grunt. "He was right about that."

Jordan came in with two bottles of Crystal Spring water and two glasses. Wilda and I both thanked her as she left and opened our drinks simultaneously. I drank mine from the bottle. Wilda used the glass.

"Gabriela said that you took to wearing hats. Is that right?"

"Wouldn't you? He learned some new procedure all right. But he learned it wrong. He used the wrong chemical on my hair. When the girl rinsed me off, I knew something was wrong. She tried to keep me seated, but I ran to the mirror. My hair was blue. Bright blue. Like a Popsicle."

My eyes widened and I tried to picture Wilda sporting wet blue hair, staring furiously into a mirror.

"But that wasn't the worst of it. Antonio tried to get me to believe that this was simply step one, and that everything was going according to plan. I knew better; I could tell by the look on his face that he'd screwed up and was just too afraid to say so. But what was I going to do? I couldn't very well go home looking like that."

"What did you do?"

"I demanded to talk to the manager. She came out, and was less than sympathetic I might add, as though things like this happen all the time. And she tells Antonio that he better fix it or he's out on his ass. I swear, that's exactly what she said. She whispered it but I heard every word. And this Antonio winks at her and makes like he's sorry, but he talked to her real close and says something about *her* ass and I caught him rubbing her butt. Like I wouldn't see that!"

"Did he fix it? Your hair, I mean."

"I didn't want Antonio to touch me again, but he insisted. Told me I was overreacting and that everything would be fine after another twenty-five-minute processing. I was blue, you know? What else could I do? And none of the other stylists there wanted anything to do with me at that point."

Wilda took another long drink of her water before continuing.

"So, I'm a little worked up, to say the least, but Antonio assures me that I'll be back to a real color in no time. So I wait. And I have this cream all over my head, and it's wrapped in a plastic bag. I'm under the dryer now because he says that will make the natural blonde take better. This time, when they go to rinse me out, I'm watching the eyes of the girl real close, and I'm telling you there's nothing so . . . frightening as seeing a person's reaction when something horrible is happening. Especially when that horrible thing's happening to you.

"My heart about stopped beating, I think. And she calls over Antonio, except her voice is almost screaming. I grabbed my hair and I . . . I felt my scalp. My scalp! I shouldn't have been able to feel that! And little bunches of hair, like lumps. I ran over to the mirror—" Wilda interrupted herself then. She was reliving it as she spoke. Her face suffused with pain and the tears poured freely down her face. "My hair was gone. Almost all of it. There were only some patches left. Like . . . like . . . one of those Japanese trees. Chunks of blue hair stuck out, but otherwise my head was completely bald."

I was beginning to think there might be more to Gabriela's story than I originally assumed, as I logged my impressions in my trusty handheld voice recorder. Wilda's attempts to sue the salon had netted her hours of anguish from continuances, and though the case was still pending, she had clearly lost her steam. Her hair had grown out, and her attorney warned her repeatedly that costs were mounting and there was no guarantee she'd win. She stormed out of the salon that day without paying. While that move was completely understandable, she had no receipt and Antonio conveniently didn't remember the incident.

She left several pictures with me. I knew they'd make effective close-ups with her retelling the tale in a voice-over. I hoped this William was a decent scriptwriter. The blue tufts of hair sticking out all over her bald head were truly pitiful. I wouldn't wish that on anyone.

Prickles of inspiration started moving forward in my brain. I could work with this. And I had contestant number two due here in a few minutes.

In the meantime, I remembered I needed to call my Uncle Moose. I was moving out of Dan's on Saturday and could use some able-bodied help.

Aunt Lena answered on the second ring and we exchanged quick pleasantries. Uncle Moose was out, playing cards with his buddies down at the gym. A former professional wrestler, Uncle Joe had taken on the name Moose way back in his heyday, before I was born, when he'd held the title of North American Wrestling Federation Champion, which was a Very Big Deal on the south side of Chicago.

"He'll be there Saturday, Alex, don't worry. I'll make sure."

"Don't you want to check with him first? Maybe he has plans."

"Let me worry about that. He's usually just wandering around here on Saturdays anyway, getting into my hair, or into trouble." Aunt Lena took a breath, like a wind-up noise, leading me to believe that whatever came next was going to be important. "Trust me, honey, he's gonna be thrilled to help you move back home."

I stared at the phone for a few minutes after we hung up. Nobody in my family had ever liked Dan. Polite folks, they didn't slam him too badly behind his back, but I always sensed an undercurrent of "eeyoo." Even my sister Lucy

didn't much care for him, and Lucy liked everybody. That reminded me. I needed to call her and tell her I wouldn't be
there Saturday after all. I could almost picture the disappointment on her face when I broke the news.

I'd call her later.

It was almost eleven. This next chick was late. I drained
the rest of my water and decided I'd better hit the little girls'
room before my next appointment showed.

I wondered how it was that Gabriela had so many acquaintances who had hair issues. Was it just a string of exception-
ally bad luck, or what? I hadn't had a truly terrible hair
experience ever in my life. But then again, I could go months
without stepping foot in a beauty shop. I guess the law of av-
erages was on my side.

"Alex?"

Jordan met me in the doorway with the second friend. I'd
have to hold off the potty stop till later.

"Your appointment is here. This is Tammy Larken."

"Hi," I said. She looked vaguely familiar. But I couldn't
quite place her.

"You're Alex?"

Surprised both by her question and her tone, I shrugged.
"Yeah."

She didn't try to hide her displeasure. "I thought Alex was
a man."

Ooh, I could feel myself not liking this chick already.
"Nope. Sorry to disappoint you. I'm Alex St. James." I extended my hand. She shook the tips of my fingers and let go,
as though I'd handed her a fish. "Come on in. Would you like
anything to drink? Water, coffee?"

She laughed at that, a light chuckle. I had no idea what was
funny. "Uh . . . no."

"Have a seat." She did.

"When will I be filmed?" she asked.

"Excuse me?"

"The filming of the show," she said, enunciating her words. In her early thirties, she had to be the thinnest person I'd ever encountered. Not attractive-thin, she was emaciated. With short, wavy, brown hair she wore cropped close to her head, and sucked-in cheeks that showed off every bone of her jawline, I felt that nagging feeling again that she reminded me of someone. I couldn't believe her bony hands, even as they dug a cigarette out of her purse. "You mind?"

"Sorry," I said. "Regulations. This isn't a designated smoking area." It was the truth. But I knew that Bass looked the other way whenever we had someone in our offices who just had to light up to get their story out. I wasn't in the mood to deal with second-hand smoke. Especially not from this broad.

She slammed the cigarette back into the pack so hard that it bent, and then accompanied the resulting movements with several well-chosen expletives. Finally, she looked up again.

All of a sudden it hit me. Jane Hathaway. From the old *Beverly Hillbillies* show. I watched the reruns as a kid. Except Mr. Drysdale's secretary was a much gentler soul. And much prettier—which wasn't saying a lot for old Tammy here.

"What?" she asked me, and I swear, she sneered.

"I was just going to ask you about your experience at the salon," I lied.

"Yeah—and you never answered my question about when you're going to need me for filming."

"To be frank, Ms. Larken, we haven't decided yet who will be interviewed on camera and whose stories will be used as background."

"You mean I drove down the friggin' Edens all the way here for this goddamn interview and you're telling me that you might not be using my story?"

"I won't know till I hear it, so why don't we begin?"

"Why the hell should I? Gabriela told me I'd be on TV and that's what I came here for. I'm not about to spend my time with some little peon like you who doesn't know her ass from a hole in the ground."

I get these types every so often. Didn't expect it today, but hey, my luck had been going downhill lately.

I stood up. "You're absolutely right."

That surprised her.

Continuing, I gestured her to stand up. She did. "You know what? Gabriela's filming one of our ad spots right now, down at the studio. Let me give you the address."

I walked over to Jordan's desk. She was on the phone, giving me a look I didn't understand. I grabbed a Post-It note and scribbled down the information. "Gabriela's the one who's really in charge here." That was a lie I'd burn in hell for. "Take a cab . . . save the receipt, and I'll see that you're reimbursed. When you get there, tell her that we need your story on tape first, before we do any of the regular filming."

Tammy's eyes showed a touch of interest. "She can do that?"

"When she wants to. Sometimes she's a little . . . what's the word . . . persnickety? But I'm sure you already know that." I grinned, as though we were sharing a joke at the star's expense. "Push her. Hard, if you have to. She *can* do it. Don't let her tell you she can't. And then tell her to send the tape to my attention. At her earliest convenience, of course."

Jordan started to mouth something to me, the receiver still tight to the side of her head.

I smiled and winked at Tammy, sending her on her way with a cheerful feeling in my heart.

Jordan waited till she was out of earshot. "Here," she said, her low voice intense. "I think you need to take this one."

I took the receiver. "Alex St. James."

"Oh!" The sounds of a woman crying met my ear, and my first concern was for Lucy, but within seconds I knew it wasn't her. I had no idea who was calling me. Until she took a breath and spoke to me in Polish. "Alex, I am Sophie, from yesterday. My brother, Matthew . . . he's gone. He's missing."

Chapter Six

I made it to Sophie's address in just over twenty-five minutes. She lived in a tidy neighborhood on the near south side, well-known for its enduring Polish population. All the brick three-flats in this proud five-block radius, with their sparkling white trim and clipped shrubs, were a testament to the work ethic that the nationality was known for. Despite the overcast day and the scattered rain clouds that had just finished a cleansing down-pour, it was a welcoming neighborhood, the kind where I wouldn't be fearful walking alone at night.

I found her building right away. There was no place to park out in front, however, so on my second circuit around the block, I fitted into the only open space, at the far corner between two big Chevys. I loved my little Escort. Made it in with less than six inches to spare. Just as I moved to open my car door, a man emerged from Sophie's building.

Even though I was at least seven houses away, I could tell it was the burly fellow from the salon. Ro. He moved with purpose toward a dark sedan across the street from Sophie's house. There was no reason in the world for me to want to hide from him, but I got the silly sense that I should. Ole Nancy Drew kicking in again. What the heck.

Maybe he was Sophie's boyfriend come to offer his help, I told myself. But that didn't feel right. As he pulled his car into the center of the narrow street, I did two things: I noticed that the pavement beneath his car was wet, which meant he hadn't been there long, and I found a gum wrapper on the floor of my passenger side that I needed to pick up, just then. This allowed me to wait till the sound of the car passed before raising my head to check the rearview mirror. He turned left at the corner and was gone. He hadn't seen me. Of that, I was certain.

I suppose I could have gone another turn around the block and taken his recently-vacated spot, a much better one, but proud of my parallel parking efforts, I let it go and hoped the rain didn't start up again soon.

Sophie had told me to come around the back. She was there, waiting for me, standing near the support beam of her small wooden porch. Her arms folded and unfolded across her chest. Tension in her body language made her bounce.

"Alex?" she said as I walked up. Her eyes were wide and blue; she looked at me the same way Lucy does sometimes when she's gotten into trouble and needs my help to get out. "Thank you, thank you," she said in English, the words coming out like "tenk you," as she grasped my hand in both of hers and led me inside.

Sophie's three-flat had been converted, so that this floor boasted two apartments instead of one. Sophie and her brother occupied the back half of the first level. This was one tiny place to live.

We sat in the kitchen, around a four-chair aluminum table with a white-speckled Formica top. Very fifties. There were two rooms behind heavily varnished wood doors, and a hall that no doubt led to a bathroom. Everything, from the kitchen sink on legs, to the refrigerator with the freezer on the bottom, was a throwback from many decades ago. I guessed that they'd rented this place fully furnished. And I wanted to get a look at the other rooms, just because I'm a nosy chick.

"You want coffee?" she asked, getting up quickly, as though she'd made some gross mistake.

"No, no. Just sit down, Sophie."

She rubbed at her forehead, then perched her supershort thumbnail between her teeth, as if waiting for me to speak.

"Just now, out front, I thought I saw that guy from the salon. Ro?"

Her teeth didn't let go of the nail as she nodded her head.

"Is he your . . . boyfriend?"

"No!" she said, slapping both hands on the table.

Not quite the response I'd expected, I nodded. "Okay then, who is he?"

"His name is Rodero. He come here to pick up something. For work."

Remembering the altercation yesterday, I asked, "Does he have any idea where your brother is?"

"I don't tell him Matthew gone. You find him? I pay you."

"Nuh-no, wait. Hold on a minute. I don't know exactly what I can do here . . ."

Sophie pulled out my card. "I look up this word. In-ves-ti-ga-tor. It mean you find people. No?"

"Not exactly," I said.

"Not like Magnum?"

"Magnum?"

"*Magnum PI.*"

The old Tom Selleck show. Still on in reruns, obviously. "No. I work for a TV station. I investigate interesting stories . . . like the news."

Her look told me I wasn't getting through.

I switched to Polish and told her, "I'm not a detective. Not like Magnum. I investigate stories."

Sophie's lips compressed into a thin line as she nodded in a way that tore at my heart. "I don't know what to do," she said, lapsing into her native tongue.

"First of all, how do you know he's missing? Maybe he's just out for the day."

"No," she said with a vehement shake of her head. "They called me from his work this morning. He never showed up."

"Did he say anything before he left?"

Sophie's eyes welled with tears. "He never came home last night."

"You're sure?"

I watched her fight a losing battle with her emotions, her eyes expressing fear, deep sorrow, and something else. I couldn't quite put my finger on it. "I came in late last night. I had a date. And I thought Matthew was already home because he usually goes to bed early. But when I went in his room this morning, I knew he hadn't been there, because his clothes that I washed and folded were still on his bed, the way I left them."

Getting all that out in one breath took all of Sophie's energy, and she covered her face with her hands, trying to quiet her own sobs.

I let her cry for a minute. Truth was, I had no idea what to do next.

"Do you have any idea where he might have gone?"

"He only wants to help me, I know that."

I studied Sophie as she settled herself. When the tears started, her face had immediately broken out into huge red welts, and her eyes puffed up.

"Do you want me to go with you to the police station?"

She sat up as if slapped. "The police? I can't go to the police. Why do you want me to do that?"

"If your brother's missing, we can file a report. I don't know if it's too early, but it won't hurt to get his information out there. What kind of car does he drive?" I asked, pulling out my notebook.

"No car."

"Do you have a picture? We can give that to the police to help them."

"No. No police."

"Why the hell not?"

"I can't."

"Are you here illegally?" I asked.

"No," she said with tiny pride, "we have been sponsored. And we have our papers in order. I just don't want Matthew to get into trouble. He will lose his job."

No matter how much I tried to prod, Sophie had clammed up about Matthew and why contacting the police would result in the loss of a job. She insisted that Matthew had not gotten into trouble before, that he had no record of arrest.

"What about a girlfriend? Do you think he might've spent the night with someone and just forgot about work today?"

"No. No. Matthew never takes time for himself. He never tried to find a girlfriend. He is so handsome, and all the girls want to go out with him, but he want to make a good life for us here, and make our parents proud, and he never stops working. He's just trying to keep us together and strong."

"Sophie," I finally said, exasperation evident in my voice, "there's not a chance of finding out where he's gone unless you can give me some help, here. Isn't there *anyone* who might have a clue? Anyone Matthew might turn to or keep in contact with?"

"Yes . . . I don't know. Maybe."

"Okay." I wiggled forward in my chrome-legged chair, making it squeak. "Who?"

"Father Bruno. From St. Dymphna's. He is our sponsor to the United States. He helps us and takes care of us."

"Good, good. Do you want me to call him?" I asked.

Sophie bit the insides of her cheeks, and her face welted up again, as though she might break into sobs at any moment. She glanced up at the clock. "Maybe he's there now. You'll come with me?"

In for a penny, in for a pound, I thought. "Sure."

Father Bruno lived in a square-ish, brick, and solid-looking home in the center of the block. While St. Dymphna's Church, at the southern end of the street, had been built in 1968, according to the large and obvious corner-stone near the front doors, Father Bruno's home was much older. It didn't sport a year, but a concrete sign, pitted with age, sat stoically above the front door, capital letters spelling out the word "Rectory." Clearly this building had never been intended to serve any other purpose. I wondered what would become of it in years to come, as the dwindling priesthood made it difficult to justify the upkeep of so many residences across the archdiocese.

The parish name, St. Dymphna's, and even the priest's name were vaguely familiar to me. I was curious to meet him, and try to remember the connection.

Sophie, I discovered, was a physical person. She thought nothing of gripping my hand as we approached the building's cement front steps, scurrying to keep ahead of the drizzle. Even on the ride over, she touched me several times; I began to realize that she needed constant and tangible evidence that she wasn't in this dilemma alone.

The doorbell rang loud enough for us to hear it, standing outside the wood-framed door. After waiting more than five minutes, we rang it a second time, despite the hand-lettered sign that instructed to ring it only once. The pebbled glass door made seeing anything inside impossible, and the dark interior led me to believe that Father Bruno was not home.

I was surprised, then, when a flash of yellow appeared and the lock turned.

"Sophie?"

"Oh, Father," she said, sobbing, "Matthew no come home."

From her instant, high-powered cries, I gathered that the man at the door was Father Bruno. Wearing a casual ensemble of a yellow golf shirt and navy pants, the silver-haired priest should have opted for the next size after extra-large. He sent a curious glance my direction, as he took Sophie by the shoulders and led her inside. Not knowing what else to do, I followed and caught his indication that I should close and lock the door behind me.

The long, dark corridor was lined on either side with deep mahogany doors, polished to high-gloss. There were at least eight, all closed. One small light fixture, overhead, cast scant light in the area. The effect was mausoleum-ish, but I'd been in rectories before and knew that most holy men didn't spend a lot of time worried about a welcoming décor.

Father Bruno opened the first door to the right, and gestured us in.

"I apologize for the delay in answering. Emil must have stepped away again, and I was unaware." I shot him a quizzical glance, and he explained. "The rectory secretary."

The priest's face was familiar. I knew I'd seen him before, but I couldn't place him.

This room was barely an improvement over the hall. While spacious, and outfitted for both work and comfort: desk to the right, sitting room—complete with TV and DVD player—to the left, it was drab. A corner office, it had five tall double-hung windows, but the gray sky outside offered little in terms of light.

Sophie sat in a burgundy leather chair. The fancy kind

with bronze buttons lining the sides and back. I took a matching one next to her and perched my elbows on the arms. Sophie was beginning to quiet, and for the few moments that it took Bruno to pull a box of tissues from behind his mahogany desk, I thought she might have forgotten I was there. Her eyes followed the man's every movement, with huge alertness, as though ready to jump at his words. Indeed, her whole body, at first relaxed from releasing all the anguish, now tensed up again—a runner ready for the starting gun.

It occurred to me that Father Bruno must have sobbing women come visit him all the time. He gave Sophie's shoulder an avuncular pat, and set the tissue box on her lap. "Now," he said, moving to sit behind his desk, his eyes concerned behind drooping lids, "tell me what happened. What did you say about Matthew?"

Between hiccups, Sophie spoke in her halting English. Explaining the situation was so difficult for her, I could almost see her physical pain as she spoke. But I let her tell the story with no interruption, wanting to allow her the chance to get it out once again. Like poison to be purged, oftentimes the more a story is told, the easier it gets. And although Matthew's disappearance was still fresh and raw, I hoped that Sophie could find a way to face it with enough objectivity to be helpful.

They conversed in English; he had no accent, and nothing about him suggested a particular ethnicity. He was fair-skinned and paunchy, with that tell-tale gray coloring of a heavy smoker. After Sophie covered everything she'd told me, he nodded and worked his lower lip for a moment. When he turned to me, I could sense he was still pondering all she'd said.

"And you are . . . ?"

"I'm Alexandrine Szatjemski," I said providing the name I

preferred to use when covering stories. I leaned forward to offer my hand. He seemed momentarily surprised by the move, but he took it and gave a perfunctory shake. "I'm a friend of Sophie's." That was, of course, a stretch. I met the girl yesterday, for crying out loud. But that would take too long to explain, and was immaterial anyway.

"Father Bruno Creighter," he said. "Pleased to meet you Ms. Szatjemski."

Hearing his last name dropped the last piece of puzzle into place. He'd been a prominent player hovering around the pedophile priest scandal a few years back. As one of the Chicago Archdiocese's parish-level spokesmen, he'd made frequent public apologies to young victims, now grown. I'd seen his face in the newspaper plenty of times. He'd lambasted our station in one of his appearances, because he took exception to our handling of one of the stories. I decided it would be best if I didn't introduce myself, fully.

Settling himself, he studied me for a moment, then pulled a pack of Marlboro Lights from his top center drawer and apologized. "I hope you don't mind," he said, "it's a filthy habit, but I can't seem to summon the will to stop." He shrugged and gave me a wry smile. "Especially in tense situations." He returned his attention to Sophie.

"When did you notice Matthew was missing?" Bruno asked, shaking a cigarette out. He lit it with a gold lighter dug from his pocket and then tapped it against the leather blotter on his desk before resting it in his palm. A full-color enamel portrait of the Sacred Heart of Jesus decorated the lighter's top and he caressed the smoothness of the decoration with his thumb as he smoked and listened.

Cigarette lighters designed with your favorite priest in mind; now there's a marketing niche I never would have imagined.

He didn't take care to blow the smoke off to the side, as polite smokers nowadays tend to do. Each puff was savored even as his caramel-colored eyes paid rapt attention, focused on everything Sophie had to say.

Sophie tried to remember exactly what time the landscape company had called. Matthew was a gardener's assistant at a suburban shop and had been scheduled for a big project that day. "They called about ten-thirty this morning. Maybe a little later." She took two tissues from Father Bruno's stash and worked them into twisted strings. "I didn't know what to do."

"You were right to come here, my dear," he said. "We will find him."

Buoyed by his praise she brightened, visibly. Her eyes had gotten bluer from her crying and they widened with childlike eagerness. Still snuffling, she offered the priest an additional tidbit, as though hoping for another "attaboy." "Alex said we should call the police to tell them. Should we?"

He gazed up at the ceiling for a long moment, blowing a stream of smoke upward and away from us. "Let me make some inquiries first," he said. "I wouldn't want to jeopardize the boy's job. He's got a solid future ahead of him there, as long as he keeps control of his temper." His glance toward Sophie made her look away.

She bit her lip, then colored bright red before addressing me. "Matthew has been in many fights since we come here," she said. "He think some people look down on us and he get very mad sometimes." She shrugged. "But he never not come home before."

"But what if something's happened to him?" I said. "How will we know, if the police aren't out looking for him? We can't just sit around and wait and hope for the best."

Bruno took a moment to finish his cigarette, then stubbed

it out into a Star of David-shaped glass ashtray. When he spoke, he did so slowly, answering my protest with careful patience. "No, of course not. I have a few contacts who will be able to let me know if he's turned up at all. And he will, I'm certain."

He must have read the skepticism on my face, because he interrupted before I could open my mouth. Indicating me, he turned to Sophie and asked. "She is a friend?"

"Yes," Sophie answered. "I trust her."

Wow, I thought. After only one day. I must really have an honest face.

Bruno took a deep breath and let it out in a sigh. "We're able to do a lot of good for new immigrants here," he said. "I've been around long enough to realize, however, that it's sometimes better to ask forgiveness than permission." He smiled. "Matthew is one of my kids. One of the many young people I've sponsored from eastern Europe who came here for a better life." He folded his hands together on the desk, leaning forward on his arms. "A police investigation would uncover Matthew's place of work and since he's not . . . officially . . . on their books, it would ruin our relationship with that company. It's a small company, but over the past few years they've given over a dozen young men a good start." His eyes squinted at me. "I'd hate to lose that valuable contact."

I tried again. "I think I'd feel better, and I think Sophie would feel better," I shot a glance her way, urging support, "if we could do *something* in the meantime." Sophie was watching Bruno, as though measuring his reaction to my words. I continued, "Waiting is always the worst. Is there anywhere or anyone you can think of that I can check with?"

"Not at the moment," he said, shaking his head. His second chin wobbled, trying without success to keep up with the movement of the first one. "I'd be more than happy to keep in contact with both of you, though. I'll call up a few of the other boys and see what they know." Glancing at both of us in turn, he asked, "How does that sound?"

Sophie nodded, but I was unconvinced.

Bruno continued. "Matthew is an intelligent young man, but a bit hot-headed, as anyone who knows him can attest. I'm very concerned that he didn't come home last night. That's not like him. He might be afraid to face you, Sophie, if he got into another scrape."

"But," I began, whether or not Sophie was going to back me—unfortunately, in times like this, I have no "off-switch" when answers don't make sense and I want to know more, "what if he's hurt? In the hospital? How will we know?"

Sophie's eyes widened as I spoke and I regretted worrying her further, but I still would have felt better if we contacted the police. Of course, maybe even Matthew would argue that losing his job was worse than spending a night in the hospital—or the slammer.

"I understand your concerns. You're completely correct. But, again, I have many contacts." He tapped at a small gold cross pin he had attached to his collar that I hadn't noticed earlier. "One of the perks of the job."

A voice came from my far left. "Father?"

"There you are!" he said. "Where have you been?"

I followed his gaze, as did Sophie, to a second door that led to an adjacent room I hadn't noticed earlier, tucked as it was in the corner behind a wing chair.

The fellow who entered appeared bewildered by our presence. He blinked several times, switching his focus between me and Sophie as he came forward. I put him mid-fifties, scrawny, with a full head of slicked-back black hair so uniform in color that it had to be dyed. He wore a red-plaid cotton short-sleeve shirt and gray polyester pants.

He still hadn't answered Father Bruno's question.

"Emil," the priest said again, "were you . . . in back?"

Closer now, it began to dawn on me that wherever "in back" was, Emil had been hitting the sauce there. His head slightly bent, he glanced at the two of us through nervous eyes. "Sorry," he mumbled. "You need something?"

"No," Bruno said, "but these young ladies rang the doorbell twice. I wondered where you were."

Emil crinkled up his face in exaggerated apology. Why people under the influence believed they needed to react big, was beyond me. Drunks tended not to be subtle. "Oh man, I'm sorry." He scratched his head and moved close enough to lean his hip against the desk. Father Bruno's face told me he was not amused. I caught the mixed tang of alcohol and body odor and leaned back a little. "I was doing some of that paperwork that's been piling up. Hey!" he said, his eyes focusing for a moment. "That you, Sophie?"

Her body had gone rigid and she averted her eyes.

Emil's face split into a grin and I winced. His crooked teeth, brown around the edges, were tiny. Too short for his gumline, they looked as though someone had painstakingly cut them all in half.

"Haven't seen you in a while," he continued.

"Emil," Bruno interrupted. "Sophie's brother Matthew . . . you remember him, don't you?"

He nodded, again with extra effort.

"Matthew seems to be missing. He didn't call here at all recently, did he?"

Emil shook his head. "No, Father, I haven't heard from him."

"No messages you forgot to give me?"

"No, sir, none. None at all."

Sophie and I stood at the same time. She positioned herself close, and I felt her fingers grasp my elbow with a tiny tug. Her overbite seemed even more pronounced now, as she bit her lip. "I think we go, okay? Maybe Matthew call home already."

"Sure," I said. "I need to get back to work, too."

Father Bruno stood, polite man that he was, and held up a finger. "Ms. Szatjemski, why don't you give me your address and phone number?" He handed me a pen from a stand on his desk, and a pad of Post-It notes. Noting my raised eyebrows perhaps, he added, "Would you like me to keep you informed as well?"

"Sure," I said. "This is my parents' number. I'm staying there." Sophie grabbed my right hand as soon as I finished writing, her tugs becoming more insistent as Emil moved closer and spoke to her in low tones behind me.

"Where do you work?" Bruno asked me, canting his head in curiosity.

"In an office downtown. I'm a secretary." It was my usual cover story, one I often used when I started investigating features. The lie fell from my mouth out of habit. Probably burn in hell for that. Right now our attention needed to stay with Sophie and Matthew. A mention of my affiliation with *Midwest Focus* and that might shift. I gave Sophie's hand a squeeze, so she wouldn't contradict me, but she appeared to be oblivious to the conversation, intent instead on getting out the door.

I shook my head as we left. My boss thought I was busy with hair care stories, when really I was trying to steal back the Milla Murder story from the new hotshot on our staff. In the process of all this, I'd lied to a priest, and I'd agreed to help a young woman whose brother had gone missing. Wow, I was having a busy day.

Chapter Seven

I wanted to call Lucy from home in the morning, but my sister wasn't much of an early riser, and I needed to get rolling again on this hair story. As a researcher, my job was to take tons of information and winnow it down to a precious few ounces. Which meant my full scope of information was due on William Armstrong's desk by the end of business today, and I still had another woman to interview.

Other than Wilda Lassiter's bald and blue-headed incident, I didn't have much to go on. After Sophie's frantic phone call, I asked Jordan to reschedule my third hair victim, Angela Cucio. She'd been accommodating, thank goodness. I hoped that bode well for today's chat. Since I had nothing from Tammy Larken other than the bad taste left in my mouth from our brief, unpleasant conversation, I needed to make sure this next interview soared.

I'd made it back to the office yesterday to be greeted by Fenton, nearly apoplectic with anticipation over the file I promised him. It took me just over fifteen minutes to gather and copy all the information, but the way he behaved you'd think he waited a year. Bass had provided him with plenty of basic facts. And while nothing stopped him from researching the story on his own, Fent had spent the entire day waiting for the folder. I was certain he'd been disappointed to find that I hadn't swooped in like the good fairy and left him a fully-written report inside. Too bad.

His scriptwriter was going to have a tough go, but David

Gonzales was a talented guy. I wouldn't have minded being assigned to him, now that Tony was gone. But I figured that maybe this William might be good, too. I'd find out soon enough.

I flipped through my calendar to see when my next free day might be. Lucy always liked to have the date to look forward to, and I knew how much she'd been counting on seeing me this Saturday. Even though I was pretty anxious to grab my junk out of Dan's place, now that we'd made the decision to split, my letting Lucy down gave me a queasy, sad feeling, as though I was making a poor choice and I knew it.

The Wrigley Building across the river showed nine o'clock through a lingering mist that looked to be burnt off any moment by the sun rising over the lake. Time to talk to Lucy. I picked up the receiver.

My door opened, without an announcing knock. "Alex?"

Fenton actually called me by the correct name. I was impressed enough to hold off dialing, but I kept the phone close to my ear in a "don't make this long" maneuver.

"What's up?"

"I talked to Bass. He's giving me an extra week on the Millie story."

My lips compressed as I bit back correcting him on Milla's name once again. I'd have to stop in by Gonzales to make sure the poor girl's name wasn't massacred in Fenton's notes. "Another week?" I asked, and I know incredulity squeaked out in my voice. "This is one of the hottest local stories out there. Why in the world would you want to hold it for a week?"

Fenton was wearing yet another pair of Dockers, dark gray this time, with a pink golf shirt. It had one of those "I paid a lot for this item" logos embroidered in yellow on the chest, small enough that I couldn't quite make it out, but from where I sat it looked like a pig being hoisted up by its middle.

He flipped his hair back, jutting his chin out in an insolent way. "Because," he said giving an impatient wiggle, "you haven't been exactly forthcoming with information. I'm in a bind here, you know."

I stood up, and although the room stretched between us, I noticed he took a tiny step backward. Just enough to make me feel like I had an edge. "Guess what, Fent? I've got a story to research too. So, your best bet is to figure out how to do your job and get it done. Nobody here is gonna hold your hand."

"You know, that's another thing."

"What?" I asked. He backed out of the doorway to allow me to pass.

"The way you talk to me. I'm Genevieve Mulhall's nephew, you know."

"Yes, I'm fully aware. And I remember Hank telling us to treat you like everyone else. Just like any other member of the team. And you know what? Each of the players on this team holds up their end, and I don't think we should start making exceptions. Do you?"

His brown eyes blazed.

I made a show of looking at my watch. "I have another appointment scheduled soon. For *my* story."

"The hair care story." His mocking voice dripped derision.

"The hair care story." I answered him in kind.

"Well," he said, "it's obvious they know which of their researchers to give the important stories to."

This guy was a total idiot.

"You can look at it that way," I agreed, forcing a smile on my face to let him know just how pissed I was. "But then it only reinforces the fact that you won't need my help. Not one little bit."

I've always wanted to flounce away from someone. It's such a neat, strong action. So, I shot him another insincere smile saying, "And next time you come to my office, remember to knock first," and turned my back in a grand gesture of dismissal, not realizing that William the scriptwriter was right behind me, yet again. I flounced all right. Right onto his left instep while the knee of my other leg rammed into his thigh.

"Geez!" I exclaimed. I was so embarrassed that my immediate reaction came out sounding annoyed rather than apologetic.

"I'm sorry," William said, grabbing me by the elbow, keeping us both from falling to the ground in a heap. He managed to keep me upright and still hang onto a manila folder tucked under his right arm. Chalk one up for being coordinated. Him, not me.

I heard Fenton snicker.

I backed away, murmuring my excuses, feeling clumsy and off-kilter.

"I was just coming to see you," he said to me. His eyes flicked over my head. I turned and watched the Nephew retreat back to his office. "But if you were on your way out . . ."

Totally frazzled, I stood there, attempting to collect my composure. "No, actually, I was just trying to shake Fenton."

He gave a look then; his eyebrows raised a notch and his mouth twitched. It could have been amusement, or it could have just been an acknowledgment that I'd spoken. I wasn't sure, but I headed back into my office after checking with Jordan to be sure my nine-thirty hadn't cancelled, and motioned William to follow me.

"Come on in," I said, with an expansive gesture toward the two chairs by my desk. Having met him only twice and both times being under less than ideal conditions, I felt an inexplicable need to impress him. As if to prove I wasn't quite the twit that I appeared to be at first, or even at second glance.

"Hmm. Different setup," he said, taking in the side-set desk. "Interesting chair."

The black leather chair behind my desk was about as comfortable as they come. High-backed, with cushy arms, it came with the office and it was beginning to show its age.

"Yeah. It's a keeper."

The man, it seemed, didn't smile often, or maybe it was just that he didn't like me much. Not that I could blame him at this point. But I got a better look at him as he settled himself across from me. Just as handsome as I remembered, maybe even more so now that I could assess him without little streaks of panic distracting me.

"So," I began, "how are things going, so far?"

"Good."

"Starting to settle in?"

He nodded. "Yeah."

His brevity unnerved me a little. It made him harder to read, but I got the distinct impression that there was more to him than met the eye. Still waters run deep, so they say. Mr. Armstrong carried himself with an air of confidence that I found compelling; I sensed there was much more to this man than his laconic responses would suggest.

I tried again. "Is it a lot different here than at the *Sun-Times*?"

Amusement. I swore I caught a flicker of amusement in his eyes. As though he knew I was trying to jump-start conversation, and he was having fun watching me flounder. "I'm adjusting."

I waited.

"I worked at the *Times* about eight years, wanting to write, but copyediting mostly. I knew when I started that there was a hierarchy in place and that if I wanted to make a name for myself, I'd have to play by their rules. I knew that, and I was prepared for it."

He gave a self-effacing shrug. "I wanted a feature column, worked hard to get one, and did lots of writing with no byline because my boss at the time promised that my cooperation and team spirit would pay dividends down the road."

"But . . ."

"Yes. But." He raised his eyebrows in a helpless gesture.

William Armstrong was anything but helpless. I'd gotten the lowdown on him over the past couple of days. From everything I gathered, he was a respected and valued team player. No shortage of glowing reviews there. There was however, one small glitch.

No one would tell me why he left the newspaper. Like it was some big secret. Or maybe, no one knew.

I'm nothing if not direct. "But," I repeated. "You left. How come?"

The breath he expelled as he leaned backward told me this was a difficult subject. "It's a long story."

I opened my hands. "I'm a good listener."

"Some other time, perhaps." His blue eyes seemed to intensify, almost as though he was gauging my trustworthiness.

"Okay, then. Whenever you're ready."

"Thank you," he said with a nod. And then, he smiled.

When he did, his entire face transformed. Tiny crinkles near his eyes and around his mouth deepened. I could tell these were lines that got lots of use; it just so happened that I was seeing them for the first time. I felt my stomach flip-flop as my face began to warm. Yowza. I'd better hope he didn't smile at me too often or I'd never get anything done.

"About this hair story," he said, his eyes traveling down to the manila folder on his lap. "I thought maybe you could bring me up to speed? Give me an idea of what else is coming? I have *some* information. Not a lot."

I wondered that he had any at all. I hadn't done my homework on Wilda Lassiter's interview yet. "What do you have?"

"Let's see." He dug out a sheet of paper, and placed it at the edge of my desk. "Ah, yes . . . Ms. Tammy Larken."

"Tammy Larken?"

"The name rings a bell with you?"

I couldn't tell if he was making a joke, or slamming me. His face was back to being devoid of expression, so I decided to tread with caution. "How do you know her?"

"She came to visit me yesterday—around noon. Apparently she made a trip down to the studio to see Gabriela, based on your suggestion." I cringed; I could tell this anecdote wasn't going to have a happy ending. "What you didn't know when you sent her, was that Gabriela had rescheduled the shoot. Nobody there but a couple of techs."

"Ouch."

"Yeah. Ouch."

William let the words sink in. I half-dreaded what he might say next, but I had to know.

"She came back to see you?" I asked, a gentle prod.

"Actually, she came to see *you*. But you were long gone by then, so the staff directed her to me."

"I'm so sorry."

"Don't be. Once she calmed down, she really was a good interview. Had a terrible experience and is quite . . . animated . . . when she speaks."

"I'll bet. I really *am* sorry. She was just so—"

"Incorrigible?"

"Pretty much."

"And is that how you usually treat incorrigible guests?"

I was certain his lips twitched that time. It was a gentle rebuke, one I deserved. "No," I said, genuinely sorry now. "That was unprofessional of me. It's just—" I stopped myself.

The truth was I'd been frustrated with my failure to find my adoption records, with losing the Milla story to creepy little Fenton, with bad hair issues, with Dan, and with knowing I still had to disappoint my sister. It all weighed heavily on my mind, but William didn't need to hear the history of my sorry life. I wasn't making a very good impression on this fellow and yet a niggling feeling in the back of my brain was telling me I ought to try and remedy that. "Just a bad day," I finished. Wow, that sounded lame. Bet I impressed him.

He gave a short nod, as though in absolution.

"So . . . Alex." It was the first time he'd used my name to address me. Hearing it gave me a tiny wave of pleasure. As unexpected as my reaction to his earlier grin. "Is that a nickname?"

"Yep. Short for Alexandrine."

"That's an unusual name. I like it."

"Thanks, I do too," I said, smiling myself, hoping to coax another one out of him. I was a glutton for punishment.

"In any case, about Tammy Larken . . ."

I heaved a mental sigh. Back to business so soon.

"She told me her story. And it was pretty intense." He glanced down at his notes. "She seemed like a good candidate for the camera, too," he added, answering my next question. "But I thought you might want to make that assessment yourself. I didn't want to step on your toes." He looked at me. "Although I almost did that out in the hall just now."

Tiny smile that time. My heart gave a little lurch in response. He did have a sense of humor.

"Thanks. I appreciate that. More than you know. I'll give her a call."

"Actually, she's stopping by again today. If you're free around one-thirty, I'll walk her over."

"One-thirty?"

"I offered to take her to lunch," he said, getting up. "Figured it might help to smooth her ruffled feathers."

"Oh. Sure. Lunch was probably a good idea." I nodded to William as he left, and wondered why all of a sudden I felt a whole lot less ebullient than I had just a moment before.

Jordan popped her head inside the doorway. "Angela Cucio's here."

With the name Angela Cucio, I'd expected a raven-haired Italian beauty. I wasn't even close. She turned out to be short and stocky, like someone had jammed a full-grown woman into a kid-size body. Her frizzy strawberry-blonde hair hung past her shoulders, an unusual style for a woman in her mid-fifties. Everything about her gave me the impression she hadn't had an easy go of life. As she came in and took a seat, I caught the unmistakable scent of stale cigarettes. Judging from the wrinkles around her mouth and the yellow of her teeth when she smiled, I would have to guess she nailed at least three packs a day.

Where the other two women had been dressed to the nines, accessorized and polished, Angela wore snakeskin cowboy boots, low-slung jeans and a peasant blouse. When she shifted in her seat, the hem of her shirt came up enough to let a roll from her belly hang over her silver "Harley" belt buckle.

Jordan brought in two bottled waters and set them on the desk, held up from walking out again by Angela's hand on her arm. She looked up at Jordan. "Don't forget to call now, y'hear?"

While she didn't have anything even remotely resembling a Southern drawl, the "y'hear" suited her. Jordan gave the woman a solemn nod, then headed back to her desk. I'd have to find out later what that was all about.

"I really appreciate you rescheduling on such short notice," I said, by way of an opening.

She brushed aside my thanks. "Not a problem," she said, the word coming out "prollem."

She seemed so unlike the other two that I couldn't help myself asking, "So, how do you know Gabriela?"

"Gabby? She's my niece."

"Really?" I said, astonishment apparent in my voice. "She didn't mention that."

"Yeah, well, I'll betcha she didn't want me to mention it neither."

"No?"

She uncapped the water bottle. "Nah . . . you know Gabby. She knows I'd get a kick out of being on TV, even if it is for something like this. And she prolly'd figure that if it got out I was her Auntie, then everybody'd start accusing her of playing favorites." Grinning at me, she recapped the bottle, without having taken a drink.

"Auntie Angela—" I had to say it out loud.

"Call me Angie. Everybody does. Haven't been called Angela since I was a little plaid-skirted brat back in grammar school. And back then it was Angela O'Toole."

"Cucio's your married name?"

"Well, yeah. My last one. Been married twice. Won't likely do it again, but both were fun. While they lasted." She took a deep breath as she sat back in her chair and I worried for a moment that I was about to be treated to a play-by-play of her love life.

"So Angie," I said, easing back into interview mode, knowing I'd have a hard time keeping the unbelievable idea that she was related to Gabriela out of my mind, "you had a bad experience in a hair salon?"

"Oh yeah," she said, her voice taking on an amused growl. She uncapped the water bottle again, and took a long drink, making a glugging sound as she downed the liquid. I waited till she finished. "Happened a long time ago," she said.

"I gathered. Your hair seems to be a good length . . ."

"Yup."

She put the bottle on my desk and skooched herself forward, close enough to lean her forearms against the edge and to look comfortable doing it. "Fifteen years ago last August I decided to try a new place everybody was saying was the best. It was real high-priced, real chi-chi pooh-pooh, you know what I mean? They didn't just cut your hair, they 'designed' it. I know everybody uses that term nowadays but back then it was still like some big deal."

The fifteen years ago caveat troubled me. While a hair emergency is a hair emergency, I didn't know if the distance of time would be an issue. Maybe Gabriela *was* playing favorites by putting Auntie Angie up here. But the woman oozed genuineness. I liked her already. A rough-and-tumble woman, you could see her participating in an athletic event, not winning, but having the biggest cheering section in the stands.

Her eyes were so light, I couldn't tell if they were green or blue. I imagined that could change, depending on what she was wearing. All earnestness, she continued, "This place was known for its 'different' approach to styling hair. They didn't use hairspray or mousse. Too common. They used seaweed and mud and the essences of exotic plants . . . whatever that means. I thought it was a bunch of hooey, of course. Just a creative way to milk more money out of gullible people, you know?"

"So why did you go there?"

"Honestly? I can't remember. Been too long. But I think I had a mind to show all those folks who raved about the place what goofs they were for falling for such crap. I got the money, so high prices didn't bother me none. I wanted to come out and say, 'Hey, I been there, I done that, and I don't want the T-shirt.' "

She smiled at that, amused by some sort of private joke.

"Did you have a bad reaction to some of their unique methods?"

"Bad reaction? Not exactly. This place, they're a franchise now—believe it or not—they also specialized in advanced techniques, and shit like that. Well, they didn't use scissors, not much at least. They were 'artistes' and they only cut using razors. Gave me the worst cut of my life."

"But it grew out," I said.

Angela smiled, and her face went all craggy as she did, but I sensed she was amused. "Nope," she said. "Never grew back. Never will."

With that, she lifted up one side of her hair and showed me her perfectly slashed right ear. The entire curved top was missing.

She laughed. "Not exactly Van Gogh, huh?"

Chapter Eight

I grinned at the expression on Dan's face when he answered the door. All of a sudden, the long trek up Lake Shore Drive with a senior citizen behind the wheel didn't seem such a bad way to have spent the morning. I'd had second thoughts about the ride, knowing Uncle Moose's proclivity for hanging in the right lane doing twenty miles under the speed limit. But I felt like I was going into hostile territory and I wanted him there, both for moral support and for the use of his big-trunked Cadillac. Even though that meant I had to ride shotgun to Mr. Magoo.

"Hey, Dan," my Uncle Moose said, fairly bulldozing his way into the condo, using the empty boxes in his arms as a battering ram.

"Joe," he said, and I swear he stammered the single word. "What's up?"

I followed Uncle Moose in, enjoying myself. Though they'd only met a couple of times, Dan, Mr. Schmooze himself, never seemed entirely comfortable with my former wrestling champ uncle.

Standing dead center in the living room, Uncle Moose affected a look of pained curiosity. Working at it, I could tell. Trying to look as obvious as possible.

Still in relatively good shape despite his advanced years, he was just short of six feet tall, with broad shoulders and a full head of hair that he kept dark by working used coffee grounds through it every night before bedtime. I wondered how my aunt handled it. No wonder she could doze off in a heartbeat. Smell that every night of your married life and boom, caffeine ain't gonna bother you anymore. "How long you lived here?" he asked Dan.

"Five years."

"Five, huh." Uncle Moose wandered through the spacious area, his head swiveling this way and that, taking it all in. Dressed in his old blue jeans with bright red topstitching—a popular trend back in the seventies—he scratched the side of his head. Total affectation. I had to admit, I was enjoying the show. "The place look like this when you moved in?"

I saw the condo through my uncle's eyes. He of the patterned fuzzy rocker that reclined with the touch of a button and accompanying mechanical "thunk." Dan's home, with buttery brown leather sofas imported from Italy, and jacquard draperies whose precise fringes framed the room-width windows, was a little out of my uncle's league. Far below, Lake Michigan rolled in with tiny white-tipped waves and I could see north up the Drive. For just a moment, I remembered how much I enjoyed the movement of headlights and taillights shimmering below on rainy nights. Raindrops would glisten against the glass, blurring the view till it looked like a Tom Lynch watercolor.

And then I remembered how much more I enjoyed those evenings when I'd been up here alone.

"No," Dan said, with a bit of a huff. "It was a brand new building. I saw to the decorating myself."

"Ohhh," Uncle Moose said, drawing the word out into two syllables and rolling his eyes at me.

My beeper went off, forestalling further comment. Which was good. I sensed, looming, a delicate question, indelicately put.

The voicemail was from Maria. A Chicago cop and friend of mine since high school, I'd called her the day before to put the word out on Matthew's disappearance, despite Sophie's objections. It wasn't an official missing persons' report, but I needed to do something. I listened to her terse message. "Got your call. I'll see what I can find out, but I need some information. Give me a ring. I'll be here till noon."

"Work?" Dan asked.

"Kinda," I lied. With a smile, I led Uncle Moose to the second bathroom. The one I'd used. Dan had commandeered the master bath and I made it a point never to encroach on his territory. It was one of those unwritten rules he had. Still, even in this bathroom there were a couple of things that belonged to him. "Pick out all the girly stuff, okay?" I got a huge kick out of Uncle Moose's low whistle as he took in the Roman Bath-themed room.

"You sure this guy doesn't . . . you know . . ."

"What?"

"Swing both ways?"

I patted him on the shoulder. "Don't forget. Just the girly stuff. But . . ." I winked at him, "if in doubt whether the girly stuff's mine or his, go ahead and take it."

He nodded, then glanced around to make sure Dan wasn't in the immediate area. "I always wondered about that guy."

Dan touched my arm as I emerged. He shot a wary glance toward Uncle Moose and backed away from the room, pulling me along. "Listen. I think I'm gonna go out for a while."

"Sure. Want me to leave the keys somewhere?"

"No. Use them to lock the deadbolt. I'll get them from you later. We're still going to see each other, right? Occasionally?" He winked.

I knew he meant it to dazzle, in that sort-of "let the poor thing down easy" way. But it did nothing for me. Nothing. Surprised, and suddenly giddy with that realization, I grinned back at him. "Sure," I said.

He chucked me under the chin. "Good. That's my girl. Nice to see you smiling again."

"Oh, yeah," I answered, but my sarcasm was lost on him.

I grabbed one of the boxes I'd brought, and headed to the bedroom, pulling out my cell phone again. I got Maria on the first ring. She was rushed, so I got straight to the point. I gave her Matthew's description and a short synopsis of the events leading up to his disappearance. Swinging the door till it was nearly closed as I chatted, I moved to the closet and began pulling out armloads of clothes.

Maria listened, asking questions at such intervals that I could tell she was taking notes. "Hey, one other thing," I said before we hung up. "These people knew the murdered girl, Milla Voight. Sophie works at the same place she did. I don't know that there's any connection, but I figure it doesn't hurt to mention it."

Maria's voice was tight. "You're right. It might be important. And I'll see what I can do. But I gotta go. My partner's giving me the evil eye. I'll touch base later."

Just as I hit "end," movement outside the bedroom door caught my attention. I figured it was Uncle Moose, not sure what to take, what to leave, and reluctant to interrupt my call.

Throwing open the door, I looked, but he was nowhere to be seen. "Uncle Moose?" I asked, heading toward the central living room. "Oh."

Dan was pacing the Persian area rug, making footprints in the deep pile. He looked up at my entrance, with a question in his eyes.

"What?" I asked.

"You're still on the story, aren't you?"

"What? No." Then realization dawned. "You were listening in on my phone call, weren't you?"

"It's my bedroom. I have a right to be there."

"So you did listen."

"You lied," he said with an expression that strove for "hurt" but came off as "pissed."

"I didn't. I am off the story."

"Then explain that phone call."

"I don't have to explain a goddamn thing to you."

We hadn't shifted positions since the conversation began. He stood in the middle of his expensive rug. I was at the entrance to the bedroom corridor. Uncle Moose's sturdy frame suddenly appeared in the opposite hallway.

"Everything okay, honey?" he asked me.

"Just ducky," I said, staring at Dan.

He looked over to Uncle Moose, licked his lips, and scooped up his keys from a nearby table, affecting a tiny swagger. "You know, maybe we won't be seeing much of each other, after all."

I felt a bubble of laughter work its way up my chest. "Well," I said, in a mock-serious tone, holding back as long as I could, "I'll try to control my disappointment."

The giggles started and I couldn't stop them. Not for anything. Not even when he stormed out of the apartment and slammed the door.

Aunt Lena was there when we got back, to help me sort and settle in. I whispered a prayer of thanks that the house was decent. My family and I often joked that we had to get the house "Auntie Lena Clean," before we'd let her visit. Today, it wasn't quite up to that standard, but at least it wasn't a pigsty.

I didn't really need the help setting up, but she enjoyed taking over the motherly role. Both of her kids lived out of state and, since my folks did too, it was a good fit for both of us. Close, but not too close. Before she left, I gave her a run-down about my unsuccessful trip to Springfield, knowing she'd keep that tidbit to herself. A long time ago, I'd asked her about my roots, hoping she knew some of the secrets, hoping she'd share. But no luck.

I was six when the light had finally dawned on me that I'd been adopted. It came less of a shock than a feeling of a cog settling into place. My parents hadn't been secretive about the origins of my birth. They told me that I'd been "chosen" when I was only two days old. But, despite their attempts to be open, there came the moment when I finally understood what they meant.

They say that the age of enlightenment is seven. I don't subscribe to the Catholic Church teaching that at age six you can't sin, but just wait till that seven-candle birthday and whammo, you're in the big leagues. At seven, you can not only commit venial sins, but mortal sins are now on your agenda as well. Bunk. We're all enlightened at different ages. And though I might have grasped the significance—and had my eyes opened at age six about my adoption—I'm still yet to be enlightened on plenty of other topics.

Growing up, I looked more like my best friend Rene McLaughlin than I did my fair-haired sister. Back then, I had no clue where babies came from, and the fact that I didn't re-semble my parents, nor Lucy, nor any of my Polish cousins had never bothered me.

All of a sudden it did.

My mom answered my slew of questions, but there was much she didn't know about the woman who'd given birth to me. All Catholic Charities had said was that my biological parents were young, unmarried, and at that point, healthy. Nothing else.

At about age ten I came up with the idea of searching out

my birth parents, spending long nights planning the new quest. All the Nancy Drew books I was reading at the time inspired me to find mysteries everywhere, and here was one, involving me, that I could attempt to solve. I was thrilled.

Bounding into the kitchen one morning full of excitement, I laid out my strategy to find my birth mother. I was five minutes into an explanation about how I planned to accomplish this, before I noticed the look on my mother's face.

With one of those smiles that can tear your heart out, she nodded, listening. Standing next to the kitchen table, the aluminum pot tilted, ready to pour hot Cream of Wheat into my bowl, a small saucer of brown sugar ready for sprinkling over it, she bit her lip and smiled. The smile didn't reach her eyes, which had taken on a glassy look. A lot like she looked when my Nana had died, just a couple of months before.

Across from me, her elbows firmly on the table, Lucy, eager to share my excitement, kept asking me what I meant. Offering to help, too, with whatever she could do. Neither my mom nor I answered her, and, after a few moments she stopped asking, sensing I suppose, the heaviness that had settled in the air.

I never mentioned finding my birth parents again.

But I never forgot, either.

Now, by myself, I walked through the house I grew up in and saw it through new eyes. This was no longer my parents' place. This was my house, my home. I was in charge and in control. For the first time, really, I was alone, too. When I'd gone to college, I had roommates, and even when I got my first apartment after I started working full-time, I had to share it to make ends meet. For a short time, I had the place to myself when Becky moved out to be with her fiancée. But then Dan had suggested I join him, and that was that.

This was a small house, by any standard. A tiny cottage, it

was sandwiched between a stolid, brown Chicago bungalow and a red-brick two-flat on a short city block that boasted only six homes and a gas station on the corner. The street outside was fairly busy, and I remembered my mother's angst any time we wanted to play out front.

Two bedrooms, mine and Lucy's, took up the west side of the home, while the living room, bathroom, and kitchen lined the east. My dad built a third bedroom in the basement for him and my mom right around when I was eleven.

My parents had taken most of the furniture to Arkansas and there were big, rectangular spaces on the living room carpet where the deep-brown rug was clean and never walked upon, like ghost images of what had been. It was just as well. I had money saved from not having to pay rent, and I wanted to give the house a bit of a lift, anyway. I preferred light colors and cheerful décor. My parents had redecorated in the seventies and hadn't bothered to change it since.

They'd left the kitchen pretty much as it was, furniture and all, and my kitchen table wasn't all that different from Sophie's: Formica top, chrome sides, and matching chairs that squeaked when you sat in them. My dad took it upon himself to update the set a decade ago, so now all four chairs sported Naugahyde covers and casters that made you careful about sitting down too quickly. I went sailing across the floor a couple of times myself.

Although I'd been sleeping back in my own room for the past couple of weeks, it looked different to me now, too. I stood in the doorway, remembering the many years of writing in my journal, of talking on the phone, of agonizing over how to rearrange the room so that I maximized its limited space.

Back when I was about twelve, I'd realized that I could touch two walls from anywhere in the room. Not only was the square footage so minuscule, but because of built-in cabinets in the kitchen, a bumped-in pantry on one side, and a set-back from the hallway door, it was a very odd-shaped room.

It was something I was proud of, in a strange way. That I could find myself comfortable in such a small room, that I had the smallest room in the house, by far. As a teen, I'd covered the walls with white latex, then used masking tape to delineate the lines for a rainbow of colors I mixed myself. Still here, cheering up the room with faded versions of color, they made a complete and active circuit and it made me smile at the memory. It was dated, but I liked it. And I wouldn't change it for the world.

I stood now, in the very center of the room and touched one wall, then reached to touch another. I grinned with the lighthearted memory of life being easy. I felt transported back. I was home again. Some things never changed.

And then the phone rang.

I thought about not answering it, but I hadn't hooked up an answering machine yet, and my parents had never gotten Caller ID.

It rang again, intrusive in its own way.

I sighed and reached for it, thinking it had better be important to ruin my reverie. Damn important.

It was.

A hysterical Sophie told me in halting, crying tones, that they'd found Matthew . . . dead.

Chapter Nine

When I got to her apartment, I didn't understand why she'd called me. The place was filled to capacity—milling groups of young women, all busying themselves with the mundane tasks of cooking, cleaning, and phoning that accompany a death. Smells of simmering Polish foods—spicy sausages, tangy kraut, and the tomato sauce of cabbage rolls—permeated the small area. Coffee percolated on the stove.

They looked up at me, as one, when I walked in the open door. Some faces were vaguely familiar from the salon, and I smiled at them—hesitant.

When, through hiccupping cries on the phone, Sophie had said that Matthew had been found, apparently murdered, the shock hit me first. Then the sorrow. Remembering our conversation from the other day, I rushed over, not knowing what I might be able to do for her, but knowing that I had to try.

There must have been at least a dozen people in the apartment, and in the close quarters, they passed each other amid bumps and murmured pardons. It was a cacophony of Polish speech, but the mood was subdued.

One of the young women, a petite girl with very straight, light brown hair, approached. "Are you Alex?" she asked.

I nodded.

I could tell that she'd been crying by the redness in her eyes and the dark smudges of mascara beneath them. She gave me a serious smile, however, and took my arm. "Tenk you for coming for Sophia. I am Helena. We are best friends."

Helena was a pretty girl. Not beautiful, nor voluptuous in the same way Sophie was, but tiny and pert, with pale eyes and pale skin that should have made her look washed out, but didn't. There was an undeniably foreign look to her, and her accented English let me know that she hadn't been in the States very long at all.

"There are a lot of people here," I said, for lack of anything else.

She nodded, understanding at once. "We take care of Sophie. It terrible thing for her. She take care of Maciej," she said, exhaling a breath that seemed to shudder out of her. "She like mother to him. She feel—how you say? Like her fault."

I hadn't seen Sophie in the crowded room, and Helena now led me to one of the doors toward the back of the apartment. "She in the bedroom. She not good. Maybe you talk with her? She think you maybe are able to help?"

"Of course," I said, having no clue of what I was in for.

Sophie's whisper as she called my name sounded like "Ah-lex," and held just enough hopefulness and desperation to put a lump in my throat. I eased the wooden door behind me till it was nearly shut.

Darkened, the room's shades had been pulled to keep the late-afternoon sun from bringing any brightness to the room, but a slice of gray-blue light shot in, angling across the bed. There was enough daylight to see, though everything had that sort of non-color blur like flashbacks in a mood-movie. I could see a heavy dresser, covered with assorted makeup essentials and toiletries, and the old-fashioned double bed where Sophie reclined. She pulled herself up onto one elbow when I came in, and I sat in a kitchen chair that someone had thoughtfully left there. I was sure each of her friends had been taking turns sitting with her, hoping to comfort, all the while knowing it was too big, too much to bear.

"Sophie," I said, taking her outstretched hand. It was cold and clammy, and where there should have been fingernails, were crusts of dried blood. "What happened?" I asked her.

"A police officer came to my door." Sophie's face was coming more into focus as my eyes adjusted to the lack of light. Her face had welted up again and her hair had ratted behind her, from tossing on the pillow, no doubt. She spoke slowly, in Polish, as though pushing out each word, punctuating every sentence with hiccups and sobs. "I was afraid. I didn't answer the door when I looked out the window and saw him. But he saw me and he knocked and knocked and called out to me until I opened the door. I was very afraid, Alex."

A niggle of curiosity wormed through my brain. Why would she be afraid of the police coming to her door? Especially if she'd been anxious about her missing brother.

"What did he say? What happened?"

"Maciej was my baby brother. I should have been more protective. I should have taken better care. It's all my fault. He is dead and it is all my fault."

She broke down again, her words coming out with a high-pitched, keening sound. I could hear low mumbles outside the door and I had no doubt they could hear Sophie. I wondered why no one came in. They all appeared to know each other, but they didn't know me. Why they trusted me here, I didn't understand.

Her grief, even her blaming herself was understandable. I gave her hand a squeeze. "Tell me what they told you."

"The policeman was very nice to me. He asked me for a

picture of Matthew, and he took me down to the station and asked me many, many questions about Matthew's friends and where he might have gone. He asked me why I didn't call them when Matthew didn't come home, and I didn't know what to say. I just cried. They took me to the morgue for me to identify him. And then they let me come home. The policeman brought me home."

I nodded. "But they think Matthew was murdered?"

Sophie sat up in the bed and pulled the covers away. I noticed bruises on her uncovered arms and bare legs. "What happened?" I asked.

She pulled the quilt back, in a defensive move. "I hurt myself. At work."

She was lying, but I didn't push it. "What about Matthew?"

"They found him in some place. Near the road. In a bad neighborhood. They took all his money and they hurt him." The words coming out of her mouth made her cringe in pain as she said them. Her face contorted as she tried to hold back while she spoke, but she couldn't manage much more than a whisper. "They hurt him, Alex, they broke his neck. And he was just trying to help me."

It wasn't the first time she'd used those words, that Matthew was trying to help her. It had piqued my interest the first time. Now, with her hand squeezing mine and her eyes on my every move, I knew there was no better time to get information from her. "What was he trying to do, Sophie? What do you mean he was trying to help you?"

I felt her reaction as much as saw it. Her hand went limp before she let go completely. Dropping her head backwards onto the pillow, her eyes searched the ceiling for answers to questions I couldn't even begin to guess at. I wanted to find whatever it was that caused the vacant stare, and a tiny flicker of fear in her eyes, but I knew I had to tread lightly.

"Sophie?" I asked, keeping my voice soft.

"I have done many bad things."

Her words were so quiet that I had to lean forward to hear her. She turned to me, fat tears quivering in the wells of her eyes.

"What?"

She pressed the bitten-nail fingers of both hands hard against her face. I waited till her breathing shifted from erratic to some semblance of normal. "I will tell you," she said. She sat up again, sending a nervous glance over to the bedroom door. I got up to close it completely, turning the knob to keep the sound quiet. The hum from the kitchen outside remained a constant, touching reminder that life went on.

"Matthew, my Maciej, did not approve of my . . . job."

I conjured up my recollection of the Hair to Dye For salon. "Why?" I asked. "Did they take advantage of you somehow?"

She smiled then, but a more pained smile, I've never encountered.

"I have wanted to be a hair stylist since I was a small girl in my village outside of Krakow. I have wanted nothing else. Back in Poland, I could not follow this dream. I could only work in the factory, with metal and punches and stamping. I never even knew what I was making. I only knew that there must be a better life. And the machinery frightened me. I didn't want to lose my fingers the way many of my friends did. Then how would I ever realize my dream?"

I kept eye contact with Sophie, knowing that if I let my gaze wander, it might break the spell. There was more; I watched and waited.

"When Father Bruno came to our town and told us of the opportunities here in America, I wanted to come here right away. But Matthew, though he is younger . . . was younger . . ." she drew a ragged breath before continuing, "he insisted on coming with me, to protect me. And my parents were happy. They were so afraid that they would lose their little girl. And now they have lost a son."

She shook her head. "America is a land of hope and dreams. And I was so happy when Father Bruno found me a position at the salon. I went to school at night to learn, to get my license. And I have done a good job. I am proud of my work." She focused high on the wall again, as twin tears made their way down her cheeks. "But, the owner of the beauty shop does not hire us because we are good hair stylists."

"She hires you because you're new to the country and you work for minimum wage?"

Sophie's smile was one of deep sadness. Though she was younger than me by a good five years, I had the sudden feeling of being in the company of a much older, more world-weary woman, explaining the sad facts of life to me. "No," she said, in English. "We are . . . what is the word? *Prostytutka.* We are their whores."

Chapter Ten

Bass leaned back in the orange plastic chair, crossing his feet on an upturned wastebasket, which he kept in this mini-conference room for that express purpose. He'd chosen the only chair of the stackable set that didn't wobble, and had dragged it to the head position nearest the door.

Windowless, this minuscule section of the office had lived a prior life as a storage area up until several months ago. After much debate, the station had buckled under pressure from the constant complaints of frustrated employees about impossible-to-dig-out files. When space opened up, the administration leased more capacious facilities five floors above us.

Our staff meetings, which Bass called from time to time with no discernible pattern, were always held in here, despite the fact that the large, windowed conference room was nearly always available. I sensed that Bass liked the close quarters; being in a smaller pond undoubtedly made him feel like a bigger fish. While I'm not claustrophobic, I disliked the tight, airless warmth of these meetings. I wondered if Bass did that on purpose. Keeping us uncomfortable ensured our time here would be brief.

Styrofoam cup of coffee in hand, Bass read his notes from the leather portfolio on his lap. He favored wide-striped ties and those blue shirts with white collars that went out of style when I was a teenager. But no matter what he wore, he looked scruffy and unkempt. If I had the chance to pick the perfect outfit for him, I would have gone with a navy blue bow tie and red plaid short pants. Maybe even a red clown nose, too.

William sat next to me. We'd taken the two seats farthest away from Bass. To my right was David Gonzales and two seats away on William's left was Fenton. There were three empty chairs, no longer needed, now that the research and writing staff had been pared down to just four. And in the center was a long, low table, ridiculously out of place in a business meeting. It might have been someone's coffee table from a fifties living room. Brown, with fake wood grain, it sported long, matching angled-out legs with tiny gold caps at the feet.

"Everybody here, then? Let's begin," Bass said unnecessarily. He leaned forward to place his cup on the squat table. His voice, just a couple of notches too high, took on an ominous quality as he dropped his feet to the floor and began his next conversation with a long, wound up, "Ohhhhkay."

I'd attended Bass's meetings for a long time. So had David. We exchanged sidelong glances. When Bass went "feet to the floor," it was never a good sign. Next to me, David put his notebook on the table, then leaned back, interlacing his fingers across his stomach. While not an enormous man, David was big. A consequence of possessing an unhurried demeanor and a love of all things edible. On the few occasions we'd gone out to lunch together, I'd been amazed at how much the guy could put away. His dark hair, dark eyes, and olive complexion, however, more than made up for the added weight. Taken as a whole package, David was a hunk.

Bass shot an angry glance at each of us in turn. "So, what's up? Why aren't we producing stories here? Have you all gone on vacation and forgotten to let me know?"

Fenton wasted no time. "You gave me an extra week on the Millie story. Remember? I told you all the problems I was having, and you told me not to worry."

Bass telling somebody not to worry was like the Pope asking new converts if they might not like to consider Judaism before taking the baptismal plunge.

"I told you to get the research done so that Gonzales here has something to write about. You told me you wanted an extra week. I never agreed. How much you got, Gonzales?"

David didn't move from his position of feigned relaxation. "Not enough. I've got the stuff that Alex did. All the background. Very thorough, as always, Alex." He gave me an abbreviated nod. "But a lot has happened on the story since it switched hands. From that point on, I got nada."

Bass turned to Fenton. "What have you been doing?"

"You know, she could have given me a little help here. It's not like she's working on anything real important or anything. I asked her. She won't do anything for me."

Oooh. A tantrum. This might turn out to be a fun meeting after all.

Bass let the question of my involvement slide, instead shaking a finger dangerously close to the Nephew's nose. For a short fellow, Bass had some major *cojones*. "You are one lucky punk. I got a call this morning from Hank. Just found out we've got political specials we need to run." He addressed his spiel to the rest of us. "Elections are coming up and some of the small, local races are garnering interest. Hank's got Gabriela set up to do interviews for the next airing."

David sat up. He loved political stuff. Really excelled at it.

As though anticipating the question, Bass raised a hand. "No, not like that. These are going to be all pabulum. Pre-set questions provided by the candidates' headquarters. Sincere, well-crafted answers to help educate the voting public." He rolled his eyes. "We're just the vehicle."

David grimaced and reclined again as Fenton shot me an expression of one-upmanship. "I still think that since Alex isn't doing anything important, she ought to pitch in on mine."

"What do you say, Alex? You want to show Fenton the ropes on this one?"

The beauty of Bass's remark was not lost on me. With a weeklong delay due to the candidate spots, it was going to take some real clever angle to get people engaged in Milla's story again. Dan's station had done a small introductory teaser on it, touting it as an "ongoing investigation." Which meant that they either had some big revelation in the works, or they were scrambling to come up with one.

Bass wanted help. Badly. I could tell from the politely-toned request. But I wasn't about to fold.

William had been very quiet. He had all my information-to-date on the hair care story, and as yet, I hadn't been assigned anything new. I often juggled multiple stories at once. As a matter of fact, I'd grown accustomed to the pressure, and when I had only one story to focus on, I tended to get bored. Which led me to my request.

"Actually," I said, "I have another story I'm working on. Entirely new."

"What is it?" Bass asked.

William shifted in his seat, in a way that made me think I might have piqued his interest. Problem was, I didn't want Fenton to know anything about my private investigation into Milla's death. Or about the alleged prostitution ring Sophie told me about.

So, I hedged. "I'm going to ask you to give me a little leeway here, Bass. Trust me on this one." I had nothing to back my claim, other than a gut-level feel that I'd scratched at the surface of something big. "It's too early to get into it all. There are lots of variables, and I need time to investigate before the story comes clear. This extra week to finish off the hair care story is going to make all the difference for me."

He'd acquiesce. I could sense it.

"Nope."

My mouth dropped open. "What?"

Bass shook his head. "Not good enough. Fenton needs your help on the Milla Voight story. This is the one we've been waiting for."

Though I kept my eyes on Bass, I could see, in periphery, Fenton's gloat. I wanted to tell him that he could kiss my ass before I'd jump in to help pull this off. "No way," I said. "You took me off that one."

"Yeah, well I've got another story for you in mind if you're so set on working a different one. You know that homeless story we've been batting around for a while . . . ?"

He let the sentence hang, but the threat was there. The homeless story. The story that he pulled out of mothballs to hold over our heads every time he needed something done. Nobody wanted the homeless story. It was one of those that could be done any time, fit in any place, but involved traveling down to the depths of Lower Wacker Drive to interview recalcitrant, not to mention smelly, people who would prefer to spit and throw things at you than to answer your questions.

Not to be baited into an argument, though one was gathering like a storm in my brain, I deflected the tangent of the conversation. "I'll tell you what. Give me the leeway I'm asking for on this new one, and I'll make it work. *Up Close Issues* will be eating their hearts out. But I'm going to need time."

Maybe it was my imagination, but I believed Bass maintained a grudging respect for me. I watched indecision work its way through his face, and I sensed his reluctant trust. "Okay," he said at last.

I let out the breath I'd been holding and tried not to laugh when Fenton jumped out of his chair to start whining.

Bass snapped at him, effectively shutting him up with a rebuke. "Cut it out. You do your job; let Alex do hers." He turned to me then. "But you better come up with something good. Otherwise, I *will* assign you that homeless story."

William cleared his throat. "One thing you might want to consider," he said. Focusing his attention directly toward Bass, he gave me a nice profile to watch as he talked. The sheer difference in size between the two men was staggering. William was tall, trim—a man who kept himself in great physical condition. Bass was short, pale, and, though not overweight, he enjoyed the life of middle-class sedentary hedonism and had just enough flab to prove it.

"What's that?"

William gave a nonchalant shrug. "Homeless stories tend to be the black hole of ratings. We did a couple of them at the paper and nearly sank the ship both times." His eyes flicked my direction for a split-second before he continued. "I know we're hungry for ratings here. Thought that might help."

"Yes, well, thank you," Bass said, but I'd bet he was gritting his teeth as he spoke. William had effectively taken the wind out of Bass's sails of threat. Politely too. I caught William's glance and smiled. He raised his eyebrows in a gesture of innocence and went back to studying the files on his lap.

I visited Sophie again at her apartment right after our staff meeting adjourned. For the first time this season, the air held a bit of a chill. Navigating the narrow gangway that separated one tall three-flat from its neighbor, I was blasted with a twisting breeze that swirled my hair around my head and made crispy brown whirlpools out of the fallen leaves that crunched when I stepped on them.

Up above, beyond the top of the bricked walls that made

up the two structures beside me, I stared at the blue in my narrow view of the sky. Days like this made it hard to believe that such beauty and such sorrow can exist on the same planet. Matthew's wake was scheduled for the next evening, Tuesday. I'd make it a point to attend.

Sophie had told me over the phone that she was afraid she didn't have the funds to give Matthew a proper burial, but that Father Bruno had made arrangements on her behalf with a mortician friend. Except for the relatively minor price of the grave, and the marker, if she chose to purchase one, Matthew's funeral would cost her nothing.

We sat at the kitchen table again, with two steaming cups of coffee sitting between us. Behind Sophie, a large, double-hung window offered a view of the next-door brick wall.

"Her name is Lisa Knowles," Sophie said in a halting way, writing the name down for me in curlicued foreign script. "But is maybe not her real name. A man call her Vicky one time and she answer. I pretend not to listen. She no know I hear that."

Her admission the night before had thrown me off-kilter, and I had to fight off a vague sense of disillusionment. She told me that most of the young women who came to help her—the women I'd met the night before—were her colleagues. Not all of them. But most. And several worked at the north side hair salon as well.

My best shot at helping her, and at making Bass sit up and take notice, was to withhold judgment. Who was I to decide other peoples' life choices? Still, the idea of that kind of intimacy with strangers for money made me cringe.

Sophie's tentative English was comprehensible, but slow. As she spoke, I could feel her weigh every word, analyze her syntax, and be more concerned about how she phrased things than about what she was saying. I urged her to switch to her native language and I pulled out my small tape recorder. If worse came to worse, I had a whole family of folks I could rely on for translation.

Sophie's odyssey had begun two years earlier, when she had come to the United States under Father Bruno's wing. When he interviewed her, she said, he'd been happy and proud to find out that she had goals and aspirations.

"Matthew," she said with a sucking breath that threatened to be let out in a sob, "came to protect me. My parents were afraid to let me come to a new country on my own. We hoped to bring our parents here someday, too. He wanted them to have a good life." She paused again as tears moved down her pinkened cheeks. "But this is the life that killed him."

"You can't think like that, Sophie. Dangers are every-where. It isn't your fault."

Her lips tight, she simply shook her head.

"Do you know what he was doing in the neighborhood where he was found?" I asked.

"They killed him there."

"I mean," I said, "do you know why he went there? Did he have some business? Friends who live in the area?"

I watched her struggle for control. "Matthew didn't go there," she said at last. "Someone took him there. They were afraid that he was going to go to the police. They had him killed."

Afraid that Sophie had lost her grip on reality, I said, in as gentle a voice as possible, "You realize all the evidence at the scene suggests a robbery gone bad." I'd squeezed in a call to Maria to see what she could come up with. The fact that Mat-thew had been found in a neighborhood known notoriously for its high-crime and that he had nothing left on his body of value, made it likely Matthew was simply a random victim. The only way they'd been able to discover his identity had been my alert to Maria earlier. She caught the connection and put two and two together.

"You don't understand."

"I'm trying to," I said.

Sophie's frustration seemed less aimed at me and more toward an unseen entity near the ceiling. "You remember the girl who was murdered? Milla Voight? Milla worked at the salon, but she would not prostitute herself. She refused, despite a great deal of pressure." I watched more heavy tears gather, trembling in Sophie's eyes. "She was going to be fired soon. Miss Knowles was very angry with her.

"But then Milla found she was pregnant. And only after that did she learn that her beloved Carlos was a priest. A priest! What would Father Bruno say to that?" Sophie hugged her arms around herself and gave a shudder. "Even when she found out, I think she would have kept it quiet, except then she heard he had slept with many of the girls. And paid for it." She gave me a meaningful look. "He knew what we were. Just as he knew Milla was really just a girl in love. And he used that. He used her. He was part of Miss Knowles' organization."

Sophie's face wrinkled up again.

"She was never going to get an abortion. I knew that. She would never go through with something like that. She only went there to confront Carlos. I think he would have liked her to get rid of the baby, if you want to know the truth. But he was there, demonstrating, with other clergy, and he had to make a show of stopping her."

The story hurt for Sophie to tell, as was obvious from her constant shifting and from the way she bit her nails after nearly every sentence. I wanted to hold her hands down on the table, to keep the poor fingers from losing their nails entirely, but I held tight to my mug and sipped my coffee instead.

"She discovered later that he had planned all along to lure her into prostitution. I can't tell you how much that tore her apart. I swear she lost her mind. She'd given him her heart. A woman does not do that lightly."

"No," I agreed, "she doesn't."

"She threatened him, then. She should never have done that. She told him she was going to go to the authorities. To let everyone know what kind of a priest he really was. She was so hurt, herself, she wanted to hurt him."

"But that would have exposed all of you."

Sophie shook her head. "Milla only wanted to frighten him. She wanted to make him understand the kind of fear she was feeling."

"But then she was killed?"

"Yes," she said, taking a deep breath. "Matthew disapproved of my involvement. Even though it put food on our table and paid our rent while we tried to make a life here. He believed someone killed Milla before she could reveal the truth about Miss Knowles' organization. He wanted to find proof and show me, so that I would leave."

"But you didn't believe him?"

"No, of course not. I didn't want to believe that at all. Miss Knowles and Rodero protect us. They take care of us. They don't want us hurt." Her words were coming out fast. She stopped for a moment, shaking her head. "Or, I didn't think so. I felt safe. And I didn't want to disappoint Father Bruno. If we left, what would he think?"

"How did Father Bruno react?"

"To Milla's murder? He was saddened. Deeply saddened. He takes care of us like we were his children. He found out about the pregnancy after she died, and he grieved for all the lives that were lost or were broken in this tragedy. He did not know about the prostitution. He only knew that Carlos was the baby's father. Still, he felt responsible. After all, Carlos was his protégé."

I made an unladylike sound.

Sophie continued, "Milla's was the most touching funeral I have ever been to. And he is angry at Carlos for leaving the United States. But his hands are tied."

I gauged her reaction as I asked, "What's the story on that fellow, Emil? From the rectory."

"Why?"

"You froze up the minute he walked in. And he either had a good drunk on him, or he's under some major-league medication. Something's wrong there."

Sophie's gaze dropped to the mug in front of her. It was still full to the brim, untouched. "He works with Miss Knowles to make arrangements. He was my . . . date . . . once."

I resisted the overwhelming urge to exclaim disgust. "And you're telling me that Father Bruno isn't aware of all this going on under his nose?"

Sophie's eyes were wide. "I will tell you this. Miss Knowles has made it clear. Very clear. If any of us ever say anything to Father Bruno, she will make sure we are sorry. He brings many girls to her from Poland. She knows that he will stop if he ever finds out the truth."

"She's threatened you?"

Again, another shrug. "She has shown her displeasure with some of the girls."

"How?"

Sophie shook her head. "We just know better."

The coffee had been strong, and hot, exactly the way I like it. I'd sipped as we spoke and had made it about halfway down the mug. Sophie spied the emptiness and jumped up to get the pot for a refill. It gave her something to do and I didn't mind the extra buzz from the caffeine. I could use it.

When Sophie returned to the table, I saw that she brought my card along with her. Fingering it, she bit her lip in concentration. I felt an unexpected pang at the look on her face. I remembered how much she and Matthew had resembled each other. And now he was gone.

Sophie kept her eyes on the card as she spoke. "I know you aren't the kind of investigator who goes after criminals. I understand that. But I need to find out who killed my Matthew. And I'm not able to go to the police. Not with my . . ." she took a deep breath, then looked up, ". . . my occupation. But I know you have ways of finding things out. Will you find out who killed Matthew? Please?"

The request shocked me. But my reaction shocked me even more. Pure temptation; I wanted to do it. "I work for television," I said, cautioning her. It was only fair to let her know the risks. "If I do look into this, you understand that a lot may come out? And there's no guarantee that I can do anything."

She nodded slowly, once. Then compressed her lips. "If I tell the police, they will only take me and use me to uncover the other girls. Then what? Miss Knowles will disappear and start all over again. Milla is dead. Matthew is dead. I can't let this happen any more. I want Miss Knowles and Rodero to be uncovered. They are the guilty ones here. And . . ."

I looked at her. "And . . . ?"

"And now, I am very afraid. Will I be next?"

Chapter Eleven

I nearly turned the car around. Twice.

What the hell was I getting myself into?

Considerably west of LaGrange Road, I was far enough south to have had cornfields as my companions for the past several miles. A developer's sign on my right told me it was just ten minutes further to the Noble Ridge subdivision, featuring custom-built homes and Chicago water.

Houses out this way were bigger than their urban counterparts—sprawling, mansion-like structures, so far apart that their owners probably took the car to visit the next-door neighbors. Some of these homes, with turrets, three chimneys, and walk-out basements, were so magnificent that if I didn't know better, I'd have thought they were small hotels. I thought about my little house with its tiny bedrooms and single bath. What did these people do for a living anyway?

Gravel kicked up to ping under my car as I pulled over to the side of the road. There were no other cars in any direction. Just miles and miles of brand-new homes dotting the expansive land. It was quiet. So quiet that all I could hear was the steady rumble of my car engine and the wind making soulful sounds as it plucked leaves from the outstretched arms of nearby trees to dance across my windshield.

Through my open window I caught the unmistakable scent of burning wood, which, coupled with the poofy white clouds in an otherwise clear sky, suddenly made it feel like fall. The time of the year I liked best, with its sweaters in subdued colors and caramel apples with nuts—curling up with a favorite author's book at night, the breezy wind rattling my old windows. Knowing I was safe inside.

Life didn't get much better than that.

But right now, hands gripped on the steering wheel so tight my knuckles were white, I knew I was anywhere but safe. I stifled a little shudder, more from nerves than cold.

I had Lisa Knowles' address and phone number on a small scrap of paper, even though I memorized them both. Her home was nearby, but I wanted to verify the street before I got any closer. I wiggled the note out of my back pocket with effort. My jeans were a little too tight, my shirt a little too low-cut. I'd pulled these clothes out of the far reaches of my closet, searching for just the right look. I couldn't believe they still fit.

And I couldn't believe I was about to apply for a job as a prostitute.

"Heaven help me," I said aloud.

The wind whipped up again, sending a blast into my car, mussing my hair. Not that it mattered. I was going for the out-of-work young woman look. And I hoped my meager acting skills would carry me through.

With a quick look in the rearview mirror, I put the car in drive, and headed for my interview.

I turned right onto Shade Lane, deep into the brand-new subdivision. Young trees, set at precise intervals, lined the parkways of the homes set far back from the street. The numbers were easy, single and double digits, which had to be tough for emergency teams if they ever got called out here. How the hell do you find Six Shade Lane out in the middle of nowhere? If it hadn't been for Sophie's explicit directions, I'd have been lost.

While Lisa Knowles' home wasn't the most opulent residence on the expansive, curvy street, it had a unique look. The home was done completely in white brick, with all sorts of detail work at the structure's corners and above the windows. The bricklayers had spent lots of time designing the curves and patterns, and that hadn't come cheap. It was a two-story home with a backyard that sloped away from the house, offering a walkout basement. I caught a glimpse of a white vinyl fence and the edge of a sparkling in-ground pool as I pulled to the curb. Still open, even this late in the season. It must be heated.

A horseshoe-shaped driveway wound past a four-car garage. We were talking some big bucks, here. Not bad for the owner of a lone hair salon that never had any customers.

What set this home apart from the others was the color combination. The rest of the neighborhood made do with cream color, brown, or the obvious favorite, red brick. And all had coordinating roofs of either shingle or tile. Tile roofs equaled big bucks. Even I knew that.

The bright white brick of Lisa's home was topped with an equally bright pink tile roof. I'd love to know what her neighbors said about it behind her back. It resembled a garish birthday cake and I wondered if she'd had it designed that way because scantily clad women popped out of it so often. Personally, I didn't think I'd like living next to a pink and white house. Just looking at it gave me the heebie-jeebies.

Showtime, I told myself. Quelling the nervous energy that made my stomach jiggle and my breath come faster, I pressed the doorbell and bit my lip, too late remembering the double dose of red that I'd caked on my mouth before I left. Lipstick has an unmistakable flavor, one I detest. I wished I had a stick of gum.

With all this grandeur, I expected a maid or butler to

attend the door. But the chimes, which had rung so loudly that I could hear them, were answered by Lisa herself.

She in no way fit the mental picture I'd conjured up.

I put her in her early forties, maybe even older. She had clear, tanned skin, and brown eyes that drooped a little in the center. Pulled back into a haphazard ponytail, her dark hair, streaked with red and gray, was curly and thinning. She was a big girl, a head taller than me and probably fifty pounds heavier. Czech, I thought, or maybe Russian.

She tilted her head, with a smile that didn't reach her eyes, striving for "friendly," but I could tell she was busy formulating assessments already.

"Alex?" she asked.

"Uh-huh. Are you Lisa?" I asked, with a look I hoped telegraphed both young and eager. On a good day, I could pass for mid-twenties and I worried that there was an upper age limit on the girls she'd hire.

"Yeah," she said, her eyes raking me from head to toe and back again. "Come on in."

She wore a stretchy dress of deep red in an African pattern. Rows of minuscule beige animal silhouettes started at the low gathered neckline, growing in size until a parade of hand-height giraffes marched across the calf-length hemline. Her bare feet sported purple polished nails and she wore a silver toe ring with attached charm that jingled as she walked.

She led me through the marble-floored hallway with a soaring staircase that headed up into an expansive second-floor loft. To the right of the hall was an enormous living room with white leather furniture accessorized in an Oriental motif.

I kept listening for sounds of others in the massive structure. But heard nothing. No sign of husband, kids, or even an annoying little dog. Maybe these digs were hers alone.

The dining room sat on the left of the hall. It, too, was decorated with a Japanese theme. Lisa, however, was a brisk walker, I didn't get much time for the kind of scrutinizing observation I like best.

"If you come back here again, I'd appreciate if you'd use the alternate entrance." She turned toward me and smiled. This was not a happy woman. "Did you see that door, set back next to the garage?"

"No, I didn't."

"I'm surprised Helena didn't tell you about that. She's been here often enough." Tiny frown and then the insincere smile returned. "Don't worry, though. It's okay . . . this time."

"Sorry," I said, already beginning to feel like the hired help.

She ignored my apology, wending her way to a sizeable office area that, by my estimation, sat directly behind the garage. She passed through open double pocket doors, turning to slide them shut behind me once I stepped into the room. It gave me a moment to make my own assessments. Lisa Knowles was either a clean freak or she kept a maid on retainer. The place was spotless. Even this office, her work area, was pristine.

This room had two entrances. The one we'd used, and an outside door, which I figured must have been the entrance she mentioned. I never would have noticed it from the street.

Furnished like any typical office, the room was spacious enough to handle the massive desk and accompanying chairs, a wall full of filing cabinets, and a meager bookcase full of accounting textbooks. I caught sight of only one novel, a well-worn copy of a paperback titled *Sandra*. I sat down in the chair where she gestured.

She sat behind the desk and I felt her eyes on me again. Assessing me. Shrewd. This woman had an intense air about her. I'd have to be cautious.

Behind her, a bright picture window had been painted with bold sweeps of color. The faux stained-glass had a religious feel to it and, while it provided privacy for her, it did nothing to keep the afternoon sun from shining directly into my face, effectively blinding me. She must have sensed my discomfort, but she didn't offer to pull down the shade.

I switched seats. It helped. Lisa appeared amused.

"Your name is Alexandrine Szatjemski?"

I nodded. "Yes."

"Helena tells me you're looking for employment. She gave me a call, suggesting I interview you right away." Lisa's voice matched her body to perfection. Low and raspy, she sounded like a heavy smoker, but she didn't look like one, and I neither smelled, nor saw, any evidence of cigarettes in her home. "But when I started to ask her about your qualifications, she really had no idea about anything. How long have you two known each other?"

I gave a nervous, self-effacing laugh. "Not long. I really just met her. I'm actually a friend of Sophie's. Sophie Breczyk?"

Lisa nodded. I thought I saw one eye squint, just a bit.

"Well," I said, launching into the spiel I'd rehearsed, "I just got fired about a week ago and I don't know what to do. Sophie's always been good to me and she always seems to be able to make things work, you know?" I widened my eyes, trying to look like I'd given the matter deep thought. "She's always got—not a lot of money—but enough. And she's helped me out some. So, I thought maybe, if there were any openings where she was, I could give that a try. And I wanted to ask her to kind of introduce me and all, but then . . ."

I purposely let the sentence hang.

Lisa raised her eyebrows, but stayed silent.

"This whole thing happened with her poor brother and now Sophie's all broken up—not that I blame her—" I shook my head and shot her a sincere expression, then grimaced, for effect. "But I got a bunch of bills and I don't know how I'm going to keep my head up if I don't find something soon. You know?"

When she nodded again this time, I sensed she'd accepted the story. At least in a grudging way, so far.

Lisa picked up a pen and played with it a moment before pulling out papers from her desk drawer. From the manner in which she held it, this was one heavy pen. Gold and silver designs snaked up and down the barrel and they formed a picture, but from my vantage point, I couldn't tell what it was.

In a way, I was surprised at her hands. Long-fingered and smooth, their nails were manicured and polished in a shade that matched her toes. I'd originally put her in her early forties, but her hands were young and supple.

Of their own accord, my eyes shot back to her face for a reassessment. Perhaps she and I were closer in age than I thought. Could be her line of work that added the lines and wrinkles.

"I like to take notes, if you don't mind," Lisa said, with a smile devoid of warmth. All business, this woman.

"No, no, not at all," I said, thinking that I'd better be careful to remember everything I told her.

"Spell your name for me, please." Her hand was poised above the sheet. Was she trying to check me out? I chose to use my undercover name, my parents' original last name, Szatjemski, the one that never showed up on *Midwest Focus*'s rolling credits.

"*Czy mowi pan po polsku?*" she asked.

I hesitated. The question in Polish surprised me, but in a

split-second decision I feigned confusion, with a shrug. I could tell by her pronunciation that she was probably as fluent as I was. It would be smarter not to let on that I understood, just yet. My chances of learning anything significant might be better that way.

"Was that Polish?" I asked, biting my lip to convey concern that my answer wouldn't meet with her approval. "I don't understand it," I lied. "Well, a couple of words and phrases is all."

She nodded, regarding me closely. "You don't look Polish."

"I guess I take after my mom."

From what I could tell, looking at it upside down, she was recording her notes on a form. Neat blank sections with bold print titles. I could see the top section, where my personal information ought to go. She looked ready to start a question and answer session, when I asked, "Is that the job application? Do you want me to fill it out for you? Make it easier?"

"No. I prefer to get information on you first. Make my decision. Then, if we come to an agreement and it looks as though we could have a good working relationship, I'll make sure that section's completed."

"Okay."

"Phone number?"

I was ready for this. "I don't have a home phone. Little problem there." I shot her an embarrassed grin. "Okay, they shut it off." I dug out and held up my cell phone. "But this is paid up till the end of the month."

As I gave her the number, she jotted it down, nodding. "Where did you work before? You said you were fired?"

"Yeah." I tried to both look and sound regretful. Sticking with the truth as much as possible, I said, "I used to work at *Midwest Focus*."

"The television news show?" Her eyes widened and I felt the walls go up again.

"Uh-huh," I said, trying for nonchalant.

"What did you do there?" There was that squint again.

"Well . . ." I bit my lip, "I used to tell everybody I was a secretary there, but . . ."

"But?"

"But really, I was just kind of a gofer person. They told me that if I worked out, maybe I'd get to be one of the assistants, someday."

"How long did you work there?"

"Just over a year."

"Who was your immediate supervisor?"

"A girl named Jordan Harvey."

Lisa took notes with a sinuous motion. Even upside down I could tell that she had flawless handwriting. Clear, even, and strong. She looked up at me and asked, *"Jak sie pisze?"*

"Excuse me?"

"I'm sorry." She shot me a lips-only smile. Testing. "Spell her name for me, please."

I did. Jordan, fully apprised of my antics here today, would have my story ready for anyone who might call to check on my employment. Everything from a starting date to my skimpy salary and reasons for dismissal. I just better remember not to apply for any credit cards over the next few days. All calls regarding my recent tenure at the station were to be referred to Jordan. With the tale we concocted, my credit rating would fall through the floor.

"Why were you let go? Downsizing?"

"Yeah. That's it."

"Do you have a cosmetology license?"

"No, but Helena says I should apply for shampoo girl."

"How much schooling have you had?"

"I took a couple college classes after high school. But that was kind of a long time ago."

"What did you study?"

"This and that. You know, general stuff. I didn't know what I wanted to do yet."

"What do you want to do?"

I tried to look sheepish. "I still don't know yet?"

"Have you ever worked in a beauty shop before?"

"No."

Lisa stopped writing, leaned back in her chair, holding the expensive pen up by her lips. "Then what makes you want to work in one now?"

I was ready for this one. "At this point, I'll take anything." I took a deep breath and shook my head. "I'm telling you, I can spend money faster than I make it and I got bills up the wazoo."

A long moment passed where she said nothing but merely tapped the fancy pen against the desk top, considering. "Most of the girls I hire are recent immigrants," she said.

"Yeah. It's gotta be hard for these girls to leave home for a big city like Chicago. I'm from downstate, myself. Sophie says that Father Bruno set her up with you. She says he helped her get out of Poland and into the job market here. She's forever grateful to the guy."

Lisa reacted to the mention of Father Bruno's name with a flicker of interest. Almost imperceptible, but it was there. "You know him, too?" she asked.

"Sophie introduced us."

I was here to assess this Lisa, to get information on her organization. According to Sophie, she guarded the truth about the salon's clientele from Father Bruno. But I wanted to see for myself.

Her hiring me as a shampoo girl would be a bonus and

would provide opportunity for further investigation, but I needed to maximize this interview, now. So, I pressed further. "How did you ever get hooked up with him, anyway?"

I watched wariness slip over her eyes, like a veil. "Why?"

She'd answered a question with a question. Fencing maneuvers. I shrugged again and made light of it. "I don't know. Just curious. Father Bruno doesn't look like the type to come walking into your salon for a haircut."

"And you don't seem the type to take a minimum-wage job."

I shrugged. "It's been a tough year."

"So . . . what is this?" she asked.

I held my breath. Maybe my acting skills had failed me, after all. She shook her head, and leaned forward to rest her bare elbows on the desk. "Are you just looking for something to hold you over till a real job comes along?"

"Listen," I said, working to let the breath of relief that whooshed out of me sound like a sigh of frustration, "if I can make a pretty good buck, I'm gonna be happy. Alls I want is the kind of job so I can make enough to get back on my feet."

"Helena was right. Shampoo girl is about the best I can offer. There's not a lot of money in that."

"Sophie says that lots of girls start out shampooing, but they work their way up. If I try real hard, maybe I could move up . . . or something. You know, have more . . . responsibility?" I tried to put just the right spin on the word.

Tiny squint. Both eyes this time. "What did Sophie tell you about some of the responsibilities the girls have?"

Here it was. Sophie had made me promise not to let Lisa know that she'd spilled the beans. Though I prepared myself ahead of time for a question like this one, I still felt my mind doing a nervous tap dance inside my head. "You know," I said drawing the words out, "not too much. Even though I asked her a couple of times. She told me that you were a really nice boss and really fair. She said that, over time, you'd decide if I was good for the place or not. And if you thought I was, you'd find a place for me. I thought that sounded pretty good. Kind of like a tryout period."

The shift in her attitude was subtle. She laid the pen down and squinted at me one last time. "I like to take a picture during the interview, if you don't mind. Helps me remember who's who. I have a lot of girls I interview, you realize. This is a cutthroat business sometimes."

"Sure." I shrugged.

She pulled out a Polaroid camera from another drawer and asked me to stand against the far wall. Totally blank wall—no décor whatsoever. I bet every picture was taken against this very background. Had Milla stood here, just like I was doing now? Smiling for the camera and dreaming of a better life?

"Should I smile?"

"Please."

I did as she snapped a shot, then gestured for me to turn sideways. Mug shot time.

"You have a boyfriend?" she asked. The tone was conversational but I sensed the weight of the question. And it occurred to me that a boyfriend in this business could be a major hindrance. For a split-second, so quick I could almost pretend it didn't happen, I thought about William. And his turn-my-knees-to-jelly smiles.

Then I remembered Dan and gave a half-laugh. "No."

"What's so funny?"

Sticking with the truth, I grinned at her. "I just broke up with him."

"Feel bad?"

Total truth. "God, no."

"No reconciliation in your future then?"

"Not a chance."

"Take a deep breath and straighten up for this one." I did and she nodded, popping another flash at me. "You look better . . . prettier, when you hold your shoulders back like that. Let's take another one."

Hold my shoulders back. Hmm. Seemed what she was trying to tell me was to thrust my chest out.

Lisa finished posing me this way and that. She took a handful of shots, some close-ups, a couple full-length, but I had to admit, they made me feel uncomfortable. I didn't like the idea of my image being passed to sweaty-handed men, with money in their pockets and lewd thoughts on their minds. Men like creepy Emil.

I pushed my discomfort aside. "So, do I get the job?" I asked.

Her eyes raked over me and I caught her squinting one more time. Looking over the Polaroids she spread across the desk, she ran her tongue over her lips. "I can probably find a place for you temporarily. After that, we'll see how it goes. Fair enough?"

Chapter Twelve

Dan's message on my voicemail at work first thing Tuesday morning asking me to dinner was a shocker. I'd left him a quick message Sunday, reminding him that I still had his keys. I planned to drop them off at his station by mid-week unless I heard from him otherwise.

I expected that he would want to meet for the exchange; Dan was particular about his keys. I had no problem with that, but I also didn't want to go out of my way to return the things, either. I figured he'd make a quick stop by my office on Monday or Tuesday and that would be that.

I punched in his number and sat back, waiting for his voicemail to pick up on the fourth ring, like it always did. This morning, my office window gave me the kind of view I live for. From the azure sky with picture-perfect clouds dotting the expanse, to the sharp focus of the buildings and the river, it was a sight that made me, for just a moment, pretend that the window was a painting on the wall instead of a glimpse into the real world outside. I'd like to have been able to freeze the moment, take a snapshot, and use that as my view on days I needed a boost.

He answered the phone himself, on the third ring. "Dan?" I said, sitting up. Even I heard the surprise in my voice.

"You were expecting someone else?"

I sat back again. "I expected your voicemail."

"Well, then, I guess it's your lucky day."

I rolled my eyes, wishing he could see me. "Yeah."

"So, how about it?"

"How about what?"

"Dinner, tonight. Say, seven o'clock?"

A knock at my office door interrupted. "Hang on," I said, then called, "Come in."

William walked in, opening his mouth as if to speak, but he stopped short when he noticed I was on the phone. I invited him to sit down with a hand motion toward my chairs, then turned my attention back to Dan.

"I can't. I have a wake to go to." Matthew's. And I didn't think I'd be able to just make an appearance and run at this one. "Why don't you just stop by the office after work and I'll have them for you? Or I could leave them with the receptionist."

He was silent.

"I promise to put them in a sealed envelope."

He wasn't amused. Or so I gathered from the grunt on the other end of the connection. I shot a quick smile over to William to let him know I'd be right with him.

"What about lunch?" Dan asked.

"I've got another hair appointment this afternoon," I said, "and my schedule's packed."

Dan was quiet. So quiet I could almost hear the gears working in his brain. He wanted something. Otherwise he would have taken any excuse to pick the keys up without having to "visit."

"Where's the wake?"

I glanced at the notes in my calendar. "Why?"

"I thought maybe we could have dinner afterward," he said. Then, as if the thought just occurred to him, asked, "Who died?"

"A friend's brother."

"Sorry to hear it," he said without conviction. "Maybe we can meet for drinks afterward?"

Oh, now that appealed to me. Just what I wanted to do after an evening of mourning the dead. Go out for drinks with Dan.

"We can make it quick," he said, perhaps sensing my reticence. "I have something I want to talk to you about and I'd rather do it in person."

I felt energy drain out of me. "Fine," I said. I didn't want to go traipsing back downtown after a long day, so I told him he'd have to meet me at a neighborhood restaurant near the funeral home. "No drinks, though," I cautioned. "The strongest thing they offer there is coffee. Let's make it around nine, okay?"

"Great." The absent-minded tone of his voice told me he was writing the address down. "Whose funeral did you say this was?"

"Gotta go," I said. "See you then."

William brought his attention back from looking out my window as I dropped the receiver into the cradle with a bang. "Hi," I said, massaging my temple.

He shot a glance toward the phone, giving me the impression he was curious about the call, but he got down to business right away. "How did your interview go yesterday?"

"I start next week."

He gave an appreciative nod. "You're good."

I laughed. "Let's just hope I don't get myself into a situation where I have to prove *that*."

Ooh. Slightly bawdy remark on my part. Slipped out. His grin and raised eyebrows told me he'd caught the humor, and my instant flush of warmth was less from embarrassment than from his smiling reaction to it. What the hell was up? I was finding myself attracted to a man I barely knew. Very unlike me. Time to start squashing these instant physical responses to his presence.

Yeah, like I had any clue how to do that.

The blue eyes staring at me turned serious again. "I've got most of what I need on the hair care story. You're getting some impressions today from that salon where Angela Cucio got her ear sliced, right?"

"I'm scheduled for noon. Only time I could get in, and only because of a cancellation. The place books weeks in advance."

"Nervous?"

Movement outside my window pulled my eyes that direction. The Michigan Avenue Bridge was rising to allow passage of a tall-masted boat. Late in the season, but maybe they pushed their luck while the weather was good. "A little, I guess. I'll make sure they only use scissors on me." I grinned. "See that bridge? I never get tired of watching them raise and lower it. And I must have seen it happen a hundred times. Amazes me every time."

William walked over to the window to watch. I got up and stood next to him, marveling at the elegant sweep of the pavement as it moved to point skyward. Both upper and lower Michigan Avenue moved together, the only real time they were in sync. Back in place, in their ordinary roles of providing passage over the river, business-suited commuters and tourists strode along its length in the sun. Directly underneath was reserved for vagrants, the homeless, and the smart drivers who knew the secret of avoiding traffic snarls above.

Yellow flashing warning gates and clanging alarms had cautioned pedestrians and cars to halt at the bridge entrances in both directions. Until the boat cleared and the streets were lowered, the noise and lights continued. I pointed.

"You see right there? I guess some woman got her car stuck in the mechanism once. She went too far forward and, when the bridge came down, it squashed her hood. Closed down the Magnificent Mile for hours."

William turned to me. "Did you get to see it?"

My eyes were just a trace higher than his shoulder. Nice height. I tilted my head up, suddenly realizing that in my enjoyment of the show, I stood closer to him than the concept of "personal space" generally dictated. Not that I minded. But he might.

"No, unfortunately." I moved back to my comfy chair, warning bells still clanging from the street below. "Missed it when I was out on a story. But I would have loved to have seen it," I said, then amended. "Nobody got hurt, you understand."

"I figured, from your level of enthusiasm."

Running my fingers through my hair, I thought about the story again. "I'm hoping for some background on the shop. I plan to ask a few pointed questions. See if anyone there knows what happened. Not that the girl who did a number on Angela's ear would still be there."

"About the other story. The prostitution ring. Any idea how big? How far-reaching?"

"No. This Lisa's pretty close-lipped."

"If she thinks you're unemployed, how come the delay? Why not start sooner?"

"You're gonna love this," I said.

Pleased with the mirth in his eyes as I said that, I continued. "I have to go for a physical." I waited a beat for the import to sink in. "To be a *shampoo* girl. She insists that I get a clean bill of health and told me not to be concerned with the emphasis of the exam on sexually-transmitted disease. How did she phrase it? 'You may not realize it now, but this can be an intimate business. I want to be sure my clients feel safe in our hands.' "

"She said that?"

"Her exact words."

"Nothing like a double meaning, huh?" William expelled a breath of disbelief. "We're going to nail this story quick, aren't we? Before things heat up for you?"

"Oh, yeah," I said with gusto. "I don't plan to find myself in any compromising situations. No story's that important."

"Good." He gave a short nod. "Well, I was just checking in. You let me know if you need an assist on anything, all right?"

"Sure," I said. It was an automatic response, but the offer had surprised me. Tony had never volunteered help on my end of the story. I investigated. He wrote. And never the twain shall meet, or however that saying went.

"Good," he said again as he stood. "This one's just begging to be followed. I'm looking forward to working with you on it. And, hey, thanks for the show." He lifted his chin to indicate the window. Back in place, the bridges again allowed passage of walkers, bicyclists, and traffic. "My view is . . . a wall. But it's an attractive wall." He smiled again and I deliberately fought the whump that resounded in my stomach. He gave my office a once-over and, despite the mountains of files on every horizontal surface, he said, "This is nice."

My brain screamed to say something clever, to invite him to visit anytime his little heart desired. Something like that. Instead I cleared my throat. "Thanks."

I dragged open the restaurant door and took a deep breath of its aroma. I smelled food. Burnt coffee, unidentified fried meat, late-night scrambled eggs. Yum. The day had run away from me and I hadn't had a chance to eat since I grabbed a bagel and coffee in the morning.

I was starving.

It didn't matter that the scent of kill-all-germs-in-the-radius-of-a-mile disinfectant wafted from the adjacent bathrooms into the dining area. My stomach responded to the availability of nourishment with an anticipatory growl.

Pausing for a moment at the cashier's stand, I recognized the back of Dan's head. With business slow at nine o'clock at night, the woman in charge of seating patrons had taken a perch near the kitchen, leaning one ample hip against the tall counter as she spoke in a foreign language to a sweaty man behind it. They kind of matched one another, in a middle-aged, swarthy sort of way.

At my appearance, she boosted herself to a standing position until I waved her back. I'd find my way over to Dan without interrupting her yak session. She pointed to the stack of plastic menus, then settled back against the counter and winked at me as I grabbed one, not stopping her conversation the entire time.

Dan looked up with alarm when I slid into the booth opposite him. The place was fairly quiet. Three or four occupied booths out of about thirty. And only one person at the long Formica countertop nearby, an elderly fellow reading the paper and smoking a cigarette. I noticed the ashtray at our table.

"Why didn't you ask for non-smoking?" I asked.

Dan seemed confused. He looked at me for a half-second longer than the simple question warranted and shrugged. "Didn't think of it."

I grabbed my menu again. "Let's switch over to the other section then," I said.

"Nah, I kind of like it here. Less crowded."

I shot him my "what are you, nuts?" look and turned my

coffee cup over for the swarthy hostess-turned-waitress to fill, which she did almost immediately.

"Nice hair," he said.

The remark might have even been sincere. Today's trip to the salon where Angie had gotten her ear whacked had been a win-win situation all around. The girl who styled my newest " 'do" hadn't been around the place very long, but the woman at the next station had. I asked a few innocent questions about things going awry in salons, and admitted, in a conspiratorial whisper, that I'd heard about a woman who lost an ear there.

The older stylist, Luanne, was only too happy to repeat the tale for the three of us rapt listeners: me, the younger stylist, and Luanne's client. I got plenty of background that would add flavor to the story William and I were building.

A protracted squeak alerted me to the door to the women's bathroom opening, sending another gust of hyper-disinfected air my way. A blond woman emerged, carrying a laptop and a purse. Dressed like she just stepped out of a power business meeting, I watched her make her way toward a far booth in our section, digging a cigarette out of her cunning designer purse. Looking out of place in a neighborhood dive like this, she had an air about her that roused a pang of envy. I wished I could look that polished this late at night. Right now I felt run ragged from the events of the day, and it was a sure bet I looked it, too.

I'd snuck out of the funeral home before the end of the wake. Sophie had plenty of friends there for support and, while I could tell she was touched by my presence, she still had so many mourners to greet that I knew she wouldn't notice if I left.

Having gotten there around seven, I'd been eager to get out of there when, at eight on the nose, Father Bruno made his bulky appearance. I altered plans, making an instant decision to stay. The guy intrigued me. Priest, confidant, protector of poor eager immigrants, he had all the right qualifications to be a saint. But I wasn't quite sure I liked the guy.

Maybe it was just me, I reasoned, and I decided to stay and see if I couldn't muster up grudging respect for him.

Sophie latched onto his arm the minute he showed, breaking out again into the soft, sobbing rhythms that had punctuated each guest's arrival. He patted Sophie on the back and spent a long moment kneeling next to the casket, head bowed, eyes clenched.

Rising with the grace that a lifetime of carrying excess weight bestows on a man, he became the shepherd of the flock, surveying the gathered mourners in slow motion. Lifting his chin, he called out in a louder voice than necessary, "Please be seated."

Within moments, amid creaks and mumbles, the room fell silent and everyone had a seat. I perched at the edge of a brocade couch. One of four matching ones that lined the walls, it was close to the rose-and-carnation arrangement with the fake clock in its center, to indicate Matthew's time of death. I wondered how the sender had decided on eleven-thirty.

Bruno gave the crowd a smile. Of appreciation for the immediate response to his request, I guessed. His eyes seemed to take in every person in the room. Opening the little black book that looked somehow insignificant in his hands, he cleared his throat and led us all in prayer for the next half-hour.

After the service, drained from the boredom of repeating identical words en masse, I stood up and made a show of checking out the flowers. Why not take a quick look at who was thoughtful enough to send them? My close proximity to

Matthew's coffin also gave me a great vantage point for watching Father Bruno interact with those who came up to talk with him, to touch his hand, and look up at him with trusting eyes.

Sophie was still holding the priest's arm, her gaze directed at Matthew's tranquil form. "He look like he is sleeping, no?"

Bruno had glanced up and we made eye contact. At Sophie's question, he turned his attention back to her. "He looks like an angel, Sophia, because now your brother *is* an angel."

I couldn't help but think that it sounded so . . . scripted. To the man's defense, he no doubt attended many more wakes and funerals than the average lay person, and I was sure he had to rely on a cache of comforting murmurs to help the bereaved get through their heartbreaking ordeal.

Sophie's face crumpled in on itself, reddening as she tried in vain to stem the tears again. Helena took her by the shoulders and Bruno extracted his arm in a smooth movement. He turned to me and smiled, effectively cornering me into conversation.

"Alexandrine, isn't it?"

"I'm surprised you remember."

"You were a friend to Sophie when she needed you. It would be more unlikely that I would not remember."

"I know Sophie is happy you were able to come, Father," I said. "She hoped you would."

"I'm certain your presence here is as welcome as mine. How are you? Everything going well in your life?"

"Well, no. And yes." I shot him a grin and launched into my charade. I might as well strive for consistency. "I lost my job. I kinda knew I would, but it still hit me when it happened."

His brows furrowed.

"That's the bad news. The good news is I asked Sophie if maybe she'd talk to her boss for me. See if there's any place for me where she works."

"Well, that is good news." He smiled, in a distracted, thoughtful way.

Conjuring up a look of concern, I bit my lip. "Is that okay? I mean, it just dawned on me this minute that you might not be happy about it. If that takes away a job opening that you can use for one of the kids from Europe . . ." I let the sentence hang for just a second before interrupting myself. "I never thought of that till just now. I can really use the job, but I don't want to mess things up."

"No, that's quite all right, my dear. Good luck in the new job. I know you'll do well."

A lineup of women waited to talk to the good father. I made my excuses and left. The prayer vigil and subsequent chitchatting left me no time to stop home, and I headed straight to meet Dan.

Sitting here in the booth now, my stomach made another insistent growl, causing Dan to cock an eyebrow at me. It was so loud I wondered if the waitress heard, because an instant later she stood at the table's side, pen poised over her order pad. What I wanted was a Reuben sandwich, fries and an iced tea, but I'd already downed a cup of coffee and it was pretty late at night for heavy food.

"I'll take two eggs, over hard, with rye toast," I said. "And bacon."

Our waitress turned to Dan. He shook his head. She eyed our half-empty mugs and headed back toward the kitchen.

"I thought we were just here for coffee," Dan said. "I didn't know you were going to eat."

I shrugged, in an effort to dismiss his complaint. What difference did it make? "Oh, here," I began, digging into my purse for Dan's keys.

"Not yet," Dan said, reaching forward, touching my hand. From the look on his face, it was more a restraining move than a romantic one.

"What's with you?"

He smiled. "I just don't want you to get the wrong idea. I wanted to sit and talk a while. If that's all right?"

"Sure," I said, adding a tiny bit of half and half to the coffee. It didn't make a dent in the deep brown liquid, so I added more. "What's up?"

Dan made an effort at small talk, asking polite questions about the shake-up at the station, and about William in particular. I could tell something important was on his mind. A pair of lines formed between his eyebrows, a sure sign of his concentration. His eyes held mine in a way that used to make my heart beat faster, but now, even the neat symmetry of his face, the model-perfect look he wore with grace and style, wasn't enough to even give me pause. I got the feeling he wasn't concentrating on my simple answers to his questions; he seemed to be elsewhere.

He leaned forward, arms resting on the speckled silver tabletop. "Whose wake did you go to tonight?"

"I told you, a friend's brother."

"What was his name?"

"Why?"

My food arrived, the heavy stoneware plate thudding as the waitress dropped the end one second too early. I watched the steam rise from the buttery fare, and thought the shiny grease on the hash browns was about the best thing I'd seen all day. Starting in, I forked in a mouthful of eggs, then salted them lightly before moving on.

Dan didn't seem to be in any hurry to answer my inquiry.

"Why are you asking me?" I repeated.

The expression on his face was one of muted anger. "Because," he said, leaning back in the booth and folding his arms across his chest, "I think you're still on that Milla Voight story and you've been lying to me all along."

Anger rose up with such vehemence and such power that I dropped my fork with a clatter.

"What the hell is wrong with you?"

"You went to Matthew Breczyk's wake, didn't you?"

"And what if I did?"

"You're still working the story."

We were getting progressively louder, and I hissed for him to keep our voices down, then added, "I'm not."

"Then why the hell were you there?"

"That's none of your goddamn business," I said, thinking, *asshole.*

"I think you owe me an explanation."

My stomach squirming, I looked down at the food. All of a sudden it looked like mishmash swimming in a pool of grease. I couldn't touch another bite.

"No," I said, with as much calm as I could muster, "but *you* owe me." I stood up, bright lights of anger going off like flashbulbs in my head. "This one's your treat. I'm outta here."

I grabbed my purse and was out the door in an instant, my mind registering at once that Dan hadn't followed me.

I wanted him to, and it bothered me that I did. Not because of any hoped-for reconciliation, but for some tangible evidence that I'd ever meant anything to him.

My car was parked at the far end of the small parking lot. I stopped at my back bumper and turned around. It was cold. It was dark. And the surrounding area was silent, except for the buzz of the restaurant's neon sign and the hum of the streetlights above.

Supremely pissed, I jammed my fists into my sides and stood there a long moment, imagining all the scathing comments I could have made if I would've thought of them before I stormed out. A quick, cool breeze drew past me, lifting the ends of my hair, almost in a caress. I blew out a breath of frustration and watched as it swirled and dissipated into the night air. He wasn't worth the energy I expended on him.

Deep down, I knew I was better off that we'd gone our separate ways. I supposed the thing that bothered me most of all was that he didn't realize I'd had such a change of heart. That I was glad we broke up. Part of me wanted to ram that knowledge down his scrawny little throat. But my more logical, less emotional side fortunately took control and reminded me that his belief that I still carried a torch for him was no real skin off my nose. And in time, it would fade.

Deal with it, I told myself.

With that, I got in my Escort and, about to start the engine, I came across Dan's keys. I'd forgotten about them entirely.

I muttered under my breath at my lack of concentration, and made my way back into the restaurant with his house and car keys in hand.

The hostess was back at her perch against the counter, but the look on her face as I walked in was one of apprehension. Maybe she thought I came back to make a scene. I smiled at her, hoping to give her reassurance, and started toward Dan's table.

And then I understood the waitress's reaction.

My side of the booth was now occupied by the polished blonde in the stunning business suit. She and Dan, their fingers entwined, were engaged in animated conversation, so much so that neither noticed until I stood next to the table.

I plastered on my best fake smile. "Hi. I'm Alex St.

James," I said, extending my hand. To her credit, she let go of Dan long enough to shake it, though with only the very tips of her manicured fingers. I got immense pleasure out of the fact that my sudden appearance seemed to have rendered her speechless. "And you are?" I asked.

She blinked, shot a furious glance at Dan, and then her poise returned enough to answer. "Pamela Ricketts."

"Pleasure."

I turned to Dan, wiggling the keychain high so that it made a nifty metallic musical sound. "Almost forgot to give you these."

Pamela Ricketts said nothing, but if looks could kill, Dan would be dead on the floor.

Stunned, but somehow cheered, I turned to leave. Dan grabbed my wrist, effectively stopping me. "The reason I wanted to meet with you tonight—which I was going to tell you before you got all huffy—is because I have some information about that guy, William Armstrong, who just joined your station."

I pulled my arm out of his grasp. "Uh-huh."

"I know why he left the *Sun-Times*."

"Good for you," I said, the big smile still in place. "Have a nice night." I gave a jaunty little wave, fought an irresistible instinct to bolt, and took my sweet time walking out the door.

Chapter Thirteen

Today was going to suck. Big time.

I hit the snooze alarm three times, but didn't avail myself of the additional opportunity to sleep. I dozed a bit overnight, but I never fell into a sound enough slumber that would provide the attitude and energy I needed to pull my sorry butt out of bed this morning.

Fingers laced behind my head were now turning numb, and my gaze fixed on a volcano-shaped crack in the ceiling. I shivered. In my vain attempts to find the right position all night to coax myself to sleep, I twisted and turned until my sheet and blanket looked like some giant had wrung out his wash. Right now, shucked to the side, the bright rainbow-quilted bed cover, which survived the eighties about as well as I had, did nothing to protect me from the morning's chill.

The idea of attending Matthew's funeral was enough to make me want to burrow in and forget that I'd gotten involved in this mess. That and Dan's new girlfriend. How blind was I?

I felt emotions swell and, like waves of an incoming tide sweeping me along, though my body remained perfectly still, I was stunned. The idea that he so casually brought us together in such an underhanded way bugged me. If he wanted to go for a late night tête-à-tête with luscious little Pamela, why didn't he just have her there at the table, so we could meet like civilized folks?

I was hurt, in a vague way. He'd made a concerted effort to

157

keep Blondie secret and I didn't understand why. Although she obviously did.

Mostly I was angry at myself for letting the jerk's actions bother me. And I was annoyed that he said something about William. Something that led me to believe that whatever the scoop was on his leaving the *Sun-Times*, it was not going to put him in a good light.

Asshole.

Dan, not William.

I tried to convince myself that Sophie could get through today without me. I'd so much rather just stay in bed. Of course, that wouldn't be fair to Sophie, even if she had good old Father Bruno there to hold her hand.

Father Bruno. Now there was a man I wanted to know more about.

My energy thus engaged, I swung my legs around and planted my feet on the cold wooden floor. It was only after I started the car to head for the service that I realized it was a priest who'd gotten me excited enough to get out of bed. I was starting to scare myself.

"Hi," I said, holding my hands against William's doorjamb, "got a couple of minutes?"

"Sure," he said, glancing up with what seemed like downright disinterest, "what's up?"

When William told me that his view out the window was of the building next door, he didn't mention that it was so close-up, so near, that if he broke the picture window and reached out, he could touch the cool, white marble. I never knew what a lousy vista there was from here. The office's prior occupant had been an older guy who swore, complained, and smoked. He kept the dark drapes pulled across the window's expanse—always. Now I knew why. It still smelled faintly of stale cigarettes, and the formerly white walls had an uneven stain of brown up near the ceiling, where the old guy's exhalations had settled and left the equivalent of a tobacco-water line. William kept his back to his window, which, despite the bland view, was bright. Very bright. He sat almost in silhouette, until I got up close and moved to a blue, nubby, upholstered office chair. Another reservoir of leftover smoke, it shot a gust up to engulf me as I sat.

"How do you stand the smell in here?" I asked.

"Bass promised me a cleaning crew would be in one of these days to spiff up the place." He shook his head. "Every night I go home, my clothes reek. I've been keeping the dry cleaners happy, let me tell you."

Like a tantalizing puzzle to be solved, I studied our Mr. Armstrong. My expertise was reading people. I excelled at it. Which is how I managed to keep Bass happy—by providing plenty of in-depth research on a steady stream of interviewees. But, except for small glimpses into William's personality, which I suspected he doled out when the mood struck, I couldn't read this fellow, despite my senses being on red alert every time he was nearby. And he didn't seem to be in the mood to dole out much right now.

I brought my attention back to work matters. "I went to Matthew Breczyk's funeral this morning."

Grimace of commiseration. "Yeah. How did that go?"

"It was a funeral," I said, with a bit of sarcasm. I didn't know precisely why annoyance had crept into my words, but it had. Something uncomfortable had crawled into my heart and was sitting there. I couldn't quite get a grip on what it was. Not that I expected him to do backflips when I sat down, but he had a look on his face that made me sorry I stopped in. Matthew's funeral had taken a lot out of me, and Father Bruno had conducted the affair in such a sincere, heartbroken manner. I wondered if I *had* misjudged the man. Emil hadn't shown up, thank goodness; he was probably guarding the rectory and downing the stash of altar wine.

Maybe I was seeing things through an unpleasant filter. I'd come in, half-tempted to broach the topic of his departure from the *Sun-Times*. Make no mistake—I was curious. But this didn't feel like a good time for the subject. Maybe I was just cranky. In that case, the best bet would be to stick to business. "Did you get the rest of the hair care story research I left for you?"

"Yeah."

That was it. "Yeah." From this point on, William would be in charge of writing the script, working with the talent co-ordinator, and attending the taping. I don't know what I was hoping for. An invitation to be part of it, perhaps? But I wasn't about to ingratiate myself where I might be considered a hindrance rather than a help.

Pushing against the arms of the chair, I stood, eager to get out of tobacco heaven. "Okay, good. Let me know if you need anything else."

"Alex? Is that you?"

Father John Triphammer stopped raking the leaves that covered the rectory's side yard like a raggedy blanket. Colorful yet muted, the ground moved and shifted with every twist of the wind beneath the wispy, gray afternoon sky. This yard, which brooked the thirty-foot distance between the rectory and my grammar school, had always been off-limits to the students. We had another yard for recess, on the other side of the school. This one, with its shrine to Mary, complete with a weatherproof kneeler dead-center amid all the trees, was meant for meditation. But no one ever really used it.

Father Trip, as he was affectionately known, leaned on the

rake's handle, his eyes crinkling up as he smiled. I always thought he was a handsome man and I had a massive crush on him back when I was in grammar school, blissfully unaware that having crushes on priests was a no-no. He reminded me a lot of Dick Van Dyke in those days. My parents always watched the black-and-white reruns, and I think I fell a little in love with Rob Petrie. Tall, with a narrow face and an easy smile, Father Trip wore his hair cropped short, and just these past few years, white hair won the battle for his head. Nowadays the priest still resembled the actor, but now he looked more like the *Diagnosis Murder* version. When he said Mass, standing below the bright overhead lights, he often looked to be encircled in a halo.

Not that Father Trip was any kind of saint. I'd seen him at social gatherings, where he blended in and traded barbs with the parishioners. He could be sharp-tongued when piqued. While he never stepped over the priestly line with anyone, he came about as close to being a regular guy as a man in a collar could get.

Right now, he had a blue flannel shirt on, with the sleeves rolled up past his elbows. His hooded gray sweatshirt lay discarded over the cyclone fence that surrounded the yard.

I stretched my arms out, feigning inspection of myself. "Yep. It's me. In the flesh." I was in jeans and a T-shirt. On my way out the door, I'd grabbed an oversized sweatshirt for warmth. Maroon, with my university crest in gold across my chest, it made me feel comforted whenever I wore it, engulfing me both in warmth and memories.

Father Trip grinned. "You need something." It wasn't a question.

Embarrassed cringe on my part. "That obvious?"

"Well, let's see. Except for Christmas and Easter, the only time I ever see you anymore is when you have a Catholic question." His eyes shifted, suddenly serious. "You know, Alex, you don't have to be afraid to come visit. I'm not going to try and drag you back into the fold, or convince you to start attending Mass again."

"I know," I said, gazing around at the enormous maple trees that dotted the small yard. He'd never get all these leaves raked up today. Not alone. "You got another rake?"

He turned to glance back against the side of the rectory wall. "I must have known you were coming."

Grabbing it, I started in. "Scary," I said. "Maybe you have ESP."

"Or a direct line to the Almighty?"

We worked in silence for a short while. Overcast, the gray sky was still bright. Enough so, that when I looked up, the branches of the trees that had gone bare made a pattern against the brightness. The sight of it made me sad for some reason I didn't understand. I caught a flit of red—a cardinal alighted on one of the branches and chirped its distinctive call. Leaves pulled and pushed against each other in a soft shush, lulling me into silence. It seemed almost wrong to break the rhythmic quiet of our task.

Within minutes, I'd shucked my own sweatshirt as a gleam of perspiration came over my face and onto my arms. It felt good to move.

I walked over to the cement Madonna and brushed errant leaves off her head.

"So, what are you investigating this time?" Father Trip asked, never stopping his movement. "Milla Voight?"

"God!" I said, amazed. Immediately, I was embarrassed for my exclamation.

"Taking the Lord's name in vain, Alex? And in front of a priest, no less." Father Trip's question was half-admonishment, half-tease. "Maybe you had better think about coming back to confession one of these days."

"How did you know what I wanted to talk with you about?"

"Keep raking," he said. "It'll be your penance."

I listened to the twin scrapes of our wiggly fingered rakes against the uneven stubble of the ground for several beats. "How *did* you know?"

"The Church is taking Father de los Santos' escape to South America seriously. Very seriously." His head down, Father Trip's eyes met mine; his voice lowered a notch. "They don't want a repeat of the scandals from a few years back."

I moved closer, toward the base of a tree nearer to him, lowering my voice as well. "You mean they think this might not be an isolated incident?"

He shrugged, but I noticed that he dug deeper into the piles of leaves as he spoke this time. "I pray to God that it is. But the fact that Milla Voight is dead, and so conveniently, is making the media sit up and take notice." He glanced at me, and I felt the weight of his words. "All I hope for is that the truth comes out. But I'm afraid that people will see a conspiracy where there is nothing but the very bad judgment of one priest, and the unfortunate death of a young woman."

He stopped raking. "The Church values human life. Life is sacred. There is no man in the Catholic clergy today who would so callously end another human's life to protect himself from scandal. This I believe. I would stake my vocation on it."

"Do you know Father Bruno Creighter?"

I paused in my raking, but Father Trip's quick glance of reminder got me started again. He nodded and began again, too.

"We've met, briefly, several times, but I know him by rep-

163

utation more than personally."

"He was Father de los Santos's—umm—boss? For lack of a better term. What's the word on him?"

A strong breeze shot past, flipping my hair into my mouth and twirling away the top layer of leaves off the pile I created. I reached my rake out to recapture them.

"From what I understand, Father Bruno is heartsick. The man is well-known as a staunch proponent of the Catholic Church, and he abhors anything or anyone who sullies the Church's good name. This is particularly hard for him, because the young priest was one of his golden boys. A candidate for eventual pastor. What with the shortage of young men entering the priesthood, the granting of a parish to someone with his qualifications is no longer unheard of."

"Leaves a bit of a hole in the organization?"

"Not only that, but Bruno's a career priest." Father Trip must have caught my raised eyebrows, because he quickly added, "Don't misunderstand me, I'm not minimizing his devotion. But with his media contacts, he's got a shot at Bishop and, from there, a clear path to Archbishop. Maybe even Cardinal. He's proven his usefulness, his dedication. And he's a go-getter. He's overseen the ordination of more young men than anyone in years. And he's got friends in high places." He smiled as he paused for a moment.

"Such as?"

"He's technically a citizen of the Vatican. Was born in Italy to devout parents and made lots of useful connections before he was sent over here."

"Creighter isn't an Italian name."

"Italian on his mother's side. Doesn't matter anyway, he's got the drive, the network, you name it."

"So if he's such a Catholic catch, why hasn't he moved up already?"

Father Trip pulled out a big brown lawn bag and began scooping armfuls of debris into it. "Could be any number of reasons. Timing being key. You realize that no one can move up until a position is vacated. And with life expectancies going up all the time, there's not a whole lot of turnover at some of those higher levels."

"Is there any dirt on him?"

"Alex!" Father Trip's reaction came out sharp, but a look at him told me he bordered on hurt. His tone softened. "There aren't a whole lot of secrets in the Church. Not anymore. And that's a good thing. I think if there were anything about Father Bruno that could tarnish his reputation, I would have heard about it by now."

"Okay, okay. But there's a guy who works for him. Emil."

"Emil?"

"Yeah, he's the secretary or something. I'm not really sure. But he works for Bruno—"

"Father Bruno."

"Sorry. He works for Father Bruno and he's—I don't know—icky."

"Well, there's an objective observation."

A leaf fluttered down over my head and landed on my right shoulder, its scratchy edges hanging tight to the fabric of my T-shirt. I brushed it away. "What I mean is, he works for the Church, but I get a bad feeling from him. He's got connections, I think, that he shouldn't."

"Connections?" I could hear the skepticism in his voice. I wanted to avoid telling Father Trip about the prostitution ring. It didn't yet feel like my story to tell; the fewer people who knew about it, the better.

"Something's wrong. There's not much more I can tell you, just yet." I bit my lip. "Would you mind checking around? Just a little?" I pulled the leaves closer to the big pile

165

that had accumulated, obscuring the bright white of my Reeboks. Keeping my attention to task, I waited.

It wasn't until I heard him sigh that I looked up. "Have you really become as cynical as you sound?"

I stopped scraping the leaves. "Not cynical," I said slowly, meeting his gaze. The look in his eyes was pained concern and I hated the fact that I put it there. "Just less willing to take things at face value."

He gave me a lopsided grin, and with it, a sense of willingness to lighten the mood. "Whatever happened to that little girl who trusted everybody?"

Looking at the big pile of leaves, curled corners of brown and red and orange, I couldn't resist. I sat down with a sigh of pleasure, feeling the crunch beneath my butt as a puff of mossy autumn smells enveloped me. I covered my blue-jeaned legs, just like I used to do as a kid. "She's still here," I said, smiling up at him. "But life changes people. And she's grown up."

"Grown up?" he asked, and he held my gaze a moment before averting his eyes. "Or grown away?"

Chapter Fourteen

The following morning I cancelled my employment physical. Despite the fact that Lisa had given me the address of an established medical group in the area, the idea of submitting to an examination for a job selling sex made my skin crawl. I wanted to go undercover, but not under those kinds of covers. The nurse who handled my phone call asked me if there was any sort of problem, or if later in the day suited my schedule.

My suspicious mind raced, wondering how if any of the staff of this place were on Lisa's payroll as well. The nurse's voice was so sincere, yet she pressed.

"I have an opening tomorrow, if that would be any better. A cancellation at ten? How's that?" Her voice sounded mid-fifties, brassy, eager.

"Umm," I hedged.

"I'm just trying to help, you understand. I see from the notice here, that this is for new employment, and we try to do our very best to expedite when we can." I could hear the smile in her voice as she said that.

"Yeah," I said, thinking fast. There was one excuse that would make sense. "But I got my period today. Totally unexpected."

"Oh," she said, stringing the word out into two syllables. "Don't you hate when it does that?" A page flipped and she hummed. "Okay, what about a week from today, same time?"

"That'll work," I lied.

"Okay, thanks for calling, Miss Szatjemski. We'll see you then."

The rest of the morning I spent at the library, looking up local news stories for any mention of Lisa Knowles. Fruitless venture.

Back home, I left the car in the garage and walked across my own small yard to the house. Leaving the gray sky and the sharp wind outside, I pushed open the back door, lifting it slightly so it didn't scrape the landing, and felt the home's welcoming warmth. The heat must have just kicked on, with that recognizable, comforting smell of the summer's dust burning off in the vents.

I flicked the overhead light on in the kitchen and thought about making some hot tea as I leaned over to check the answering machine on the counter. No messages. With a grin I remembered Lucy's exclamation whenever there were no messages on the machine when we got home. "I guess nobody loves us," she used to say. Yep. With my parents gone, Lucy safely ensconced in her new home, and Dan out of my life, that about summed it up. Even the telemarketers had thumbed their noses at me.

Gearing up for more research, I settled myself in Lucy's old room, where I'd hooked up my computer and peripherals. I surfed the Net, using every search pattern I could think of to find something, anything, about Lisa Knowles. My intense concentration and unswerving stare at the monitor for over two hours netted me little more than a pounding headache. The kind that made a starburst of light appear with each throb. I massaged my temples and sat back, waiting for the hammering to subside.

It didn't make sense. *Everybody* could be found on the Net. I got a slew of hits on the name Lisa Knowles, over five hundred. And I tenaciously clicked and followed every promising lead. Unless Lisa was a flyfishing aficionado in Oregon, a McDonald's manager in Colorado Springs, or a librarian in Utah, I was outta luck.

Another thing nagged at me. I'd left three messages at Sophie's and hadn't gotten a reply. I started out with a brief inquiry, expressing my concern and hopes that she was doing well after yesterday's ordeal. The second and third messages I left were more imperative, requesting, then insisting, she return the call. I was sure there'd be a quick "Hello, everything's fine," when I got home.

Starving, I meandered back and forth from the bare pantry to the nearly-bare refrigerator, half my mind deciding what to eat from my meager supply, the other half of my mind worried about the lack of word from Sophie.

I was coming up empty on both.

On the countertop, next to the answering machine, were three taffy apples, tempting me from their clear plastic "keep-em-fresh" display packaging. Not exactly a healthy meal, but I was getting desperate. Telling myself I'd make up for my poor eating habits later, I tore open the crackling package and downed two of them, licking the caramel off the stick of the second one as I eyed the third.

My appetite not quite satiated, I checked the answering machine again. As if it might have lied to me earlier, hiding a message. Still nothing.

While Sophie had been forthcoming on much of the story, I sensed that there were things she held back, things she was reluctant to admit to. And since she seemed equally reluctant to return phone calls, I decided I'd take a quick ride and visit her. Granted, I told myself, as I pulled my university sweatshirt over my head again, enjoying the fragrant outside smell as the cushy inner lining conformed to my shape, she could be recuperating from yesterday's long day. Maybe she was sedated. It wasn't unheard of.

Still, I hadn't gotten this far in life by not listening to my gut. Trotting back out to the garage, I started to feel the sugar high from the taffy apples kick in. Just what I needed right now.

I knocked on Sophie's door four times. When I'd been here before, I spent little time at her doorstep. Now I had a moment to look around while I contemplated my next move. This first-level landing of the three-flat had been painted a semi-gloss gray. As though a cleaning crew had been in moments before my arrival, the place was pristine. And if that shade of gunmetal gray had been even a little bit lighter, I would have said the place sparkled.

As it was, the cleanliness was almost depressing.

I could have sworn I heard movement in the apartment after my first knock. I put my face close to the heavy paneled door and called to Sophie, hoping that she'd answer if she knew it was me. I remembered her description of the police officer who came to tell her about Matthew and I stepped out of the little vestibule onto the porch to peer into her kitchen.

Not much there.

I tapped at the glass, and took a slow inventory of the room as I waited, the condensation of my breath on the glass fogging it up so I had to shift positions every few seconds. Everything in place. If cleanliness is indeed next to godliness, this woman was destined for sainthood.

A delayed realization caused my eyes to swing back to the kitchen table. One mug. One chair slightly askew. In my house, disorder of this magnitude would be cause for celebration. There was usually half a week's worth of dishware on the table or near, though never *in* the sink.

Sophie, however, would not have left the table looking like that.

I knocked again at the glass, hoping to catch her moving about in the apartment. Nothing.

With resolve, I headed up the creaking gray stairs to the second floor. It didn't matter that I had no idea who lived above her, I was beginning to get a bad feeling and I had to do something. Or at least feel like I was doing something.

No answer at that door.

One more flight up. If I had no luck, I could try the front door. At least there were doorbells there. As I climbed the steps, my feet making quiet smacks against the black lining, I noticed how much warmer it was getting up here. They say warm air rises, and this was no exception. At the top of the stairs, I was surprised to find yet another short flight that obviously led to the attic.

The gray and white paint combination ended abruptly and the look of bare wood, dark and kind of creepy, began as that last flight led upward. I didn't see any need to explore the attic, not now. And the hot, musty air that poured out from above didn't give me added incentive.

I peered up around the steps and realized there was almost no natural light up there. Probably a slew of spiders, though.

Before I could knock at the apartment on this floor, the flat, solid door opened with an abbreviated squeak and I found myself face-to-face with an equally solid woman. Over sixty years old, she was about five and a half feet tall, and nearly as wide. Her dark brown hair had been pulled around gray metal rollers and secured by big pink plastic pins, so tight that if I reached over to flick at the hair stretched out, I was sure I'd hear a "ping." Her face was pudgy and squished up, like a bulldog's, and she peered at me through rhinestone-studded glasses.

"Hi," I said.

She spoke to me in rapid-fire Polish, so fast that I couldn't keep up at first. What I gathered was that she didn't want to buy whatever I was selling and she was taking the opportunity to let me know how very put out she was by all the comings and goings in the apartments lately and didn't people even try to keep quiet anymore? I got the impression that she thought I had a direct line to all door-to-door salespeople and Jehovah Witnesses nationwide and that I'd pass the word along to quit showing up at her door.

I waited till she quieted her tirade. When her head tilted back and she looked at me more closely, she asked if I spoke Polish. I was getting asked that question more in the past few days than I had in my entire life.

I shrugged. Punted. "Sophie?" I asked, pointing downstairs.

Behind the woman, a man shuffled toward the stove where a percolator sat, making its musical coffee announcement and sending the delightful aroma out the door toward me. The woman gave me a look that could have been suspicion, could have been lack of comprehension, and turned to the man, who poured himself a cup and was making his soft-footed way to the table. This apartment was full-size. These were probably the landlords.

She spoke to the guy in Polish, which caused him to look in my direction. I felt his assessment, though he kept himself bland-faced. Placing his cup on the table with unhurried care, he shuffled to the door. "Yes? You ask about Sophie?"

I explained that I'd been concerned about her. That I hadn't seen her since the funeral yesterday. "She isn't answering her door, or her phone," I said, looking from his face to hers, and back again.

The man turned to his wife and conversed in low-toned Polish. I caught that their names were Mabel and Casimir. They'd been concerned about Sophie, too, from what I could gather. They *were* the landlords and had been debating going into her apartment to check on her.

"I looked in the window," I said. "She left a cup of coffee on the table."

He translated and they both raised eyebrows at that. The man nodded to me and invited me in. "I get keys. You wait."

Why on earth the woman decided to talk to me while we waited for Casimir to meander to the back bedroom for the keys, I didn't know. I feigned ignorance, but I picked up as much as I could.

There'd been a disturbance this morning. Standing on the landing above Sophie's apartment, they eavesdropped, hearing shouts, sounds of furniture moving around. Not wanting to get involved, they waited upstairs until things quieted down. It was Sophie's boyfriend again; they'd seen him often enough, knew he was trouble. Wished she'd break up with the guy already, because one of these days he was going to smash something or cause damage and who would pay for that?

Worried more about the state of the first-floor apartment, it seemed, than Sophie's well-being.

Maybe I was too quick to judge, I thought. Mabel here was yammering on and on in Polish, unaware that I understood her every word—a woman who didn't hesitate to vent when she felt like it. And the way she shook her head when she said Sophie's name made me wonder if perhaps she was concerned for her, but masked those feelings in concern for her material goods.

Maybe I was providing a means to go check on Sophie and this was Mabel's way of working out her anxiety. Not sure.

And I wondered if the man they'd seen was that Rodero guy.

She held up the percolator, raising her eyebrows in the universal gesture of "Want some coffee?" I shook my head, tempting though it was. Mabel poured herself a helping so full that I was sure it would spill over the top before she raised the delicate china cup to her pursed lips. In a curious juxtaposition, she slurped the black coffee noisily, while keeping the cup aloft, and her pinky extended in a show of elegant manners.

Casimir returned, still wearing his brown slippers. They whished against the tile floor, signaling his re-entry to the kitchen. Taller than Mabel, he was slim enough to make the gray pants and blue shirt he wore look like they'd been hung on a clothes rack, and none too carefully. A set of keys, at least thirty of them, were attached to a silver ring, with a long matching chain that dangled down. He searched for the right key with intent—there was some method to his organization, apparently—and within seconds, he singled out one. Blue eyes met mine from under bushy gray brows. "You come too?"

"Sure," I said. Like there would be any way I'd stay back.

Casimir knocked at Sophie's door, almost as hard as I had. He called out to her in Polish, asking if she was all right. Waiting a beat, he knocked again, then announced that he would come in, unless he heard from her.

He handled it all in a polite, no-nonsense way. Dad-like, almost, and I wondered if he had any idea of Sophie's true employment.

Casimir was not the kind of man who changed facial expression often. After he unlocked the door, he creaked it open a little, then wider to allow us into the kitchen. We both stood, looking at one another, and I realized at that point, I didn't quite know what to do. I dipped my pinky finger into the abandoned coffee in the mug, but there was so little in the bottom that the coldness didn't surprise me.

Casimir gestured toward the bedrooms. "You look," he said.

I headed for Sophie's room, noticing at once that the door was shut all the way. Chances were she was sleeping.

Wrapping my hand around the glass knob that looked like an oversized diamond, I rapped on the door and whispered Sophie's name.

Nothing.

Casimir took a couple of steps backward, which was curious. I wondered what he was afraid of, then realized that the altercation he and Mabel overheard earlier might have been much more violent than I originally assumed.

With a sense of urgency, I twisted the diamond and pushed my way in.

The room was almost exactly as it had been when I visited Sophie the day Matthew died. She was in the bed, but had her back toward me. The shaking of her shoulders gave me instant relief. Losing a loved one, particularly when one feels responsible, can often push people to the brink, and I'd been worried. I let out the breath I'd been holding, then reached out to touch her shoulder.

"Sophie," I said, in a soft voice, "it's Alex."

Her silent cries transformed into a wracking moan as her body froze for a moment before beginning to shake. Casimir, who'd shuffled up to the doorway to peer in, gave a quick nod, as though he'd seen enough and everything was all right now. He waved a hand at me to indicate that he was going back upstairs. A second later, I heard Sophie's back door shut with a click.

She resisted my attempts to turn her toward me, at first.

"Sophie, come on," I urged.

Her words were muffled, unclear, like she was speaking to me through a mouthful of marbles. In Polish she begged me to go away and leave her alone.

I had few experiences with grief in my life, but this reaction was ringing alarm bells. Sure, everyone handled death differently, but something was wrong.

Grabbing her right shoulder, I squeezed. In warning, I supposed. An attempt to get her to turn of her own volition one last time. She fought me again, but with less resolve this time.

With effort, I turned her to face me.

It took a few seconds for the full realization to sink in.

"Sophie," I said. And though my voice was soft, the words sounded like a scream to my own ears. "What happened?"

Despite the scant light, her injuries were obvious. Her face had purpled and was swollen around her mouth and along the entire left side of her head. Dried blood from her nose and a cut crusted her lip; she'd bled all over her pillowcase. Her left arm was discolored and she held it against herself in a way that let me know she was in pain.

Her blond hair was plastered to the side of her face, a combination of blood and tears locking the tresses, as though some four-year-old had just made a doll picture and glued the strands of yarn in the wrong places. She spoke in English.

"I go see Lisa," she said, her voice cracking. I strained to hear every word. "I tell her I finished. I no work any more."

Sophie licked at the open sore on her lips before continuing.

"When I come back . . . Rodero here. At my apartment. He wait for me."

Chapter Fifteen

"No hospital!"

Though battered and bruised, Sophie maintained enough strength to sit up in her bed. She let me look at her arm. It didn't appear to be broken, but I was no doctor. She swore it was merely bruised, that I shouldn't worry, but what broke my heart most was the way she kept her face slightly askance as she spoke. As if to keep me from seeing the damage done. I wondered if she'd been beaten before.

I tried repeatedly to get her to agree to have her injuries looked at, just in case. But Sophie was adamant. With no other options, I soaked a few washcloths and brought them, dripping, from the bathroom to help her clean herself up. She patted at the blood on her lips, and the side of her face, and I winced every time she did when the terrycloth stung her raw skin.

She shook her head as she worked, speaking in Polish so quickly and so quietly that I had trouble following her. She lamented the fact that she'd ever been lulled into this life. She mumbled between sobs, about how she should have listened to Matthew. She called herself every dirty name in the book and cried about how ashamed she was.

And now, she seemed to believe she couldn't get away. Now, when she finally realized what a mistake she'd made, she was stuck in this life, for as long as her body and her looks held out. And she called out to Matthew, and she knew he didn't hear her.

I listened for a long time. The pale light that brightened the room when I first got there now nearly dissolved in the late afternoon. Shadowy, the room was dim enough to warrant turning on a lamp, but I sensed that doing so might make Sophie more self-conscious.

We talked in the dark. Despite her many pleas for me to go home, I knew that there was no way I could leave her here in this condition, despite my belief that Rodero wasn't going to be coming back for a while.

"Did you tell Helena?" I asked in Polish.

"Oh, no!" Sophie said. "Rodero would go after her if I did. That's why you shouldn't even be here. If he finds out that I told anyone, he'll kill me."

"Then there won't be a next time. Come home with me," I said. "At least let me keep an eye on you tonight. You shouldn't be alone."

"If I leave here, Alex, where do you think they'll look for me?" Sophie's mind was still working; I took that as a good sign. "They'll ask Helena, but she can only tell them the truth, that she doesn't know. And then what? They'll come to you. They'll come to your house. No."

"Alex? Twice in as many days? Should I take that to mean that the Holy Spirit has moved you in some unusual way? Or—?" Father Trip's jovial greeting was cut short. Undoubtedly by the look on my face.

I caught him at home. His rectory, a converted red brick bungalow, was much smaller than the imposing structure Father Bruno lived in, though both had been built in the same era. Father Trip answered the doorbell moments after I rang it, which was good, because leaving Sophie alone in the car unnerved me.

She was crouched down in the passenger seat, her eyes

wide and terrified, looking even bluer than normal against the angry purple bruising of her face. I'd pulled to the curb and hurried around to head up toward Father Trip's, despite her protestations not to leave her alone. The poor girl shook, holding her hands tight together, jammed up close to her chest. I assured her that I wouldn't let the car out of my sight.

About to swing the door wide to admit me, Father Trip halted his movement, asking, "What? What happened?"

"I need a favor," I said.

I watched his eyes flick toward the car. "What happened?" he said again.

"Do you trust me?" I asked, hoping I knew the answer.

The two-second delay in his response didn't seem to indicate hesitation. More like he needed to gear himself up to accept whatever information I was about to impart. "Yes," he said. "Of course."

"There's a girl in my car. A . . . friend. And she's in serious trouble. For reasons I can't explain right now, I can't take her home, nor to a battered women's shelter. There can't be any attention drawn to her."

Except for another quick glance in the direction of my car, Father Trip kept his eyes on me, his face devoid of expression as he waited for me to continue.

"I know that you've helped people in the past. You must have connections. And she needs to be hidden. For a little while." My brain took a moment to catch up with my actions. I wondered how I'd play Sophie's disappearance to Lisa, should the subject come up. And I had no doubt that it would. Coupling that with my decision to cancel the scheduled doctor's appointment could make me suspect in their eyes. I thought of Sophie's poor swollen face and my stomach churned. For both of us.

All of a sudden Father Trip looked old to me. As though

the smiling lines around his eyes I'd grown used to all these years had suddenly become age-telling wrinkles. He nodded, very slowly, and I could almost hear him weighing my words against his need to caution me about my involvement here. He rubbed his face, and the late afternoon stubble caused a rasping sound at the movement in the quiet chill of the air.

"Bring her in," he finally said, tilting his chin that direction. The simple imperative gave me immense relief.

I trotted back to the car, then bit my lip when I saw that I'd startled her by opening the car door. "Come on, Sophie," I said, "a friend of mine will help."

Jordan caught me by the arm as I made my way through the hub the following morning. "Bass is on the warpath." That didn't seem like news to me, but it obviously did to Jordan. A couple of the other administrative assistants were watching us, their able fingers poised above their keyboards, their body language telling me that they wanted in on this conversation. Okay, they got my interest now.

"What's up?"

Jordan looked both ways, just like the criminals do in old movies, and steered me directly to my office. Her brown fingers held my arm with the sort of grip that gave me the impression that if someone, Bass perhaps, were to step out into the hub at that moment, she'd pull me under the nearest desk.

Shutting the door behind us, she tilted her head and wagged a finger at me. "You gotta do something," she said, her brown eyes blazing. "Bass is pulling the Milla story. Says that we're gonna be outclassed by *Up Close Issues* anyway. Because Fenton didn't do squat on it. And all *he's* been doing is bitching and moaning that you screwed him over." She glanced toward the window that separated my office from the hub and peeked out through the white sheers. "And now Bass sees you gone for the past couple of days, and thinks that you're messin' with him . . ."

She let the thought hang.

Just what I needed. To have to hold Bass's hand today. I swung my purse toward the credenza behind my desk and flung it into a corner. "Shit," I said.

Jordan put a hand on one hip and sauntered closer to my desk. "He's making life living hell around here, lemme tell you. Even made two of the girls cry today." She shook her head. "Mary and Vivian."

"There you are," Bass said, bounding into the office without knocking. Jordan jumped at the noise as the door hit the rubber stopper at the wall and bounced back to close. Shooting me a look of compassion, she eased herself out.

"Bass."

"Where the hell have you been?"

His fury broadcast itself through the twin tendons that stood out, bright red, on his neck, and from the vein that popped out right in the center of his forehead. Flustered, and spewing complaints at me that ranged from my recent absence, to Fenton's inept handling of the Milla story, which made me gleeful though I kept my face straight, he got so excited that little bubbles of spit gathered at the corners of his mouth.

I knew better than to interrupt. And I knew better than to sit down.

His short body nearly danced with barely-contained frustration. "I should never have told you about the week off for the political story. You just thought it was free ride time, didn't you? Taking advantage of the station's money to go get your hair done at some fancy salon. Skipping out on the work. Fenton could've used some help here, but did you give him any? No."

Bass held a manila folder stuffed with papers in his hand. He waved it up toward my face for a moment, then dropped his arm as he began to pace. The rug in my office had been there since the fifties, short-napped and a nondescript gray-brown. It never wore out, although Bass was giving it his best shot right now. He'd left his suitcoat elsewhere, and his shirt had puffed out, as though he'd been doing lots of overhead work and had forgotten to tuck it back in. It bloused at the waistline like a rumpled balloon, making him look much wider than he was.

As he paced, his voice quieted. Just a bit.

I still waited.

"What am I going to do?" he asked. Rhetorical, I waited for my moment. "They give me this idiot kid who can't find his own asshole with two hands and a map, and they want me to babysit. They let all the veterans go, the people who knew what they were doing . . ."

He had his back to me at this point, but I raised an eyebrow at his comment. Almost as if I'd called out, he looked over. "Okay, okay. Not all the veterans. You and David know what you're doing. I don't know about this Armstrong fellow yet."

At the far point of his pacing he turned, set his hands on his hips, still holding the manila folder, now nearly bent in half at his waist. He looked out the window and I watched a forced calm come over his features. He shook his head—frowned at me. "What am I going to do?"

"Have a seat," I said.

As though all the life had drained out of him, he sat. The look on his face was a combination of anger and tentative hope. I knew he expected me to solve all his problems on the very story he'd taken me off of none too ceremoniously. And I knew I could do it, too.

But not without a price. I was going to get full cooperation, whether Bass realized it at the moment or not.

He scratched the top of his head with the tips of his fingers. More of a stalling move, than an answer to an itch, I'd wager.

"Okay," I said. "I have some leads on a story. But let me call William in here," I said, lifting the phone. "I think maybe the three of us need to discuss this one anyway."

"Is it a good story?" he asked as I hung up. The tone of his voice was pitiful. Hopeful and wary at the same time.

I didn't answer, choosing instead to ask Jordan to hold all calls except for any from Father Trip or Sophie. Bass raised his eyebrows at the mention of the priest's name. "Patience," I said.

"Remain faithful to your regulation," he whispered. Barely moving his lips, he spoke so quietly, I almost didn't hear.

"What?"

His eyes, having wandered away along with his mind, apparently, snapped back to meet mine with apprehension. "What?"

"What did you just say about regulations?"

Bass tried to shrug the sheepish look off his face. "Nothing. Just something I need to remember when things get tense."

I repeated the phrase to myself in my head. *Remain faithful to your regulation.* Sounded like an ad for a laxative. "And that helps you?" I asked.

"Just drop it."

William knocked, then came in, easing into the unoccupied seat across from me.

Bass's lips moved, though no words came out. It occurred to me that he performed some sort of daily affirmation, or repetition of a mantra, to help calm himself. Interesting. He didn't strike me as a New-Age touchy-feely sort of fellow.

I glanced over at William, who seemed to be catching the same vibes from Bass that I was, based on the guarded look on his face. "All right," I said to Bass, "remember that story I mentioned to you the other day?"

He nodded, fractionally. Tension emanated from him like heat. Sitting at the edge of his seat, his feet were firmly planted on the ground, but his one leg kept bouncing, and his eyes shot back and forth between me and William, like a wary animal's, waiting for a strike.

I took a deep breath. "The hair care story—"

"This is about the friggin' hair story? For crying out loud, Alex, you knew we agreed to that to shut Gabriela up. It's filler, for crissake."

Both my hands shot up, index fingers pointed skyward. "Didn't I tell you to have patience?" Bass nodded. He was angry, I could tell, but at least he was silent.

In periphery I saw William's eyebrows shoot up.

"Here's where we are," I began.

I told him about my ulterior motive in visiting Hair to Dye For, about Matthew's disappearance and subsequent murder. I cautioned him that I was basing much on speculation and conjecture, but that things were beginning to add up and that I had a gut-level feel that I was following the Milla story, after all. That I'd bring a whole new angle to the exposé, and I told him, in detail, about my undercover antics with Lisa and the alleged prostitution ring. And I told them about Sophie: safe, at least for now.

He sat back when I was finished, his face and body relaxing for the first time since he'd come in. "How soon?"

"Bass . . ."

William cut in. "There's a lot here, and Alex and I haven't

even had a chance to work through the next steps."

Just then my cell phone rang out from the depths of my purse. I pulled it out, and glanced at the Caller ID. Lisa Knowles. "Quiet," I said in a terse enough voice that they both silenced at once.

When I answered, Lisa's voice was all business. "Is this Alexandrine Szatjemski?"

"Yeah." I lapsed in to what I hoped would pass for a standard down-on-her-luck, yet eager, woman.

"Lisa Knowles calling. I'm so sorry," she said, though her voice sounded anything but. "There's been a mixup. I somehow hired two of you for the same position. And since there's only one opening, currently . . ." She didn't finish the sentence. She didn't have to.

"You mean I'm out?" I was stunned—"Why?"

Lisa heaved a sigh. Total affectation. I could tell that even through the phone lines. "I'm very sorry."

At this point, I realized my acting talents weren't going to make much difference. My undercover plans had been shot sky-high. Politeness took control over my disappointment. I thanked her and hung up.

"Shit!" I said.

Bass held his hands out; they might have been trembling. "What? What happened?"

As I related the conversation, I felt an enormous rush of disappointment. Even though I had no plan to get "promoted" past the level of shampoo girl, I had intended to gather information for as long as I could. Something changed that killed that chance for me. The timing was lousy and I could only wonder what had triggered Lisa's move. Because I didn't for a moment believe her story about accidentally hiring two girls for one job.

Bass was quick to point out that it left us with a hole in our investigation. Except he didn't use the word "us." He'd stood up to pace, gesticulating as he walked. Coming to my side of the desk, he looked ready to spit as he warned me that this was a serious problem. He pointed in the general vicinity of my chest. With anyone else, I would have taken it to have sexual overtones. With Bass, he was just too agitated to notice how close he was. He told me that I was going to have to come up with another idea. And I better be pretty damn quick about it.

"Listen," William said, "we don't know who killed Matthew Breczyk or Milla Voight. That's true. But there is a story here that we can explore. Sophie isn't going to go on camera for us. We know that. And we wouldn't want her to. But we can tout this as an ongoing investigation. Alex has contacts with the Chicago Police Department. I do, too. What if we throw out a net?"

Bass's skeptical look was gentle, compared to the tone of his voice. "Net?"

"We're not the authorities; we don't have to play by the same set of rules. We can talk about the alleged prostitution ring, we can talk about the exploitation of immigrant girls who've come to the United States for a better life, and we can write a kick-ass show, without using a single name or identifiable reference."

"This is a net?" Bass asked again.

"Sure. Because what do you think will happen when the show airs? Some of the girls are going to start to worry about getting caught. They're going to wonder if they'll go to jail when the full story gets out. And that's when some of them might step forward. And they're more likely to step forward to a television station than they would to a police department. Especially if we guarantee anonymity."

We'd never done anything quite along those lines. It was a

bit chancy. Bass, seated again, was making that very argument, and since I had no doubt about what he would say, I let my mind wander a bit. While I'd been skittish about what to do if they'd ever try to set me up on a "date," I also knew that there would have been no better way for me to gather information. I wondered again about Lisa's reneging on the job she'd promised me. I still wished there was some way to exploit the undercover angle.

"Hey," I said, half to myself.

They both looked my direction, Bass's mouth half-open, mid-sentence. He wiped at the tiny beads of spit around his mouth.

"What? You think William's idea will work?"

I sat up, excited, buying myself a moment to allow the thoughts that had jumbled in my mind to find some order. "Okay, what if . . ." I realized I was thinking out loud, which sometimes gets me into trouble when I don't take the time to edit myself ahead of time. But the ideas needed to be spilled. The two of them could help me sort through and massage the plan into place. "What if we went undercover after all?"

William cocked an eyebrow at me, but said nothing. Bass frowned. "How are you going to do that? You can't be a hooker anymore; they just fired you."

"Yes, but . . ." I had my hands up, gesturing, working out the energy I felt so that my brain could remain calm enough to explain. "The problem with my plan, even if it had worked perfectly, was that I depended on overhearing conversations to build our story."

They both nodded. Good.

"To actually prove that a prostitution ring existed, to actually prove that Lisa exploited young girls, I would have had to cooperate, and whenever she would have set me up with my first 'date,' I would have fled. End of our stream of information, right? Because it would have been too dangerous for me to actually follow through on that."

Again, the double nod, though Bass seemed less certain than William.

"We could still prove the prostitution ring. Without Sophie's cooperation. Keep her completely safe."

I felt my own eyes widen as I spoke and my words came out fast, like they always do when I'm excited. "What if we sent in an undercover *john*. We have him contact Lisa to set up a date for himself. Then capture the whole exchange on videotape."

William's quizzical look forced me to add, "I don't mean that he'd actually go through with any . . ." I struggled for polite phrasing, ". . . physical contact. But if we could set up the hotel room ahead of time, and our guy could get her talking . . ."

"Yeah," Bass said. The word came out with a slow, thoughtful bob of his head.

William leaned forward in his chair, waving the pen in his hand to interrupt the flow of conversation. "What about the girl? We air any of it and she's toast."

"No, no," I said, jumping back in. "We can do this, I think, without them ever realizing what went down. We get enough information and we hand it over to the police. They take it from there. We've worked with them before in some of our investigations. They get the arrests, we get the exclusive story."

"Okay," he said, "but, remember that the reason you started to follow this story in the first place was because a young woman was murdered. And now Matthew Breczyk, who purportedly tried to bring the organization down, is dead too. If your suppositions are correct, we're dealing with some dangerous people here."

"Which is why we'll be extra careful," I said.

"Right," Bass chimed in. He looked back and forth between us and licked his lips.

I tapped at my teeth with a fingernail. "Let's say for a minute that we do this. Who do we send in?"

Bass shook his head in a move that communicated that the answer was obvious. He pointed. "Billy here, ought to do it."

I heard William's sharp intake of air.

Billy? I thought. Since when was he "Billy"? I shook my head. "I was thinking we'd hire someone. Like an actor or something—"

"Why?" Bass asked. "This isn't the kind of story we want leaked, is it? Of course not. Other than the three of us here, I don't think anybody else should know about it. We keep it safe that way."

"What about William? What if they find out he works here? Then what?"

William cleared his throat. "This situation is no different than the one you put yourself in when you applied for that job with Lisa. You were taking a risk."

"Yeah," I said, "but . . ."

I caught myself. I'd been about to say that the difference was that this was my story, not his. But then I remembered his offer to help out. I'd been on my own so long in this job that I wasn't used to dragging anyone else through the quagmires I inevitably created.

In an effort to cover up the near-blurt, I said, "But . . . are you willing to go through with something like this?"

Something akin to pain crossed William's features, and he gave an abrupt nod. "What I need to know is, what then? Where do we take it from there? Once we get our feature?"

Bass's eyes flickered with nervousness. "What do you mean? Once we get the story we're done, right?"

William turned to him and I felt a chill in his gaze. "These people are preying on vulnerable young women. Women who've come here for a better life and who made a bad decision. Look at what happened to Sophie. She tried to get out. Are we in this for a story? Or are we in this to make a difference in these peoples' lives?"

William's voice had grown quieter even as it intensified. I had to admit it—the little shiver that ran down my spine as he spoke had nothing to do with the ambient air temperature. Wow. I liked this guy. Couldn't have said it better myself. We both waited for Bass's reaction.

With trapped-animal jumpy looks toward both of us, he nodded, a bit too enthusiastically. "We want to make a difference in their lives," he said. Then added, "Of course."

Chapter Sixteen

"Father Trip," I called, stopping him mid-stride.

He was crossing the parking lot adjacent to the church, likely on his way to the school for his daily check-in. I knew that Mass was celebrated every weekday morning at nine-fifteen, so my appearance here just before ten was no accident.

I caught up with him, encouraged by the fact that he was smiling. Chances are nothing was wrong. And I was over-reacting.

"Alex! Good. I was going to call you later."

He resumed his brisk walk toward the school. Wearing black pants, black gloves and a black polyester jacket with the furry collar turned up against the chill, he could have been a cat burglar.

"Everything's okay?"

He wiped at his red nose. "Yes, of course. Sophie had an uneventful night." One hand snugged the collar a little tighter as he pointed toward the convent with his chin. "The sisters took care of her. Made sure she felt at home."

"Where is she now?"

He stopped walking. While his expression remained calm, his eyes flickered with a touch of alarm. "At the convent. I checked on her early this morning. She was up at dawn, helping the nuns with their chores."

"She's not there now."

"Are you sure?"

"Sister Mary Mildred told me she 'went to go see

Father.' " I looked at him. "I assumed she meant you."

Dead center of the asphalt lot, we were a perfect target for the biting wind. I could hear it whistle as it streaked past my ears, leaving the tops of them feeling that first numb of the season. My nose ran a little, and as I wiped at it, I was glad I'd worn a pair of knitted gloves. My hair felt as though it was being twisted by a cyclone and my eyes watered. Even though Father Trip's hair was short, the tiny silver ends lifted up as we stood there. He looked away, his jaw set, his eyes inscrutable.

Though the elements made for a cold, harsh discussion venue, neither of us moved. Father Trip puffed out his cheeks, then blew out a pursed-lip breath that curled out white before him. "No. Not me."

Despite the many layers I wore, I swore I could hear my own frantic heartbeats. "Where would she go?" I asked, knowing even as I did that Father Trip would have less of idea about that than I would.

"Maybe she just went home to pick up a few things?" he said.

He sounded about as convinced as I did when I replied, "Maybe."

He walked with me back toward the convent, where we asked Sister Mary Mildred what time Sophie had left. Both Father Trip and I were surprised to find out she'd been gone for over two hours.

"Damn," I said as we left the convent.

We stood for a moment at the front stoop. I watched some of the remaining leaves try to hang on tight against the wind's plucking fingers. They twisted and turned, like wind socks, some holding firm, some losing the battle—catching a ride on the wicked breeze.

I wanted to talk to Sophie. To get some insights as to how

William should approach Lisa Knowles. If there was some sort of code, or bit of knowledge that would keep him from raising the woman's suspicions. The undercover operation had been the only thing on my mind since our impromptu meeting. I was worried about the story. Worried about making it work. But mostly worried about William. Not just about safety issues either; he seemed to want to tell me something as the meeting wound up. He'd left me with a meaningful look I didn't understand, and the cryptic line, "We need to talk."

"Alex," Father Trip said, breaking into my thoughts. His words, gently spoken, cut through the soft autumn sounds in a lonely way. "I'm sorry."

"It isn't your fault," I said.

He put his hand on my arm and I felt the priestly paternal squeeze. "Sophie's a grown woman. She decided to leave, for some reason. And just because she did, doesn't mean that anything's happened to her. She may be on her way back, right now."

I nodded. "Thanks, Father."

Father Trip smiled. "Whatever I can do to help, let me know."

I drove back to Sophie's apartment, without a lot of hope of finding her there. Mabel and Casimir were surprised at my knock, but they hadn't seen Sophie this morning either. It might have been the look in my own eyes that alarmed them, but Casimir asked me to please let them know when I found her, and Mabel pressed a note with their phone number into my hand.

The fifteen-minute ride had given me ample opportunity to think, however. The nun who told me Sophie left, said that she was going to see Father. When I questioned her further, Sister Mary Mildred remembered Sophie digging out change for the bus before she left. Which meant that she hadn't been going to see Father Trip after all. Which is why I was now on my way to visit Father Bruno.

Emil answered the door. Rumpled as ever, he wore a different flannel shirt than he'd been wearing the first time I met him, but I swore it looked as though he'd slept in it. His face, pinkened on one side, and his constant blinking gave me the impression that my surprise visit woke him up.

He scratched at the side of his face, near his temple, as though trying to massage a headache away. "Don't I know you?"

His breath backed me up a step, but I smiled. I wanted information, after all. "I was here the other day. With Sophie?"

Dropping the hand from his temple, he used it to point at me. "Oh yeah," he said with what sounded like pleasured approval. "I remember." His eyes raked over me from head to toe and back again, and he gave a small frown when he looked in the direction of my chest. "I hate winter."

Puzzled by the non-sequitur, I was just about to ask about Sophie, when he added, "Makes people wear too many clothes." And then he winked at me.

Thank God for down jackets, I thought. What an idiot.

"Have you seen her?" I asked, changing the subject.

It seemed to take him a second to make the leap, to understand what I was asking. "Sophie?"

Exasperated, and wishing I could get away, I bit the insides of my mouth. "Yeah, has she been around?"

"Oh, she's been around, that girl. Let me tell you . . ." His eyes lit up, and I interrupted before he could go any further. The gleam in his eyes made me want to retch, right there. And aim for his face.

"I mean, did she stop by here this morning? To see Father Bruno?"

"I dunno, she might have. Bruno headed over to the church early this morning and said he needed to meet with one of the girls. Coulda been Sophie."

"One of the girls?" I decided to press, just a bit. Dealing with Emil made my skin crawl, but he might have useful information. "You mean one of the girls he helped come over from the old country? The ones he's gotten . . . jobs for?"

Wariness jumped into Emil's expression. I hadn't thought him capable of it.

"What do you mean?" he asked.

I forced a smile. "You know what I mean."

His eyes raked over me again. "You a working girl?"

I ignored the question. "What would Father Bruno think of it if I was?" I asked.

He shook his head as a small smile played at his lips. Which he licked, twice, before beginning to answer.

"Emil!" A voice from the sidewalk interrupted our conversation.

I turned to see Father Bruno make his way up the concrete steps. He shot me a chilly smile.

He wore old-fashioned black robes. Skirt-like, they hung out below the bottom of his beige winter jacket, swishing around his legs as he climbed the stairs. Atop his head he wore a fur hat, Russian style. I couldn't be sure, but it looked like real fur to me, and I wondered how many of God's creatures had given up their lives in sacrifice to his head-warmth.

He puffed as he crested the top stair, years of smoking taking their toll. "Alexandrine," he said with what seemed more like surprise than pleasure. The pale brown eyes, watery from the cold wind, didn't communicate the welcome his smile seemed to strive for. "We were just talking about you."

I tried to tamp down the jolt of optimism. "With Sophie? She was here?"

"Yes, of course," he said, pushing past Emil through the rectory's open door. I followed, catching a whiff of the secretary's body odor as he swept his arm to guide me in, in what looked like an attempt at a gallant gesture. I wondered if the man ever bathed.

"Where is she now?" I asked, holding my hand up near my nose in a reflexive action, though it did no good whatsoever. "At church?"

Bruno pulled the fur hat from his head. Silver hairs stood out in all directions, and he wiped a beefy hand at them, coaxing them down. He headed into the same room where we'd met the first time. I thought it had been dark before. Now the dreariness was overwhelming. If parishioners came here for guidance, I wouldn't wonder that they left more depressed than they were when they came in.

Making his way around his desk, Bruno stripped the jacket off and tossed it on a chair with the hat in a smooth motion.

Grabbing a Kleenex, he blew his nose, several times. Robust blows, one nostril at a time, keeping an eye on me as he did so.

"I don't know. She left after our meeting," he said with a small frown. Impatience, it seemed. He hadn't taken a seat. I took that to indicate that he wanted this interview over quickly.

Relief that Sophie was apparently all right gave me the freedom to stay a few moments longer to find out more. "What did she say?"

Bruno leaned on his desk, his fingertips bearing his weight. "What did she say?" The incredulity in his voice was palpable.

"Did she tell you what happened to her? Did she tell you about her . . ." I didn't know how to phrase it. Emil stood in the open doorway behind me, listening to every word. ". . .

Her problems?" I kept it vague. Very vague.

"Alexandrine," Bruno said, in a condescending tone. "Aren't you a good Catholic girl?"

I nodded.

"Then I shouldn't have to remind you that what is divulged under the sacrament of reconciliation is protected. What Sophie shared with me is sacrosanct, and I will thank you never to ask such a question again."

Anger shot through me like a white hot knife. "I wasn't aware she'd come to confess, Father," I said, in as calm a voice as I could muster.

He nodded, benignly. As if granting absolution. But I hadn't asked. And I wasn't sorry. He smiled. "Do you need anything further?"

"No."

"Well then, if you don't mind, I have a busy morning planned," he said, easing himself to sit.

My cue. On my way out, as I neared Emil, still standing sentry in the doorway, Bruno called to me. "Alexandrine."

"Yes?"

"How's the new job?"

I flashed him a lips-only smile. "Bad break. Ms. Knowles couldn't use me after all."

He returned my smile in kind. "I'm sorry to hear that. But I'm certain something else will turn up."

"Sophie, you had me worried."

She'd made her way back to the convent, unaware of the angst she caused by disappearing the way she had. Her face had cleaned up well; the cuts on her lip appeared to be healing already. Residual swelling still marred the left side of her face, giving her an elephant-man look. Purplish bruises on her chin and cheeks exacerbated the image.

She favored her left arm, resting it in her lap as we spoke. The four nuns who occupied the convent made themselves scarce, bustling about at their business, letting us know that we had complete privacy here in the dining room to talk.

Sophie and I sat at the far end of a long table, me at the head, she at the first side chair. The blond wood table, made in the fifties, but looking brand-spanking new, lent a certain surreal feeling to our discussion. We kept our voices low. Even though no one was nearby, the large room, and the silence that pervaded it, caused us to whisper.

"I had to go see Father Bruno," she told me in Polish. Her right arm rested on the corner of the table and she didn't meet my gaze. I watched as she rubbed her thumb against the side of her index finger, eyeing it.

"But why?"

Her hand trembled. She continued to rub. "He has been like a father to me. He has taken care, good care of me, since Matthew and I arrived from Poland. And I have done the worst thing I could do. I gave in to temptation. The temptation of money."

As though there were answers coming down to her from above, she focused on the ceiling. Her right hand lost the battle she'd been waging and she raised it to her mouth, biting her thumbnail while she gathered her thoughts further.

"If I'm careful, Lisa and Rodero won't hurt me anymore. But I'm in trouble. I know I am. And if something happens . . ."

"Like what, Sophie?"

"If . . . if I should die . . . I can't go to heaven with my Matthew if my soul is stained with such mortal sin."

Pulling her fingers from her mouth, she put her head down on the table as though drained of energy. Her hair spilled onto the tabletop like a blond waterfall, obscuring her face. I got up, reaching to put my arm around her, and I could feel tiny tremors in her back as she cried.

She calmed after a bit, and when she sat up, I told her about Lisa's call reneging on the shampoo girl's job. Her eyes widened and she buried her face in her hands, as though in prayer. "Thank the Good Lord. Jesus, Mary, Joseph, thank you, thank you," she whispered. Looking back up at me. "You will be safe now. And I will be, too."

"Father Bruno's going to help you get away from Lisa, then?"

Sophie bit her lip.

"Sophie? What did you tell him?"

"You want to know my confession?" Her horrified look that I would ask about her confessed sins could have been humorous had the situation not been so grave.

Her thumb had gone back up to her mouth.

"No, of course not," I said. "What I want to know is how much Father Bruno knows about Lisa's organization now."

"He knows my sins."

"Did you tell him about your job?"

Blue eyes held mine as she nodded her head.

"Everything?"

"No. Not everything. I made it sound like I work for someone else that he doesn't know—doing the . . . things I do. I didn't tell him where I was staying, either. I just told him enough to get his forgiveness."

I felt energy drain out of me with startling immediacy. "Let me call him," I said, standing. "I think he needs to know that Lisa's behind this." My mind was going two-forty, recalling that he asked me about my job this morning. *After* Sophie had talked with him. I wished I would have paid closer attention to his reaction to my disclosure that I lost the position. He'd seemed angry and quick to dismiss me. But his de-

199

meanor could have a lot to do with the magnitude of Sophie's news, too.

I reached the phone in the adjacent kitchen, just as I became aware of Sophie behind me. She reached, dragging at my arm. "No."

The nuns had one of those old-fashioned dial phones with the hang-up hooks that people always fiddle with in movies when a connection has been lost. Sophie attacked it now, slamming it down with the palm of her hand.

"No." She said again, wincing in pain at her sudden movement.

I felt like a little kid caught making a prank phone call— the mom staring at me with folded arms, and angry. "Why not?" I asked with more than a touch of anger, myself.

"He made me promise to tell no one else."

I stared at her, my disbelief apparently evident on my face, because her Polish explanation came out fast and nervous.

"Father Bruno sat down with me, not even in a confessional. He took me to the back in the sacristy, where we could talk without anyone hearing us and where I could see him. It made it easier, you know. To see his face. I was so worried that I would hurt him because he has done so much for me."

I was getting pretty damn tired of hearing what a saint Father Bruno was. Because of her undying loyalty to the man, Sophie had never said a word of the real work she did for Lisa Knowles. In my opinion, the man should have had the reality of the situation presented to him a long time ago. The girls' complicit agreement to keep him protected boggled my mind. He should be aware. If he wasn't already. Father Bruno didn't seem like a man who'd bask in ignorance or naïveté.

Sophie leaned back. There was a chrome-edged countertop that ran three-quarters of the way around the airy kitchen, which still sported the aqua cabinets that had come with the fifties-designed building. One small window to my left and an overhead fluorescent fixture gave us ample light, and I listened to the lamp's buzz as I waited for Sophie to continue. She seemed to take strength from the support of the counter behind her, leaning both hands on its top, fingers over the edge. But I noticed she still put no weight on her left arm.

"He was very understanding. He didn't make me feel . . . dirty. He made me feel good about myself. What kind of a special man does that take to make someone feel good about themselves when they have done so much that is so bad?"

"He made you feel good?" I asked. I didn't know whether to be impressed or repulsed by that. "What did he say? Exactly?"

She shook her head and sent a long look out the window before turning back to me. "I don't remember all his words. What I remember is that he took my hand and said that God would forgive me. That the temptations of material wealth is something we all face every day. And that I had taken the right steps to try and fight the temptation by telling him."

Sophie shrugged before continuing. "He said he will help me find who killed Milla and Matthew. I know you're disappointed, because it will ruin your television story, but this is what I had to do, Alex. I hope you understand. And you aren't planning to investigate any more, are you?"

My hesitation seemed to exasperate her.

"Alex, please. I know I wanted you to find who killed Matthew. But I am so afraid. And I am so sorry, because I know you tried to help me and you won't have your good story anymore."

Shaking my head, I was about to interrupt, but she continued.

"Father Bruno will take care of it. And when he does, I will be free from Lisa and from Rodero. I have to take care of myself. There's no one else to take care of me anymore."

It wasn't like I was a private investigator who'd just been pulled off a case. Sophie hadn't hired me; she simply had asked me to look into the situation. I could continue to look into it; I saw no need for me to let up. Not yet. Of course, I also saw no need to let Sophie in on that nugget of information.

I hated lying, but it didn't stop me for more than a heart-beat. "Listen, Sophie, even if I don't continue following this story, I'd like to know how everything worked out. So, I'm just going to stick around for a little bit. You can understand that, right?"

She nodded, but she had a skeptical look on her face.

I left her feeling more than a smidgen of disquiet. Great word, "disquiet." It summed up exactly the buzz going on in my brain, thoughts jockeying for position like bees in a summer hive.

Driving back to the office, I replayed some of our conversation. I asked her about Emil, but she had no further information on him. But asking about him helped me understand the steps William would need to take to contact Lisa. I was convinced, however, that Emil played a significant role in this drama. Otherwise how could Father Bruno remain oblivious? And there was no doubt in Sophie's mind that he *had* been oblivious, up until she'd bared her soul.

I wasn't so sure. I wished I could have been there.

The only other enlightening tidbit I gleaned from her with regard to Father Bruno was that he'd asked her about my involvement in all this. Which I found curious. Maybe I shouldn't.

He piqued my interest—maybe I piqued his as well.

Chapter Seventeen

This time it was William at my office with his hand on the doorjamb. I'd left the door open for a change, purposely hoping for company. There are times when the grit of my job feels like sandpaper chafing away my humanity, and I need personal contact with those I care about to bring me back to believing that the world is good.

I tried to call Lucy, but she was in a home economics class and I didn't want to disturb her. Swept up in the week's intrigue, I'd utterly forgotten to call her, and the fact that I had bothered me deeply.

I'd half-expected Jordan to pop in; I wanted to grab some good girl-talk while I let the ingredients of my story simmer in the back of my head like a stew.

Instead, I got William.

"Hi," he said. "Got a few minutes?"

No smile, again. In fact, it seemed as though his eyes narrowed a bit when I answered, "Sure." I wondered what I was in for.

He came in, shutting the door in a move I would have sworn was stalling, except for the fact that *he'd* come to see *me*. I heard the metallic click as it closed. Turning back to face me, he shot me a lips-only smile, as he grabbed the back of one of my chairs and pulled it away from the desk before he sat. Distance, I thought. He's putting distance between us. This can't be good news.

"How's Sophie?" he asked.

I related the morning's events and was pleased to see his reactions match my own on every point. I dug out the notes I'd written and copied for him. With a quick glance at them, I pointed. "Here's the number Lisa uses for business. She's wary of new clients at first, but Sophie says she doesn't like turning them away, either." Before the recent confession to Father Bruno, Sophie had been very upfront with all aspects of the business. "As a matter of fact, beside the contact information, she also gave me a few names of men she's . . . been with." I looked up. William seemed uncomfortable. "First names. You might be able to bluff your way through by using one of them."

He nodded. Took the notepaper and folded it into precise quarters. Again, it looked like a stall tactic.

William wore a muted blue two-button polo shirt and dark pants. The look said "casual" though he seemed anything but. With the note tucked into his pants pocket, he nodded again.

"So," he said, raising his eyes to meet mine. I was taken aback, again, by the vibrant shade of blue. Darker today— their color seemed to vary with his demeanor like a permanent pair of mood rings.

I waited.

"There's something you need to know before I go on this undercover investigation."

"Okay," I said, striving for an encouraging tone.

He stared at something at the edge of my desk for a moment, then looked at me again. "Have you heard the scuttlebutt about why I left the *Sun-Times*?"

Thoughts of Dan sent a rush of relief that he hadn't had a chance to have his say about William the other night. "No," I answered truthfully.

"Let me tell you, then. At least, let me tell you my version." He sat forward in his chair, and pulled it up a few inches to allow him to rest his arms on the edge of my desk.

"You ready?" he asked. The words were tentative, but his body language was assured.

"Yep."

With a nod, he began. "I was there for five years, working for a fellow named Bernie. About a year before I left, he hired someone new, a woman. Chloe."

His brow furrowed for a split-second. "I know I don't need to ask, but I'd appreciate it if you didn't share this information with anyone."

"I won't," I said. And I wouldn't.

"She was tough as nuts. A real hard-driver. At first I respected that, thought she'd infuse new life into the department. I mean, she had spunk and a willingness to get the job done. And don't get me wrong . . . she was good. Damn good."

"But?"

I felt power surge from those blue eyes and I realized that whatever was coming next carried weight with him. "But after a while it became apparent that she had her own agenda. The good of the group meant nothing to her. We'd been a nice, tight team. We looked out for one another, helped each other along. That's so rare nowadays. But we had it. We were more than a team; we were friends."

He shot me a look before continuing. "But, like an uncontained virus, her influence spread. She backstabbed constantly, convincing others that there were conspiracies that didn't exist. Before we knew it, the spirit that held us together was gone. People started to leave. Good people. And, of course, Chloe was there, ready to move up as each one departed.

"She went from beat reporter to byline in less time than

anyone else I'd ever known. She's a contender. No doubt about it. Talented. Voracious in her desire to claw her way to the top. Or the perceived top."

Claw. Interesting word choice.

William took a breath before continuing. He turned to stare out my window for a moment. It seemed to me that he needed a break before continuing. "This really is a great view," he said in a voice that bordered on melancholy. I followed his gaze, and though the top of Wrigley was covered in gray fog, the pedestrians all head-bent under dull umbrellas taut with wind, and the river water choppy and black, I had to admit, he was right. I felt a twinge of guilt, remembering the outlook from his office.

"The Powers That Be at the *Times*," he said, picking up the story again but still watching out the window, "decided to create a new section. All new features. Big splash debut. It would start out on Sundays only and eventually move to twice a week. This was big time. Very big time. And they wanted a writer/editor for this new feature section. Bernie had been grooming me from day one for an opportunity like this. It was mine to lose."

"And you lost it?"

"I had help."

His face contorted, almost of its own volition and almost imperceptibly, but it was there. I got the impression that this was a man in total control of his emotions. And yet this story was difficult for him to relate.

"This is long, and it's ugly, and I don't like telling people about it, because no matter how I say it, the words sound resentful and bitter. Though I suppose that's appropriate." He gave a wry laugh, and dragged his gaze away from the window to turn to me.

"What it boils down to is this: Bernie brought the team together—what was left of the team, that is—and let us in on the plan for the new Sunday section. He told us that my promotion to features editor would be announced by the paper to coincide with the section's debut, about a month down the line. There were five others besides me left in the department, and at the end of the meeting, four of them came up to congratulate me on the promotion."

"Not Chloe?"

William pursed his lips, letting a whistle-like sound escape his clenched teeth. "Nope. She did them all one better."

I raised my eyebrows in anticipation. I had no idea what he was about to say.

"First thing the next morning, she circulated a memo, achingly written," William's face tightened, "apologizing for not bringing it up sooner, but letting the administration know that she'd filed a lawsuit against the *Times*, and against me."

"For . . . ?" My hands flew out, in an expression of frustration.

"Sexual harassment."

"What?"

"It was perfect," he said, shaking his head. I could tell that he'd left me, that he was reliving the incident as he spoke. His words had gone quiet, almost as though he was talking to himself; he wasn't seeing me any longer. "It was so manipulatively worded, I could almost believe it was true myself.

"In the memo, she explained how she tried to bear up under the strain of working with me, but that my lewd and obnoxious behavior had gotten progressively worse. And while she'd repeatedly spurned my advances, she didn't know how long she could work under such dire circumstances. My impending advancement to features editor, she claimed, would only increase my power over her. She wanted to trudge on like a good soldier, but the strain was too much. In a very vulnerable and polite way, she let the administration know that, unless they rethought my promotion, she'd move forward with the lawsuit and pull the *Sun-Times* down, along with me."

The key to this man's soul was his eyes. He told the story entirely deadpan, but his eyes blazed with anger.

I was speechless.

William looked at me with an expression of anticipation. "Bet you didn't know I was a lech, huh?"

"But you're not."

He leaned forward again, his head canting slightly. "How do you know? Maybe I am."

I held his gaze. "No," I said. "You're not."

He blinked an acknowledgment and sat back in his chair. "Thank you."

"And so they fired you? But it was her word against yours, right? You'd been there for a long time. How could management take her claims seriously, if they knew you?"

"Management had a responsibility to investigate her claims. And as much as it burned me to cooperate in the farce, I understood their position and complied. But the feature was gone. They couldn't start a whole new series under the sword of Damocles. Their hands were tied. That's the beauty of all this. They did know better. All the players in this little drama knew the truth. But they decided that promoting me wouldn't be in the paper's best interests at this time."

"So you left?"

"So I left. Right away. Chloe immediately dropped the lawsuit. Surprise. Surprise. I took a few months off, traveled a bit, wore down my retirement savings and rainy day money because it felt damn good to do it, and then I wound up here."

I nodded. And completely understood.

"The reason I'm telling you all this now," he said, reading my next question off my face, perhaps, "is because—having had a sexual harassment suit slapped on me—I'm a little uncomfortable with this undercover assignment with a prostitute."

"Geez," I said, running a hand through my hair, gripping it atop my head. I let go almost immediately when I realized how attractive that must look. "We'll get someone else. That's not a problem."

"No. I'll do it. At this point it would be tough to bring someone up to speed who could get the information we're looking for. I'm up for it." He leaned forward. "It's just that I thought you ought to know."

I was shaking my head, trying to come up with other ways to handle the situation. He interrupted me.

"Listen, I've already talked to the film crew and they're going to digitalize my appearance so that if we broadcast the tape, I'll be completely unrecognizable."

I leaned forward on my forearms in a clear spot on my desk. My hands were crossed one over the other in body language that meant I was "serious." "William," I said.

"You know, you can call me Will."

I gave a tiny sigh of impatience for the interruption. "Will," I shot a smile at that, "there's no need—"

He placed his hands over mine. Their warm weight sent an immediate rush of blood up into my chest. "Yes, there is. I want to do this. If I let her stop me, then she's won, again. I just wanted to let you know. I thought you deserved to know."

For one more heartbeat, maybe two, we stayed connected, hands and eyes, until he pulled away. I sat back too.

He asked me, "Do you remember the other day when you stopped by my office?"

I remembered. Right after Matthew's funeral. "Sure."

"I'd just gotten off the phone with Bernie about five minutes before you came by."

"And?"

The amusement in his face this time was tinged with sadness. "They're bringing out that new Sunday section again. Next issue. And guess who's the new features editor?"

The front door creaked.

It never creaked. Not when it was closed.

I'd been home for at least ten minutes, my jacket thrown over the back of one of the kitchen chairs, and I headed to my room to change out of my work clothes into jeans. Just as I pulled my long-sleeve gray T-shirt over my head, I heard it.

This was the house I grew up in. I knew every regular noise: the groan of the octopus-like furnace in the basement, the blast of the fire as the gas came on, the click-hum of the refrigerator that was as old as I was, and the rattling sound of the windows when a sturdy breeze hit. This noise was different, and though quiet, it stood out like a misplayed chord in a familiar melody.

A definite creak. And I realized with alarm, that it was the sound of my front door opening.

Two seconds earlier, my bare feet appreciated the cool, varnished wood beneath them. Now, they just felt cold. And no light coming from outside my window made the house seem dark. Very dark.

For a moment I was frozen in place. I couldn't move, couldn't speak, couldn't think. But somewhere in the depths of my brain, I remembered I brought my purse in the room with me, and I dug out my cell phone to call 9-1-1.

Then stopped. For crying out loud, I was about to call to report a noise. That wouldn't exactly bring the fleet flying over.

I listened again, but heard no footsteps. My house was old enough to broadcast any movement with a cacophony of wood squeaks. Unless an intruder could make himself weightless, I had to believe there wasn't anyone was in the house with me. Yet.

Trying to calm the frantic beating of my heart by taking a few deep breaths, I wandered around the corner of my door, cell phone in hand, 9-1-1 keyed in. All I needed to do was hit "send." As I came around the corner, and all was clear, I realized that I'd be better off dialing from my home phone. At the very least, they'd have my address if I suddenly got disconnected.

I tiptoed to the kitchen, grabbed the portable phone, and cursed myself for not having programmed it to speed dial in an emergency. I'd do that right after this, I promised myself.

The front door *was* open. Wide open. It moved with minuscule swings as air pressure coming through the aluminum screen door pushed it back and forth, as though on an invisible string. I inched toward it, making plenty of squeaks myself, questioning how this could happen. I rarely used my front door, except to check the mail. And I never forgot to set the deadbolt.

Closer now, I saw the marks. Deep grooved scratches at both the doorknob and deadbolt levels. Someone had pried my door open. Today.

I dialed 9-1-1 in a hurry.

Two officers arrived minutes after my call. I was surprised at the speed, actually, because I'd told the female dispatcher that though it appeared my home had been broken into, I didn't believe anyone was inside. Still, they showed up, one coming directly to the front door and the other walking around the back of my house before joining us.

Officer Cross, a tall, black man wearing a navy blue winter

uniform jacket, stood in the center of my living room. "What's been taken?"

I had to give both officers credit, I thought later. They were extremely gracious as I walked through the house with them. Nothing appeared to be missing. Not the TV, not my VCR, not my laptop. Nothing. Not even a gold earring off my dresser.

They followed me from room to room, down to the basement, and around the perimeter of the house as I checked everything. I was apologetic, almost disappointed, that nothing appeared to have been disturbed other than the front door.

Both men took a close look at the scratches by the lock. They exchanged a look and asked me if the marks were new. I assured them that they were.

Despite the fact that I could tell they were convinced I'd simply neglected to shut my door completely, they were professional and courteous. And free with advice. My deadbolt, they informed me, was not very high quality, but they gave me the brand name of another type that was. And suggested I have them installed both front and back. My back door was accessed by a long, round key into a old-fashioned keyhole—the kind people usually try to peep through. Once inside, I had a bolt I could throw, but seeing it through their eyes now, I was embarrassed. A quick hip hit against the door, and even my arthritic neighbor lady would be able to break past that wimpy barrier.

"My guess is whoever broke in was frightened away. They probably just got in the door and heard you coming in through the back and ran off," Officer Cross said, shrugging.

His partner, a middle-aged white man with dark hair, brown eyes, and a five o'clock shadow that made him look like Fred Flintstone, nodded in agreement as he inspected the scratches once again. I felt foolish and paranoid for having called them. About to apologize, I wondered if he'd read my mind when he said, "You did right calling us. You can never be too careful."

Officer Cross added, "You know I thought I saw movement down by the alley when we drove up, anyway. Coulda been the guy getting away."

The other officer, Ellis, turned to me. "You live here alone?"

I nodded.

They exchanged a look again. I wondered if they thought they'd be making more trips here in the future. That I might be the type who jumped at every little indistinguishable sound. I hoped not.

"What do you do for a living?" Officer Cross asked. He'd already snapped his notebook closed, so I guessed he was just making conversation at this point.

"I work for *Midwest Focus NewsMagazine*. I'm a researcher."

Ellis raised his eyebrows, impressed. "Do you know Gabriela Van Doren?"

I nodded.

"She's something," he said with gusto. "Man, that woman's a babe. Smart too. I like those smart ones." He shook his head, a faraway look in his eyes that made me not want to try and imagine what was going on in his mind. "She's gotta be something in real life too, huh? Is she as gorgeous in person as she is onscreen?"

"I'm not the best judge of gorgeous women," I said, smiling.

"Oh yeah," he said. "But she *is* smart, isn't she?"

I opened my mouth, and caught the snide Gabriela-bashing reply before it hit my tongue. Why ruin this guy's impression of our anchor? "She's a major asset to our station," I said.

"I thought so." He grinned. "Maybe you can get an auto-graphed picture sent to me?"

I smiled and said I'd do what I could.

Officer Cross looked around again, offering, "There's a chance too, that whoever broke in here was looking for some-thing specific."

"Like what?" I asked.

"Don't know. You'd be a better judge of that than we would. Maybe something to do with your work. And maybe they looked around but didn't find it." He gave a grimace. "Although usually, when a guy's looking for something, they toss the premises. And your place looks—lived in—but not disturbed."

I got the distinct impression that I'd wasted their time, but they were trying to not make me feel like such an idiot. I ap-preciated the gesture, and as I saw them out, Officer Ellis re-minded me, "It wouldn't hurt to get those locks changed, you know. The quicker the better."

Five minutes after they left, I hauled out the yellow pages and left messages with several different locksmiths' an-swering services.

Which is why, when the phone rang twenty minutes later, having just shoved an Oreo cookie in my mouth, I never ex-pected it to be Father Bruno.

Chapter Eighteen

It took a couple of beats for me to switch my brain trajectory and I stutter-stepped my first words, trying without much success to mask my bewilderment.

"Father Bruno. How are you?"

While we exchanged pleasantries in polite pretense, faking the tone of voice the people do when they're happy to hear from one another, my mind raced. I knew I gave him this number, and my address, but I didn't expect him to do more than shove the information into his desk to be tossed out some day when he forgot who that Szatjemski chick was.

A protracted silence fell over the line after we exhausted scintillating observations about the weather. I waited. After all, he made the call, he must have had a reason.

I expected him to ask how Sophie was doing. Instead, he cleared his throat and went a different direction. "You were baptized at Good Shepherd Church in the fall of . . ." I heard paper shuffling, and then he named the year. The right year. "That's correct?"

"Yeah," I answered, too stunned by curiosity to even consider anything but answering truthfully.

"Would you be free for a brief meeting say, sometime tomorrow?" he asked.

"Tomorrow?"

"If you can carve a half-hour or so out of your busy schedule?"

I massaged my eyebrows, then pinched the bridge of my

nose. His question about my baptism had thrown me. "What about?"

A noise came over the line—lip-smacking. "Just a half-hour of your time."

"Well . . . let me check my calendar." I stalled, trying to figure out what was up. But who was I kidding; of course I'd meet him. "Sure," I said. "I can come by the rectory . . ." I felt the gears click into place as my brain finally engaged itself. "Or, how about if we meet for lunch somewhere? My treat." I had no idea what was up, but all I could think about was avoiding that dreary room at the rectory, and keeping my distance from Emil. Particularly if I hoped to glean any information from Father Bruno about the little pervert.

I heard a short laugh over the phone, which could have meant nothing, but felt like condescension. "Lunch. What a delightful idea, Alexandrine."

Odd, how he emphasized my name just then.

We arranged to meet at one o'clock the following afternoon at the same neighborhood diner where I'd met Dan. My idea. Might as well just have one place for all the screwed-up meetings; better than sharing the wealth.

I stood in Will's door early Saturday morning. "Hey," I said.

Other than the two of us, and Bass in his office down the hall, the place was quiet. The rest of the staff had the weekend off, like normal folks, but we'd agreed to meet this morning, to keep the momentum going on this story.

"Alex," he answered, with a pleasant lilt to his tone.

The cleaning crew hadn't made it here, yet, but I refrained from commenting on the pervasive smoke smell. If an item didn't affect Bass personally, he didn't attach much weight to it, and situations such as this one could go on indefinitely unless Will pushed it. I might throw out the hint that he engage a cleaning crew himself and bill the station for it on an expense account, but that would have to wait. I had other things on my mind.

"Were you able to reach Lisa?"

He answered me with a look.

"And?" I asked.

"She's something else, that one. Prostitution with the personal touch."

"What do you mean?" I was about to take a seat in front of his desk when he stood up.

"Tell you what," he said. "I was thinking about grabbing a cup of coffee downstairs. You want to join me? I'll bring you up to speed."

The Emperor's Roost, downstairs, was a throwback to a time before I even toddled around my parents' coffee tables. Dark, with sooty pictures of Napoleon in various battle poses decorating the cheap, paneled walls, it had crescent-shaped seating arranged in semicircles around a bar and along the perimeter. We chose a scuffed-white booth far from the two boozers hunched over the bar, drinking their early lunch. The place did a great business during the week, especially when the weather was either too hot, too cold, or too wet, which in Chicago is nearly every day. Eating here at The Roost, as cheerless as it was, was often preferable to braving the elements. Today being a Saturday, the place was desolate and the dinginess overwhelming.

Our waitress, a redhead who looked like she could be an advertisement for Lisa Knowles' organization, swish-swished over to us. The sound, I realized, came from her large support-hosed thighs rubbing together as she walked. She wrinkled her nose when we told her we were there for coffee only. "Fine," she said, turning her back to us and returning moments later to fill our upturned mugs.

Will and I added cream to our coffee as she left. He stirred, I didn't. I preferred to let the light brown clouds take over in their slow-motion ballet. Holding the cup close to my lips, I blew a short puff of air downward to facilitate the process. Wisps of steam curled above the cup and I looked over the rim to see him watching me. "You first," he said.

I gave him a quizzical look.

"Something's happened. Something's on your mind," he said.

My look shifted to one of disbelief. "How the heck could you know that?"

He put his hands out. "It's a gift."

I took a sip of the coffee, enjoying its warmth and aroma and the comforting way it eased down my throat, savoring the pleasure of the moment before I shot him a wry smile. "My house was broken into yesterday."

"What?" he asked, his cup returning to its saucer with a clatter. "Are you okay? What did they take?"

"I'm fine, actually. And believe it or not, not a darn thing was taken."

"You reported it?"

"Right away. And," I said, forestalling his next question, "I got all my locks upgraded. Right now my house is so well-protected, you'd need to detonate explosives to get in without a key."

"*Nothing* taken?"

"Not a thing."

"That doesn't make sense," he said.

"The police think that I might have frightened them away as I came in through the back. It's a possibility."

"You don't sound convinced."

"I guess I'm not." I held off while the waitress came by to

refresh our coffee. "Why go to all that trouble to break in and not take anything? Think about it. My house is small. Really small. The television and DVD player are right there as you walk in. Even if they heard me coming, they could have yanked them both out in a matter of seconds."

"You think the break-in has something to do with your story?"

I shrugged. "What purpose would breaking into my house serve?"

"Scare you off?"

"Maybe." I took a long sip of the coffee. "The police said that maybe the thief was searching for something in particular, but didn't find it. But, what could I have that anyone would want? And like I said, nothing's missing."

We were both silent for a long time. Forty-year-old springs beneath my white vinyl seat were straining to escape, and I shifted to find a comfortable pose. "So? You talked to Lisa Knowles . . ."

"Quite the businesswoman."

"Are you on?"

His jaw tightened a bit as he nodded. "Tonight, at ten."

"Bass arranging everything?"

"As we speak."

I let my mind wander a bit. Bass would be working as liaison between our investigative department and the media group. The administration liked to keep abreast of undercover operations. Bass, as manager, had the authority to request technical support. Of course, that meant he had to come along for the ride, too.

"So," William said, apropos of nothing, "you're good friends with some of the people over at *Up Close Issues*?"

Now that was a peculiar question. Other than Dan, and his boss, Roy, I knew perhaps three or four people at that station well enough to say hello, but that was about it.

"Not particularly, why?"

William seemed a bit unsettled as he took a drink of his coffee. Putting it back down, he shrugged. "Oh, nothing. It's just that . . . ah . . . nothing."

"You can't do that to me," I said, half-laughing, half-annoyed. "If it's nothing, then it's no big deal to tell me. . . . So, tell me."

"Okay. Dan Starck."

"What about him?"

"I heard that you and Dan were an item . . ." He let the sentence hang.

"Not any more," I said. "Why?"

Maybe it was my imagination, but he seemed pleased by my answer. Still the question felt odd, more inquisitive than conversational.

He shrugged, as if unsure. "I was in the parking garage, earlier. I stayed sitting in my car, listening to the end of one of my favorite songs and I saw somebody hanging around there."

Just then Bass walked in, looking wild-eyed with worry as he scanned the restaurant's interior till he spotted us.

"You're here," he said unnecessarily, but with obvious relief.

William's face changed in a way that made me realize that whatever he'd been about to tell me wasn't something he cared to share in front of Bass. So before he had a chance to sit down, I suggested, "Why don't you let the waitress know you're joining us?"

He gave a thoughtful nod. "Good idea."

I turned back toward William.

He shrugged, but spoke quickly. "It was Dan. I've met him a few times, so I knew what he looked like, and I'd heard that you and he . . ." He let the sentence trail off. Again.

It took me a second to get what he was implying. I fixed him with a hard stare.

William looked down into his coffee cup, then continued with another shrug, this one apologetic. "I followed him. I figured he was meeting somebody, and at first I wondered if it might be you."

"Well, it wasn't."

Bass gestured toward the washroom. I nodded, then turned back toward William. "Sorry, go ahead."

He nodded. "I was afraid to get too close, in case he saw me. He got into a car with somebody. I couldn't get near enough to see who."

"What kind of car?" I asked.

William gave me a peculiar look at the question, and it dawned on me that I probably sounded like a jilted, jealous lover, scrounging for scraps of information. I put my hands out. "You've got me curious now. I don't see why he'd have any business in our garage," I offered, by way of explanation. "Anyway, I met his girlfriend. She doesn't work here."

"Hint," I wanted to say—that was a hint to let you know I'm not pining after the fellow.

Instead, I took another sip of coffee while William continued.

"I didn't notice the type of car. Navy blue, I think."

"My car's white."

He acknowledged that piece of information with a nod. "I waited a few more minutes, then started to feel foolish. So I came up to the office."

William drained his coffee cup. Buying himself time, I suspected.

His eyes met mine just as he placed the cup down onto the saucer with a little clink.

A momentary thought that Dan might have been there to spy on me flashed through my mind. But that couldn't be it. But the fact that William had been curious enough to find out if Dan and I were an item made me smile.

Bass emerged, rubbing his hands together as the men's room door swung shut, blocking out the whirring of the hand dryer. As he made his way toward us, I turned to William. "You sure you're okay with this operation tonight?"

He averted his gaze. "I can handle it."

I touched his hand across the table, a move that didn't quite startle, but seemed to grab his attention. "I appreciate this, you know."

He smiled, but I knew it was for my benefit. My heart gave a little lurch of unease as he shook his head. "Don't you worry about me."

Back in my office I sorted through e-mails and went over the details Bass had provided regarding the evening's plans. Peppering his conversation with words like "reconnaissance" and "stake-out," he gave us the scoop. As William headed for the pre-arranged hotel room tonight, Bass and I would reconnoiter nearby to watch. Jeff, one of our premiere technicians, volunteered for the after-hours escapade. His wife was out of town and he wanted the overtime. One of our older techs, he had to be over forty, but no one had a handle on the state-of-the-art video equipment like he did. Bass was pulling out all the stops on this one, and for a moment I worried about something pulling the plug before this story came to fruition. Jitters.

Alone now, I called up a file I'd created and password protected, just in case Feudin' Fenton ever got his greasy paws on my computer. To keep life simple for me, I used only three passwords for all my documents. One for business, one for

personal, one for really, really personal. Made it easy to remember, but if any of them ever got out, my life would literally be an open book.

I wore comfortable clothes today, since it was the
weekend. Jeans, T-shirt, and a hooded sweatshirt I periodi-
cally took off and put back on, as I moved from place to place
and the ambient temperature changed. I rubbed my hands on
my legs, thinking, thinking.

I wanted to record everything that happened so far. And
within forty-five minutes or so I had a decent rendition of the
events that had transpired, up to the minute. A quick glance
at the empty hub unnerved me. The only sounds were the re-
frigeration compressor on the water cooler and the lonely
whoosh of warm air coming through the large vents overhead.

Passwords were hard to break, and if something should
happen to me . . .

Rotten thought. I pushed it out of my head at once. But
still . . .

Finished, I dragged my coat on as I made my way through
the darkened hub and to the glass front doors. I supposed it
wouldn't hurt to let William know about my meeting with
Father Bruno. And while I was there, I could clue him in on
my business password, just in case. I trusted him.

Turning back, I headed for his office, convincing myself
that this was the right course of action. Sheesh. Not that I had
a death wish or anything, but as long as someone else was in
on it, it wouldn't be needed. That's the way jinxes worked, I
told myself. The way to break them.

I came around to his open door and realized he'd gone
home. Turning back, I leaned against the adjacent wall, and
shook my head. The super-quiet was getting to me. And it
was nearing my meeting with Father Bruno time. I had to
go.

★ ★ ★ ★ ★

"Alexandrine!"

He greeted me with the effusiveness of a long-lost friend, and I felt my body tense when his beefy hands grasped my upper arms. If he'd been about to pull me into a hug, he'd apparently gotten my "back-off" message, because he let go almost immediately after I froze in place.

There was a younger hostess today, and several teenage waitresses. With weekend business brisker than that of late night, I supposed they could afford a bigger staff. I felt a little thrill of victory when I beat Bruno to answer her question, "Smoking or Non?"

With a bland smile that looked to be pasted on, he picked up a briefcase set near his feet that I hadn't noticed earlier, and followed me and the hostess to a far booth in the "non" section.

Once my iced tea, his coffee, and a basket of assorted rolls were settled before us and our orders sent back to the kitchen, I leaned forward, arms on the table, and smiled. I decided to take control of the moment. His phone call to set up this meeting had thrown me off my game enough to make me uncomfortable. And discomfort doesn't help me maintain my equilibrium in wacky situations such as this.

"I was surprised to hear from you," I said in an attempt to take the reins and guide the conversation. "I can't imagine what you need to see me about."

Bruno was wearing priestly garb: black pants, black long-sleeve shirt with the stark-white notched collar that let everyone in the restaurant know a holy man was present. He acted as though he hadn't heard me, instead moving his gaze around the murmuring diners, obviously catching an eye now and then. Giving "priest nods"—those innocuous head gestures that can mean anything from "hello" to "you are blessed," but probably meant nothing in this case more than, "Hey, I'm a priest. Did you notice?"

Attendant Catholics acknowledged, he returned his attention to the table. He pulled a wrinkled handkerchief out from inside his black sleeve and blew his nose copiously, eyebrows raised, his face reddening in the process. This man plodded. He took his time. And if he was hoping to set me off-kilter again, it was working. Of course, I wasn't about to let him know that.

Time to be direct. "So why exactly did you want to meet with me?" I asked.

Tucking the soiled hanky back into its nook, he shot me a short-lived smile. "Alexandrine Szatjemski."

I felt my eyes squint, wary. "Yeah."

His face broke into a large smile. A scary one, because his eyes picked up the overhead light and glittered when he spoke again. "Also, Alex St. James?"

Damn. He'd made the connection. "Sometimes," I said, and shrugged as if to say, "no big deal."

With slow movements, designed no doubt for maximum suspense, he slid his coffee cup far to his right and brought his black briefcase up, opening it on the table, with a snappy click-click. He had it angled in such a way that I couldn't see what he pulled out, other than to know it was papers. Several papers.

"You neglected to mention the real reason for your interest in Sophie."

"My real reason?" I affected confusion.

"Come now, Alex. And you do usually go by Alex, don't you?" He didn't wait for my answer. "It wasn't that hard to find out about you. I suppose most people who you interview and whose stories you tell on *Midwest Focus* simply don't take the time to discover who they're dealing with."

Another smile. Another jolt of unease for me.

"Or maybe," he continued, "you don't need to affect a different persona for your other stories."

I'd lost control of this one. That was obvious. Now I needed to decide the best way to regain my footing. I opened my hands in what I hoped looked like a gesture of abdication. "Okay, so you found me out. What are you planning to do?"

"I'm going to do what I do best, my dear," he said. Everything about him oozed condescension. The gentle, yet not-so-kind look in his eyes. The tilt of his head that to onlookers might seem as though he was engrossed in my words, but to me looked like ill-concealed smugness. "I'm going to protect my children."

Our young waitress arrived with his open-face pork sandwich—a mound of meat and accompaniments swimming in gloppy brown gravy so carelessly ladled on, that thick globs dripped off the side of the plate. She slid my small dinner salad in front of me. Ranch dressing in a silver cup on the side, just like I requested. She asked if there was anything else we needed, in a voice that expected we'd say we were fine.

"We're fine," I said, eager to turn the conversation back to Father Bruno. As soon as she left the side of the table I asked, "How?"

He closed the briefcase again, returning it to his side on the booth's seat as he turned his attention to food. His doughy face had broken into a smile, and I half-expected him to rub his hands together before diving into his meal. But he picked up his knife and fork, checking them for spots, it seemed, and started in with gusto. I didn't think he heard me.

"How?" I repeated.

"How . . . what?"

"How do you plan to protect them?"

Condescension again, this time blatant. "Eat," he said

gesturing with his now-dripping knife. "Plenty of time to talk when we're finished."

We locked eyes for a moment or two, him daring me to push it, I thought.

The idea of eating right now went beyond surreal. His arrogance glittered from small eyes peering out over flabby cheeks. This man across the table from me, leering at me not with lust, but with power, was a priest. A priest who made my skin crawl. I tried not to think "asshole" and "Father Bruno" in the same thought, because doing so would probably guarantee an eternity in hell, but it was tough.

Small talk wasn't coming easy for me, but Bruno didn't seem to mind. He paid little attention to anything other than the massive plate before him and his coffee, which he drained at least four times while he shoveled the pork roast and dressing in, at an impressive clip. He asked me once where Sophie was staying, but I didn't answer and he didn't press.

He cleaned his plate, using the last bite of a sesame seed roll to sop up the remaining gravy. Tiny bits of cooked pork goo remained near the inside curve of his platter and he stamped at them with the bun, trying to pick up every last one, before shoving the arrangement into his mouth. His bottom lip was droopy in the center, I noticed. Like a baby pout, the middle hinged downward. With bits of food that he worked from between his teeth, the lip got lots of exercise.

I dropped my fork into my unfinished salad. Now that he was done, we could talk, and I was more interested in that than cleaning my own plate. Our server, in a bit of waitress-understanding, moved up to clear the plates right away, then swung back moments later to refill our beverages and drop off the check, which I grabbed. This girl was good, and I'd have to remember to tip her well.

I brushed crumbs off the end of the table with the side of my arm. "So," I said, prompting, "the reason for our meeting today?"

This time he kept the briefcase on the seat next to him as he opened it. "Alex. Alexandrine."

I waited.

"Lovely name. Alexandrine P. Szatjemski. What does the 'P' stand for?"

"My middle name," I said without humor.

"Yes. Yes," he said, taking his sweet time, his eyes focused downward, to the side. On something inside the briefcase, no doubt. He had my attention, that's for sure.

After a few moments of noisy shuffling, he looked up at me. Gone was the beatific smile and kindly demeanor. "You're an intelligent young woman, Alex. And a beautiful girl. You have the potential to go far in this world." His eyes never left mine. "If you make good choices."

The ranch dressing began to curdle in my stomach. I cleared my throat. "What kind of choices am I looking at?"

His smile didn't reach his eyes as he answered. "Now, now. Not to worry. There's nothing sinister in what I'm about to propose."

The restaurant seemed almost to fade away, and I was unaware of any movement or sound beyond Father Bruno's sonorous breathing as he settled his girth in the booth and leaned forward to explain. He pulled his head low, and arranged his voice even lower. "I told you that I protect my children, did I not?"

He got me to nod.

"And I sometimes do so at great personal risk." The timbre of his voice suggested this was an "important point" he needed me to grasp. "If *Midwest Focus* does the story I envision, then many, many good people will get hurt."

"Many good people are getting hurt, now," I reminded him.

"There's a lot you don't understand."

"Why don't you enlighten me, then?"

Leaning back, he expelled a breath that could have been frustration. "Oh, Alex," he said, shaking his head and taking a long drink of his coffee as he glanced around, grimacing. His voice changed—petulant. "I really do wish we'd sat in the smoking section."

"Why?" I asked. Anger and frustration got the best of me. Unable to stop myself I added, "Getting nervous?"

That brought him back to the table, in a hurry. His eyes blazed. "No. I'm not nervous." His words were quiet, precise. "Because I know who, and what, I'm dealing with. These girls come over from the old country and they're not going to make it. Not unless they get help. And so I help them." His voice rose. "And if they make choices that aren't . . . ideal, that's their decision. What I do is ask myself, do they have a better life because of me? I like to think they do. No. . . . I *know* they do."

I pulled away a little at the tirade, taken aback by his vehemence. From the corner of my eye, I noticed a couple of other diners sneak a peek in our direction. I doubt they heard his words, but his body language was clear.

With a protracted downward glance, Bruno pursed his lips, gathering his poise, it seemed. A smile twitched at his mouth before he raised his face to look at me again. "My apologies. I'm sure you can tell that I care deeply about these young people and that I am passionately concerned for their well-being."

I wanted to laugh in his face. My back straightened and I sat up, restraining myself from spitting an argument back at him. Realizing I'd learn nothing by fighting him, I waited, every nerve in my body taut, wound like a spring ready to attack.

"You're a woman of good character, Alex. I can tell these things."

"You can," I said. Not phrased as a question.

He ignored me. "I know you would be a woman of your word. Am I right?"

A web began to spin around me, but I couldn't find a way to prevent it. I gave a reluctant nod.

"Good." He smiled a genuine smile for the first time since we'd met at the door. "You and I are in a position to help one another." His voice had lowered. There was no way anyone else in the restaurant could hear him. I had to bring my face closer to the table to catch everything, myself.

"Do you know what would happen if you run your television program?" He wasn't looking for me to answer, so I kept silent. "Sophie, who escaped the harshness of destitution in the old country, would be deported." He squinted at me. "In an instant. Her life would be ruined. Do you understand? Ruined."

"But you're sanctioning—"

"Alex. Listen. Jesus forgave Mary Magdalene. What you're suggesting is that one of my children is committing sins as grave as hers."

"You obviously haven't paid attention to all the news programs lately," I said with some enmity. "Mary Magdalene wasn't a prostitute after all. She's of royal descent."

He heaved a theatric sigh. "Oh yes, all that. The big Catholic cover-up." He rolled his eyes. "My point, however, is still valid. Jesus forgives. Who am I to second-guess Jesus, if indeed any of this is true?"

"It is true. You know it is."

"I know that Sophie is a good Catholic. I also know that

she works hard in her job. There's nothing I can do to stop her from pursuing other means of support when she's out of my sight."

"But Sophie trusts you. I'm sure all the girls trust you. You could be their champion."

"All the girls?" he asked, and I couldn't decide if the surprise on his face was genuine or an affectation.

"Yes, all the girls. The girls you placed at Lisa's salon. If you would confront Lisa Knowles, it could make all the difference to them. It could change their lives."

He stared at me for a long moment, with eyes I couldn't read. "You think you have a story here, don't you?"

"I think a lot of innocent people are getting hurt."

He heaved a sigh. "You aren't listening with the right attitude. You don't know Sophie the way I do. I know what's right for her. All I'm asking is for you to look the other way. Just for a little while."

"You must be joking."

"No," he said, drawing the word out.

"I can't do that."

"Like I said earlier, Alex. We are in a position to help one another."

I shook my head, not understanding.

Bruno reached down, pulling a slim manila folder from his briefcase. He placed it on the table between us, his fingertips poised atop it like a spider as he pressed it firmly in place. The message was clear. "Don't touch."

"I've done my homework on you Alexandrine Szatjemski. And I've been able to pull some strings. Some very important strings."

I waited.

"I would be willing to hand you this folder, right now, if you give me your word that you'll kill the story."

I had to know. "What's in the folder?"

He gave a long, slow smile. "Just a few pieces of information." Picking it up, he opened it so that it formed a wall between us. "Let's see here . . . Your date of birth is November eighteenth, correct?" I felt my mouth open as he continued. "I have that right here. And a couple of names. Mother, father, attending physician. Your real name."

I heard, more than felt, the sharp breath rush into me. Surrounding lights and noises dimmed and a rush of blood shot to my brain, sending sparks of fear, anticipation, and hope ricocheting through my body like knives, making tiny cuts as they flew.

"I have contacts with Catholic Charities, to answer your question. It took some effort, but when I assured the administration that this was of the utmost importance, they took me at my word. And I will take you at yours, if you give it to me."

His stare bore into me, as he took his time before speaking again. The fact that I sat speechless did not deter him. The part of my mind that tenaciously tried to remain objective understood that I was giving him the precise reaction he'd expected.

"As I said, we are each in a position to help the other." Closing the folder, he placed it on the table again, this time using his smoke-stained fingertips to inch it closer to me.

I couldn't take my eyes off it. Inside were all the answers I wanted. My mother's name. Who she was; who my father was. The questions I'd had for decades, questions I'd suppressed. All the answers were right there. Within my grasp. All I had to do was look the other way where Sophie was concerned. And how simple that sounded right now, how very easy.

My hands gripped each other tightly in my lap, but I couldn't tell if they were working together to prevent grabbing the folder or if they were pained in anticipation. I didn't know anything.

"Alex," Bruno's voice was soothing, like a lullaby, as I stared at the answers to my dreams on the table before me. "You'll be helping Sophie, you'll be helping all those she cares about. If they've chosen their path, their eyes are open. And they're hurting no one. Would you strip from them the very lives they've created? Just to exploit their stories for the nation to see? For your own need for recognition and accolades? Think about it, Alex. What will happen to them, if they're exposed? Even if nothing of what you claim is true, their lives will be forever tainted by your actions. Can you live with that guilt for the rest of your life?"

My mind tried to catch up with my emotions. I ignored the shots of adrenaline that raced my heart so hard and so fast that I swore it would burst. I knew I should refuse. I knew that. I tried to distance myself from my own desires. To analyze the situation. But, like a dream where you're being chased by a shadow, and your feet are suddenly frozen in place, I struggled against an unseen force.

Concentrate, I told myself. Don't react. I conjured up enough chutzpah to say, "It isn't just Lisa's . . . organization."

He raised an eyebrow.

I took a deep breath. But I had to know. "Milla," I said. "And Matthew. Were their deaths—"

He held his hands up, positioned eerily like priests' are during the blessings over bread and wine. "Alex." His voice was low, warning. "Don't."

"Why?"

Once again, the kindly priest mask settled over his features. "Because you are a news investigator. You see connections that don't exist. You'll bring more to the forefront than belongs there, all in the name of exposing the truth. But there is nothing there. We may all be sinners in the eyes of God, but there is no one more devoted to protecting the sanctity of life than I am."

I wanted to believe him. For Sophie's safety and for my own. But I had to know.

"If I refuse?"

His face hardened, for a brief moment. He pulled the folder from the Formica tabletop, in exquisite slowness. My heart wanted to reach out and grab it from him before he tucked it back into his briefcase. "If you pursue your story, I will use whatever means necessary to prevent the segment from airing. I have many important contacts in the city, and I'm confident I'd be successful." He paused a long moment. "With that in mind, why not take advantage of my offer and make it easier on both of us?" He shut the briefcase with a tiny double-click and eased himself out of the booth. Tapping the table in front of me he smiled in a way that made my stomach squirm. "Think about it."

Chapter Nineteen

The very last time my parents took us to the drive-in theater, we'd gone for the requisite double feature. Kid movie first; some Disney offering, as I recall. Grown-up film following. The arrangement worked like a charm as far as my parents were concerned. Dangling the carrot of a drive-in before us ensured our angelic behavior for at least half the day leading up to it. A perfect family outing. Especially since, at drive-ins, no one complained about Lucy's incessant chatter.

Once the kid-friendly movie finished, my parents expected us to go to sleep, pajama-clad in the back seat, like we always had in the past. They collected our empty candy and popcorn containers, let us take one last sip of our sugary pop, and settled us in during the peppy, animated intermission.

Lucy complied, snoring softly, in three minutes flat.

That time, for some reason, I couldn't. And though the idea of sneak-watching a grown-up movie held allure to my ten-year-old sensibilities, I quickly found it boring. My parents, engaged in the talky drama, didn't notice me doing what I liked to do best, which was, even at that age, watching other people.

The young couple in the car next to us, very close, were engaged in some heavy petting, though I didn't realize it at the time. I kept my head low, peering over the edge of the door. Half-open to allow for air movement, my window made a nice place to rest my forehead as I watched. I kept having to ease my sweet-sticky fingers up to smear away my breath's condensation, but I moved in stealth, knowing without knowing why, that my parents wouldn't quite approve of whatever this couple was doing.

I vividly remember trying to figure it out. Obvious to me that these two weren't interested in the flickering movie either; they seemed instead to be moving their bodies in un-natural gyrations. He sat facing forward, in the back seat. She faced him, looking to be perched on his lap.

I found it curious, fascinating. Little did I know. Judging from their faces, I decided that whatever the activity, they both found it enjoyable. And they kissed a lot.

When he pulled her shirt over her head, exposing her bare chest, my attention was riveted. I couldn't drag my eyes away, no matter how much I knew I should. I watched them smile and kiss and rock in increasingly quicker motions until she arched backwards, letting out a high-pitched moan that grabbed my parents' attention from the screen.

Within seconds Dad looked at them, looked at me, threw the big old metal speaker out the window, and slammed the car into gear.

My parents never spoke about the incident, and didn't answer Lucy, even when she raised her groggy head to ask, "What happened?"

Never went to the drive-in again.

And a little bit of my innocence was lost.

That memory popped up now as I sat with Bass in the night's darkness, with a silver-framed plasma screen set be-tween us. The slight scratchiness of the audio, the closeness of the car's interior, and most of all, the anticipatory feeling of voyeurism transported me back to that moment. At once I felt eager, guilty, and uncomfortable.

We were across the street from the Romantic Voyage motel. Its amber sign blinked in loud precision buzzes, advertising four-hour naps available round-the-clock. Cicero Avenue had plenty of traffic, but we'd picked this particular establishment because a quiet parking lot across the street afforded us opportunity to watch the place while William's encounter would be recorded. The shrub-shaded lot we sat in now had no overhead lighting. Tall yews and the dark night guaranteed our near-invisibility to the traffic zooming by. This parking area butted up to a squat brick animal clinic—office hours over since noon.

I'd driven my Ford Escort, at Bass's pointed suggestion. His roomier Lexus SUV would have been a better choice, but he claimed car problems and insisted we use something "more dependable." Known forever as a car-babier, I suspected he simply didn't want his precious vehicle involved in the undercover operation for paranoid reasons of his own.

Tech-Jeff walked us through the process earlier. He was a handsome man, over six feet tall, not a spare ounce on him. Ten pounds more would have been a smart investment, in my opinion. Men need a little bulk. His full head of dark hair had the monochromatic sheen of dye. Long, slim fingers worked the gizmos he'd demonstrated, and I swore that his nails were manicured and polished. He went over each step of the taping process with clear explanations and caveats. From our perspective, things were easy. Bass and I would sit in my car, watch the monitor, and whisper the occasional direction to Jeff via our walkie-talkies. But only if necessary.

Jeff had parked in an adjacent lot a block down; the van he drove had a number of odd gizmos attached to it, and we didn't want to attract undue attention by parading it along busy Cicero Avenue. Should the need arise, we had a code word, "Voyager," that would bring him front and center to help out.

When we first arrived, I left Bass in the car long enough to take a quick walk around the place, to get a feel for it. As "nap" motels went, the Romantic Voyage did a nice job of keeping the cheap-looking clean. Faux-classy, the white-washed two-story structure had red trim and pink doors that boasted gold room numbers against wooden red hearts. The light from the flashing neon sign, thirty feet tall, washed over the building in blinks, causing it to alternate in color between cool night-white and a sorry shade of yellow. The parking lot, surprisingly free of litter, even boasted two small plantings of shrubs that someone cared enough to trim. William's car sat to the far right of the lot. He'd rented one. In case anyone bothered to check, he would appear to be merely a traveling businessman.

William had gotten to the motel a short while before we did. He and Jeff had set up four tiny cameras in strategic places around the room. We watched William now, on the plasma screen squeezed in the narrow space between our two laps, the color display split into four views. Jeff had a similar set-up—with one notable exception. From his screen, wires led to a busy recorder, filming events as they took place.

Watching William wait for his date made me irritated, the same way I feel when my hands are dirty, or my clothes are too tight.

He paced the motel room. Tiny, utilitarian, it had one bed—large, though not king-size. The orange floral spread was short on one side, fitting unevenly so that a corner of a beige blanket hung out the end, an extended rip along the hem. A television perched, suspended from the ceiling—stationary on a solid metal bracket. Two chairs, that neither matched each other nor the bedspread, straddled a small table by the draped picture window. A far door at the rear of the room led to the bathroom. William walked toward it and turned on the light, giving it an up and down glance before shutting the light back off. He looked our way again. "It sure ain't Buckingham Palace," he said.

Up to that point, he'd been silent in the white noise, and it jarred me to hear him speak. He shucked his jacket, dropping it near the pillow end of the bed, and shook his head with a look up to the camera that I knew was meant for me. My heart gave a little lurch.

Silent, Bass and I watched him pace the motel room floor on the different viewpoint monitors. The effect was strange. As he walked away from one camera, he walked toward another. If I shifted my attention from right to left, and back again, and timed it just right, it appeared that he was walking away from me, over and over and over again. Both cameras were capable of zooming in and out. Jeff worked the controls from his location, while Bass snapped orders, pestering him to test the effects before our quarry arrived.

The fourth camera, a wide-angle mounted atop the suspended TV, provided a bird's eye view of the entire room. Unless either William or the girl went to the washroom, they would be in our sights the whole time.

I checked my watch and, in periphery, noticed Bass do the same. Just ten o'clock now.

At a knock, we all reacted. William's attention shot up toward the camera. I watched him square his shoulders before he strode to open the door. He couldn't see us, of course, but I still smiled encouragement at him. Bass yelled, "Wider, wider," to Jeff over the phone, so loud that I found myself shushing him like a kindergarten teacher reminding a child to use his "inside voice." Evidently the message went through loud and clear, because the close-up shot from the first monitor widened abruptly, but not before I caught William's look. I bit my lip.

She was both exactly and nothing at all what I expected.

When she walked in, my heart went out to her. Petite and blond, she carried herself like a young girl, a tiny bounce in her hesitant steps. "I am Candy," she said, in heavily accented English. She canted her head. "You are John?"

William nodded and stepped far enough away from her that we were able to get the full effect of her appearance. We would cover her face in post-production, but her clothing would be clear. Wearing a short black and white zebra stripe skirt, and a fluffy white coat that came to her waist, she looked the part of a hooker. Right down to her spikey heels and the small pink purse clamped to her side like a security blanket.

"You bring money?" she asked.

William pulled out several bills from his back pocket and handed them over.

Candy counted them, twice, tucked them into a zipper compartment of her purse, and shot William a tiny smile when she finished.

Pulling the fuzzy coat off, she draped it over her purse, along the back of one of the two chairs. I shivered at the skimpy spaghetti strap top she wore on a cold night like this one. Bright pink and shiny, it clung to her body like a glove. No bra. When she drew away from the fuzzy coat, something caught her attention and she moved back for an instant, re-arranging it so the sleeves wouldn't rest on the floor. A possessive move, made all the more poignant by the fact that this coat had been out of style for decades.

Patting the garment with affection, she turned to William, as if asking him to take the lead. When he smiled at her, she nodded, reached back into her purse, and pulled out a condom. "I bring. Is okay?"

"Oh," William said, shaking his head, "no."

"No?" Her squeaked reply told me she hadn't expected that answer.

"What I mean is—why don't we talk for a while first?"

She tilted her head, puzzled. "Talk?"

I leaned forward, as though that would somehow make the sound clearer, the picture more crisp. "Candy," no doubt a name chosen as hooker pseudonym, just like Sophie's "Cherie," put the condom on the bed, and smiled at William. She pulled her left arm over her right, massaging her right wrist, as she glanced downward. A surreptitious check of her watch, from what I could tell.

"We get cozy first," she said. And in a smooth move, she'd closed the distance between herself and William, to press her body against his, averting her face. Her hands splayed out on his chest and moved upward in a trained way, till she'd connected her fingers behind his neck. "We talk later, yes?"

Leaning away, he reached around to pull her hands away, gripping her forearms. He stepped back. I couldn't see her face at this point, close as she was to William, but it seemed he reacted to an expression he saw there. "Please, just for a little while . . ."

She stepped back and canted her head at him. "I no understand. You pay for two hours, yes?"

William took a seat on the bed. Perfect positioning. He patted the mattress next to him, offering an avuncular smile. "I want to get to know you. . . ." he stammered a bit, ". . . before."

She sat, but her lower lip jutted out in a manufactured sulk. Her chin down, big eyes stared at William. "You no like me?"

"It's not that. You're a very beautiful girl."

And then he smiled at her.

Her expression softened. William had charmed her, as we

241

knew he could. But the smile he'd shot her was the same sort of smile that had knocked me for a loop in the past.

A shiver ran up my spine, even though the car's interior had warmed. Despite the fact that this had been arranged, even scripted in parts, despite the fact that there would be no physical intimacies happening here tonight, watching William's interaction with this woman made me squirm. I didn't want to see him work his appeal on her. It bugged me. It shouldn't, but it did.

Bass shouted, "Close up! Close up!"

His small-man voice echoed in my car, tinny and shrill.

"For crying out loud, Bass," I said, "keep it down. Jeff can hear just fine, you know."

By the time I finished speaking, he'd gotten his close-up of "Candy." Small-boned, with nice features, she had the unmistakable look of a foreign girl about her. One that would have told me she was off-the-boat Polish, even before she opened her mouth to speak. Large eyes and a wide mouth were trimmed with excessive makeup. She wore false eyelashes and way too much eyeliner. Her lips, red and wet-looking, still had a childish pout to them, and it seemed wrong for this tiny person to be coming on to William in a cheap motel room.

A knowing smile came over her features, shattering the little-girl look, almost with a crash in my brain. "Ah," she said, giving him the once over, slowly. "First time you come to us?"

William sat up straighter, obviously startled by the question.

She smiled, again a shrewd look, as she played her fingertips on his knee, then walked them up along his thigh. "I mean, you first time to pay for it?"

He pushed her hand away, in a move so awkward that it

made me think he was trying to be gentle about it. "I just want to be comfortable first."

"Oh, yes . . . cahm-for-tahble . . ." She grinned. "I help." Her hands began to move his way again, but he leaned back and she stopped.

"Candy." William grasped her hands, effectively stopping their movement. "I paid for two hours of your time, right?"

She nodded.

"Then, let's talk. I want to get to know you."

A tiny smile played at her lips, sending yet another shiver down my back. "Other girls tell me about men like you." She shook her head as though amused. "I never meet one before. Okay. We talk."

"Good." He released her hands, and I released a breath I hadn't realized I was holding.

Our pre-arranged script came to my mind, and I could tell from the slight loosening of William's shoulders that he was ready to get underway. We'd decided that coming at one of Lisa's girls full-force with questions about the organization could be counter-productive. At best we might get prevarication. At worst, outright hostility. We had almost two hours. William was an attractive man, with a sincere smile and gentle demeanor. With any luck, he'd be able to get her to open up about her life, and smoothly move the focus to her involvement with Lisa.

I frowned at the screen. Bass caught me. "Something bothering you?" he asked in a smart-ass tone of voice.

"What do you mean?" I asked.

"Oh, come on," he said with a grin, his eyes moving from me to the monitor and back to me again. "Like I can't see the way you look at him."

I folded my arms across my body, and shook my head. "Just drop it."

"Well, just remember my personal policy on inter-office dating," he said.

I shot him an angry glance, which he ignored. I swore he gave a smug wiggle as we watched William launch into investigative mode.

"What you want to talk about?" Candy asked.

"Well," he asked, with a self-effacing shrug, "what's your favorite color?"

She gave him a peculiar look—but she answered.

"Purple."

He asked her a few other simple questions, on innocuous, safe subjects, designed to loosen her up. That had been the plan. As we'd expected, she came in pretty loosened already, though not necessarily to talk.

Deep into their conversation, she laughed at an anecdote William told her about a dog he had when he was young. She responded with a pet story of her own, from back when she lived in the old country.

As she talked, she scooted back on the bed, making herself more comfortable as she warmed to her subject. She folded one leg underneath her and tugged at the hem of her skirt in an absent-minded, demure move. The words flowed, Candy's face becoming more animated as they chatted.

Bass spoke into the microphone to Jeff, "Close up on these two, okay?"

Seconds later her face took up one view, William's another. We still had two wide shots that showed body language. Candy was beginning to relax.

"No," Bass said, his voice threatening to rise again. "Too close. You lost the shot of her tits."

"Bass!" I said.

The shot widened almost instantly.

"What?" Bass said. "You think people are going to tune in

to see a hooker's *face?* Come on, little girl, grow up. Sex sells, remember? We need ratings. This is gonna get 'em for us."

I wanted to tell him what he could do with his ratings, but the drama on the screen pulled my attention once again.

Like hearing a deftly written script performed by a seasoned actor, William segued into asking if she still had family back there. She did. Candy's face tightened a bit, and she became hesitant. With a glance toward William, who nodded encouragement, she admitted that she missed her parents and siblings very much. Her parents believed she'd made a success of herself. They were so proud of her. And her littlest sister, Josie, wrote her letters asking when she could please come visit.

"Will you go back to see them?" he asked.

The tiny face softened. She bit her lip and focused on the dark brown carpeting, shaking her head. "How can I?" she asked. "They all so proud of me. They write letters and say how happy it is I came here. If they know what I do, they will cry. I break my parents' heart. I break Josie's heart. I can no go back."

"But didn't you know what you were getting into, here?"

"No!" she said, with vehemence. "I am good girl." She gave a sad sigh. "I *was* good girl. I no even have boyfriend in old country."

"How did you get involved in the business, then?"

She hesitated. Her eyes dropped again to the carpet, and her mouth compressed into a tight line.

"Candy?"

A deep breath. A shrug. "Two years ago, my parents meet man. A priest. From America. He bring gifts and food and money. He said that life in United States much better than life in Poland. He tell them that he can get jobs for girls who work hard. Cleaning lady, or hair style lady, or factory work."

She pulled her gaze back up to meet William's. "He promise that we meet wealthy American men, that we live like queen. My parents tell me go with him. I no want to go. I no want to leave. They say it will be better if I go. It will be a dream come true. For whole family."

"He sponsored you?"

She rolled her eyes. "Yes. He introduce me to Lisa. She tell him she hire me to clean houses."

When Candy didn't continue immediately, William asked, "Does this priest know what you really do?"

She shook her head and shrugged at the same time. "He only get me job. Then he no come by no more. I think he see we all doing well and he no need to know more."

"But he has to know."

Candy shook her head again. "Is all Lisa. She make me work cleaning houses. She tell me that I could make more money if I do more for her. The other girls tell me what she mean. So, I say 'no.' " Candy bit her lip. "Lisa very angry. The next house I go to, is not empty. A man is there. Lisa's boyfriend. He make me do many things. He hurt me."

"What's the priest's name?"

Candy seemed about to answer, then stopped herself. "Why you ask?"

William backed off. "Just curious," he said.

"Damn it!" Bass bellowed. "This is dynamite and he's blowing it." Bass pressed the walkie-talkie button. "You getting this, Jeff?"

"Yeah, Mr. Bassett. I'm getting it all. Don't worry."

I shot him a look meant to keep him quiet. I didn't want to miss any of the conversation.

Mollified by William's answer, Candy continued. "Is no good I tell you. You already talk to Lisa, you know Lisa. You dom need to know priest."

"Why don't you leave?" William asked in a low voice.

Candy's eyes shot up, alarmed. "You no understand. No one can leave. When you talk to Lisa, you arrange all this?" She made little circles with her index finger, encompassing the room.

"Yes."

"Wait . . ." Candy moved back to dig the money out of her purse. She counted it out on the bed between them. When finished, she picked up one of the bills—I couldn't make out what it was—and tucked it into her shirt. The remaining cash sat there between them. "This for me," she said, patting her chest. "The rest, Lisa. She make lot of money and she do nothing but tell us where to show up. She dom let nobody go. Not while we still can work."

Bass pressed the wrong button on the phone. It gave a screech of protest. Unflustered, he said, "Keep it steady on her face, and keep the chest in there," Bass said to Jeff. Then, a moment later, "Yeah, that's good."

"Did you ever try?" William asked.

The world-weary look in her eyes shot through to my heart, as she gathered up the cash again, to put it away. "Others try. But they change their mind."

"What happened to them?"

For a breathless moment, we all waited.

Candy stared for a moment, then gave a shrug. "This dirty business. They know we no able to call police. Lisa's boyfriend come visit if we no behave—if we try to get away. I smart enough not to try."

"I'm very sorry," William said.

Bass shouted again, too loud for my car, "Shit! He's turning this into a freaking soap opera." He punched numbers into the cell phone.

"What are you doing?" I asked as a phone in the motel

room scene rang. "Bass! What are you doing?"

"Giving him a clue about how to proceed," he said.

"Don't!" I said. He ignored me.

William, visibly startled, grabbed the cell phone from his jacket pocket. Flipped it open. "Yeah?"

His voice was angry, terse and in stereo—coming as it did through the display and Bass's phone—with about a half-second delay.

"You need to push her, Armstrong," Bass said, thankfully quietly enough. I could only hope his voice wouldn't carry for Candy to hear. William must have had a similar worry because he stepped back, near the washroom, putting distance between him and the girl. "We need concrete information, you understand? Push the broad. Quit being such a marshmallow."

At Bass's rebuke, William stiffened. His back went straight, and Jeff chose that moment to go for the close-up. I watched William work his jaw, as though to fight internal tension. "Yes," he said, a fake-friendly tone to his voice. "Thank you for letting me know."

He slammed the phone shut, jamming it back into his jacket before Bass could react.

"That son of a bitch," Bass said.

Candy tilted her head. "Who call you?"

"My boss."

She shot William an inquiring look, but didn't push.

I thought I saw one of William's hands fist and flex, but it might have been screen distortion.

Candy tilted her head the other way.

"You no want sex, do you," she said. It wasn't a question as much as a realization.

He shook his head.

Next to me, Bass made an impolite sound.

248

"Is okay," she said. "Why you spend money, then?"

William looked away for a moment, then turned back to her. "My name isn't John," he said.

"I no think so."

Apoplectic, Bass shouted, "What's he doing?"

"Shh," I said. I understood. Or at least I thought I did.

"My name is William. Will."

Candy nodded acknowledgment. "My name," she said, shy all of a sudden, "is Katrina."

"Hello, Katrina."

When she smiled, I saw the baby face in her again. William must have seen it too, because a flicker of sadness crossed his eyes, enough to translate through the camera.

Bass broke the silence. "Shit."

"What?"

"Just look at these expressions we'll be missing if we obscure their faces."

"If?"

He broke his stare from the monitor to look at me. "You know what I meant."

I glanced at my watch, having to tilt it toward the screen for enough light to read the time. We had just under fifteen minutes left before Candy's meter ran out.

"So," she asked again, "why you want to meet here?"

"Can I ask you something?"

She nodded.

"Would you like to get out of this business?"

Her guard went up in a flash. She leaned away from William. "What you mean?"

"Don't worry. I'm just asking. If you could, would you quit if you could?"

"You have job for me?"

"No, I don't. I just want to know if you'd take the chance."

"I dom know," she said with a shrug. "I no able to get away. I no think about it."

"But what if you could? Would you? Would the other girls?"

Katrina seemed to examine the question for a long while. She stared at the floor. One foot bounced with tension.

She looked to William with innocent eyes, a glimpse of the girl she had been, and for a moment the trashy clothing faded away; she seemed more like a child playing dress-up, mixing and matching things that clashed but made her feel grown-up.

"Me? Yes. I get away if I can. Maybe some other girls too. Not all. Some think they no can do anything else. Some think this better than working. I can do many things. I good in math at school in old country." She wrinkled her nose, as though to stem tears. "I work hard. I like work hard. I like to try."

She sucked on her lower lip, and sniffed deeply. When she spoke again, her voice faltered. "I nineteen years old. I here now, two years. I think I come to United States, I meet nice American man." She shook her head. "You first one I ever meet who nice to me, not just for sex. I want some day to have babies and have house and nice life."

"Maybe I can help you," William said.

She gave him an amused look. "You want to marry me, give me babies, and money?"

"No."

She lifted her chin. A touch of defiance, curiosity. "How you help me, then?"

William pulled out a business card from his pocket. "My work phone number is there." He pulled out a pen and scribbled on the back. "My cell phone number too." I winced. Wow, he was going out on a limb for this girl.

She scanned the front of the card. Even if she couldn't

read, our station's logo was unmistakable. "You work for TV?" Her guard shot up again. The fear in her eyes was palpable.

"I won't do anything to put you in danger."

She stood up. "I no be on TV."

"Katrina," William said, in a voice so deep and powerful and soothing that it would have stopped me at the sound. He repeated himself, slowly. "I won't do anything to put you in danger."

"They kill me."

I heard my own sharp intake of breath.

"Katrina—"

"No!" she shouted, her eyes shooting between William and the door as though to gauge the prospect of escape.

"You don't understand," William said, as he moved to angle himself, effectively blocking the door. He apparently sensed, as I did, that Katrina might bolt any second. "I won't let that happen."

I believed him. I only hoped she would too. We'd gone off script, but I had no doubt in my mind that he'd stay true to his word.

"Shit," Bass said again. "He's losing control of this."

"I sell body, yes?" Katrina nodded, angry panic shooting her voice up two octaves. Advancing on William, he seemed forced to nod in agreement. "But I no sell my life. I no sell my soul." She shook the card at him. "You keep this. They find it, I dead. You understand that? I dead."

"Katrina," he said. "We will protect you."

"No. No one can protect. No one. You understand? Even if you get me away from them, what? What about my friends? What about other girls? You can no protect us all. You no know what you doing here. You no know who you dealing with." Some of her hooker, tough girl persona made its way to the forefront; her voice lowered and strengthened. "No," she said, her gaze hard. "You get away from me. You no call again. You no ask for me again."

"But we can—"

"No!" she shouted, crumpling the card and throwing it at him. Her voice warbled with hysteria. Grabbing her purse and fluffy white jacket, she moved to get around him, out the door. "You let me go. Now. Time is up."

"Awww, hell," Bass said.

His face impassive, William stepped aside.

She wrenched the doorknob and literally threw herself out of the room, faltering a bit on wobbly high-heel feet. Bass swore, loudly, and I got out of the car, to watch her scuttle down the metal stairs. Even across the street, we could hear the stilettos clank as she ran all the way down.

Neither of us knew how she'd arrived, so we watched from between the six-foot bushes for about ten chilly minutes while she paced, hugging herself against the cold, until an extended-length gray passenger van approached. As Candy/Katrina opened the door to jump in, the interior lights went on. At least four other girls occupied the back seats, each sitting alone. Each leaning against a window, staring out.

"Now what?" Bass asked.

I ignored him to glance back inside the car. The monitor gave me four versions of William, sitting perfectly still on the edge of the bed, eyes averted, jacket gripped in his hand. Waiting for the signal, no doubt. The gray van had pulled far down the street, gotten a green light at the intersection, and was gone. I held my horn down, for two long blasts.

On the monitor, I watched him sigh and shake his head, right before I slammed the car door shut to hurry across the street.

Chapter Twenty

Leaving Bass with a stern admonishment not to move from my car, despite his furious sputterings, I made my way across Cicero Avenue. Several late-night speeders and a semi-trailer truck rumbled past, making me wait, the cold more biting than earlier. And me fresh and warm from my toasty car. Why the hell did this street still have so much traffic late at night? A half-block of emptiness finally opened up, giving me an opportunity to scamper toward the motel before the next wave of headlights neared.

The night clerk, a middle-aged woman with tight perm-curly brown hair and a bulldog's dour expression, watched as I passed the office. Leaning on the high countertop with flabby arms, she held a page of a magazine, mid-turn, her attention on me.

I ignored her, heading for the metal staircase. My first few steps clanged, announcing my presence, so I ran the rest of the way to Room 212 on tiptoe.

William answered before I had a chance to knock a second time.

"God, I messed up," he said when he saw me.

"No you didn't."

He stepped back, allowing me into the room. Exactly the scene I'd watched onscreen, but different. It disturbed me. Like I'd stepped into a movie, real, but not real. The still-made bed with the floral cover askew and the ripped hem, mocked our plans. Two-dimensional, they'd represented

253

background for a set-up-story with a prescribed, predictable ending. One that I'd been able to watch from a safe distance, on a sterile screen, the players performing for me, for my viewing and story-developing pleasure.

But here, the musty smells of old linens and stale cigarettes mixed with those of sweet perfume, reminding me that reality is often far different than that which we perceive.

"I should never have let her go," he said.

"You didn't have any choice."

He shot me a meaningful glance. "No?"

Having removed three of the cameras from their locations, William worked on the fourth. I got the impression he needed something to do with his hands, to work out whatever tension the night had wreaked upon him.

He knelt on the matted carpet to reach under the window, where he had difficulty extricating the final camera from within the tight alcove between the heating unit and the wall.

A couple of bumps, like a person punching a wall, came from the room next door. I turned my head that direction for a split-second. A silly move. Like I'd suddenly been given x-ray vision or something. Rhythmic thumpings, now accompanied by female exclamations, were barely muted by the thin wall between us. Amid whump-whumps and pleasured groans that neither of us could ignore, William looked up. Our eyes locked for an oh-so-brief moment.

It was strangely stirring.

And I think I held my breath.

The woman's voice shouted a couple of choice expletives. Then, sudden silence.

Just me and William and whatever thoughts might be traipsing through our minds at the moment.

"Cold in here," I said, glancing away, and then back.

He raised an eyebrow. "Yeah. I shut the radiator off when

I got in. The smell and the heat were too much. Plus," he nodded to the bookcase-sized contraption next to him, "listen."

He reached around, flipped up a hinged black cover and hit the "on" switch. The wheezing blast of heat surprised me to the point that I took a step back. Like a downtown musician gone bonkers on a set of upside-down kitchen pots, this baby rattled and shrieked to its own beat. So loud, the din was almost painful. Dust and fuzz and who-knows-what-else blew upward out of the top vents. Finishing with the last camera, William stood up, gave a wry smile, and shouted, "We wouldn't have been able to catch a single word over this thing."

"Shut that off," I said, straining to be heard, but by the time I got the sentence out, he'd already hit the switch.

The quiet was immediate, and welcome.

Another bang from the wall next door. Just one this time.

I looked that direction again. No way.

"Keep it quiet in there, wouldja?" a male voice shouted.

William rolled his eyes.

"You watch the whole thing?" he asked, placing the camera equipment pieces back into their carrying case.

"You were amazing," I said, sincerely. "I couldn't believe how much you got her to open up." I winced at my choice of words, but he didn't seem to notice.

"Oh, yeah," he said, his tone sarcastic. "Real good job. And for what?"

I heard clanging in the background again. Someone on the steps outside. Busy night.

"Listen," I said, "it's a place for us to start. My friend Maria on the police department might be able to . . ."

I stopped when I saw the look on his face.

"We'll have to deal with Bass first," he said. "I doubt he's too pleased."

"It wasn't your fault."

I'd left the door slightly ajar. Bass banged in at that moment, his face red. Possibly from the cold, possibly from the exertion of walking up the stairs, but most likely because he'd whipped himself into a frenzy. He wore the overcoat he'd shed earlier. Unbuttoned, he held the open flaps in place and twisted his neck, struggling against the half-in, half-out collar.

"What the hell happened here?"

Unruffled, William turned to me with a shrug. "What did I tell you?" Then, to Bass, he asked, "What took you so long? I'd have bet you'd be over here before Candy hit the bottom step."

"Okay, smartass. Why the hell didja let her go?"

"What did you expect me to do? Tie her up?"

"You should have pressed that issue about the money. About how much she gets, and how the call-out thing works. You handled her with kid gloves, for Christ's sake."

"*You* didn't have to look into her eyes."

Bass waved dismissively in front of William's face.

I heard William mutter under his breath.

"What?" Bass asked, "What did you say?"

"Nothing," William said. He walked around to the far side of the bed, where his coat lay.

Bass gesticulated, talking loudly. "We'll hardly be able to use any of this," he said. His voice reached fever pitch. "Didja even think about that before you let her walk out of here?"

"What about you? Did *you* see her? Did you hear *anything* she had to say?" William's eyes widened and I watched his body tense up. He hadn't put his coat on yet, and every muscle I could see had grown taut as he faced Bass.

256

"Uh-huh. And guess what? I checked with Jeff. Perfect sound. Perfect visual. Couldn't ask for a better recording. And for what? Nothing. Shit. Can't use any of it because you couldn't get her to cooperate."

Someone banged on the wall again. "Shut up!"

"Bass," I said, keeping my voice low, "let's talk about this later. You're upset, I understand that. But maybe we'll find some way to use the tape after all."

"Sure," he said, propping the door open while he spoke. "Some use." He turned to William. "Maybe you want a copy to keep at home; get your jollies with it."

"Bass," I said, "you're talking like an idiot."

He took a step back into the room. The door swung shut, but didn't close completely. "What do I have here? Nothing. Nothing." He started to pace. "You two get to have fun making goo-goo eyes and playing secret agent, and what do I get? Expenses up the ass and no story to justify them."

William shot a quick glance over to me, apparently for an explanation of the "goo-goo eyes" comment. I shrugged, like I had no idea.

Bass, not finished yet, kept pacing. Shouting now. "I trusted you. I trusted both of you—"

The door banged open again, with a swirl of cold air. "Is there a problem here?"

An enormous Hispanic man, six and a half feet tall, minimum three hundred pounds, with slicked back hair and one very long, very bushy eyebrow, took a couple of steps into the room. His black leather jacket had sleeve patches near his shoulders that said: "Security." The embroidered name on his chest said: "Nick." His round face moved slowly one way, then the other, his eyes taking in the three of us angry people.

I could only imagine what was going on his mind. What he might have thought this situation could be.

"We got complaints." He gave us each the once-over. "Noise. And the owner here says that you're abusing room privileges." He propped the door open with his extended right arm. From beneath it, behind him, I saw the woman from the front desk peeking at us.

"Her," the woman said, pointing. "She isn't the same girl who came earlier. That first one left right before she came in here." The woman's voice, like a rusty pipe, from a lifetime of cigarettes no doubt, took me aback. "There was no trouble till she got here."

The Hispanic man scratched his chin. "That true . . ." he looked at Bass with pity, then at me with contempt, "Ma'am?"

I'd about had it. "We're getting ready to leave. Right now, as a matter of fact. Will that be okay?"

Security-Nick glanced down at the woman. "What do you say, Ms. Carney?"

Right at the level of his armpit, she piped up, "All right. Just as long as nothing's broken." She swiveled her head, taking a quick survey of the room, as though making sure we hadn't played hot potato with any breakables. The still-made bed appeared to fluster her; she blinked several times before muttering, "I gotta get back to the desk anyway."

At least the interruption had silenced Bass's tirade. William hoisted the briefcase and we started to trudge out the door. The security man restrained William with a hand on his arm. "Whatcha got in there?"

"Personal stuff," William said.

"Drugs?"

"No," we all said in unison.

Oh, I bet that made us look innocent.

"Why don't you let me take a look for myself?"

"You have no jurisdiction," I said, standing closer to him.

I had no idea if he had jurisdiction or not, but I thought it sounded authoritative enough to bluff.

His wide face split into a grin. A mouthful of crowded, yellow teeth. "You know, we can make this easy, or we can make this hard."

Visions of the place swarming with police, because Nick here thought he had detained some big-time drug dealers, made me shudder. Just what we'd need, the *Midwest Focus* staff, a ménage à trois, headlining the morning news. Updates at four, six, and ten.

"Fine," I said.

William bounced the case on the bed, and snapped open the latches. Nick began to inch forward, keeping an eye on me and on Bass as he kept a hand poised over his right hip. It didn't look like he had a gun, so he either had pepper spray, or it was total affectation on his part. Whatever. I'm sure Bass and I looked like we could take him and he was real worried.

When he spied the cameras, each fitted into their respective gray Styrofoam casings, I watched his big black unibrow shoot up. "Ohhh . . ." he said, turning toward our little group, and shaking his head. "Man . . . That's sure some kinky shit, but Ms. Carney downstairs runs a nice little place here, you know? She don't want none of this seedy stuff going on. You take your cameras someplace else from now on, got it?"

Too tired to fight, too tired to argue, I said, "Sure."

He walked with us down to the parking lot, a bit more amiable now that we weren't drug dealers and looking at me with something akin to disbelief. Generally I didn't mind my wholesome image. But I hated to think that I came across as incapable of inspiring passion as the look on this fellow's face seemed to convey. So much for my Mata Hari aspirations.

William handed him the key. "Turn this in to old Ms.

Carney for me, would you, Chief? Spare her having to deal with us any more."

As Nick trotted off, William turned to us. "I'm outta here."

"What about the debriefing?"

"Not tonight, Bass." He made a dismissive gesture similar to the one Bass had given him upstairs.

"Listen, Armstrong, you screwed up big time in there. This is no time to be getting high and mighty with me."

"I told you, Bass. Not tonight." He spoke very slowly . . . I caught the glitter in William's eyes, a reflection of the overhead neon and anger. Definite anger.

"You'd better grow up, junior, if you want to succeed in this business," Bass said, waving a finger up near William's face. "And don't forget, I gave you a second chance, too."

William took a step back, but I sensed spring-coiled tension in the movement. He spoke quietly. "There's a difference between succeeding and exploiting. There are some lines I won't cross."

Bass snorted. "Well, when you've been in second place for as long as we have, maybe you'll grow a set of balls."

The insult seemed to stun William, and for a moment I thought he might punch Bass. I think he might have thought about it too. He looked at me, blushed, then handed me the suitcase and headed to his car without a backward glance. I followed him. "Will," I said. "Do you want to go somewhere?" I asked, knowing my words sounded weak even as they tripped over my tongue. "To talk about all this?"

He'd eased into the space created by holding the driver's side open just a bit, and now had both hands on the top of the door. His right hand gripped the ignition key. "Right now, I just want to go home."

"Isn't there anything I can—" I placed my hand over one of his.

He pulled away with a sharp movement. "Alex . . ."

I felt like an idiot. So I said nothing.

"If I stay a minute longer, I'm going to punch that little jerk's lights out." He shot me a smile, not a happy one. "And then where would I be? Two lawsuits in the same year: one sexual harassment, one physical assault. That wouldn't look so good on an unemployment form, would it?"

I nodded, bit my lip. As he reached out to grab the door handle, pulling it shut, I took my hand off the car's window frame. Seconds later, I watched his red tail lights turn—the opposite direction the gray van went.

Bass sidled up next to me, his breath making short cloud puffs ahead of him. "Where's he going?"

"Home."

"Damn," he said. "I wanted to go over this now." He stamped the ground.

"He already told you, not tonight."

"Yeah . . ." he let the word hang there, and I realized Bass knew even less what to do next than I did.

The night's stillness and the cold of the evening brought everything into sharp focus. Bass, his hands shoved deep into the pockets of his charcoal gray overcoat, shifted his weight from side to side, whether from impatience or cold, I didn't know. I got the distinct impression he waited for me to give him direction. Maybe he finally felt a little remorse over his ridiculous behavior up in the room.

"Beside the hair care segment, I don't know that I'll have a story for this week's show," I said, mostly to break the silence.

"No shit, Sherlock." Bass danced a bit more.

A beat-up Chevy pulled into the lot, cruising into an open

spot near the bright, all-window office. Only the guy got out. Young. White. Good-looking, with a solid build. An athlete. Late teens. When he opened the car door, the interior lights illuminated his female passenger, a slightly plump brunette, with straight, stringy hair, who blinked and grimaced until the door shut again. Twice tonight, I'd caught glimpses of people who would no doubt prefer to remain invisible. And right now, I wouldn't mind fading into the background, myself.

"Actually, I don't know if this story will be ready, ever."

Bass looked up at me, not in anger, not in impatience, but in utter denial. "Then you better start figuring out what will be ready. I've got a twenty-minute spot open for next Friday. Twenty minutes—one feature. And that sucker's got your name on it."

The young guy emerged from the motel office, wearing a triumphant grin and shaking a room key high in the air toward the car where his companion waited. He gave us a look of quizzical disinterest and motioned her out, like a dog trainer holding a treat aloft for his eager charge. She didn't disappoint, squirming out of the car to join him. Giggling, she attempted to take his arm. He leaned away, shaking her off. When she frowned and stopped walking, he said something to her. She glanced back at the car, as though having second thoughts, then gave a little shake and followed him again.

A maid emerged from a far corner of the motel, pushing a cleaning cart. She headed directly to the room William and Candy had occupied, and entered, presumably to tidy up. Not much work for her in there tonight. I found it curious that she didn't knock first. I couldn't imagine why she'd want to risk catching tardy patrons in *flagrante delicto*.

I wondered what Bass and I looked like to the young lovers

and the maid, or to anyone peering out the motel room windows. Maybe an odd-couple romance? Or maybe some chick trying to weasel a raise from her boss? I shook my head, grimacing at the thought.

Soft shushing sounds forewarned me seconds ahead of a cold blast. "Let's go," I said, hunching my shoulders against the wind.

Bass followed me across the wide avenue. Traffic had slowed markedly. I kept my head down as we crossed. Bass talked. I ignored him.

Until he said, "Use what we have."

I'd just cleared the evergreen dotted berm we'd used for concealment. My shoes made a tap-tapping sound on the asphalt parking lot. I stopped. "What?"

"You have to get your friend Sophie to agree to cooperate."

"Ain't gonna happen," I said. "She's convinced that both Milla and her brother were killed by someone in the organization. And after hearing this Katrina tonight . . . well . . . if they're right, Sophie would be stupid to appear on TV. It'd be like signing her own death warrant."

"Don't be so melodramatic. This is what William talked about, isn't it? The 'net'? We'll use as much as we can."

"Yeah, right. With no release?"

"We'll claim First Amendment. Broadcast all of it, but edited for time, you know. It'd be like exploding a bomb in a lake, and all the dead fish float to the top. Right?"

"That's not a net. That's unnecessary killing."

"I was being symbolical."

Symbolical? "Bass, you never cease to amaze me."

"Anyway, we're talking about fish."

"We're talking about people!" I said, my voice a notch below shouting. I moved in closer to his personal space. I knew he hated that.

He backed up. "We'd mask the girl's face . . ."

"Didn't you hear what she said? They'd kill her. She wasn't play-acting when she freaked out like that. She was terrified. Even if we mask her face, then what? She gets nailed because somebody recognizes her outfit? That pitiful jacket of hers?" Angry, I headed back toward my car. Bass stood at the passenger side, waiting for me to finish, I guess.

I shrugged, looking up at the night sky to quiet my frustration. The stars and moon were in sharp focus. Too bad my mind wasn't. "I'll talk to my friend Maria at the police department. She'll give us some idea of where to take this."

"Sure. I'll tell you exactly where the story will go, then." He blew out a breath so loud and forceful that its wispy grayness traveled across the entire top of the car before it dissipated. "Cops are gonna laugh you outta the station. What? You think they're going to give a shit about some Polock hustler?"

He was right, as much as I hated to admit it. In the darkness, I couldn't read his expression. Not that it mattered. I felt annoyance. At him, at myself, at the situation. At William for leaving so abruptly. "Well then, I don't know. I don't know anything."

That wasn't entirely true. An idea bubbled in my brain, but I didn't have the words for it, yet.

Bass got back in the car before I did. "Hurry up, would you? It's cold in here," he yammered at me as I stopped, just for a moment, before lowering myself into the driver's seat, giving my idea a chance to congeal.

Snapping the car door shut, I suppressed a chilly shudder. Bass had his leather-gloved hands wedged between his knees for warmth, like a little kid. It was cold, but not that cold.

I blew out two cloudy puffs of air, but didn't start the car.

"What are you waiting for?" he asked.

"What are you going to do with the footage we just recorded?"

He shook his head and looked out the window. "I don't know," he said with just enough resignation in his voice that I knew he understood that we couldn't air it. "Jeff's already headed back to the station. I'll get it from him Monday. I'll hold onto it, I suppose," he said, turning toward me again. "She might change her mind, you know."

"She might," I said. Not a chance, I thought. And even if she did, she'd thrown the phone numbers back at William. No way for her to contact us.

"And you're gonna work on getting Sophie to cooperate, right?"

"I'm going to work on the story, Bass. But I'm not guaranteeing that Sophie will be part of it."

He looked over at me and I saw weariness, anger, and shrewd impatience in his eyes. "You got till Tuesday. To wrap this one. I think you better start leaning on her."

Dejection settled over both of us. I felt it in a physical way, like a blanket of lead draped over my shoulders. Bass didn't push me to get moving, and I don't know how long I sat there before keying the ignition to head back.

Chapter Twenty-One

I spent a restless night wrangling with my covers. Too hot, too cold, too bumpy—the bed provided no comfort as memories from the night's adventure mingled with snippets of dreams, flickering through my brain like a poorly-edited movie. Odd combinations: Candy's walk, Bass's shouts, William's face. My own feelings of disquiet where he was concerned.

The late-night daydreams finally dissolved into sleep. But not a restful one. My mind replayed all the evening's images, and went on to create some new ones of its own. I woke up in the dark: alone, disoriented, and not knowing where I was. It had been so real.

Bass's warning still rang in my ears when the morning dawned. I went out to the back porch, my feet chilled on the cold linoleum, making quiet, sticky noises as I walked. My neighbor's backyard tree, now nearly bare, stood staunch in the late October wind. It reminded me of a scary movie, where branches come alive to reach in and grab and snatch and steal.

Lucy had always wanted a tree house there. With it not being our tree, my father had taken time to explain that we couldn't build a tree house. She claimed she understood, but I'd seen her wistful looks. That memory tugged at my heart, reminding me I hadn't called her. Worse, I hadn't even planned to see her this weekend. I knew she missed me. I missed her, too.

When she went to live there last month, I vowed that she'd

never become a statistic—one of those poor souls sent to live in a home by well-meaning relatives who never managed to visit. And yet, despite my best intentions, I'd made it there only once, so far. This goddamn story, Bass's goddamn pressure, and my own driving need to see it through were blinding me to everything else.

Conjuring up ambitious resolve, I decided I would spend next weekend down there. Once this story wrapped. Allowing my guilt to snowball, I toyed with the idea of taking a week off from work, bringing her home. Like old times. It would be a high energy, high tension week for me, but I knew Lucy would love it.

I leaned on the windowsill with the heels of my hands, elbows locked. Stretching, I stared at the tree. Everything was screwed up. I needed to regain control. Cloudy grayness cast a pall over the orange and yellow leaves caught in mini-vortices near the ground. Brown, gray, cold. The world felt as bleak as it looked.

After my second mug of coffee, I called Sophie.

A nun answered. "Just a moment."

A well-being check, I told myself. But not the truth.

Confession, they say, is good for the soul. I wanted to come clean, to tell her what we'd done the night before; but I also half-hoped that Katrina's story would spur Sophie to action. Action that could include her helping me with the story.

Guilt and unease made me chew my lip while I waited. I'd gotten involved because I wanted to help Sophie, I told myself. But that wasn't entirely true. I'd gotten involved because I couldn't let go of the Milla Voight story. I needed to push. Calling her now seemed like just another exploitative move. I cringed at what that said about me.

Sophie had tried to get out of the organization, but had

been beaten up for her efforts. Like a fly caught in a web, the sticky snare tightened around her with every move, keeping her unable to extricate herself. Everywhere she turned, she faced those who would be her friend, but only for a price.

Maybe I was no better, after all. I wanted this story. So badly, I could taste it. Cradling the phone on my shoulder as I rinsed my mug under the spray of warm water, I had a disturbing notion. What if this was it? What if this was as good as I got?

She came on the line, interrupting my mental self-flagellation.

"Alex," she said, in a breathless voice. "I going to Mass now, over here. I call you back later?"

A quick glance at my watch. I remembered the Sunday schedule from the days I used to attend Mass at Good Shepherd. Next one was at eight-thirty. About fifteen minutes from now. Father Trip usually said this one. I'd be late, even if I left this minute, but, what the heck.

"I'll meet you there," I said.

There was something almost soothing about the rote responses my mind directed my body through during the Mass. This early service had no choir, no music at all. Father Trip led the sung responses and hymns himself, and he winced at the flatness of his own voice at every opening note, exactly the way he'd done for as long as I could remember.

Afterward, he stood in the church's narthex, shaking hands with the thirty or so elderly parishioners. Sophie and I hung back, waiting for the small crowd to disperse.

If Father Trip had been shocked to see me, he gave no indication. Afraid of scaring me off from future visits, perhaps.

"You have a few minutes?" I asked him.

Sophie looked at me.

"Sure. Let me get changed out of my vestments," he said, holding his arms out to indicate the long, embroidered tunic he wore. "And I need to check on the altar servers. I'll be right back."

"Okay, we'll be in there."

I moved toward the "crying room," a small, sound-proof enclosure that could seat about ten devoted parents and their wailing babies at any given time. The crying room boasted a wide picture window view of the entire church and sound piped in through big speakers overhead. With the neighborhood demographics having changed so drastically over the past decade, I wondered if the room ever got used anymore.

I snagged one of the squeaky folding chairs and sat, more to calm my restlessness than anything else.

Sophie reminded me that she planned to return to her apartment the next morning, and I was in the midst of trying to convince her otherwise, when Father Trip returned.

Talking fast, I brought them up-to-date on the undercover operation gone wrong last night, and Katrina's reaction, which I knew would hit a nerve.

Father Trip took a seat. The three of us faced one another in a skewy triangle, on creaky chairs that echoed in this semi-darkened room. With all of us speaking in low tones, I felt the familiar tingle that always hit me when I used to kneel in the confessional and tell the good father what I'd done wrong that week.

Three Our Fathers, three Hail Marys. Standard penance. Less than that, and you felt pretty good about avoiding all those venial sins all week; more than that, and you knew you'd blown it.

Right now, having told him all about the prostitution ring, and having him realize that he'd been harboring a hooker in the parish convent without knowing it, made me believe that I was going to get the Good Book thrown at me. But Father Trip didn't react. Not outwardly, though I thought I detected sadness in his eyes.

"She tell you her real name?" Sophie stooped in her chair, as though the news had punched her in the gut.

"She did, and her story is perfect. It can make all the difference. Help you and all the other girls break free. If we can just get her permission to air it—"

Sophie's fingers massaged her temples. She stared at the floor, talking to herself. "If anyone ever find out that she give her name . . ." Sophie stood, glancing up toward the door. Exactly the way Katrina had the night before. "Oh, Alex," she said, her voice dropping, full of despair. "How could you do this?"

"Sophie, listen, you were right. They killed Milla. They killed your brother. I'm sure of it, now. But we need to prove it."

Sophie sat down again, as though all the bones in her body had turned to rubber. I decided to press.

"Do you know this Katrina? She's small. Tiny actually. Blond hair?"

A sigh. "I meet her coupla time."

Trying to keep anticipation out of my voice, I prompted, "You did?"

"She work for Lisa as cleaning lady. When she need hair done, she come in. No charge. That how we know she one of Lisa girls."

"Can you talk to her?" I kept my voice low, as gentle as possible. "If we can just get her to agree to come on camera—"

Sophie shook her head, with vehemence. Her large teeth bit hard on her lower lip. "She will never."

"What about you, Sophie?" I said, in measured tones. "Maybe *you* could?"

"I wrong, Alex. How you no understand?"

"After hearing Katrina, I know you were right."

Sophie looked like an animal, trapped and panicked. Nowhere to run. "Please," she said. "Please, you don't do no more."

I turned to Father Trip. "Were you able to find out anything about Father Bruno?"

Sophie asked, "Why?"

I pretended not to hear her. She leaned forward, to tap me on the arm—Father Trip hesitated before he answered. "I don't know what you were looking for, Alex. Bruno Creighter is well-respected, well-known, and every person I spoke with couldn't say enough about the man."

Sophie stopped tapping. Now she grabbed my arm, at the wrist. "Why you ask about Father Bruno?"

The time had come to lay my cards on the table. Even though I knew neither of them would like what they saw.

"Katrina said that a priest had come to her village. . . ." I let the thought hang.

Sophie said nothing, but Father Trip fixed me with a stare. I forgot how piercing his gaze could be. There were times he actually stopped a weekday Mass to chastise misbehaving school kids. Worked like fast magic to whip them back to attention.

I forged ahead. "This priest convinced her to return to America with him."

"So?" Sophie said, in a high voice. I could see her sit straighter, her back getting up. She wasn't a dumb girl; she knew where this was going.

I tried to keep my voice gentle. "She was talking about Father Bruno, wasn't she?"

Father Trip interceded. "Alex, everyone in the Archdiocese knows of Father Bruno's work to help bring young people to the States for a better life. He's sponsored more people, and achieved so much success, that they've created an award for him. For his work on behalf of humanity."

I chose my words. This almost hurt to say aloud, not for fear of sullying old Bruno's reputation, but for what damage I was about to do to both Father Trip and Sophie's outlook on life. "I'm convinced Father Bruno is involved in the prostitution organization. In a big way."

There. It was out.

I worried for Sophie. I worried for Father Trip. I hadn't exactly been forthright with him about Sophie's profession when I asked him to shelter her here. He was definitely getting an earful today.

Sophie stood up, rested her forehead against the window facing the church. The little bit of light that came into our small room from the doorway was enough to let me see the reflection of her face in the glass. She personified misery.

Father Trip shifted in his chair. Looking from Sophie to me again, he said, "I don't think so, Alex. A man of God wouldn't ever get involved in such a scheme."

"You wouldn't," I said. "But I believe *he* would."

I explained Father Bruno's "deal," to let me have a copy of my adoption folder in exchange for my silence on the story. At that revelation, Father Trip got up. Hands behind his back, he walked toward the doorway and stood, facing out.

Feeling icky and vulnerable, I stood, too.

After a moment, Father Trip cleared his throat. "I did find information about Emil."

Trying to keep my voice neutral, I said, "You did?"

I watched the back of his head nod.

"His full name's Emil Schober. And he's not the sort of individual I'd expect to find working in the church," he said, hesitation in his voice. "The few people I talked to shied away from the subject. It seems he falls in the 'let's not discuss it' category."

"Isn't that the attitude that got the Church in trouble not so long ago?"

When he turned to look at me, I wished I'd held my tongue. "Yes," he said, "you're absolutely right, and precisely why I pushed further than I originally thought necessary."

"I'm sorry," I said.

He didn't acknowledge my apology as he sat down once again. "I don't know how to rationalize it," he began. "Father Bruno has everything going for him in his position at Saint Dymphna's. He's the kind of priest the higher-ups point to and suggest we emulate. Emil appeared on the scene a couple of years ago."

"Who did you talk to?"

"Friends. Many of the fellows I attended the seminary with have their own friends among the higher-ups. As a grapevine, it's pretty reliable. And it seems our friend Emil has been in and out of jail a number of times, and continues to fight a losing battle with alcohol."

"And yet Bruno keeps him on?" I said.

Sophie waved a finger our direction. "Father Bruno tell me. Emil was homeless man downtown, but Father save him. Give him work and home. And he such a good priest, he won't turn a back on him now, even though he don't work no good."

Father Trip waited, took a breath, and then continued. "That's partially true, Sophie. Emil drinks. But the story about Bruno saving him from a life on the streets is not."

I canted my head, waited.

"I hate to give you this information, Alex, because I know you'll believe it feeds directly into the conclusions you've drawn. I beg you to be objective and to understand that connections don't always exist, even when it seems like they must."

Déjà vu. Didn't Bruno use almost identical logic on me yesterday?

"I won't jump to off-the-wall conclusions," I said. "I promise."

Father Trip blew out a breath. "Emil is a transplant. He worked on the West Coast till the late nineties, before he made his way here. While there, he got in trouble with the law. A lot."

"For?"

He hesitated, again.

"Pandering."

I jumped immediately to several conclusions, even though I'd promised not to.

Sophie looked at me quizzically. I explained in Polish.

"No-oo," she said.

"And you still believe Father Bruno is utterly oblivious to the fact that Sophie and the other girls he sponsored are . . ." About to say, "Selling their bodies," I veered to the safer, but less expressive, "Involved in this organization?"

Father Trip averted his gaze. "I don't know *what* to think, anymore. And maybe it's my own personal prejudice. None of those involved in the pedophile scandal were colleagues I knew personally. In some ways perhaps that's how it spiraled out of control the way it did; we didn't see the problem. It's the fault of all of us who simply can't conceive of one of our own doing the unthinkable."

"So you're telling me that you now think it's possible that Bruno is a major player in this little drama?"

Sophie stood up, nearly knocking her chair backward. It clanged against the empty one next to her. "No! I tell you no!"

"Then why would he want me to silence the story?" I asked her. "Why would he try to buy me off?"

She shook her head while I spoke. I was certain she hadn't heard a word, staying deaf with stubbornness. "He help me. I believe in him. My family believe in him. Matthew believe in him."

It was the sound of the bereaved trying to prove to themselves that their dead loved ones were alive, somehow. Convincing no one, yet trying, till it hurt.

I was still digesting Father Trip's words, when he continued, "I have a meeting at the Cardinal's residence a week from tomorrow," he said. "There will be several other people there who might have a better grasp of the situation."

"Next week?" I said, too sharply, betraying my frustration. Sophie, all set to move back to her apartment, would fall under their control again. Maybe she could give up, but I couldn't. Plus my story was due in William's hands this Tuesday. I didn't have time to wait.

"I know," Father Trip said, "but it would be uncharacteristic of me, and call undue attention to the situation, if I were to contact any of these men now."

"Listen," I said, "I had an idea last night, after everything went sour with Katrina."

Sophie, wary, watched me. I knew her emotions were running high and it disconcerted me momentarily. "You no put Katrina on TV?" she asked.

I shook my head. "The key here is to nail Father Bruno," I said. Reacting to Father Trip's stern look, I added, "*If* he's guilty, of course. There's a chance he's not."

Both waited, alert, for me to explain. The tiny, dark room gave me the sense of profound loss, like I'd stepped into a morass with no lifeline. But I plunged in. "I've got one of those little handheld tape recorders. All I have to do is get a couple of key pieces of information on tape, and we're in business."

I held my hand up to stop Sophie's protestation.

"What I want to do is go visit Father Bruno. I'm going to lay it all on the line. Ask him directly about his involvement, talk about the adoption folder, everything. I'm leaving nothing out this time. But this time, I'll set it up so that our friendly conversation is all on tape."

Sophie whimpered. "You no understand. He not guilty. If he find out, he gonna talk to Lisa. Then, they know I told you. Then they come for me. This time they find me."

"This time?" I asked.

Her eyes widened, and a scarlet flush washed over her face.

"Were they here, looking for you, Sophie?" Father Trip asked. "Why didn't you tell me?"

Like a cornered animal giving up the fight, her entire body slumped. "I talk to Helena. Lisa come talk to her to find me, and later she overhear some things, too. They wonder where I am. She lie for me. She tell them that I feel sad about Matthew and go visit relatives. Helena tell me that Lisa say that okay, but they want to make sure."

I prodded, "And . . . ?"

Sophie dropped her head. "Helena say that someone break into your house, to check if I there."

My jaw dropped, just a bit. Of course. They'd been looking for Sophie. Thank God, I hadn't taken her there. No wonder nothing was missing. They weren't looking for TVs or VCRs.

"Now I safe. I am," she said, with emphasis. Perhaps responding to the look on my face. "They don't know I hiding." Shiny wet wells pooled in her eyes. "I frightened."

"Sophie," I said, in as gentle a voice I could muster,

"Father Bruno knows. He as much admitted that. I just need to get proof, now. And then this will all be over."

"I talk with him, then," she said.

"No!" I said.

"He will listen to me. He will tell me the truth."

"Don't," I said. "Let me handle it."

"He not guilty. I know it."

"I wish I could believe that," I said, "for your sake more than anyone else's."

Father Trip leaned forward. "If what you suspect is true, Alex, I will support every effort to have him brought to justice. But let me reiterate. I don't know how to explain all you've discovered, but I'm confident that Father Bruno is not guilty. It just isn't possible."

I canted my head, silently expressing my skepticism.

He set his mouth in a line. "But if Emil is involved, then Father Bruno needs to be informed. From that viewpoint, I understand that you're doing what you have to do."

"I go back now," Sophie said, in a small voice. "I no feel good."

She walked out, her shoulders slumped, her feet making soft dragging noises on the floor.

Father Trip squeezed my shoulder as he stood up. "I'll be praying. For both of you."

Chapter Twenty-Two

Back home, my attempts to reach Bass netted me no more than opportunities to leave messages, which I did. Twice. I tried William, both at home and on his cell. No answer, no machine. "Damn," I said after the third try, pacing my kitchen like a caged animal. I wanted to pounce hard on Bruno, scratch him till he bled, and watch him cry out, begging for mercy.

Vindictive? Me? Nah, I was a pussycat.

A feral one.

A glance at my watch made me jumpier. Why couldn't I reach them? I needed someone to discuss this with, and though I would have much preferred William over Bass, at this point, I would take whomever I could get. The dead-end ringing on William's phone made me believe that he still harbored strong feelings of unpleasantness from last night's encounter. I was part of that. An integral part. I wondered if he knew it was me and simply chose to ignore the call. I probably shouldn't blame him. But I did, anyway.

Nearing noon. Father Bruno's last Mass at his parish ended soon. I'd been playing telephone wallflower for the past hour and a half, using the time to send William an e-mail, asking him to call as soon as possible. I gave him my home and cell phone numbers, even though I'm sure he had them. Just for expediency.

I dialed again. Waited again. Nothing.

"For crying out loud," I shouted at the phone. Like that would help.

But watched pots and phones neither boil nor ring, so I tapped out my frustration with piano fingers on my countertop, with thoughts of a backup plan. I knew I had to move. And I had to move today—before Sophie put herself back in harm's way, sitting like a clay pigeon in her apartment, content to let Father Bruno and his friends take aim when they would.

As the second hand of my kitchen clock marched with soft steps past the twelve, I decided not to wait any longer. Pulling out the list of numbers from the night before, I called Jeff on his cell phone, praying he had it turned on. He picked up on the second ring.

"Hello?"

Poor guy. So relieved to have reached him, I launched immediately into an explanation of what I needed.

"Whoa," he said. "Who is this? Alex?"

"Sorry, Jeff. Yeah."

"Slow down and tell me again what you're talking about."

By this point, I'd moved onto the back porch with the phone. Staring out the window, I caught a glimpse of the sun, attempting to burn its way through the heavy cloud cover. A good omen, I told myself. But the air on this cool porch after the welcoming warmth of the kitchen made me shiver.

I plotted my idea out to Jeff, told him about my plan to tape Father Bruno on my handheld recorder, and asked him about the viability of the plan. If he had any suggestions to help me get a quality recording, I'd be happy to hear them. Even though I didn't have a go-ahead from Bass, it wouldn't hurt to get all my technical ducks in a row.

"So you're going to go meet this guy? This priest? And you want to get a quality tape from a recorder you shove in your pocket?"

"Not going to work?" I asked.

"Hard to tell, without seeing the recorder," he said. "But I'm guessing it'd be a long shot. You'd get conversation. Maybe even most of it, but no chance you'd have recognizable voices. What you want is something more sophisticated."

"So what do I do?"

"Tell you what. I've got some time before I have to be out at O'Hare airport. I could set you up with some state-of-the-art stuff. When are you meeting him?"

"I haven't set it up, yet. It might not even materialize, but if it does, I want to be ready."

Silence for several long moments on his end. Then, "And you say that Bass has no idea that you're planning this?"

"I can't get a hold of him. I left him messages."

"Sticky," he said, then added, "I don't know the law all that well, but I think if you get caught wearing a wire without him knowing, it's your ass on the line, not the station's. It'd be better for you if Bass gave his blessing. Hang on one."

I did, but I listened, even as it came clear that he'd cupped his hand over the receiver. Another voice in the background, male. Brief conversation, none of which I could make out. Then Jeff returned.

"Sorry."

"Okay, so I don't officially have Bass's approval," I began. Jeff could be a stickler about things. I knew that. He treated every piece of the station's equipment as though it was his own. Good for the station, but bad for me if he was going to be a rule-monger about this. "But I need to do this. And if I can get it arranged for today, will you help me?"

He heaved what sounded like a thoughtful sigh. "Yeah. I got a couple of ideas. Call me back when you get your time squared away."

★ ★ ★ ★ ★

The next call went to Father Bruno. The surprised pleasure in his voice took me aback.

"I'm so happy to hear from you. I didn't get the chance to thank you for the delightful lunch yesterday."

I frowned at the phone. What? Did he think we were buddies now?

"I'm glad you enjoyed it," I said, blandly. "The reason for my call has to do with our discussion, as a matter of fact."

"Oh?" I heard the flick of a lighter. The Sacred Heart of Jesus one, no doubt. Then a long pull of breath.

"I've had a chance to think over your offer," I said.

He exhaled. "Have you, now?"

I couldn't make out anything from his reply. Inscrutable, at least over the phone. He might have been expecting it. But my call could just as easily have knocked him for a loop. A careful man, he let none of his reaction show.

"I did," I said, trying to project just the right balance of hesitation and eagerness. "I think I'd like to have a look at that folder. That is, if the option is still available?"

"As a matter of fact, I have it on my desk right here," he said. "A complete copy, which I'll be delighted to give to you. To keep. Assuming we both understand that my goal here is to protect my charges from malicious scandal."

"That's exactly what I want to discuss with you," I said.

"Excellent."

He inhaled again, and exhaled, as I chose my words. "Would you have time this afternoon?"

"This afternoon?" he chuckled. "A bit eager, are you Alex?"

I smiled. "A bit," I said.

If he only knew.

★ ★ ★ ★ ★

Tight timeframe. Jeff needed to be on his way to O'Hare Airport by four o'clock and it was already nearing one. Father Bruno had several meetings scheduled for the day; though he agreed to fit me in between appointments, I needed to meet him at a church on the north side.

When Jeff answered his cell phone, I jumped right in again. This time, at least, he was prepared for my call.

"Okay," he said, slowly, after I outlined the plan. "I won't have time to get down to the office, but I have equipment here that we can use. My own stuff. Actually, that'll work out better. If you get the proof and we use it, it's my property and somebody'll have to cough up some big bucks for it."

If Jeff could make a few extra dollars on this one, I was all for it, as long as I got my story. I remembered Bass saying how perfect the recording with Candy had come out. I wanted that kind of clarity. "Will we get clear reception?"

"Listen," he said, with a tiny bit of pride in his voice, "this isn't just my job, this is what I do. The stuff I've got here will kick ass."

His confidence encouraged me. We agreed on a meeting place and I hustled to get a few things done before I left.

Still no answer on Bass or William's phones. Annoyed the hell out of me. With limited time, I wrote them both quick, but explicit e-mails, explaining the plan and hoping neither would take offense that I moved forward without them. I tried calling Sophie too. Sister Mary Mildred told me that Sophie went back to her apartment to clean up, but she'd be back soon.

I called her there, but nothing. She could be en route, or she could just as easily be spending some time with Casimir and Mabel upstairs, getting herself settled again. And I didn't have time to waste tracking her down.

I knew I should wait until I talked with Bass, or William. But even if everything went perfectly, I needed to get this story finished. Pronto. Tuesday's deadline loomed. Even if I could corner Bruno, get him to admit to his guilt on tape, I still needed to follow up with my cop friend Maria, to wind up our story with a triumphant arrest. That all took time. Lots of time.

Ignoring the doubts dancing around in my head, I set off to meet Jeff.

Fullerton Avenue buzzed with activity. I exited northbound Lake Shore Drive to head west, passing nineteenth-century brownstones interspersed with brand-spanking new loft homes on both sides of the street. Traffic crawled, doing its peculiar city movement. Coasting forward while the distant traffic light was red, and coming to a complete stop whenever it turned green.

I pulled into the parking lot of a bustling Starbucks Coffee shop, lucky that a motorcycle pulled out, opening a spot for me. Jeff was there, waiting for me outside the glass doors, sipping from a steaming cup.

"Wow. Nice neighborhood," I said, as I got out of my car.

"Yeah," he answered, looking around as he nodded. "Moved up here about five years ago. My kid went off to college and I finally talked the wife into living somewhere with a little night life."

Not particularly interested, I still strove for polite. After all, the guy was helping me out on his day off. And without getting Bass's approval first. "And how does she like it up here?"

He grinned, half of his mouth turning up. "She doesn't. Which is why she spends so much time visiting her sister in Atlanta. She prefers a 'normal' life, whatever that is. And, hey, the weather ain't bad down there, either. 'Course, I can't really complain today. Nice day for October, isn't it?"

It was. A warm front had washed over the city in the wee hours of the morning, and I'd taken off the winter jacket, getting along with an open, zippered sweatshirt over a casual T-shirt. A gentle breeze kicked up my hair, and I noticed gray clouds in the distant, southerly horizon. It would cool off again, soon enough. "So, what do I need to do?" I asked, prodding a bit.

"C'mon, I've got it all over here."

We walked about fifteen steps to a blood red convertible. One of those cars that wears only a logo, no name, so that you have to know cars to figure out the brand. I was pretty sure it was a Mercedes. But it could have just as easily been a Beemer. Whatever. "Nice car," I said. Geez, maybe we were paying this guy too much. North side homes in this area didn't come cheap and neither did cars like this one.

"Belongs to a friend of mine," he said, using a handheld control to beep the trunk open. "He let me borrow it this morning. Here." He reached into a duffel bag and grabbed a slim plastic case. It reminded me of the kind of pencil pouches I used as a kid. Clear on one side, silver on the other. Reaching his narrow fingers into the top opening, he plucked at the device inside with a pinching motion and extracted a thin wire, with a tiny silver button at the top. Like a very long, flexible straight pin, it wobbled in the breeze as Jeff handled it.

"You're sure you're going to get this guy to admit to prostitution in the Catholic Church?" he asked, skepticism abundant. "Seems unlikely that a priest is in charge of something like this."

"He's not in charge," I said. "A woman named Lisa runs the show. But I know that Bruno is involved. If I can just get him to admit to a few key things . . ." I had no doubt about being able to get Bruno to admit to the bribery and to his complicity in the prostitution ring. Feeling like Scarlett O'Hara, I swore to myself that if I had to lie, cheat, steal . . . I'd figure out a way to make Bruno's admission work for me. To nail the bastard. Because it wasn't going to be over until the fat priest sang.

"Okay then," he said, "and like I said, this is my own personal equipment. It's actually superior to the stuff we have at the station. We used some high-quality stuff last night, but I have a few extras here. State-of-the-art."

"That's great."

"I mean," he said, blinking as he continued, "I like to keep up with the newest products. Guys my age are nosed out of the tech fields if we don't keep up. Okay, here, let me explain how this works."

Digging back into the duffel, he pulled out a roll of medical tape, the cross-hatched white kind that's almost clear. His eyes raked over my chest. "Good size," he said.

"What's a good size?"

"Your breasts."

He wasn't leering or making a joke, from what I could tell, but I didn't understand his comment, either. It rendered me momentarily speechless.

Squinting at my chest again now, he added, "I'd suggest you lose a layer . . . Too much fabric could interfere with the signal."

"What does the size of my chest have to do with anything?"

"Cleavage," he said, turning back toward the trunk for more pieces. "God's perfect invention for the eavesdropping trade. We hide the microphone in there, you'll get great reception."

His assessment of my build had been forthright, almost clinical, but the "we" part of setting up the microphone made me apprehensive. Producing a small metal box, about half the size of a pack of cigarettes, he explained the controls that took up its top. "This is the actual transmitter." He pointed. Turning the device over in his hand, he continued, "It'll pick up everything from the microphone—totally wireless. But you have to keep the transmitter within, say, arm's reach. You smoke?"

"No."

"You do, now," he said, pulling out a fake cigarette pack. "Isn't this sweet? Tuck the transmitter in here . . ." he opened the bottom of the open pack to demonstrate, then closed it again, "and see, it looks like ordinary cigs." He pointed the top toward me. Open, it looked like an almost-full pack of smokes. All half-cigarettes, they must have been glued in place because they didn't fall out when he gestured. "Stick this in your purse, keep the flap open. It's powerful enough to grab whatever you get and send it out to me. No one will ever know."

A steady stream of people walked by, some openly curious about our intense concentration directed at my chest. Others ignored us completely.

I looked skeptically at the long needle-y contraption. "I just tape this in place."

"Yeah," he said. "Try not to let the tip touch any fabric, or your bra or anything. Scratchy noises will interfere with your reception. And I'm assuming you won't have to shave your chest before you affix the tape." He grinned at his own joke. "I'm telling you . . . cleavage is the perfect hiding spot."

He taught me how to test the system myself before I left. I paid close attention and made him run through it twice, just to be sure. "This is a lot different than the mini-tapey device I was going to use."

He made me pull it out and show him.

"You know," he said, "this is a nice little recorder. Not great, but not bad." He made a so-so movement with his head. "It's your call, but I like redundancy. It wouldn't hurt to keep this running during your interview too. You never know when you need a backup."

I raised my eyebrows. Hadn't considered that idea. "Yeah, I'll do that. Sounds good."

"Where're we going anyway?"

I told him.

Making a face, he looked at the blood-red car again. "I don't think I want to take this baby into that neighborhood. My friend has a van that'll be perfect, though; I'll get that and meet you up there. Keep an eye out. It's white and a little beat up, with a blue company logo on the side. 'Cable Partners.' It'll blend right in."

"Okay," I said, checking my watch. Time would be tight.

"When you get what we need, I'll take off. I've got that stopoff at O'Hare when we're done, but then I'll head back to the office. Start making copies for you. Don't let any of the other techs at the station in on this, okay?"

"Why not?" I asked.

The question apparently took him by surprise. He answered, flustered. "I don't want anyone messing with my stuff," he said. Looking at his watch, he added. "Time to move."

Chapter Twenty-Three

What must have been a magnificent church at one time, now sat like a dethroned queen in the midst of the unwashed masses. Our Lady of Perpetual Sorrow had the architectural lines of those built in the very early part of the twentieth century. Heavy European influence. I spotted the massive structure when I was still four blocks away, its tall spire a majestic presence above the half-bare trees. I didn't notice its shabby condition till I got close; the façade looked like a jigsaw puzzle with scattered pieces missing, the cement steps sloping so far down and to the left that they reminded me of a funhouse attraction.

The church dwarfed the rundown buildings surrounding it; small homes, most were single level structures with broken siding, all in desperate need of paint and structural repairs. Or, better yet, a bulldozer.

After driving past it, I parked in the church's lot, a half block away. Small, asphalt, it hadn't been resurfaced in a decade, judging from its many cracks and indentations. The sun had disappeared behind new gray clouds, and a breeze had kicked up. Pulling my jacket on, I headed into the wind and toward the front of the church.

The Milla Voight–Matthew Breczyk story had taken over my life. I thought back and tried to recall the moment it happened. The moment I'd reached the point of no return. I knew without a doubt that if I were able to nail Bruno today, I'd have the key to all the answers I sought.

I reached in my jacket for the hundredth time since I left,

to verify that my microphone sat safe in place. Without time to go home and change, I'd been reduced to stripping off my T-shirt and now wore nothing under my hooded sweatshirt except my bra. Brought a whole new meaning to underwire, I thought, feeling half-naked. The tiny microphone head sat snug between my breasts, taped in place, deep enough that it couldn't be seen despite the sweatshirt's zipper front pulled low. No chance of any contact with fabric. Thank goodness we were meeting indoors, I thought. In this whistling wind, I'd never make out a word of the conversation when I got back.

Keeping my head down, negotiating the uneven sidewalk in front of battered and shuttered homes, I shivered. I saw nothing but dirt, everywhere—the tough, dusty kind, that kids didn't even like to play in because digging produced only misshapen, rocky lumps. I couldn't see a patch of grass anywhere, though that had little to do with the onslaught of fall. Tiny city parkways were nothing but hard earth, scuffed and littered with debris. Even the weeds had been frightened away, apparently. Beer cans and bottles, used diapers, and discarded piles of furniture were strewn everywhere.

A group of young men loitered across the street, the wind bringing their quiet conversation whipping past my ears so fast I couldn't make out anything except that they spoke in Spanish. The area made me nervous and as long as they ignored me, I'd ignore them.

Judging from the long white streaks running down its walls, pigeons made their home in the church's upper nooks. Now the cooing creatures circled a bit of food out front, eyeing me warily, waiting till I was less than a yard away before they flew off in a flapping huff. They'd been pecking at a fried chicken leg. I looked up at the rooftop they'd scattered to. "Cannibals," I scolded them.

The church's crazy house steps leaned downward to the left, and as my hand skimmed the cold iron banister, I felt it wiggle in response. A quick look around and I realized that any handicapped, wheelchair-bound parishioners would have a devil of time getting into the structure for Mass. And a slow-moving elder could easily get caught in this neighborhood's gang cross-fire. Thank goodness for Channel 50 and the *Mass for Shut-Ins*. Maybe by watching from home, they'd save their hides as well as their souls.

The church could have been quaint. Like a diamond in the rough, however, the setting robbed it of grandeur. Had it been magically transported to a sprawling meadow in England, with misty fog surrounding it at daybreak, there would be no end to the tourists lining up for a peek inside.

The huge front doors were recent additions. Tall, they were made of shiny ribbed steel. The uneven surface designed to fend off graffiti attacks, I supposed. Whoever decided on that had been only marginally successful. There were a couple of slogans that were distinguishable, if you tilted your head a certain way. "Jesus Loves the Savior Souls," and "Gangstas for God," were my two favorites.

"Hey, *chula*."

The raised voice came from across the street. Kitty-corner from the church. A group of four young men watched me, with apparent interest. I looked up. The speaker, a rangy Hispanic fellow, pushed himself up from leaning over the side of a rusty red pickup truck. Two of the others, both average in height and weight, kept their eyes on him, as he started to saunter around the vehicle. While I would call the fourth guy heavyset if I were trying to be polite, the truth was he was fat. Real fat. He sprawled across the pickup's open bed, one leg dangling off the back as he watched us, his mouth hanging open, making him look stupid.

Ignoring the gangbangers, I tugged at the closest, left-hand door. Locked.

The leader spoke again. "You too late for church, baby. Maybe you come over here, and I give you something to pray for?"

Loud guffaws from the three other guys.

The worst thing, I knew, was to show panic. All four of these guys sported the same red knit hats, worn tight against their heads. The fat guy's long wavy black hair strung out, messy, and long enough to drape over his shoulders.

Looking around the immediate area, I strained for the sight of a slightly beat-up white van. Nothing. I fixed the speaker with my best withering stare. "Thanks for the offer, but I'll take a rain check." Oh, that was smooth, I thought.

He turned toward his friends and shrugged. I knocked 'em over with my wit, yup. But the movement stalled him long enough for me to try the right-hand door.

Locked, too.

"You pretty for a *chica blanca,*" he said to me, starting across the street again. "Maybe I come over there, help you out?"

The three other fellows straightened, moving around from the far side of the pickup like a pack of wolves, gathering behind him. The big guy hoisted himself forward, gingerly putting weight on one foot. I could tell he didn't really want to move unless he had to.

"I'm fine, thanks," I said, feeling a tremor in my throat, hoping it didn't sound as bad as it felt.

So far the conversation wouldn't do more than make Jeff curious. I looked around again but still didn't see the white van he drove up here. I hoped he was near. We'd separated on Lake Shore Drive and I kept him apprised of my location as I drove, wishing we had come up with some sort of two-way communication. But with this wind whooshing about, whipping my hair, he might not be able to hear me, regardless.

Half a block away, my car wouldn't do me any good. Even if I tried to run for it, I'd still have to fumble with the keys and unlock the door before climbing in. I swore my next car would have automatic locks and one of those remote control openers.

If I lived long enough to get a next car.

Smiling through my rising panic as the fellows approached, shuffling across the street, as though they had all the time in the world, I thought twice about the fact that people thought gangbangers were basically stupid. I had no doubt that these fellows knew precisely what they were doing, exercising exquisite psychological torture on me, knowing I had nowhere to run and nothing to do except watch them get closer.

I widened my smile, as though dismissing them, as though utterly unafraid, but hearing the pounding of my heart in my ears, a panicked thrumming. I headed instead to the farthest set of doors.

On the way, I noticed it. A doorbell.

A doorbell on a church.

I didn't have time to analyze how very peculiar it was that there should be a doorbell sitting prim on the edge near the right center door, I just pushed it and hoped that the fact that it was cracked didn't mean it wasn't working.

I pushed it twice more, listening intently, hoping to hear the chimes reverberate in the church to send someone, anyone, scurrying over to answer my plea.

Nothing.

The four guys made it to my side of the building, and continued to shuffle my direction. As they neared, I noticed that all four of them wore long blue jeans flared out in wide bell-bottom hems, the right leg of which skimmed the sidewalk, fraying the dirty bottoms even further. White strings from the ragged fabric dragged behind them like tiny streamers across the filthy street. Their left cuffs were turned up, doubled, exposing the light blue inside of the denim. All four. All the left side. Some sort of gang allegiance, I figured. They spoke in Spanish, and something they said caused one of the two slimmer fellows to smile, showing a gold front tooth.

"Maybe she don' like dirty Mexicans," gold-tooth said, pronouncing the word "Me-hee-cans." "Wha' you think, Rico?"

Rico, the leader, made a long noise of assessment. "I think maybe you right. Maybe we should teach her a lesson, eh? Show her what a Latino lover can do for poor, lonely white babe. Give her big treat, eh?"

Three of the guys sported teardrop tattoos on their faces. The fat guy didn't have any, but the guys that did had at least two each. I'd heard once that teardrop tattoos signify a killing. If that was true, between the three of them, they'd killed seven.

Deep breath, I told myself.

Even if Jeff were nearby, he probably couldn't pick up their words, so he might not know the panic that rose in my chest, though I bet the microphone was close enough to pick up the thumps of my frantic heartbeat. I half-wanted Jeff to appear, but I knew that his presence could impede my plans. "I'm okay, Jeff," I said quietly, hoping he was listening.

Standing as close to the doorbell as I could, I leaned on it again, like a lifeline. At the same time, my mind raced, trying to come up with a plan to talk my way out of this confrontation.

"Hey, wait a minute," I said. Where this chutzpah was coming from was anybody's guess. I acted on pure instinct. The tougher prey appeared, the less appealing it was. Or so the Discovery Channel claimed, in their special on the hunting rituals of Amazon wildlife.

Rico got close enough that I could smell fried food on his clothes. His eyelashes, straight and black, sloped downward, giving his brown eyes a relaxed, yet no less sinister look. His dark leather jacket flapped open, and beneath it, despite the cold, he wore a silk shirt, unbuttoned halfway down. A heavy gold charm, Christ on the cross, hung right where the buttons started, in the center of his hairless chest.

The back of my brain chose this moment to chastise me for not ever investing in the pepper spray my friend Maria kept nagging me to buy. I could hear my own voice, tsk, tsking, telling me what a fool I'd been to wander about a known rough neighborhood without any means of self-protection.

"Yeah?" Rico said.

"You aren't gonna mess with me."

The four of them laughed. "Oh yeah? And why not?"

I fixed my gaze on the gold crucifix at Rico's chest as I tried desperately to remember the lessons from a single self-defense class I'd taken four years ago. Eyes, groin, knees. I thought those were the places I ought to target. Or maybe not. I couldn't remember. And that half-hour class had assumed a one-on-one attack. Not four on one.

The fat guy hung back a bit. Maybe three on one. "Holy ground," I said, opening my hands, a little. Not too wide. I wanted to keep all my body parts out of harm's way. "Bad karma. You don't want to mess with hurting folks on God's turf."

"Okay," he said, glancing around, as though the Almighty would choose that moment to wing him with a bolt of lightning or something. His three friends watched him, as though for guidance. He reached out and touched my hair, letting it fall around his fingers. "You right." He lifted the crucifix from his chest and touched it to his lips before turning to address the fat man. "We take her back to your place, eh Fernando?"

I sucked in a bit of breath.

Then I heard it.

A wonderful noise. A metallic chunking vibrated next to me as the front door opened.

I never thought I'd be so happy to see Father Bruno.

In a quick second, he assessed the situation. The four guys backed up. "Alex, is there a problem?" Bruno asked.

"Don't worry about it, Padre," Rico said. "This a domestic here. This my woman." He grabbed my arm so fast that I didn't notice Bruno opening the door wider, again.

"Let go, asshole," I said, forgetting my self-defense lesson as I tried to wriggle out of his grip. My foot shot out, and I almost connected with his knee. And I would have, if he hadn't backed up just then.

Turning around I saw the reason. Ro. Big old nasty Ro. The same gorilla who'd beat the bejeezus out of Sophie just a couple of days ago, had moved close, to stand next to me.

"Rico," he said in a low voice. "What'd I tell you about comin' on this side of the street?"

I could tell by the way Rico's grip loosened that the bold look he wore was mere bravado. When his three buddies started to move off, Rico shook my arm for attention. "Why don' you tell me you belong to this mother?"

Rico flung me away, muttering in indecipherable Spanish. I watched them depart, heading back to their perch around the red pickup truck.

"I'm sorry about that," Father Bruno said. "But I trust you're not the worse for wear?" He waited for my nod before continuing. "Good, let's get inside then. It's frigid out here." He extended his fleshy palm toward the open metal door. "After you."

Chapter Twenty-Four

I led our little three-person parade; Ro brought up the rear.

I hadn't expected *him* to be here. I knew Ro worked for Lisa. His presence sealed the connection I knew existed all along. I felt a tiny thrill of victory, but an unexpected sense of menace as well. The sooner I got the audiotaped proof, the better, and I'd be on my merry way.

Ro gave the door a mighty pull to shut it, and the sound of the heavy, solid metal swinging home reverberated throughout the empty church. Though dark, I could make out stairwells leading upward to the choir loft on either side of the vestibule where we stood.

Father Bruno rubbed his hands together. I'm sure he did so to generate heat, but in the low lighting, with just the creases of his face lit up by the small double-paned windows, it seemed a maniacal gesture. "There's a meeting room off the sacristy," he said by way of explanation, gesturing with his chin.

A set of double doors opened to the main church. Entering, I was reminded of a religious picture I saw once, of Jonah inside the whale. Graceful, curving wooden beams arched above, to meet at the peak of the ceiling, and though it was almost too dark to make out the very top of the church, the whole image was reminiscent of being inside the bones of the big sea mammal.

Tall, stained-glass windows lined both sides of the area, the dimness of the day outside causing their bright colors to meld and seem flat. Dark bars lined the pictures from the outside, in an effort to prevent vandals from breaking through the antique designs. Only slightly successful. There wasn't one single picture left unmarred by shattered glass. The light that came in from those open sections still wasn't bright enough to illuminate the huge area, though my eyes were beginning to adjust. I could make out the fact that both the ceiling and the walls had enormous patches of peeling paint. Just like the rundown homes outside, this place needed a makeover.

Our tapping shoes echoed as we made our way down the marble center aisle. I skimmed my bare hand over the worn tops of the varnished oak pews. If I hadn't been in church, I would have considered whistling. Just to convince the others that I was perfectly at ease, and had no fear whatsoever. Truth was, I wanted to convince myself. The semi-altercation outside had left my knees a little weak.

No one spoke until we neared the shadowed altar. Decorated in whites and golds, there was a plethora of plaster statues on both sides of the main center stage. Mary, the mother of Jesus, gazed down at me, one hand touching her own heart. From her placement, I knew she had to be the church's patron saint. Our Lady of Perpetual Sorrow. But she didn't look particularly unhappy. I would have characterized her expression as "content"—maybe even pleased. Joseph, her statue-husband, took up a prominent position at the far end of the area. In between were a couple of other saints and holy folks; some I could name, others I hadn't a clue.

A long, wide brass railing, two feet high, separated the altar area from the pews, with a wide red cushion running its length at the base. This used to be where folks would come to kneel to receive communion. Back in the "say it in Latin" days. Back when lay people never ventured into the back rooms of a church.

At the front, just past the first pew, Bruno grasped the railing, as his right knee skimmed the cushion in genuflection. Standing again, he veered right. "Over here," he said.

We passed another long shelf of holy people, these much smaller. One of them was the Good Shepherd, Jesus with a lamb around his neck and another at his feet, looking up adoringly. The patron of my home church, it gave me a moment's peace remembering that the Good Shepherd always watches out for his flock.

Of course, wasn't that simply to keep them safe from the wolves, so they could be slaughtered in sacrifice later?

"In here," Bruno said.

He opened a door off to the side. Invisible when shut, it blended into the wall, and had an indented handle. If he hadn't opened it to allow yellow light to spill out onto the cold floor, I never would have noticed it there.

Inside looked like a typical old-fashioned kitchen. Wacky place for it, I thought. Along the faded green walls, unadorned except for dirt streaks where someone might have tried to wash them once, were a sink on legs, a stove, a refrigerator, all looking like they should have been left out at the curb three decades ago. I caught sight of the ancient metal-edged oak table and chairs, my adoption folder, and a full ashtray centered atop it. Good, I thought. Shucking my coat, I sat down to launch into my charade.

"So, Father," I began, not wasting any time, "how about we get down to business?" I placed my purse, with the hidden handheld recorder set to voice activation, on the table next to me. Made sure the flap-top was open. Redundancy, Jeff had said. Worth the extra effort.

"My," he said, "aren't we eager all of a sudden? After our conversation at the restaurant the other day, I was certain you'd never come around to see the wisdom of my offer."

"I guess you could say I saw the light," I said forcing a smile, congratulating myself on my cleverness.

Bruno lowered himself into the chair opposite me. It protested his bulk, creaking until the large man had settled himself. Ro stood behind me, making me itchy, uncomfortable. But I tried to ignore that.

"Yes, I suppose you have." Bruno's piggy eyes ran up and down my face several times before he leaned back, causing the chair to creak again. Pulling a pack of cigarettes and his lighter out of the inside pocket of the black suit jacket he wore over his robes, he took his sweet time lighting up. His gaze seemed to settle on my breasts. The half-open sweatshirt was exposing not just a little bit of cleavage. I could feel myself blush. This guy was a priest? Seems like he was pretty selective about which rules he chose to follow and which he didn't.

Glancing over my shoulder, I shot a pointed look in Ro's direction. A wooden soldier, he stood expressionless, arms folded, in front of the door. Turning back to Bruno I lowered my voice. "Wouldn't it be better if we spoke alone?"

"Of course," Bruno said. He glanced over my head to the big man but didn't say a word. Moments later, I heard the soft whoosh of the door shutting and a tiny click of the latch.

"Thank you," I said. "I know he's one of Lisa's people. Sophie says he's Lisa's boyfriend." I waited, but Bruno neither confirmed nor denied the bait. My voice had dropped to a whisper in my excitement; remembering the audiotape, I raised it a few notches, and hoped Jeff was reading me loud and clear. "We have a lot to discuss." I leaned a bit further on the table, a shade closer to Bruno. I didn't want to miss a word.

"We do?"

"Let me ask you a couple questions, if you don't mind," I said, shooting him what I hoped came across as a conspiratorial look. "Since we're agreeing to this trade, it won't hurt for you to enlighten me a bit on a few things I'm curious about."

I heard the soft tick tick of the wall clock behind him, as a smile broke over his face. "What do you want to know, Alex?"

A tiny nag of doubt, vestiges of my "Catholic priests are near to God" upbringing, gave me a moment's pause. But I knew the truth. I just needed it spoken aloud so that others would know as well.

"Our agreement is that you'll give me this adoption information," I slid my eyes to the manila folder between us, "if I kill the story I've been following."

"Mm-hmm," he said.

"Sophie is a prostitute," I said.

He nodded.

Crap, I needed him to verbalize.

"You know that?"

He nodded again.

I had to stop asking yes or no questions. Some investigator I was turning out to be.

I tried again. "How long have you known?"

"About Sophie's line of work?"

I nodded, then caught myself. "Yeah. And the other girls."

"Some time."

I wracked my brain for a more clever approach. "Some time," I repeated. "How do you justify bringing new girls to Lisa when you know the kind of life they'll be facing?"

"Alex," he said, chastisement on his lips, "you really aren't seeing things clearly. You forget that our Father in heaven forgives."

"So you keep telling me," I said. I dipped down into the reservoir of desperation. "But what about Milla Voight and Matthew Breczyk?"

"What about them?" His tone was flippant. Like we were sharing a joke.

"I believe they were killed because they threatened to expose Lisa's organization."

"And?" he asked. One eyebrow snaked up, just a fraction of an inch.

"That doesn't bother you?" I asked, my voice climbing higher than I would have liked.

"Of course it bothers me," he said, both eyebrows furrowing in anger. "It more than bothers me, Alex." He pulled both hands, clasping, to his chest. "It hurts." He squeezed his hands together, so tightly that the pudgy stretched skin went white. "I knew both of them. I watched over them. They were like family to me."

"Then who murdered them?"

"Why are you asking me?"

"You know why, Father. I think you're up to your Roman collar in this mess."

"That's a very serious accusation," he said, with unnerving calm.

"Then you have to want to help me. Help Sophie. Help all of them."

"I already do help them," he said. "Any way I possibly can." His gaze dropped. It took a moment for it to register that he was staring at my cleavage again. An instantaneous burst of adrenaline shot through me, wondering if the mike had become visible. Frozen in fear, I didn't move.

Then he gave a sigh, and raised his eyes to meet mine again. "I enjoy helping young people. But you're here on business, unfortunately."

Realization of his meaning washed over me with a shudder of disgust.

A fear trilled in my heart. Could it be that he'd been one of

Lisa's pawns so long that he could now so cavalierly ignore his vows? I knew the fervor with which my good friend, Father Trip, embraced his lifestyle, embraced all that the church taught about life and morals and God's will. Even if Bruno wasn't half the priest Father Trip was, there still had to be some glimmer of goodness in him. He'd brought these girls into a life of prostitution. Perhaps not knowingly at first, but now, he must be aware. Surely he felt remorse.

"Give me Lisa," I said. "Give me enough to shut her organization down and put her away, and I promise I'll do everything I can to keep you and the church out of the story."

His mouth went through a series of gyrations, as though he wanted to laugh but struggled to be polite, since I wasn't in on the joke.

"Pride before the fall," he said.

"What?"

His hands gestured, in a smooth, practiced way, as though to encompass the entire room, the entire situation. "You are so supremely confident you have all this figured out, don't you?" he asked, his eyes squeezing in condescension.

"I do have this figured out," I said. "Trust me. I can help you. Together we can put an end to Lisa's group."

"Trust you?"

"Yes." I took a breath before continuing. "If I play this right, in our feature, I can protect both you and the girls. I'm serious. With what you know and with what I know, we can assemble a story, and perhaps even a case against Lisa and Ro for the murders of Matthew and Milla."

"With what I know, and what you know," he repeated.

"Yes," I said, trying not to clench my teeth as I spoke.

"What is it you think you know?"

I heaved a long sigh of frustration, and stared at the corner of the room near the ceiling, where a spider had spun a thick web. Several dark shapes dangled in the fragile pattern, leading me to believe he'd been successful in trapping his prey.

"Alex?"

My eyes flicked back to meet his.

He tapped the ash-laden end of his cigarette in the tray, then brought it to his lips again. "Take the folder." I heard the smoke escape with his words.

I looked at it, weighing my choices. But I couldn't take it. Not yet. He hadn't said nearly enough. His beady little eyes watched me as I struggled to rephrase my question. He hadn't admitted to anything. I needed a whole lot more. And I needed it fast. This interview wasn't going the way I'd hoped. He took another drag on his cigarette as I opened my mouth to start my next question. But he interrupted.

"What's stopping you, Alex?" he asked, blowing smoke out his nostrils.

I looked at him.

"The file is here, just waiting for you to grab it and go." He shrugged, and I swore I saw a flicker of dark amusement in his eyes.

"Listen," I said, "I'm offering you a chance to tell the truth. Then walk away. And let all the girls you've brought over here walk away too."

"So what you're proposing here, is to offer me *tabula rasa?*" He took another long drag of his cigarette, and exhaled off to the side. The smell of the burning tobacco and the gray cloud that began to envelop us started a tickle in the back of my throat.

"A clean slate? Yeah. That's exactly what I'm offering," I said. The fact that he seemed willing to talk now, encouraged me. "A new beginning. And," I smiled, bold enough now to make a joke, "you know what they say about confession being good for the soul. Why don't you let me in on all of it? It'll make you feel better."

He nodded. "Now that we're alone," Bruno said, sitting up, "I do have a few things I can tell you." He stubbed out his cigarette in the ashtray and leaned forward on his forearms, his voice low.

I moved forward, mirroring his position, bringing my head down near his, to hear, and, more importantly, to bring my chest near enough to his voice so that the microphone wouldn't miss any word of it. "Good," I said, attempting to keep my excitement level under control. About time.

He stared down at my chest again for several seconds, then he smiled as his eyes met mine.

"You're right, on several counts."

"I am?"

"Yes, of course." He tilted his head. "You seem surprised."

My mouth opened but no words popped out. His admission came too fast. I blinked, then asked, "So, you're telling me that you recruit young people from poor villages in Poland—"

He interrupted. "And other places as well."

I hated the tiny stammer in my voice as I continued, "Okay. You recruit these girls and bring them to Lisa. She puts them to work as prostitutes. And what, she pays you? Offers you a percentage?"

Bruno's eyes glittered. Amusement, again. But he didn't answer.

"How . . ." I asked, "how does a priest get involved in this sort of scheme?" I sat back a little—it was an involuntary movement, but one that took the microphone further away. Remembering, I scooted forward again and shook my head, instead. "This goes against everything the church teaches.

Everything the church stands for. I can't understand how a man who's taken religious vows can be involved in such . . . such . . . vile activities."

"Ah, Alex. I told you once that you weren't looking at it the right way."

The stammer in my voice was gone. Anger bubbled up in my chest, and I worried for a moment that my heartbeat would drown out our conversation on the tape. "There is no other way."

"Yes, there is." He pushed the folder closer toward me again. "And so, here we are. *Tabula rasa.* I have fulfilled my part of the bargain, have I not?"

I looked down at the slim manila file under his splayed fingers. Tiny bits of whitened skin brightened his knuckles, making them stand out on his reddened hand. Tension. He pressed down harder than I would have thought necessary.

"I guess you have," I said. I tried to slide the file out from beneath his pressed hand, but he held fast. "And now I'll take this and be on my way." Maybe it would be enough. I couldn't wait to hear the tape. I thought of Jeff outside. And I hoped he'd gotten it all.

Giving me a peculiar look, Bruno lifted his hand straight up, allowing it to hover for a second over the folder. "Be my guest," he said.

"Thanks." In one motion, I'd stood up, pulled the folder to my chest and grabbed my coat from the back of the chair. Sliding my arm through the sleeves, I headed for the door.

"Why don't you open the file now? Read it before you leave?"

I hesitated. "You said it was mine to keep."

"I did."

"Then I'll read it at home." I shot him an insincere

smile and began moving again.

"Alex," he said.

I turned.

"Open it now."

I gave him a withering glance, as though he was a fool to doubt my intentions. "Why?"

"Because I want to see the look on your face," he said with a grin. "I enjoy it when things come together as well as they have today. I revel in it."

"Thanks, but I'll wait."

His smile faded. "Humor me," he said.

My conscience prickled with the thought that I had just made a deal—given my word. I promised that if I got my adoption information, I'd hold back on the prostitution story. The folder felt tingly in my hands. I had no intention to look inside. In my own convoluted logic, that allowed me to continue my investigation without sacrificing my ethics.

Facing Bruno now, I had to reassess. His calm demeanor belied anger deep inside. I could almost see it simmering out of him. He doubted my sincerity. With good reason, I might add. But the fact remained that I needed to prove my good intentions.

"Fine," I said. I promised myself I wouldn't really read the information. That I would focus on something other than the information that tempted me more than anything else in the world. I faltered a moment, knowing how much I wanted this information, trying to rationalize a way for me to have my information and nail Bruno, too.

With a short sigh, as though impatient to get moving, I opened the file.

A blank page stared up at me.

I looked at Bruno. "What is this?"

"I guess you could call it my version of *tabula rasa*," he said. "A blank slate."

"I don't understand."

"Yes, you do."

Beads of perspiration burst out from under my arms and down my back, leaving trails of sweat that suffered immediate chill, despite being covered by my big down jacket.

"No," I said, unable to come up with a better response. "I don't."

"I know."

"You know . . . ?" I asked. "What?"

"I know why you're here."

The room became close all of a sudden. From the look in his eyes, I knew he didn't mean for the supposed trade. I was momentarily speechless.

"Give me your recorder."

"Excuse me?"

"Don't play coy, Alex," he said. "You're not good at it."

I moved, bumping the chair, the sound of the heavy wooden seat sliding against the tile, too loud in the small room. How did he know about the recorder? Or could it be just a lucky guess? Bluff time, I thought. This meeting had gone way off track, and I knew there was no redeeming it. Not at this point.

"I thought we were here for a trade," I said, keeping my voice even. "You obviously have some other agenda going on. And I don't need to be part of it."

"Sit down."

"Sorry," I said, moving again toward the door. "Give me a call when you're ready to do business. This has been a waste of my time."

All I could think of was getting the hell out before Ro came back.

"Aren't you the least bit curious?" he asked, as my hand grabbed the inner doorknob.

I turned. "About what?"

"About how I knew you were planning to tape our conversation?"

I had enough. Time to go. I thought about Rico and his buddies outside. Which was the frying pan and which the fire? I wondered. I'd take my chances and beat a path to the car. And I still had Jeff as a backup. If worse came to worse, he could call for help.

I jerked the door open and was immediately halted in my tracks. Sophie, her bright blue eyes wet, and surrounded by circles of red welts, stood before me, blocking my path. Ro loomed behind her, giving her a shove that brought me back into the room, stumbling backwards.

I flashed my attention towards Bruno. He hadn't moved; his large arms still rested on the table, and he watched me with interest from his chair. He'd lit another cigarette and puffed on it, the picture of relaxation. He oozed serenity. Of course. He held the cards now.

I'd been a fool.

"Now that's loyalty, Alex," Bruno said. "My dear child, Sophie, came to visit me this morning at my parish, so convinced of my innocence, so willing to protect me, that it took almost no effort to pull details of your plan out of her."

She'd been crying quietly, with soft ragged pulls of breath, but when Bruno spoke, she began to blubber in earnest, sobbing out an apology. Till Ro clamped a big hand around her mouth.

"One more yelp out of you and I'll off you right here. Understand?"

Her bright blue eyes widened over the edge of his callused hand. She nodded, and when he let go, she hiccupped softly, her gaze flicking in fear toward the gorilla-man with every inadvertent sound she made.

Bruno pulled himself upright.

"You thought you were so clever, didn't you? I warned you, didn't I? You could have taken the information . . ." he tapped the folder again, ". . . the real information—when I offered it. Taken it freely and lived a long, happy life in the company of both your families. But you couldn't walk away, could you?"

I'd expected to be right about Bruno. I'd expected him to play into my hands just like bad guys do in books and movies. To give me Lisa's head on the proverbial silver platter, just because I asked nicely. But I wasn't any type of private investigator, and I'd blown it. The elation I hoped for when this story broke seemed almost a childish dream, an expectation that because I wished it, it would be so.

"There are too many people who knew I was coming here," I said, conjuring up as much boldness as I could manage. Hearing the tiny tremor in my voice. "I was the voyager."

"What?" he said, his face twisting into a puzzled frown.

"Voyager" had been our emergency word for the no-tell motel stakeout last night. I never thought to come up with a new one for today, so smug with my own cleverness. So sure that everything would go just as I intended it. But all of a sudden the water swirled over my head. I was in too deep to get myself out. "Voyager," I said again, more clearly this time, and louder. "I'm the one who ventured out here. But lots of people know about it. It would be a mistake to hurt us."

"Don't worry," he said. "There's a plan."

"What about the priest from this parish? Doesn't he know we're here? Won't that raise questions?"

"He's on vacation, as a matter of fact," Bruno said, a grin starting, his wide, full lips spreading to reveal tobacco-stained teeth. "Left me to look after the congregation in his absence," Bruno said standing now, his gaze flicking over my head again. "Rodero?"

"Yes, sir?"

"Perhaps you'll relieve our reporter friend here of her recording device."

Ro leered, stepping around Sophie reaching for me. I moved back, grabbing my purse.

"Okay," I said, "don't touch me." I pulled my handheld tape recorder out from the side pocket. "There. You happy?"

Bruno picked it up, pressed a few buttons and we all heard a playback of the last several seconds' conversation. Nice and clear. He handed it to Ro, who smashed it in half against the corner countertop.

"Did you really think such a crude attempt to trap me would work?" Bruno asked, shaking his head, smiling in a way that made me want to tear at his face. He made a "tsk" noise, then turned back to Ro. "Now let's make sure she isn't carrying any other surprises."

Ro came at me, wearing the first grin I'd ever seen on his bruiser face. I dodged around the chair, keeping it between us.

Bruno made the "tsk" noise again.

Anytime now, Jeff.

Ro made a move to his left. Reacting, I ducked to his right, but he'd faked me out. He nabbed my arm almost effortlessly, dragging me past the chair, which toppled to the ground with a wooden clatter. Tight, in a vise-grip, I felt the squeeze of his fingers into the fleshy part of my upper arm, but I bit my lip rather than cry out.

Holding me high enough that I had to stand on tip-toe, he

used his left hand to roam. I tried to distance myself from his thorough search, his rough groping. I squirmed, keeping my eyes averted, fighting hot, stinging tears of frustration as his big hands explored, squeezed, and wandered. "There are parts of this job I really enjoy," he whispered, close to my ear.

Like a trapped animal, I fought, my arms and legs flailing out, scratching, kicking, screaming. But with my every movement, his grip got tighter, his behavior more cruel, until he swung me out, crack-the-whip style, throwing me tumbling backwards over the fallen chair.

I started to scramble up, but Ro grabbed me again. The right side of my face caught the edge of the table as he pulled me roughly to my feet. My flesh scraped against the metal corner and I winced at both the sound of ripping skin, and the searing pain that followed almost immediately. Warmth poured out from a gash on my cheek. I reached to touch the tender area, but Ro pinned my arms.

He held me close enough that I felt his hot breath on my neck. My fighting had no effect on the steadiness of his breathing and I had no hope against him. I clenched my teeth, enduring violation like I'd never known before, watching long viscous drops of my blood leak to the floor.

When his hands fumbled at my breasts again, all I could do was hope that the microphone's minuscule size would prevent its detection. "Okay. Enough already," I said, fighting harder, trying to keep his fingers from exploring beneath my clothes. "How many times you need to check the same place?"

Bruno watched the skirmish with wide, eager eyes, pulling his hands out from beneath his robes as Ro finally released me. I glared at him, taking deep breaths to keep control. Where the hell was Jeff?

"Were you able to get in touch with Emil?" Bruno asked

Ro, as the big guy pushed me aside to begin searching my purse. He pulled out latex gloves to do the job, the implication of which frightened me more than anything so far. I held my breath, and took my seat again at the table, blocking Bruno's view of the bag. *C'mon Jeff.* Bruno knew I was no smoker. The fake cigarettes would be a dead giveaway.

Sophie had been terrified into silence, it seemed. She sat in a far corner chair, watching us, abject horror frozen on her pale face. I turned away from her, angry.

Not angry. Furious.

Ro stopped pawing through the bag's cavernous interior long enough to reply. "No answer at the rectory."

Bruno stuck a cigarette between his lips, pulling the Sacred Heart of Jesus lighter out of his pants pocket in a smooth motion. "Damn idiot. Probably soused up again." He stood with his back to us, as Ro resumed his examination. He spent extra time on a couple of items that seemed to interest him: my mini-flashlight, a pocketknife, and some dental floss. Great tools to effect an escape, I thought wryly.

I pulled a few tissues out from the side pocket, shooting Ro a look that dared him to stop me. They were soaked within seconds of contact with my cheek, but I held them there, unwilling to get up to look for replacements until Ro finished his search.

The fact that Jeff hadn't made an appearance, despite my obvious use of the word "Voyager," hadn't escaped my notice. Maybe he was taking his time, calling in the police . . . but maybe they couldn't just storm in. Some law or regulation might prevent their involvement without probable cause. Still . . .

"It'll be dark enough soon," Bruno said, almost to himself. "The devil does his best work in the dark." His head snapped Ro's direction. "I want her car brought around the back. We'll need it later."

Ro dug my keys out, and shoved them into his pocket. "Yes, sir."

"Make sure no one sees you. Anybody else beside those gangbangers out there?"

"Yeah. Some white guy in a van sitting out there, smoking."

Bruno's eyes flashed toward me. "Friend of hers?"

Ro considered that. "Nah. Cable guy or something. I had Rico and the boys chase him off."

My heart dropped.

Jeff.

Gone. And probably before there had been any indication of trouble here. My mind blanked for a long moment.

Ro spoke up again. "We could get Rico or one of them to drive the car, you know."

Bruno stared at us without expression. "No, I don't want them involved in this one. Too risky. They'll sell us out in a heartbeat when they get picked up for something else. I'll tell Lisa to stop for Emil along the way."

From the way Ro nodded, my big mistake became obvious. It was Bruno who called the shots. Not Lisa. She was his pawn, rather than the other way around. I closed my eyes in frustration. I'd let my Catholic-ness blind me. How could I have been so stupid to have missed it?

"Put them in the basement for now," Bruno said, glaring at Sophie and me. Our eyes locked for a moment and he grinned malevolently.

He made a sign of the cross in the air over our heads. "Not to worry," he said, his eyes triumphant. "At your funerals, I will be certain to speak of your glory. Because, as Peter says, when the Shepherd appears, you will receive the crown of glory that will never fade away."

Chapter Twenty-Five

From my vantage point in the back seat of Lisa's SUV I couldn't see the speedometer, but I could tell from surrounding traffic that she stayed well within the posted limits. She religiously used her turn signal whenever changing lanes and maintained a sedate pace on the right, switching only to the left when it became necessary to pass either a truck or an elderly driver going twenty miles under the limit. I suspected she was less concerned with qualifying for a safe driver's award than she was hoping to remain unobtrusive and avoid getting pulled over. Considering that we didn't crash, get a flat tire, or that the steely gun Ro pointed at us from his twisted perch in the SUV's passenger seat didn't go off, the drive south on the Dan Ryan Expressway was uneventful.

Uneventful.

The word stung.

Because all of a sudden, it described my life. All too well.

I spent the ride with a wad of napkins taken from the church kitchen pressed against my cheek, staring out the side window, seeing nothing but the barrenness of the landscape as a backdrop to the barrenness of my life. Wondering at what could have been. Replaying old regrets—so many. Too many. Wishing I'd done more, seen more, experienced more.

The cloud cover from the afternoon had cleared and pinpoints of bright light twinkled above. A full moon, in such sharp focus that I could see the man in it watching over us, glinted almost silver. I breathed a shuddery sigh and wondered if I'd ever see the sun rise over the lake again.

I kept a Mark Twain quote taped to the wall next to my desk and I thought about it now. He once said that we would be more disappointed by the things that we didn't do than by the ones we did. He urged us to sail away from the safe harbor, to explore, to dream, to discover.

I'd always pictured myself as an eighty-year-old woman in a rocking chair, looking back on my life with a smile of satisfaction. Eighty always seemed so far-off. So distant. I was convinced I had plenty of time to make those discoveries, to take those chances.

I felt my life rush forward now, like the surroundings outside the window. Blurred, bleak, forgettable. Biting my lip, I fought the hard lump of ache working its way up my throat, lodging hot behind my eyes.

They'd do an autopsy, of course. A mental image of my naked body lying cold under harsh lights made me take a sharp breath. Then the scene in my mind shifted, and all I could see were my parents standing over me, Lucy asking what happened. My face caked with dead person makeup, my lips sewn tight, and my hands crossed on my abdomen. I saw the people come visit. I watched the mourners asking why and how. And—William. I never took that chance, either. I felt stabbing pain from all I missed. And in that moment I knew Mark Twain was right. I regretted all the chances I hadn't taken, far more than any mistakes I'd made. Except this one, of course.

Lisa drove with intensity. Her face flashed bright-dark, bright-dark as we zipped south beneath the pattern of street lights. Apart from an occasional glance at her rearview mirror, presumably to verify that Emil still followed in my Escort, she barely moved, and didn't speak. Her hands, gripping the steering wheel at firm ten- and two-o'clock positions, and her ramrod straight back, confirmed what I picked up earlier in her discussion with Bruno. She wanted no part of this excursion.

When Lisa and Emil first arrived, Ro and Bruno shepherded us out the back door of the church, through an alley of darkness, to three waiting cars.

Ro pushed us toward Lisa's deep green Mercedes SUV. At his shove, Sophie stumbled, skinning her knee on the ground. "Stupid bitch," Ro said, pulling her up by the collar of her jacket and throwing her into the back seat.

We looked like a troupe of stage players, performing in a lonely circle of light from one faint street lamp above. Desolate, and quiet, I hoped for a curious neighbor to come investigate what these white folks were doing in a back alley at night. But nothing moved, except for an occasional dark shadow, scurrying and scratching, near the bases of the garbage cans.

Lisa wore a black ensemble. Shoes, pants, shirt, jacket. With her dark hair, she was nearly invisible in the low light. "Hey!" she said, her voice loud, but swallowed up by the area's emptiness.

Just as he grabbed me, Ro stopped.

"No way," Lisa had said to Bruno. "They are not getting in my car."

I'd hoped Sophie would take advantage of the distraction and make a break out the SUV's far door. But instead she just sat there, mouth agape, unable to do more than watch and breathe, little post-cry hiccups punctuating the silence as Bruno raised an eyebrow in Lisa's direction.

If Ro hadn't held me by the arm, I would have run. *Don't get in the car. Don't get in the car.* I repeated it to myself like a mantra.

"I've decided. You will drive. Emil will follow." Bruno's

voice took on a tone of authority.

She blinked at him several times. "What about you? What will you be doing?"

"I have a pressing dinner engagement with the Cardinal in . . ." he checked his watch, pressing a small button to make the face light up iridescent green in the dim light, "thirty minutes." He held up accompanying fingers. "Two very good reasons. My parish needs assistance and I need an alibi."

Lisa ran her hand back along her head, to pull her hair back with her left hand, holding it ponytail-fashion behind her. Not the move of a power-wielding madame—this was a nervous gesture. "I'm not going to be part of this," she said. "I never said I'd be part of killing anyone."

Bruno stepped close, invading her space. "You . . ." he said. Lisa was not a small woman, but Bruno loomed large before her. His big fingers caressed, moving from her temple along her hairline, down into the neck of her open jacket. They lingered there, and he smiled. "Do you remember what happened last time you told me 'no'?"

In the night glitter-light from the pale, overhead street lamp, I watched Lisa's gaze change. I'd swear she went from rebellion to hatred, before finally dissolving into resignation. Her hand dropped from holding her frizzy hair. He tightened his fingers at her neck.

"Do you?"

With a nod, she broke away.

Giving a self-satisfied smile, Bruno looked over at Ro, who shoved me unceremoniously into the back seat alongside Sophie. "Don't bother trying to get out," he said. "Child protection locks."

I tried anyway. He was right.

Bruno went over details with Ro, Lisa listening from the open driver's side door. I strained to hear, too. Sophie, clutching my arm, started again with soft mewls of panic. With her face so close to mine, she nearly drowned out Bruno's words.

"Stop it," I hissed at her, shaking my arm to disengage her grasp. I resisted the urge to shove her away, but my anger bubbled up, boiling over. I was wrong about Bruno's position. While I'd harbored suspicions he wasn't an unwitting participant, I hadn't ever seen him as the mastermind. I'd never for a moment believed him capable of killing. What an idiot I'd been, thinking I could talk him into giving up information on Lisa and the organization. I'd been blinded from the start by my own priest preconceptions, and Sophie's unwavering devotion to him.

"How could you do this, Sophie?" White hot lights flashed in my head as I whisper-shouted, but I knew I couldn't stop the tumble of words as they spewed out my mouth. "You trusted him," I pointed to Bruno, "and now what? Matthew's dead and they're going to kill us, too. How could you do this? Why did you go to him?"

A long, deep shudder racked through Sophie's body. I watched grief and pain come over her face as she opened her mouth to speak. Nothing came out. The poor girl stiffened, then shook, her wide eyes panicked and terrified.

Immediately regretting my outburst, I took a deep breath, trying to calm the demons of anger that shot through my unnerved body. Sophie stared as though she'd never seen me before. Ashamed of myself, I relented. I put my arm around her. "Shush now," I said. "We'll get away. I know we will. Trust me."

She nodded, taking ragged breaths.

I turned my attention back outside.

". . . fatal accident," Bruno had said to Ro. With a look I could only call a smirk, he glanced up—caught me watching them. Bruno's voice cut the heartbeat of silence. "And make sure it burns."

Now, the SUV bounced hard on the uneven road, with a powerful jolt that knocked me against the door. My face bumped the side window and I felt my cut sting and stretch as it reopened. A warm welling of blood dripped down my cheek. It pulled my attention back to the present in a hurry.

Ro looked out the back, over my head. He muttered an expletive, then pulled out a two-way walkie-talkie from his jacket pocket. He pressed a button and a feedback screech echoed through the car.

Lisa jumped, then glared at him. "For crying out loud, Ro, I've got mine on, too. Get closer to the window before you use that thing."

He moved, but the gun never wavered.

"Emil, you there?"

Answering static, then, "Yeah."

"Where the hell are you?"

"Just turned off, uh, the main road, uh . . ."

"Shit, forget it. I see you."

Sophie rested heavy against my left side. She'd fallen asleep. I shook my head in disbelief. Exhausted from panic and the long crying jag she'd been through during the day, her body had simply given up. There's no way I could have slept at this point, not with the constant shivers of dread ripping through my mind. If these were indeed my last hours on the planet, I wanted to face them wide awake. But then again, Sophie was a different animal than I was, and maybe sleeping worked as her most effective coping mechanism. It must be a strong one, I thought, since the vehicle's continued bouncing didn't even faze her. I wanted to wake her up, but I just couldn't bring myself to do it. Let her remain unaware, for as long as possible.

Ro took his eyes off of us long enough to take in the surrounding area. "This is the right road," he said.

Lisa shot him a sidelong glance, then rolled her eyes. "That's why I pulled off here."

Ro missed the sarcasm. "Couple miles down that way, now," he offered, gesturing with the barrel of the gun.

"Yeah," she said. "I know."

I turned to watch my car's headlights behind us. Emil drove, but he remained invisible to me over the bright glare.

An accident, Bruno had said.

In my faithful little car.

A sudden anger welled up in me, so fast and so furious that I wanted to kick the gun from Ro's hand. Instead I took a deep breath through clenched teeth, and told myself to wait. My body tingled with anticipation, knowing that whenever the moment came, whatever it was, I'd fight before I'd go down easy.

We crossed over unmarked railroad tracks, then passed under a canopy of trees, their branches still holding onto enough leaves to block my view of the night sky. The car bounced repeatedly in the rough terrain. Lisa kept her headlights on till we reached a clearing. When she cut the motor and cut the lights, Sophie sat up, blinking, looking every direction at once. My body began to shake, reacting to the situation with a terror of the unknown. And yet, I kept a peculiar detached calm. As though I watched all this happening to someone else.

Ro opened one of the back doors and ordered us out. I heard Sophie's shallow breaths, and knew without looking that her abrupt awakening only served to disorient her further.

"Grab your stuff. You're taking it with you," he said.

I reached in for my purse, trying to think if there was anything in it I could use. Yeah, I thought, maybe I could tie them up with my dental floss.

Outside, Sophie clutched me again, wrapping her hands around my left arm, like a terrified two-year-old clinging to mom. "It's okay," I said, knowing it was anything but. "We'll be okay."

She didn't answer except to whimper.

We stood at the edge of a meadow, lit brightly by the shining moon. The wind brought the smell of burning leaves to waft by, its familiar, comforting scent hitting me with a punch of melancholy. A forested area, dense and expansive, sprawled to our immediate right. In the distance, about three football fields away, a pattern of pinkish sodium vapor lights lined a collection of industrial buildings. And right before us, a wide vastness of black, a gaping hole in the ground. So wide that its edges faded into the darkness and I couldn't see to its far side.

And then I knew exactly where we were.

The quarry.

I'd passed it hundreds of times, from the safe vantage point of the expressway above, watching the diggers and loaders and dump trucks as they worked the inside of the limestone pit, so far below they looked like toys. No one in the sporadic traffic above would be paying attention to the dark ground below, and even if they did casually glance out their windows, no one would be able to see us. We were too small, too insignificant.

"Get in," Ro said, pointing to my car.

Emil left it running. Now he sidled up to us. "I'm sorry, Sophie. But I can't . . . I can't . . ." He reached out to stroke her hair, close enough that I smelled the booze on his body.

Were they going to kill us gangland style? Shoot us in the head in my car?

"Ro," I said, facing the big man, knowing I was grasping at straws. "You're not going to get away with this. Look. You left your tire tracks and . . ." I heard my voice shake, to match the tremors of my body, ". . . footprints. With all the technology nowadays, they'll find you."

Ro shook his head. "You think we picked this place out of a hat?" He tilted his head toward the forest. "This is burn-out heaven. Kids come here to smoke dope and drink. Around midnight, there's plenty of cars, plenty of footprints. And when the drunken idiots see the fire in the pit, they'll trample all over the place. We're covered."

"Listen," I said, trying again. "Let us go. I'll nail Bruno, so he can't touch any of you, but I'll leave you out of it. I'll keep you safe. I promise."

Lisa turned away. "Just get it over with, Ro."

He directed Emil to shift my car into neutral. Then had him open the rear hatch of Lisa's car, where two plastic jugs of gasoline waited. "Did she have a full tank in that little shit car?" he asked.

Emil shook his head. "Only about half."

Without shifting his aim, Ro muttered instructions for how to add the accelerant to the car in such a way that it would look like a spontaneous blaze. While he spoke, I whispered to Sophie in Polish, "If I move, follow me."

"No!" she whispered back. "They'll kill us if we try to get away."

"For the love of God, Sophie, they're going to kill us anyway. If I go, you better be behind me. Understand?"

She nodded.

"Good," I said, gently removing her hands from my arm. "Keep your eye on me."

"Shut up, you two," Ro said, then he raised his voice slightly to Emil. "How much you got left in the jugs?"

"About half, each."

"Put one of 'em in her trunk. With the lid loose. Make it look like she kept spare gas in her trunk. For emergencies." He grinned at us.

"Which one?" Emil asked, holding the two jugs aloft.

"Get in," Ro said to us again. We stood on the passenger side of my car, about ten feet away from where Emil had poured the gasoline. "You two are gonna take a trip down to the bottom of the quarry."

"But there's gas all over the ground," I said. "Somebody's bound to notice that."

"You know what? You talk too much."

He started to push us forward, but Emil had come around the back of the car, holding out both red plastic jugs for Ro's inspection. "Which one?" he asked again.

"That one," I shouted. Dropping my purse, I grabbed the right one from his hand. I spun, splashing the open jug at the general vicinity of Ro's face, turning to run without waiting for his reaction. Praying Sophie was behind me.

I heard Lisa shout, Ro swear, and when I turned to be sure that Sophie followed, I thought I saw Emil step in front of a stumbling Ro, knocking them both off balance. It gave us precious seconds for a head start, and even as I headed for the trees with Sophie panting behind me, I had to wonder if he'd done that deliberately.

Chapter Twenty-Six

The traitorous moon illuminated the meadow like a bright spotlight, making me feel vulnerable, obvious. I felt the skin prickle on my back, knowing Ro might be aiming to shoot, even as I concentrated on the slosh-pounding of my feet on the ground through the damp grass. Keeping my eyes on the line of trees just about a hundred yards away, I listened for sounds of Sophie, but my heartbeat slamming in my ears, and my own open-mouthed panting, drowned out noises behind me.

Fearful of losing my balance or twisting an ankle, I didn't want to turn again. I knew it could slow me down, but I had to be sure.

Quick, I looked.

She was right behind me, her hair streaking backward, intensity on her face, and in that split-second glance, behind her, I saw Ro moving our direction at a rapid clip. Lisa following. The man had long legs and power on his side. Even if we could make it to the tree line before he caught up, we'd still have problems getting away. We'd never be able to outrun him.

He shouted something, but I couldn't make out what it was.

Nearer now, the trees were mere steps away, but I felt every stride in slow motion. Wind rushed at my face, howling through the trees, smarting my cheeks. My lungs burned, my eyes watered; I blinked to clear my vision, moving forward.

A loud noise, sharp, like a firecracker. But I couldn't tell if it came from behind or before us.

I ducked between two enormous trees, Sophie three steps behind.

"What now?" she asked, panicked and breathless.

I grabbed her arm and ran. I had no thought in my mind other than to keep moving.

We did, at as fast a pace as we could, through the labyrinth of trees. My eyes hadn't had a chance to adjust to the scant light. Despite the fact that the trees were nearly all bare, their dense overhead branches intertwined to allow only tiny snatches of moonlight filter through. I led the way, avoiding those bright spots, wanting to keep from becoming an easy target.

I heard another noise, faint, but steady. Ahead of us.

A combination of adrenaline, and elation that others might be in the forest, propelled me forward. We slowed down, and I tried to zigzag through the growth, quiet enough that Ro wouldn't be able to hear our movements. I tried to keep wide, shielding trees behind us, as much as possible.

Crashing sounds from where we'd just been.

Another shot.

It had to be Ro.

The faint noise ahead grew louder, more rhythmic. I still couldn't decide what it was, but I headed toward it, my mind on nothing but escape.

Then I made it out. Chanting.

The sounds came from our far right; I changed direction and headed that way. Far, through the pattern of tall, barren trees, the smell of burnt leaves got stronger and I thought I caught the flickering glow of a campfire.

I held my breath and stopped long enough to clamp my hand over Sophie's mouth to quiet her breathing, so I could listen.

I heard him behind us. Too close.

Dropping my hand from Sophie's face, I pulled her forward again.

We moved stealthily, but quickly, toward the fire, toward the sounds.

There.

Silhouetted before an enormous blaze, stretching nearly ten feet in the air, were more than a dozen figures. Male, female, I couldn't discern at this distance, but a couple of them seemed to sway, though not with the rhythm of the chanting.

Louder now, I could make out the combination of voices, repeating rote sayings, like prayers.

They sounded like devil-worshippers. Out in the forest offering animal sacrifices. If so, our presence here wouldn't be welcome, of that I was sure. But I remembered where my recent experiences with the church had gotten me and I decided to take my chances.

"Please, God," I whispered to the heavens, "keep us safe."

Tents sat at the far end of their camp. They'd chosen a small clearing, and as we broke into their midst, I saw at once they were all college-age students, mostly male, but with a couple of females sitting near the fire. Nearly everyone held a beer.

I tripped over something in the grass, falling face-first, my hands hitting metal as I broke my fall. Sophie helped me up and we moved forward again. Train tracks. Stretching from the ones we'd crossed earlier, no doubt. I stepped gingerly over a second set. These were much easier to see. No weeds obscured them. Both sets flush with the ground. No wonder I'd missed them.

Our emergence startled a few of the partiers, and it took a second for me to realize that the ones who didn't react were too drunk to realize there were strangers present. Not devil-worshippers, thank God. The smell of burning marijuana permeated the immediate area and I shouted that we needed help.

The chanting didn't stop.

In fact, it got louder.

A guy with red hair, wearing a knitted ski cap and hooded jacket, bent in half as he screamed, "I can't hear you!" to a group of about four blindfolded young men, who raised their voices at his cry.

I could make out only a few of the words as we sidled past them. Bird, clang, cow, chalk. Didn't make sense. Another group of blindfolded boys sang a song to a familiar tune, but with very different words than I remembered. I searched to find someone sober. Someone who might have a car nearby. I headed for the girls by the fire. One of them, wearing a short brown and orange jacket, was gesturing as she spoke. She looked lucid enough. I could only hope.

There was background music drifting from a boom box. A skinny guy with long, curly, blond hair intercepted us with slurred words and unfocused eyes. "Hey, we got this place staked out tonight ladies, but you're welcome to have a beer."

Drawing closer, I made an instant reassessment. There had to be twenty young people gathered, in small groups. Sitting, standing, swaying, singing. Noise and movement everywhere.

"A man with a gun," I said, loud enough to be heard over the cacophony. "Do you—"

"A cop?" the blond guy asked, his face taking on that vacuous look that people get when they're drunk, but are still trying to comprehend. His brow furrowed. "Cops never come by here. You a cop?"

"No," I said, wanting to push past him to head toward the

girls by the fire. Two of other guys who'd been working near the tents came to join the blond one.

"What's goin' on, Framp?" one of them asked. The three of them barricaded us from moving forward. "Who are you?" he asked us. Shorter than the blond guy, he carried a little more weight, and a cocky look on his face. He took us in with shrewd eyes from behind wire-rimmed glasses. When he saw the cut on my face, he glanced behind us.

In that second I knew this guy wasn't as drunk as the rest. I spoke as fast as I could.

"Do you have a cell phone? Please, call for help. Call nine-one-one," I said, my words breathless. "A man . . . trying to kill us."

I don't know if it was the open wound or the fear in my voice that made him believe me, but he blinked once in comprehension, gave me and Sophie a once-over assessment, and called out behind him, "Brothers! Trouble."

Drunk and sober alike, they mobilized, fast.

"I'm Eddie," the guy said to me, over his shoulder. "We'll take care of him."

Shit, just what I needed. Beer muscles. They'd be no match for Ro—these kids would get themselves slaughtered. "No," I shouted, but he was already taking charge of the group.

"Karen, you're in charge of the pledges till we get back. Bob, Jerry, Wayne, you're in charge of the camp. Frankie, get the fire extinguishers."

An Oriental guy pulled up the metal container next to him. "Here."

"Han, that ain't no fire extinguisher," Eddie said, ripping it from his grasp. "That's a goddamn propane tank."

Han squinted at the tank by his feet, and shrugged.

The group silenced—quiet enough that I could make out the Bee Gees warbling one of their seventies' hits.

I grabbed Eddie's arm. "The guy has a gun."

Too late.

Ro stepped out from the trees into the open area, his weapon raised, its silver-blue metal catching a glint of the moon as he aimed in our direction. The bright light from the fire danced shadows across his face and he blinked, several times, as though clearing his vision.

He'd come in a different way than we had.

"Nobody move," he said.

Nobody did. They might have been drunk, but it was early enough in the evening that they hadn't wasted themselves into total oblivion, yet.

Ro moved our direction, his attention rapt, keeping himself far enough away that he could keep us all in his sights. "You," he tilted his head to the far group of kids, "all of you move to one side. Do it now. Do it slow." He used the back of his sleeve to wipe at his eyes. Maybe some of the gas had gotten in them, after all.

Four girls, who'd stood at Eddie's call, shepherded the blindfolded boys around the crackling fire to stand with the rest of us. They held the pledges' arms and guided them, whispering to them as they moved. I could only imagine the level of fear those boys were experiencing. This was bad enough; being blindfolded had to be torturous.

"You can't kill us all," I said.

"Wanna bet?" he asked. "Back up."

He moved forward to pick up the propane tank. "This could be beautiful," he said, his eyes glittering in the fire's glow. "Headline material."

Over the high-pitched and harmonious notes of Bee-Gee voices, I heard another noise, machine-like. There were no farms nearby. And it didn't quite sound like cars.

Ro pointed to me and Sophie. "Get over here."

I told myself I could do this. I had to. My life, Sophie's life, and the lives of these innocent kids depended on my strength right now. I knew I would rush him. I knew I had to. And the inevitability of that knowledge seemed to suck away any fear. Not entirely, of course. But enough.

I knew he was strong, and wily. I needed an advantage. But what?

"Okay," I said. I grabbed Sophie's arm and edged along the line of kids who stood utterly still, watching him with wide-eyed and slack-jawed expressions of terror. I headed toward the trees where Sophie and I had come in. It was about thirty feet away from the nearest kids.

"Over here," Ro said.

Sophie started to move, but I pulled her back, behind me. "No," I said, my fear making me brave. "You want us, you come here. Keep away from these kids."

His eyes flicked from the crowd to us. And I felt the ground rumble beneath my feet.

"What's that?" he asked, looking around. No one answered for a moment. Ro clicked back the hammer of his gun. Even I knew that was an ominous move.

"Don't know," Eddie said. "The quarry company's right past the trees. Sometimes they work pretty late."

"Okay. Get by the fire. All of you," Ro shouted, as he moved toward me and Sophie.

I eased to my left, making it look as though I was about to make another run for it into the woods.

Ro made it to our side in three long strides. "Don't move." Pulling his walkie-talkie out of his pocket, he said, "Lisa. Deep in the trees. Follow the fire. Get here."

I heard answering static.

The ground rumbling got stronger. I envisioned a massive bulldozer pounding past the forest, and hoped to God the operator would see the fire and head our way.

"As soon as she gets here, the three of us are heading back to the cars. You understand?"

I nodded. Then prayed for strength.

Ro grinned. "Know what you can take to your grave?" He didn't wait for me to answer. "That all these kids would be alive, if it weren't for you, and I'm telling you right now, nobody's gonna care about the two of you when they're mourning all these dead kids. The newspapers are gonna think that the big explosion is what caused you to run off the road." He smirked. "I'm tellin' you. This is beautiful. Couldna planned it better myself."

I expected him to fall when I rushed him. To trip over the rail that I'd calculated had to be positioned right behind him. I expected him to take a quick step back and tumble. And I thought I could get the kids to run at that point.

I faked a look of alarm over Ro's shoulder, and shouted, "Emil?"

The big lug didn't turn, but his attention blanked for a crucial split-second. I hit him with everything I had, but he'd seen it coming. His empty hand grabbed me by the shoulder, taking a step back to steady himself with my added weight. But then he hit the rail, and lost his footing.

His arms flailed out, and we went down.

"Run!" I shouted to the group behind me. I pushed off Ro to stand, and shoved Sophie. "Go!"

Ro rolled to his knees in an effort to scramble to his feet as my mind registered that the kids and Sophie had started to move.

I started to go at him again, hoping to buy another second or two for the fleeing group, to give them the chance to go for help, when I felt someone grab my shoulders with a mighty tug.

Eddie pulled me back so hard that we both fell to the ground, backwards. And in that moment, I knew why he'd done that.

And Ro knew, too.

But it was too late for him.

It happened in an instant, but I could only replay it in my mind in slow motion—the disbelief on the big man's face, his aborted attempt to raise his arm in an effort to shield his eyes from the bright beacon of light—his split-second-too-late comprehension and the one step he took forward, to struggle to get out of the train's path.

The brief scream, drowned out by shrill, shrieking brakes.

And the sound of life ending, with an almost insignificant slap and the splash of blood over me and over Eddie, as we sat on the ground, quietly sick, until after an eternity the rumbling slowed, and finally stopped.

Chapter Twenty-Seven

Dan's station, *Up Close Issues*, made it to the scene before *Midwest Focus* did. Of course. The news crew joined the slew of police officers, including a tactical unit and a bunch of ambulances. Whoever made the phone call had done a thorough job. The police arrived within minutes.

Red and blue lights flashed silently through the trees with eerie crime-scene menace, even though it was over. Spotlights shone in through every opening, illuminating the campsite, making me blink each time I inadvertently stepped into the path of their beam.

A sergeant came over to talk with me, his gentle manner so welcome that I trusted him immediately and nearly lost my composure several times as I explained as much as I could, as fast as I could. He spoke to a microphone perched on his shoulder, dispatching a team to round up Lisa and Emil.

Later I found out that the two of them had apparently remained blissfully unaware of the skirmish taking place in the woods. Lisa had stopped following Ro, and waited by the vehicles. I could only guess that the campsite's blaring radio had interfered with Ro's walkie-talkie call to her.

The sergeant's name was Knight and, as he walked me toward one of the ambulances, one of his officers sidled up. "Sarge, most of these kids are underage. And there's beer all over the place. Turned up a bag of grass on one of them, too."

Sergeant Knight stopped. I tugged at his arm. "These kids saved my life," I said. "That's got to count for something."

He heaved a sigh. "Take them all down for questioning. Take your time with it. Get their statements, nice and slow. Give 'em all lots of coffee. Okay? We'll do breathalyzers on them. All of them. But, later. Got it?"

The officer gave a nod and left.

"Thanks," I said.

Sophie had an oxygen mask over her face and a blanket around her shoulders as she sat at the edge of a gurney on the ground. She was fighting the techs who wanted her to lie down. When she saw me, she ripped the plastic away from her nose, running up and hugging me so hard I thought I'd lose my breath. "Alex, you are safe," she sobbed, in Polish. "Thank you Jesus, Mary, Joseph."

I was fine, but Sergeant Knight made me get checked out by the paramedics anyway. I sat at the other end of Sophie's gurney while they took my vital signs and patched up my cut face with a temporary bandage. Eddie, being escorted to a police car, passed in front of me. I nabbed the hem of his jacket, displacing the tech taking my blood pressure. "Hey," I said.

He glanced down. "Hey."

"Thanks. I owe you," I said, reaching for my purse to give him a card, realizing belatedly I didn't have it. "Alex St. James. From *Midwest Focus NewsMagazine*."

His eyes lit up. "Cool."

"Yeah. You need anything, you call me, okay?"

He glanced at his group of friends, all being herded into waiting cars. "I'll remember that."

"Turned out to be a hell of a night for you guys, huh?"

He laughed. "Yeah. Pretty funny. It's Hell Night."

I shook my head, not understanding.

"Initiation night. Our fraternity. We call it 'Hell Night.' "

As Eddie headed off, Dan sidled up, pushing a microphone into my face. Not a television microphone, but one of those little mini-tape devices like mine before Bruno ordered Ro to demolish it. "Got anything quotable for me?"

"What are you doing here?"

"Covering the hottest story in the country right now."

"Get lost."

"Come on . . . you're a celebrity. And I want the exclusive interview. Got something meaty for me?"

I stared at him. The paramedics were finishing up, making me promise to get the cut looked at by a doctor tonight, pronouncing me otherwise fit, with only a slightly-elevated heart rate. Yeah, well, I could have told them that. Sophie, no longer in danger of hyperventilating, handed back the oxygen mask. "No," I said.

"This is a great story," he said, with a grin I didn't understand at the moment. "We're airing Friday. Devoting the whole show to it."

"What are you talking about?" I asked, as I stood up.

But he was already gone.

"Bullshit," I said.

I winced. My outburst made my face hurt. The doctor at the hospital last night had warned me it would be tender for some time. He'd taped an enormous white bandage over some new goo that took the place of old-fashioned stitches and all but guaranteed I could walk away from this encounter unscarred. But between my bruised face and my aching arm from the tetanus shot he insisted upon, I was feeling pretty battered.

Leaning back in his chair, Bass stared over his shoulder out his office window; the view was nearly identical to mine. He shook his head, then turned back to us. William and I sat across from him, both perched on the edges of our seats.

"How did they get their hands on it?" I asked.

William spoke up. "Jeff," he said. "He gave them both tapes. My video with Candy and your audio with Bruno."

"Little weasel," Bass said, "comes to me this morning, after he hears about everything that happened yesterday...." A mental picture of Ro's last seconds flashed before my eyes; I gave an involuntary shudder. "He's crying and sorry that he'd left you there alone." He picked up a pencil and tapped it against his blotter. "But the goddamn traitor had already sold us out."

"Jeff? Gave *our* story to Dan's station?" My voice croaked. "Why?"

William piped in, "Remember when I saw Dan skulking around downstairs? And I thought he was meeting with you? It's just a guess, but I gotta believe he and Jeff were setting things up. But why Jeff would do a thing like that, I have no idea."

Bass leaned forward on his elbows, still tapping the pencil. His mouth pursed, as though he'd just sucked on a lemon. "He told me that Dan blackmailed him into it."

I shot Bass a look of skepticism, and remembered the snazzy car and snazzier neighborhood. I rubbed my thumb and fingers together. "Or maybe some under-the-table bucks?"

"Could be, but I don't think so." Bass shook his head. "Not the way Jeff came crawling in here. He didn't tell me what it was, but supposedly there's something Jeff doesn't want his wife to know. I dunno, maybe he's got a woman on the side...."

Or maybe a man, I thought, remembering snippets of our conversation and the deep voice in the background when I'd called him yesterday morning. Geez. Yesterday. It seemed like a year ago.

". . . Whatever. Dan somehow got the goods on him and squeezed him for the Milla story." Bass met my eyes. "He knew you hadn't given up on it."

"You pulled me off of it," I said, my voice rising in protest.

"And see where it got you," he countered. "Why the hell did you call Jeff anyway?" Bass asked, throwing his pencil down. "You could have been killed, you know."

I'd been biting the insides of my mouth to keep from an outburst I might later regret. My healing cheek shot out a zing of protest. "Where were you two when I needed you? Huh? I tried to call you. At least ten times." That was an exaggeration, but the fury at them not being there for me, coupled with my still-tenuous hold on calm, made my voice come out a strangled strain. "For crying out loud, I could have used a little help."

"You should never have moved without my okay. And you're never gonna move without my okay again. Got that?"

I didn't answer. But I did glare.

"We were down here," he said in a softer voice. "I called William to the office," Bass said. "I'd thought of a way we might be able to use the interaction with Candy at the hotel after all, and I needed him down here to work it out."

"Without me?" I asked. My shoulders gave an involuntary slump, and I hated that they did. Bass and William had met without me. Purposely. I didn't have any idea why that fact should strike me so deeply, but it did.

"I didn't think you'd approve. You were so adamant about not using that damn video."

"Fine," I countered. "You're right, I wouldn't have wanted to be here." That was a lie. "But why didn't you answer the phone? I called and called." The hurt in my voice was obvious, even to me.

"I shut the phones off."

"Why, were you afraid I'd find out? Afraid I'd come storming down here and mess up your plan?"

"Yeah, something like that." He had the decency to look embarrassed. "I know. Bad move."

The three of us looked three different directions, silent for a long moment, deep in our own thoughts.

Bass broke in. "And here's the bad news . . ."

William and I looked up.

"We're left with no story."

"No story? Come on," I said so angry I nearly jumped out of my chair. "We've got a huge story. Hell, I was part of it."

"Dan's got Bruno," William said.

"What?"

"An exclusive," William continued. "His portion airs live Friday night."

"No," I said, hearing the despair in my voice. "Can't we do anything about this? Sue them? Something?"

Bass shook his head. "There's nothing we can do to stop them. And no way we can come up with an angle that'll hold a candle to their story. Not with both tapes and this interview with Father Bruno." He heaved a deep sigh, which went on pretty long for such a little man. "But, I've been in contact with the general manager at *Up Close Issues* all morning. They can't do the story without your name coming up," he looked at me, "so *Midwest Focus* is being named as affiliate for this feature, and Alex St. James as Dan Starck's willing collaborator. It's something, at least."

My mouth fell open.

"What did you ever see in that asshole, anyway?" Bass asked.

I sat back, hard, staring out the window. "I have no idea."

The three of us gathered in Bass's office again Friday

night. We had two screens going at once. Tapes running to record both the hair care story on our station and the "Scandal in the Catholic Church" story at *Up Close Issues*.

William and I sat next to one another on the sofa. The big bandage I'd worn for the first few days had been downgraded to three butterfly bandages. Bass sat in one of the wooden chairs and leaned forward, positioned between the two televisions, as though he could catch both programs at once. We'd turned down the sound on ours. Hell, we'd been there for the filming; we knew what it contained.

But Dan's was another story, entirely.

He narrated the feature, conducting all the interviews himself.

"Goddamn it," I whispered under my breath.

They were all there. Lisa, turning her head from the cameras, the bright lights shoved in her face, escorted on both sides by Federal agents. Her pimping service evidently crossed state lines and she faced significant prison time if found guilty. The authorities were going easy on the immigrant girls, as long as they agreed to testify. From the sound of Dan's report, most of them recognized the lifeline being thrown to them and were eager to jump at the opportunity. I talked with Sophie earlier in the week, and knew she'd agreed, too. She'd be their star witness.

And Father Trip, bless his heart, had stepped up to work with the local girls, helping find them jobs. He'd called me yesterday to let me know that he'd already placed two girls in full-time positions. A long way to go yet, but he seemed determined.

Emil held his head up as he passed through the media gauntlet. I wondered again if the slimy little guy hadn't helped us by slowing Ro down enough to give us the chance to get away. Maybe I'd never know.

During a commercial break, I let my gaze wander to the other TV. Tammy Larken onscreen. I turned the sound up. Gabriela interviewed her, woman to woman, on soft cushy seats instead of at the news desk. "Warmer," the director had told us. "Makes the audience cozy up to the victims."

Sure.

William had been right. Her story was intense. She'd been accidentally cut, jabbed in the neck with the point of sharp scissors. A tiny nick, but one that the salon didn't treat properly. It became severely infected and required prescription antibiotics for nearly a half year. Tammy lost her job, and then her husband. She sued the salon, successfully, but what she really wanted, she said tearfully to the camera, was to have her life back.

I almost didn't want to turn back to Dan's station. But I cut the sound, glancing at William as I did. "So," I asked, "you seeing her?"

His eyes flicked over to Tammy's sorrowful face, then came back to mine as they registered my query. "No."

"Good," I said.

Bruno came on, Dan seated across from him. I didn't recognize the lavish surroundings of the room they were in. Purple velvet draperies hung heavy over windows in the background behind Bruno's pudgy, smiling face. The walls were pale gold, and those furnishings I could see onscreen, ornate. Could be the Cardinal's residence, or some other fancy church meeting place. I knew it wasn't Bruno's rectory.

Dan's handsome face smiled, taking up the whole screen. "We're here at the Vatican Embassy in Chicago, speaking with the Reverend Father Bruno Creighter. . . ." He went on. Listening, I had to grudgingly admit that he did a decent job of setting the story up and making reference to Bruno's former position as media spokesperson for the Chicago

Church. After a brief interchange of small talk, Dan directed the conversation to matters at hand.

"I soundly deny all allegations of the Church's involvement in this affair," Bruno said, answering Dan's inquiry. His fat hand played with something. The lighter, I supposed. But he evidently opted not to smoke on camera.

Dan pressed the issue, asking him how this latest scandal would affect the credibility of the Roman Catholic Church.

Bruno smiled. "Mr. Starck," he said in that patronizing voice of his. "All organizations of any merit, or any significance, occasionally have a bad apple infiltrate their midst." I'd gotten to know this man so intimately that I could *feel* his need for a cigarette. "Father Carlos fled the country. Rodero, unfortunately, has gone to God and cannot be here to defend himself. But like any other eminent organization, our mother Church will survive the few who would use her protection for their own evil devices. Remember, Mr. Starck, Rodero and Emil were merely employees. Their actions cannot reflect upon our mother Church."

"What about you?"

"What about me?" His hands moved again, and his lower lip worked. His eyes, his face, his body language, exuded calm, but I knew he forced it.

"What about your involvement in the prostitution scandal?"

His hands fanned outward. "I am but a supernumerary in this little drama," he said, smiling. "That means 'bit player,' you know."

A second camera flashed Dan's reaction. Dryly, he answered, "Yes, I'm familiar with the term." The first camera focused on Bruno again as Dan asked, "Father, I have another question for you."

Here it comes, I thought.

Damn, damn, damn. This was my story. I should be the one nailing this guy.

"Yes?"

"Do the words, *tabula rasa* mean anything to you?"

Father Bruno blanched. His mouth moved as if to speak, but no words came out.

"Let me play you a tape, Father."

Dan had handled the trap perfectly. Just like I would have done.

We listened.

I replayed the scene in my mind as the words came through—with utter clarity. Just like Jeff had promised. I became aware of my own breathing as I remembered the terror that had followed Bruno's admission.

Dead silence for a long moment after the tape ended.

"My associate, Alex St. James from *Midwest Focus*, conducted that interview," Dan said to the camera before turning back to Bruno. "Do you have any comment, Father?"

Associate. That burned.

Bruno shook his head, stood. "I'm finished here."

The camera angle widened to capture both men.

I ached. It should have been me on this story. It should have been me. I must have said it aloud, because Bass grunted, "Yeah, this is the kind of story that could win journalistic awards."

"Not quite," Dan said, standing with him. "We've notified the authorities, and word is that your rectory assistant, Emil Schober, is ready to turn state's evidence. There are rumors flying about a warrant being issued for your arrest."

"I don't think so," Bruno said. I swore a smile twitched on the man's pudgy lips. "I'm quite innocent of all the charges. And I would be gratified to be able to address these issues. Alas, I'm scheduled to return to Italy tomorrow. And, unfortunately, as a citizen of the Vatican, your laws have no juris-diction to hold me."

My jaw dropped. I looked over to William and Bass, feeling hot angry frustration sear through my body. "That bastard."

The hub long silent, I worked within the warm, com-forting beam of my Tiffany lamp, paying no attention to the bright night lights of the city outside my window. I wanted to get all my thoughts, all my impressions, down in my journal before this day was through.

Bass stopped by, leaning into my office, his hand on the doorjamb. "Got a minute?"

I waved him in.

He wore his charcoal gray wool overcoat; it fell far enough below his kneecaps to make him appear even shorter than he usually did. "Your buddy William stop by yet?" he asked.

"No."

He shrugged, then leaned back to look across the hub. Peering over him, I could see William's office light spilling onto the floor outside his door. "Said he was going to come talk to you."

"Yeah?"

"If you two . . ." he pointed his head toward William's office. Then fixed me with a meaningful stare. "You know . . ."

I shook my head. Let him say it.

"Well," he pointed a finger at me, "just be discreet, okay?"

I rolled my eyes. "That's what you came in to tell me?"

Bass heaved a huge sigh. "No," he said, grabbing the back of one of my chairs.

"You look tired," I said.

He sat, making the seat "huff" as he did so. "I *am* tired. I spent the whole goddamn week fighting with the GM of *Up Close Issues* over their underhanded ways of stealing our scoop." Frustration worked over Bass's features and he looked away, as though reliving some of the discussions. "We shoulda had that one to ourselves. It would have put us on top. Right on top."

"Where's Jeff been through all of this, anyway?"

Bass shot his attention back my direction. "Fired him," he said. "Soon as he came sniveling in with his sob story."

That, at least, was good news.

Bass rearranged himself in the seat, but he looked even less comfortable after squirming. "What I really came in here to tell you is that I can't fire Fenton."

That one kind of took me by surprise. "I didn't expect you would. He's got connections."

"He's useless. Spent the whole week whining that we should of kept him involved. Told me he'd have never let us lose the story. Yeah. Right." Bass grit his teeth and shook his head again. "You know," he said, sighing deeply, "I should never have taken you off the Milla Voight story in the first place."

I lifted an eyebrow at him. "You *are* tired. And delirious. That almost sounded like an apology."

He gave a weary chuckle. "Yeah, well. Tell anyone I admitted that and I'll deny it."

"Thanks, Bass."

"I should have stuck to what I know."

"You mean . . ." I couldn't resist, "you should have remained faithful to your regulation?"

He shot me a look of dripping disdain as he stood. "I'm outta here."

I packed it up just after nine o'clock. Shut down the computer, and tugged the pull switch of my lamp. Dragging on my brand new down coat, I locked my office and headed out.

Almost as though he'd been waiting, William met me at my door.

"I lost this one," I said.

"No, *we* lost it. All of us. It was a group effort."

I smiled. "Thanks."

We walked through the shadowy darkness of the quiet newsroom toward the doors. What a couple of weeks it had been. I glanced over to William. Had I only known him two weeks? I blew out a breath. Two very full weeks.

"So . . . what do you have planned for the weekend?" he asked as we pushed open the newsroom doors to enter the brightly-lit hall. Our security guard wished us both a good evening and moved to lock up behind us.

"Visit my sister. I need to catch up with her."

"Sister, huh? She live nearby?"

"No. Pretty far, actually." I gave a wry smile. "Lucy lives in a home for . . . special folks, in southern Illinois. I'm heading down there in the morning."

"How long will you be gone?"

"I'll be back at work Monday. I'm just planning to stay there overnight. Take her out. Do a few things." I pressed my lips together a moment. "I'd hate to think that if something ever happened to me, she wouldn't know how much . . ." I let the thought hang. I'd been given another chance to avoid regrets. I didn't want to look back, ever, and wonder, *What if . . . ?* But I stopped myself, shaking off the melancholy with a shrug. Time to stop being consumed by the past. Time to look to the future. Even if I never found out who my birth parents were, I had my family, and they meant more to me than the world. "Maybe make plans to have her come up here one of these days."

William nodded. "You'll be gone all weekend, then?"

"Pretty much."

We both headed for the stairs. His question was friendly; nothing in his tone, nothing on his face conveyed more than polite inquisitiveness.

I wondered if he was considering asking me out.

Another missed opportunity?

We continued to the bottom of the stairs in silence.

Then again, maybe he harbored no romantic feelings for me. Maybe he would be shocked by any overture on my part, and politely decline. Maybe I would then have to work with him for the rest of my life feeling the sting of embarrassment from his courteous but pointed rebuff.

But maybe I needed to sail away from my safe harbor and take a chance, for a change.

"Will," I said, touching his arm.

"Yes?"

"Would you like to go somewhere tonight? Talk about all this?"

When he smiled, my stomach did its responding flip-flop.

"You know," he said, "I'd like that very much."

About the Author

Growing up in a small south side Chicago neighborhood, Julie Hyzy survived sixteen years of Catholic education, emerging from Loyola University with a degree in business administration. With three active daughters, Julie keeps one hand on the carpool steering wheel, and the other scribbling notes for stories. She can't imagine a life without writing and she can't wait to get to her computer every day. Julie's first novel, *Artistic License*, a stand-alone romantic suspense published by Five Star in 2004, was released in both hardcover and large print. *Deadly Blessings* is the first in Julie's mystery series, featuring reporter Alex St. James.

In addition to suspense, Julie's written several award-winning science-fiction short stories. In her spare time, she enjoys movies, chocolate, any food that someone else makes, and painting watercolors.